Goethe
Early Verse Drama and Prose Plays

GOETHE

SELECTED POEMS
FAUST I & II
ESSAYS ON ART AND LITERATURE
FROM MY LIFE: POETRY AND TRUTH (PARTS ONE TO THREE)
FROM MY LIFE: POETRY AND TRUTH (PART FOUR) • CAMPAIGN IN FRANCE 1792 • SIEGE OF MAINZ
ITALIAN JOURNEY
EARLY VERSE DRAMA AND PROSE PLAYS
VERSE PLAYS AND EPIC
WILHELM MEISTER'S APPRENTICESHIP
CONVERSATIONS OF GERMAN REFUGEES & WILHELM MEISTER'S JOURNEYMAN YEAR OR THE RENUNCIANTS
THE SORROWS OF YOUNG WERTHER • ELECTIVE AFFINITIES • NOVELLA
SCIENTIFIC STUDIES

Collected Works in 12 Volumes

Goethe's Collected Works, Volume 7

Johann Wolfgang von

GOETHE

Early Verse Drama and Prose Plays

Edited by Cyrus Hamlin and Frank Ryder
Translated by Robert M. Browning,
Michael Hamburger, Cyrus Hamlin, and Frank Ryder

Princeton University Press
Princeton and Oxford

The English edition was first published by Suhrkamp Publishers New York, Inc.

Published by Princeton University Press
41 William Street, Princeton, New Jersey 08540
99 Banbury Road, Oxford OX2 6JX

press.princeton.edu

GPSR Authorized Representative: Easy Access System Europe - Mustamäe tee 50, 10621 Tallinn, Estonia, gpsr.requests@easproject.com

This is volume seven in the Collected Works of Johann Wolfgang von Goethe

First published 1988
First Princeton paperback printing, 1995
New paperback and e-book editions, 2026

Paperback ISBN 978-0-691-29227-4
ISBN (epub) 978-0-691-29694-4
ISBN (PDF) 978-0-691-29226-7

Cover images: Courtesy of INTERFOTO / Alamy and Rawpixel

The Library of Congress has cataloged a previous edition of this book as follows:
Goethe, Johann Wolfgang von, 1749–1832.
[Plays. English. Selections]
Early verse drama and prose plays / Johann Wolfgang von Goethe ; edited by Cyrus Hamlin and Frank Ryder ; translated by Robert M. Browning . . . [et al.].
p. cm.—(Princeton paperbacks)
Originally published: New York : Suhrkamp, 1988 (Goethe's collected works ; v. 7).

ISBN 0-691-04342-6
1. Goethe, Johann Wolfgang von, 1749–1832—Translations into English.
I. Hamlin, Cyrus II. Ryder, Frank Glessner, 1916–. III. Titles.
IV. Series : Goethe, Johann Wolfgang von, 1749–1832.
Works. English. 1994 ; v. 7
PT2026.A1C94 1994 Vol. 7
[PT2026.A5]
831'.6 s—dc20 94-23913
[832'.6]

CONTENTS

PREFATORY NOTE

All of the plays included in this volume are original translations, with the exception of *Egmont*, which first appeared in Eric Bentley's *The Classic Theatre II* (New York: Doubleday, 1959). It was slightly revised for the present edition. The page from the score of Johann Friedrich Reichardt's 1790 composition *Jery und Bäteli* (*Jery and Betty*, see page 268) is reproduced courtesy of the Speck Collection at Yale University's Beinecke Rare Book Library.

Goethe
Early Verse Drama and Prose Plays

GOETZ VON BERLICHINGEN WITH THE IRON HAND

A PLAY

Translated by Cyrus Hamlin

Characters

EMPEROR MAXIMILIAN
GOETZ VON BERLICHINGEN
ELISABETH, his wife
MARIA, his sister
KARL, his young son
GEORG, his page
BISHOP OF BAMBERG
WEISLINGEN, ADELHEID VON WALLDORF, LIEBETRAUT — at the Bishop's court
ABBOT OF FULDA
OLEARIUS, Doctor of Laws
BROTHER MARTIN
HANS VON SELBITZ
FRANZ VON SICKINGEN
LERSE
FRANZ, Weislingen's page
LADIES-IN-WAITING to Adelheid
METZLER, SIEVERS, LINK, KOHL, WILD, leaders of the rebellious peasants
LORDS and LADIES at the Bamberg court
IMPERIAL COUNCILLORS
ALDERMEN of Heilbronn
JUDGES of the Secret Tribunal
TWO MERCHANTS from Nuremberg
MAX STUMPF, servant of the Count Palatine
A STRANGER
FATHER OF THE BRIDE, BRIDEGROOM — peasants
HORSEMEN in the service of Berlichingen, Weislingen, Bamberg
CAPTAINS, OFFICERS, SOLDIERS OF THE IMPERIAL ARMY
INNKEEPER
COURT SUMMONER
CITIZENS OF HEILBRONN
CITY WATCHMAN
JAILOR
PEASANTS
CAPTAIN OF THE GYPSIES
GYPSY MEN AND WOMEN

Act I

Schwarzenberg in Franconia
An Inn
Metzler, Sievers at a table. Two Troopers at the fire. Innkeeper.

SIEVERS. Hansel, another glass of brandy, and give us a good Christian measure.

INNKEEPER. With you it's never enough.

METZLER (*quietly to Sievers*). Tell me again about Berlichingen! The Bambergers over there are so angry, they're black in the face.

SIEVERS. Bambergers? What are *they* doing here?

METZLER. For two days Weislingen has been up at the castle with the Count; those are his guards. I don't know where he's come from; they're waiting for him; he's going back to Bamberg.

SIEVERS. Who is Weislingen?

METZLER. The Bishop's right hand, a powerful lord, who is lying in wait to cause trouble for Goetz.

SIEVERS. He'd better be careful.

METZLER (*softly*). Keep it up. (*Aloud*:) Since when has Goetz been having difficulty with the Bishop of Bamberg again? The report was that everything had been worked out and smoothed over.

SIEVERS. Aye! You try working something out with priests! When the Bishop saw he was getting nowhere and always coming up short, he started to crawl and bargain for a truce. And unbelievably, honest Berlichingen gave in, as he always does when he's got the advantage.

METZLER. God preserve him! An upright Lord!

SIEVERS. Now think, is that not an outrage? They cut down one of his pages, when he least expects it. But for that he'll give them another delousing!

METZLER. How stupid that his last foray misfired; he must have been fit to be tied.

SIEVERS. I can't remember when anything vexed him so. Just think, everything had been reconnoitered precisely, when the Bishop would leave his bath, how many horsemen he'd have, which road; and if news hadn't been leaked by some traitor, he'd have blessed him his bath and rubbed him dry.

FIRST TROOPER. What's that talk about our Bishop? I think you're itching for a fight.

SIEVERS. Tend to your own affairs. There's nothing at our table concerns you.

SECOND TROOPER. Who said you could speak of our Bishop without respect?

SIEVERS. Do I owe you questions and answers? What a fool!

First Trooper boxes his ears.

METZLER. Knock the dog dead!

They start to fight.

SECOND TROOPER. Come on, if you've got the guts!
INNKEEPER (*pulling them apart*). Can't you keep peace! Damn it all! If you have a score to settle, do it outside. In my tavern I keep things orderly and decent. (*Pushes the troopers out the door.*) And just what are you asses trying to do?
METZLER. Watch what you call us, Hansel, or we'll use your bald head for bowling. Come on, comrade, we'll thrash 'em out o' doors.

Enter two of Berlichingen's Troopers.

FIRST TROOPER. What's going on?
SIEVERS. Ah, good day, Peter! Veit, good day! Where are you coming from?
SECOND TROOPER. Take care you don't let on who we serve.
SIEVERS (*whispering*). Then your Lord Goetz won't be far off either?
FIRST TROOPER. Hold your tongue! Are you in trouble?
SIEVERS. You met the fellows outside. They're Bambergers.
FIRST TROOPER. What are they doing here?
METZLER. Weislingen is up at the castle, with his noble lord; they're his guard.
FIRST TROOPER. Weislingen?
SECOND TROOPER (*whispering*). Peter! What a stroke of good luck! (*Aloud*:) How long has he been there?
METZLER. Two days already. But he plans to leave today, so I heard one of those fellows say.
FIRST TROOPER (*whispering*). Didn't I tell you that he came this way! We could have wasted a lot of time over there. Come on, Veit.
SIEVERS. First help us beat up those Bambergers.
SECOND TROOPER. There're also two of you. We've got to leave. Adieu! (*They leave.*)
SIEVERS. Mangy dogs, those troopers! If you don't offer them pay, they won't do you a single favor.
METZLER. I could swear they're up to something. Who do they serve?
SIEVERS. I'm not supposed to say. They're in Goetz's service.
METZLER. Well! Now let's get on to those two outside. Come on, as long as I've got a cudgel, their roasting spits don't scare me.
SIEVERS. If only just once we could go after the princes that way; they skin us alive.

A Shelter in the Forest

GOETZ (*outside the door beneath a linden tree*). What's keeping my men? I mustn't stop moving or I'll fall asleep. Five days and nights on the prowl. They make you pay for it, this bit of life and freedom. For that, when I've caught you, Weislingen, I'll have satisfaction. (*Pours a drink.*) Empty again! Georg! As long as I don't lack for a drink and a bold spirit, I'll laugh at the powerplays and the intrigues of princes.—Georg!—Just send your loyal Weislingen out to visit your uncles and cousins, and let him slander me. Go ahead. I'm wide awake. You slipped away from me, Bishop! So your dear Weislingen will have to even the score.—Georg! Is the lad deaf? Georg! Georg!

PAGE (*in the breastplate of an adult*). My Lord!

GOETZ. Where were you hiding? Did you fall asleep? What the devil kind of costume is that? Come here, you look good in it. Don't be ashamed, boy. You're a bold one! Indeed, if you could only fill it out! Is that Hans's cuirass?

GEORG. He wanted to sleep for a bit and unbuckled it.

GOETZ. He has more comfort than his lord.

GEORG. Don't be angry! I took it quietly and put it on, and fetched my father's old sword from the wall, ran out on the field and drew it out.

GOETZ. And swung it about? That will have done a lot of good to the brambles and thorns. Is Hans asleep?

GEORG. When you called he jumped up and shouted to me that you called. I tried to unbuckle the harness, then I heard you a second time, a third.

GOETZ. Go, give him back his breastplate and tell him, he should get ready and look after the horses.

GEORG. I fed the horses already and put on their bridles. You can mount whenever you want.

GOETZ. Bring me a jug of wine, give Hans a glass too, tell him to be alert, things are going to happen. Any minute I hope my scouts will be coming back.

GEORG. Ah, mighty Lord!

GOETZ. What's the matter?

GEORG. Can't I go along?

GOETZ. Some other time, Georg, when we're catching merchants and plundering wagons.

GEORG. Some other time! How often you've said that to me. Why not this time? This time! I'll just run along behind, only keep an eye out to the side. I'll fetch back your arrows after they're shot.

GOETZ. Next time, Georg. First you have to have a doublet, a helmet and a lance.

GEORG. Take me along. If I'd been there the last time, you would not have lost your crossbow.

GOETZ. You know about that?

GEORG. You threw it at your opponent's head, and one of his squires ran off with it; so it was lost! Right? Have I got it?

GOETZ. Do my fellows tell you that?

GEORG. Yes! And for that, when we're grooming the horses, I pipe them all kinds of tunes and teach them all kinds of songs.

GOETZ. You're a good lad.

GEORG. Take me along, so I can prove it to you.

GOETZ. Next time, on my word. Unarmed, as you are, you mustn't go into battle. The future will call for good men, too. I tell you, boy, it will be a fine time. Princes will offer their treasures for a man they now hate. Go, Georg, give Hans back his cuirass and bring me wine. (*Georg leaves.*) Where have my fellows got to! It's incredible. A monk! Where has he come from?

Brother Martin enters.

GOETZ. Good evening, worthy Father! Where do you come from so late? For a holy man of peace, you put many knights to shame.

MARTIN. Thank you, noble Lord! I stand before you only as a humble brother, if it's a question of title. My cloister name is Augustin, but I prefer to be called Martin, my Christian name.

GOETZ. You're tired, Brother Martin, and no doubt thirsty! (*The page comes.*) Here comes the wine, at just the right time.

MARTIN. For me, a drink of water. I am not allowed to drink wine.

GOETZ. Is that your vow?

MARTIN. No, noble lord, it is not against my vows to drink wine; but because wine is contrary to my vows, I do not drink wine.

GOETZ. How do you mean that?

MARTIN. Lucky for you that you don't understand. Food and drink, so I believe, are the life of man.

GOETZ. True!

MARTIN. When you have eaten and drunk, you are as if newborn; you're stronger, bolder, more capable of action. Wine rejoices the human heart, and joyfulness is the mother of all virtues. When you have drunk wine, you are in every respect double what you ought to be, twice as ingenious, twice as enterprising, twice as effective.

GOETZ. The way I drink, that's true.

MARTIN. That is what I am talking about. We, however—

Enter Georg with water.

GOETZ (*secretly to Georg*). Go out to the road toward Dachsbach and lie down with your ear to the ground, listen whether you can hear the horses coming and get back here quickly.

MARTIN. But we, when we eat and drink, are just the reverse of what we ought to be. Our sleepy digestion attunes our heads to our bellies, and in the weakness of a gluttonous repose desires are conceived which quickly overwhelm their progenitor.

GOETZ. One glass, Brother Martin, will not disturb your sleep. You have walked far today. (*Drinks his health.*) Here's to warriors!

MARTIN. In God's name! (*They touch glasses.*) I cannot tolerate idle people; and yet I cannot say that all monks are idle; they do whatever they can. I have just come from the Priory of St. Veit, where I slept last night. The Prior took me into his garden; that's a real beehive of activity! What splendid salad greens! Cabbages to your heart's desire! and especially cauliflower and artichokes, like no others in Europe!

GOETZ. That does not sound like your business. (*He gets up, looks for his page and then returns.*)

MARTIN. Would that God had made me a gardener, or some other laborer! I could truly be happy! My Abbot loves me; my convent is Erfurt in Saxony; he knows that I cannot be idle, so he sends me forth whenever something needs to be done. I am on my way to the Bishop of Constance.

GOETZ. Another glass! To a happy expedition!

MARTIN. The same to you.

GOETZ. Why do you look at me so, Brother?

MARTIN. I am fascinated by your armor.

GOETZ. Do you fancy it? It's heavy and tiring to wear it.

MARTIN. What is not tiring in this world? And nothing seems more tiring to me than not to be allowed to be a man. Poverty, chastity and obedience—three vows, each of which, taken singly, seems to be the most intolerable to nature, so unbearable are all of them. And to crawl timidly along for a lifetime under such a burden, or else the far more oppressive burden of conscience! Oh, Lord! what are the difficulties of your life compared to the wretchedness of a state that condemns the best impulses through which we are made, grow, and mature, all out of a misguided desire to be nearer to God.

GOETZ. If your vows were less sacred, I would persuade you to put on armor, I'd give you a horse, and we would take the field together.

MARTIN. Would to God my shoulders could feel the power to bear the armor and my arm the strength to strike my enemy from his horse!—Poor, weak hands, accustomed only to bearing crosses and the banners of peace and swinging censers, how could you control a lance and a sword! My voice, only used to performing Aves and Hallelujas, would serve your enemy as herald of my weakness while he'd be overpowered by yours. No vow shall prevent me from returning to the orders which were founded by my Creator himself!

GOETZ. To a happy return!

MARTIN. That I'll drink only to you. A return to my cell is always unhappy. When you return, Sir, within your walls, with the knowledge of your bravery and strength, immune to all fatigue, secure for the first time in a long while from enemy raids, you stretch out unarmed upon your bed and reach for sleep, which tastes sweeter to you than a drink does to me after long thirsting; then you can speak of happiness.

GOETZ. For all that it comes but seldom.

MARTIN (*more heated*). And when it comes, it's a taste of heaven.—When you come back loaded with spoils from your enemies, and you remember: I knocked that one from his horse before he could shoot, and that one I rode down, horse and all, and then you ride up to your castle, and—

GOETZ. What do you mean?

MARTIN. And your women! (*He fills his glass.*) To the health of your good wife! (*He wipes his eyes.*) You do have a wife?

GOETZ. A noble, virtuous woman!

MARTIN. Blessed be he who has a virtuous woman! for so is his life doubled in length. I know nothing of women, and yet a woman was the crown of creation.

GOETZ (*to himself*). I'm sorry for him! His sense of his station in life consumes his heart.

GEORG (*rushes in*). My Lord! I hear horses galloping! Two of them! It's sure to be them.

GOETZ. Lead my horse out and get Hans to mount up. Farewell, dear Brother, may God be with you. Be bold and patient. God will find a place for you.

MARTIN. May I ask your name?

GOETZ. Excuse me. Farewell. (*He extends his left hand.*)

MARTIN. Why do you offer me your left? Am I not worthy of the right hand of knighthood?

GOETZ. Even if you were the Emperor, you would have to make do with this. My right, although not unusable in war, is insensitive to the clasp of affection, it's one with its glove, you see, it is iron.

MARTIN. So you are Goetz von Berlichingen! Thanks be to God, that He has allowed me to see him, this man hated by princes, and the hope of the oppressed. (*He takes Goetz's right hand.*) Allow me this hand, allow me to kiss it.

GOETZ. You should not.

MARTIN. Allow me. Thou, more valuable than a reliquary hand, through which the most sacred blood has flowed, dead instrument, enlivened through the noblest spirit's trust in God.

Goetz puts on his helmet and takes his lance.

MARTIN. There was a monk among us years ago who visited you when it was shot away at Landshut, he told us what you suffered and how much it pained you to be crippled in your profession and how it came to you that you had heard of someone who also had only one hand and yet served for a long time as a courageous cavalryman. I will never forget that.

The two soldiers enter. Goetz goes over to them. They talk in secret.

MARTIN (*continues to speak*). I will never forget that, how with noblest, simplest trust he spoke to God: "and if I had twelve hands and your Grace were not with me, what would they benefit me, so with one I can"—

GOETZ. Into the Haslach Forest then. (*Turns to Martin.*) Farewell, worthy Brother Martin. (*He kisses him.*)

MARTIN. Do not forget me, as I shall not forget you. (*Goetz leaves.*)

MARTIN. I felt so breathless when I saw him. He hardly spoke a word, and yet my spirit could still discern his spirit. It is a delight to behold so great a man.

GEORG. Reverend Sir, will you be sleeping with us?

MARTIN. May I have a bed?

GEORG. No, Sir. I only know of beds from hearsay, in our shelter there is nothing but straw.

MARTIN. That's fine as well. What is your name?

GEORG. Georg, reverend Sir.

MARTIN. Georg! There you have a bold patron saint.

GEORG. They say he was a knight, I want to be one, too.

MARTIN. Wait. (*He takes out a breviary and gives him a saint's card.*) Here you have him. Follow his example, be brave and fear God. (*Martin leaves.*)

GEORG. Oh, a beautiful white horse, if I ever had such a one!—and golden armor!—That's a nasty dragon—Now I'll go shoot starlings. —Saint Georg! make me grow tall and strong, give me a lance, arms and a horse, then let the dragons come after me.

Jaxthausen
Goetz's Castle
Elisabeth, his wife. Maria, his sister. Carl, his young son.

CARL. Please, dear Aunt, tell me again the story about the good child, it's really nice.

MARIA. You tell it to me, little rogue, then I'll know if you pay attention.

CARL. Wait a bit, let me think.—Once upon a time—yes—there was once a child, and its mother was sick, so the child went away.

MARIA. Not so. Then the mother said, "My dear child"—

CARL. "I'm sick."

MARIA. "And can't go out."

CARL. And gave him money, and said, "Go away, and fetch some breakfast." Then along came a poor man.

MARIA. The child set out, and then he met an old man, who was—Now, Carl!

CARL. Who was—old.

MARIA. Of course. Who could hardly walk any more, and he said, "Dear child"—

CARL. "Give me something, I have had no food yesterday or today," then the child gave him the money.

MARIA. Which was supposed to be for his breakfast.

CARL. Then the old man said—

MARIA. Then the old man took the child—

CARL. By the hand, and said, and was changed to a beautiful shining saint, and said, "Dear child"—

MARIA. "For your good deed the Mother of God rewards you through me, if you touch anyone who is sick—"

CARL. "With your hand"—it was the right hand, I think.

MARIA. Yes.

CARL. "He'll be well instantly."

MARIA. So the child ran home and couldn't say anything for joy.

CARL. And he hugged his mother around the neck and wept for joy—

MARIA. Then the mother cried out, "What's happening to me?" and she was—now, Carl.

CARL. She was—she was—

MARIA. You're not paying attention anymore—she was well again. And then the child cured the King and the Emperor, and became so rich that he built a great cloister.

ELISABETH. I cannot understand why my Lord is not back yet. Five days and nights he has been away, and he hoped to be done with this expedition so quickly.

MARIA. I've long been worried. If I had a husband who always exposed himself to dangers, I would die in the first year.

ELISABETH. I thank God that he made me of sturdier stuff.

CARL. But does Papa have to ride off, if it's so dangerous?

MARIA. That's the way he wants it.

ELISABETH. He has to do it, dear Carl.

CARL. Why?

ELISABETH. Do you remember, how he rode out last time, when he brought you back sweet-rolls?

CARL. Will he bring me something again?

ELISABETH. I think so. You see, there was a tailor from Stuttgart, he was a splendid archer, and had won first prize at a shooting match in Cologne.

CARL. Was it much?

ELISABETH. A hundred thalers. And afterward they wouldn't give it to him.

MARIA. Yes, isn't that awful, Carl?

CARL. Awful people!

ELISABETH. Then the tailor came to your father and begged him to help him get his money. So he rode out and took a couple of people from Cologne captive and plagued them for so long that they paid up. Wouldn't you have ridden out, too?

CARL. Oh, no, there's a dark, dark wood to ride through, with gypsies and witches in it.

ELISABETH. What a fine fellow! Afraid of witches!

MARIA. You'll do a better job, Carl, if you live in your castle as a pious Christian knight. On your own estates there will be chances enough for doing good deeds. The most righteous knights do more injustice than justice on their campaigns.

ELISABETH. Sister, you don't know what you're saying. God grant that our boy will be braver in time and not follow the example of Weislingen, who behaves so disloyally towards my husband.

MARIA. Let us not pass judgment, Elisabeth. My brother is very bitter, as you are also. I am more an outside observer in the whole matter and can be fairer.

ELISABETH. He is not to be forgiven.

MARIA. What I have heard about him interests me. Even your husband used to tell so much that was loving and good about him! How happy their youth was, when they were together as honor pages for the Margrave.

ELISABETH. That may be. Just tell me what can ever have been good about a man who lays ambush for his best, most loyal friend, who sells his services to the enemies of my Lord, and who tries to deceive our noble Emperor, who is so well disposed toward us, with false and foul reports.

CARL. It's Papa! It's Papa! The watchman sounds the signal. "Hurrah! open the gates!"

ELISABETH. Then he comes with spoils.

A rider enters.

RIDER. We went hunting! And we caught our game! God greet you, noble ladies.

ELISABETH. You've got Weislingen?

RIDER. Himself and three horsemen.

ELISABETH. How did it happen that you were away so long?

RIDER. We lay in wait for him between Nuremberg and Bamberg, but he didn't appear, and we knew he was on the way. Finally we got news of him, he had travelled a side road and was sitting at his ease with the Count at Schwarzenberg.

ELISABETH. That's another one they also hope will be hostile to my husband.

RIDER. I said that right away to my Lord. Off! and we ride into Haslach Forest. And it was strange, as we were riding in the night, we met up with a shepherd there, and five wolves were attacking his flock and going at it full force. Then our Lord laughed out loud and said: "Good luck, dear comrades, good luck all round and to us, too." And such a good sign made us all happy. Right then, Weislingen comes riding by with four soldiers.

MARIA. My heart trembles within me.

RIDER. I and my comrade, as our Lord had commanded, sneaked up on him as if we had grown together, so that he couldn't stir or budge, the Lord and Hans fell upon the soldiers and took them captive. One of them escaped.

ELISABETH. I am anxious to see him. Will they be here soon?

RIDER. They're riding up the valley, in a quarter hour they'll be here.

MARIA. He will be dejected.

RIDER. He looks gloomy enough.

MARIA. The sight of him will be painful to my heart.

ELISABETH. Oh!—I must go get food ready. You will all be hungry.

RIDER. Right you are!

ELISABETH. Take the keys to the cellar and fetch some of our best wine, they have earned it. (*Elisabeth leaves.*)

CARL. I want to go along, Aunt.

MARIA. Come, child. (*They leave.*)

RIDER. He'll never be his father, otherwise he'd come along to the stables.

Goetz. Weislingen. Squires.

GOETZ (*placing his helmet and sword on the table*). Unbuckle my harness and give me my doublet. It will be good to feel comfortable again, Brother Martin, you spoke the truth. You've got us out of breath, Weislingen.

Weislingen answers nothing, pacing back and forth.

GOETZ. Be of good cheer. Come, unarm yourself. Where are your clothes? I hope nothing of yours has been lost. (*To an attendant:*) Go, ask his men and open his bags, see that nothing is missing. I could also lend you something of mine.

WEISLINGEN. Leave me as I am, it's no matter.

GOETZ. I could give you a nice, clean coat, though only of linen. It's become too tight for me. I wore it at the marriage of my noble lord

Count Palatine, that time when your Bishop turned so poisonous toward me. Two weeks before then I had sunk two of his ships on the River Main. And with Franz von Sickingen I climbed up the stairs in the Inn of the Stag at Heidelberg. Before you get to the top there is a landing and a little iron railing, there stood the Bishop and he shook hands with Franz as he walked past, and shook mine too as I came after. I laughed to myself and went to the Landgrave of Hanau, who was well disposed toward me, and I said, "The Bishop shook my hand, I bet he did not know me." The Bishop heard this, for I spoke loudly on purpose, and he approached us angrily and said, "Indeed, because I did not know you, I gave you my hand." Then I said, "My Lord, I saw clearly that you did not know me, and therefore I give you your hand back again." Then in his rage the little man turned as red around the neck as a crab and ran into the chamber to the Count Palatine Ludwig and to the Prince of Nassau and complained to them. Afterwards we often had a good laugh about it.

WEISLINGEN. I wish you would leave me alone.

GOETZ. Why that? I beg you to be cheerful. You are in my power, and I will not misuse it.

WEISLINGEN. On that point I had no worries. That is your duty as a knight.

GOETZ. And you know that it is sacred to me.

WEISLINGEN. I am a captive and nothing else matters.

GOETZ. You should not speak so. What if you had to deal with princes, and they hung you up by chains in a deep dungeon, and the guard were to rob you of sleep with his calls.

The squires enter with clothes. Weislingen undresses and puts on fresh clothing. Carl enters.

CARL. Good morning, Papa.

GOETZ (*kisses him*). Good morning, boy. How have you been keeping?

CARL. I've been doing very well, Papa. My aunt says I do very well.

GOETZ. So.

CARL. Did you bring something for me?

GOETZ. Not this time.

CARL. I have learned a lot.

GOETZ. Aha!

CARL. Shall I tell you the story about the good child?

GOETZ. After dinner.

CARL. I know something else.

GOETZ. What might that be?

CARL. Jaxthausen is a village and a castle on the Jaxt, for two hundred years it has belonged to the Lords of Berlichingen by right of inheritance and possession.

GOETZ. Do you know the Lord of Berlichingen?

Carl stares at him.

GOETZ (*to himself*). He's so erudite he doesn't know his own father.—To whom does Jaxthausen belong?

CARL. Jaxthausen is a village and a castle on the Jaxt.

GOETZ. I'm not asking that.—I knew every path and road and ford before I knew what river, village and castle were called.—Your mother is in the kitchen?

CARL. Yes, Papa! She's cooking white turnips and a roast of lamb.

GOETZ. You know that, too, Sir Kitchenmaster?

CARL. And as dessert for me Aunt is baking an apple.

GOETZ. Can't you eat it raw?

CARL. It tastes better this way.

GOETZ. You always have to have something special.—Weislingen! I will be with you again shortly. I must see my wife. Come along, Carl.

CARL. Who is that man?

GOETZ. Bid him welcome. Ask him to be cheerful.

CARL. There, man! You have my hand, be cheerful, dinner will be ready soon.

WEISLINGEN (*lifts him up and kisses him*). Happy child! Knowing no evil greater than the delay of supper. May God grant you great joy in the boy, Berlichingen!

GOETZ. Where there is bright light, there is also deep shadow—yet I would welcome it. Let's see what's happening. (*They leave.*)

WEISLINGEN. Oh, if only I might wake up! and all this were only a dream! In Berlichingen's power, from whom I barely had worked myself free, whose remembrance I shunned like fire, whom I hoped to overpower! And he—the old, true-hearted Goetz! Dear God, what will be the outcome of all this? Led back, Adelbert, into the halls where we as boys would race about like hunters. When you loved him, doted on him, as on your own soul. Who can be near him and still hate him? Alas! I am nothing at all here. Blissful days, you are gone, when old Berlichingen still sat here by the chimney, when we played all about him and loved one another like the angels. How worried the Bishop and my friends will be about me. I know the whole country will share in my misfortune. What does that matter? Can they give me what I'm striving for?

Enter Goetz with a bottle of wine and glasses.

GOETZ. Till dinner's ready, we'll have a drink. Come, sit yourself down, act as if you were at home. Just think, you're once again the guest of Goetz. It's been a long while since we sat together, a long while since we emptied a bottle together. (*Raises his glass in a toast.*) A cheerful heart!

WEISLINGEN. Those times are past.

GOETZ. God forbid! I admit, we'll not find such pleasant days again as those at the Margrave's court when we still slept and wandered about together. I recall my youth with joy. Do you still remember how I got into a fight with the Polack, the one whose curled and pomaded hair-do I accidently ruffled with my sleeve?

WEISLINGEN. It was at table, and he struck at you with a dagger.

GOETZ. Well, I beat him soundly that time, and because of it you had a quarrel with one of his fellows. We always stuck together as good, sturdy fellows, and for that we were known to everyone. (*Fills a glass and raises it.*) Castor and Pollux! It always warmed my heart when the Margrave called us that.

WEISLINGEN. The Bishop of Wuerzburg started it.

GOETZ. There was a learned lord, and yet so congenial. I'll remember him as long as I live, how he coddled us, praised our oneness of spirit, and called any man fortunate who could pass as twin brother for his friend.

WEISLINGEN. No more of that.

GOETZ. Why not? When work is done, I know nothing more pleasant than to remember what's past. True, now that I think about it, how we bore everything together, both love and loss, were everything to each other, and how I supposed then it would be so our whole life long. Was that not my only comfort when this hand was shot away at Landshut and you attended me, showed more care than a brother. I hoped Adelbert would be my right hand in the future. And now—

WEISLINGEN. Alas!

GOETZ. If only you had followed me that time, when I asked you to march with me to Brabant, everything would have stayed the same. But you were held captive by the miserable attractions of court life and by the flirting and fawning of women. I always said to you, when you took up with those vain and vicious sluts and told them about unhappy marriages, maidens led astray, the rough complexion of some other woman, or whatever they wanted to hear, you would end up as a scoundrel, I said so, Adelbert.

WEISLINGEN. Where is all this leading?

GOETZ. Would to God I could forget it, or that it were otherwise. Are you not just as free, just as nobly born, as anyone in Germany, independent, owing allegiance only to the Emperor, and yet you cringe among vassals? What does the Bishop do for you? Is it because he is your neighbor? could be a nuisance for you? Do you not possess arms and friends enough to be an equal nuisance to him? You forget the worth of a free knight, dependent only on God, the Emperor and oneself. You go crawling, just to be the chief court toady for a selfish, jealous priest!

WEISLINGEN. Let me speak.

GOETZ. What do you have to say?

WEISLINGEN. You look upon the princes as a wolf upon the shepherd. And yet can you blame them for securing what is best for their people and lands? Are they safe for even a moment from the unruly knights, who attack their vassals on any highway and sack their castles and towns? Now if, on the other side, the lands of our dear Emperor are exposed to the violence of our archenemy, if he requires the aid of his estates, and if they are scarce able to defend their own lives; is it not a wise spirit that counsels them to think of the means for bringing peace to Germany, for deciding more fully the affairs of state, in order that everyone, great and small, might enjoy the blessings of peace? And you blame us, Berlichingen, that we place ourselves under their protection, when their help is close by, instead of his distant majesty, who can't even defend himself?

GOETZ. Yes! yes! I understand you! Weislingen, if the princes were truly as you describe them, we would all have what we desire. Peace and quiet! I believe that, oh yes! That's the wish of every bird of prey, to devour its plunder undisturbed. The general welfare of all! If that were the only cause for their grey hair. And they are playing with our Emperor in a disreputable way. He means well and wants to improve things. Then every day along comes a new tinker who tells him this or that. And because our Lord grasps things quickly and has only to speak and a thousand hands are set to work, he assumes that everything can be accomplished as quickly and easily. So decrees follow upon decrees, and one is forgotten for another, and whatever suits the needs of the princes, that's what they're after, and they prate about the peace and security of the state, until they get the lesser folk under foot. I'll swear an oath on it, that many give thanks to God in their hearts that the Turk holds the balance against the Emperor.

WEISLINGEN. You see it only from your side.

GOETZ. So does everyone. The question is which side has the right and the light, and the least one can say is that your moves shun the day.

WEISLINGEN. You're free to talk, since I'm your prisoner.

GOETZ. If your conscience is clear, then you're free. But what happened to the Permanent Peace? I still recall how as a boy of sixteen I went with the Margrave to the Imperial Diet. How the princes opened their yaps then, the ecclesiastics most of all! Your Bishop filled the Emperor's ear with his noise about justice, as if it had grown miraculously dear to his heart! and now he strikes down one of my pages, at a time when our affairs are orderly and I'm not thinking of doing anything bad. Isn't everything straight between us? What's he doing with my page?

WEISLINGEN. It happened without his knowledge.

GOETZ. Then why does he not release him?

WEISLINGEN. The page has not behaved as he should.

GOETZ. Not as he should! By my oath, he *has* behaved as he should, as sure as he was captured with your knowledge and the Bishop's. Do you two think I was only born yesterday, so I can't see where all this is leading?

WEISLINGEN. You're too suspicious and unfair to both of us.

GOETZ. Weislingen, shall I speak the truth, eye to eye? I am a thorn in your flesh, and Sickingen and Selbitz no less, because we are firmly resolved to die before we give thanks for the air we breathe to anyone but God and before we pledge our faith and loyalty to anyone but the Emperor. So now they stalk me all about, blacken my name with the Emperor and their friends and my neighbors, and spy around for some advantage against me. They want me out of the way, no matter how. That's why you took my page prisoner, because you knew I had sent him to gather information, and that's why he did not behave as he should when he refused to betray me to you. And you, Weislingen, are their tool!

WEISLINGEN. Berlichingen!

GOETZ. Not a word more about it, I am an enemy of explanations, a man betrays himself or someone else, usually both.

CARL. Come to dinner, Papa.

GOETZ. There's good news!—Come, I hope my womenfolk will cheer you up. You used to be quite a lover; the girls knew stories to tell about you. Come on!

In the Bishop's Palace at Bamberg
The Dininghall
Bishop of Bamberg. Abbot of Fulda. Olearius, Doctor of Sacred and Secular Law. Liebetraut. Courtiers.

At Table. Dessert and large drinking chalices are brought in.

BISHOP. Are there many German aristocrats now studying at Bologna?

OLEARIUS. Both aristocrats and merchant class. And without exaggeration, they receive the highest praise. There is a common saying at the Academy: "as diligent as a German nobleman." For while the burghers apply themselves with an admirable diligence in order to offset by talent the shortcomings of birth, the others strive, with admirable competitiveness, to exalt their dignity of birth through the most splendid accomplishments.

ABBOT. Aha!

LIEBETRAUT. Just think! What marvels to be known! "As diligent as a German nobleman." In all my days I've never heard that one.

OLEARIUS. Yes, they are a marvel for the whole Academy. Very soon some of the oldest and most skilled will be returning as *Doctores*. The Emperor will be pleased to appoint them to his courts of law.

BISHOP. That is bound to happen.

ABBOT. Do you know, for instance, a young lord?—he comes from Hessen—

OLEARIUS. There are many Hessians there.

ABBOT. His name is—he's called—Does no one among you know him?—His mother was a von—Oh! his father had only one eye—and was a Marshall.

LIEBETRAUT. Von Wildenholz.

ABBOT. Right! Von Wildenholz.

OLEARIUS. I do know him, a young man of various skills. He is especially praised for his strength in disputation.

ABBOT. He has that from his mother.

LIEBETRAUT. But her husband never wished to praise her for it.

BISHOP. What did you say was the Emperor's name who wrote your *corpus juris*?

OLEARIUS. Justinian.

BISHOP. A worthy lord! To his health!

OLEARIUS. To his memory! (*They drink.*)

ABBOT. It must be a splendid book.

OLEARIUS. One might call it the book of all books. A collection of all laws, for every case the judgment ready at hand, and whatever may still be oblique or obscure is supplemented by glosses, with which the most learned men have decorated that splendid work.

ABBOT. A collection of all laws! Well! Then the Ten Commandments must also be in it.

OLEARIUS. *Implicite* they are, not *explicite*.

ABBOT. That's what I mean, in and by themselves, without further explication.

BISHOP. And best of all, the realm could be maintained, as you say, in secure peace and quiet, wherever this system would be introduced and rightly administered.

OLEARIUS. No question.

BISHOP. To all *Doctores Juris*!

OLEARIUS. I can drink to that. (*They drink.*) Would to God they spoke that way in my homeland.

ABBOT. Where do you come from, most learned Sir?

OLEARIUS. From Frankfurt on the Main, at your Eminence's service.

BISHOP. Are you gentlemen not well thought of there? How can that be?

OLEARIUS. Strange enough. I was there to fetch my inheritance from my father, and the mob all but stoned me when they heard I was a lawyer.

ABBOT. God forbid!

OLEARIUS. This is the reason: the Sheriff's Court, which is held in great esteem far and wide, is filled with people who are ignorant of Roman Law. No one attains to the dignity of a judge but those who have acquired through age and experience a precise knowledge of the internal and external procedures of the city, along with a strong power of judgment, which applies the past to the present. In this way the sheriffs become living archives, chronicles, books of law, all in one, and they pass judgment on the citizens and neighboring populace by ancient precedent, not by statutes.

ABBOT. That is all for the good.

OLEARIUS. But by far not enough. Human life is short, and in a single generation not all cases occur. Our book of law is a collection of such cases from many centuries. And in addition the will and opinion of men can vary, today something will seem right to one person, which tomorrow displeases another; in this way confusion and injustice are unavoidable. All this is established by laws, and laws are unchangeable.

ABBOT. That of course is better.

OLEARIUS. The common people don't recognize that. However keen for anything new and different, they completely abhor whatever leads them away from their own track, no matter how much they might benefit from it. They regard a lawyer with contempt, as a disruption to the state, a cutpurse, and they are so rabid about it, that no lawyers can settle there.

LIEBETRAUT. You *are* from Frankfurt! I'm well known there myself. At the coronation of Emperor Maximilian we stole a feast on your young swains. Your name is Olearius? I do not recall the name.

OLEARIUS. My father was called Oehlmann. Just to avoid misunderstanding about the title of my Latin writings, I took the name Olearius, on the example and advice of worthy teachers of law.

LIEBETRAUT. You did well to translate yourself. A prophet is without honor in his own country; it might also have applied to you in your mother tongue.

OLEARIUS. It was not for that reason.

LIEBETRAUT. There is more than one reason for every result.

ABBOT. A prophet is without honor in his own country!

LIEBETRAUT. And do you know why, reverend Sir?

ABBOT. Because he was born and brought up there.

LIEBETRAUT. True! That may be one reason. Another is this: Because a close acquaintance with such men dissolves the halo of nobility and holiness, with which the mists of distance surround them like lies; and then they are nothing but little stumps of tallow.

OLEARIUS. It would seem that you are employed for speaking the blunt truth.

LIEBETRAUT. Since I have the head for it, I don't lack the tongue.

OLEARIUS. Just the ability to pronounce it with a certain delicacy.

LIEBETRAUT. Best apply the cupping-glass where it can draw blood.

OLEARIUS. You can recognize a barber-surgeon by his apron, and there's no offence taken for his trade. For your protection you might do well to wear a cap-and-bells.

LIEBETRAUT. Where did you take your degree? I only ask in case sometime the notion strikes me, so I can go straight to the right forge.

OLEARIUS. You are impudent.

LIEBETRAUT. And you are very inflated. (*Bishop and Abbot laugh.*)

BISHOP. Change the subject.—Not so heated, my lords. At table all things are tolerated. Some other discourse, Liebetraut.

LIEBETRAUT. There's a place across from Frankfurt called Sachsenhausen—

OLEARIUS (*to the Bishop*). What's the news from the Turkish campaign, so please your Grace?

BISHOP. The Emperor wishes nothing more than to achieve peace in his realm, to abolish feuding and to secure the authority of the courts. Then, it is said, he will proceed in person against the enemies of the realm and of Christendom. For now his private affairs keep him busy, and the realm, despite some forty local treaties for peace, is still a den of murderers. Franconia, Swabia, the upper Rhineland and adjacent territories are laid waste by bold and impudent knights: Sickingen, Selbitz with his one leg, Berlichingen with his iron hand, they mock the Emperor's authority in those regions.

ABBOT. Indeed, if his Majesty does not do something about it soon, those fellows will end up putting someone in a sack.

LIEBETRAUT. That would be quite a fellow, who could stuff the winecask of Fulda into a sack.

BISHOP. That last fellow in particular has been my implacable enemy for many years, and he annoys me beyond words, but it won't go on much longer, I hope. The Emperor is now holding his court in Augsburg. We have taken our measures, we cannot fail.—Doctor, do you know Adelbert von Weislingen?

OLEARIUS. No, your Eminence.

BISHOP. If you will await the arrival of this man, you will be pleased to behold in one person the noblest, most reasonable and most gallant knight.

OLEARIUS. He must be exceptional, who earns such words of praise from such a mouth.

LIEBETRAUT. He never attended a university.

BISHOP. We know that. (*Servants rush to the windows.*) What is happening?

A SERVANT. Faerber, Weislingen's squire, is just riding through the castle gate.

BISHOP. Go, see what he brings, he'll have news of him.

Liebetraut leaves. They stand up and take another drink. Liebetraut returns.

BISHOP. What's the news?

LIEBETRAUT. I wish someone else might tell you. Weislingen has been captured.

BISHOP. Ah!

LIEBETRAUT. Berlichingen seized him with three of his attendants near Haslach. One of them escaped to report it to you.

ABBOT. A Job's messenger!

OLEARIUS. I'm truly sorry to hear it.

BISHOP. I want to see that squire, bring him up here.—I want to talk to him myself. Bring him to my chamber. (*Leaves.*)

ABBOT (*sits down*). One more cup. (*Servants fill his glass.*)

OLEARIUS. Would your Reverence not enjoy a brief promenade in the garden? *Post coenam stabis seu passus mille meabis.*

LIEBETRAUT. Truly, sitting is not healthy for you. You'll have another stroke. (*The Abbot rises.*)

LIEBETRAUT (*to himself*). If I can just get him outside, I'll tend to his *exercitium*. (*They leave.*)

Jaxthausen
Maria. Weislingen.

MARIA. You say that you love me. I gladly believe you and hope that I will make you happy.

WEISLINGEN. I feel nothing but my love for you. (*He embraces her.*)

MARIA. I beg you, please don't. I gladly offer a kiss as a sample, but you seem to want to take possession already of what will be yours only on condition.

WEISLINGEN. You are too strict, Maria! The innocence of love is a delight to the Deity, never an insult.

MARIA. That may be! But I don't find it edifying to hear it. I was taught that caresses are as strong as chains, which they resemble, and that young women when in love are weaker than Samson after he lost his locks.

WEISLINGEN. Who taught you that?

MARIA. The Abbess of my convent. I was with her until my sixteenth year, and the happiness I felt in her presence I feel again only with you. She had loved and knew how to speak of it. She had a heart full of feeling! She was a splendid woman.

Weislingen. Then she resembled you! (*He takes her hand.*) How will I endure it, if I must leave you!

Maria (*withdraws her hand*). With a bit of pain, I hope, for I know how I will be. But you must leave.

Weislingen. Yes, my dearest, and I will. For I sense what bliss I may win through this sacrifice. Blessings on your brother, and the day on which he set out to take me prisoner.

Maria. His heart was filled with hope for you and for myself. "Farewell!," he said as he left, "I will see that I find him again."

Weislingen. And he has. How I wish that the management of my estates and their security had not been neglected by my wretched life at court! You could be mine at once.

Maria. Postponement also has its pleasures.

Weislingen. Do not say that, Maria, otherwise I'd fear you feel less strongly than I do. But I shall do deserving penance, and what hopes will accompany me at every step! To be wholly yours, to live only with you and your circle of good people, removed from the world, to enjoy all the bliss which two such hearts may provide for each other! What is the grace of a prince, what the applause of the world, compared to such simple, singular happiness? I have hoped and wished for so much, this surpasses all my hopes and wishes.

Goetz enters.

Goetz. Your page has returned. He could hardly speak for fatigue and hunger. My wife is giving him something to eat. This much I have understood: the Bishop won't release my squire, there's supposed to be an Imperial Commission appointed and a day set aside when the affair will be settled. Be that as it may, Adelbert, you are free to leave; I ask only your hand in pledge that in future you will not assist my enemies, neither publicly nor in private.

Weislingen. Give me your hand. From this moment on may friendship and trust, like an immutable law of nature, be unchanging between us. At the same time allow me to take this hand (*he takes Maria's hand*) and the possession of this noblest young woman.

Goetz. May I say yes for you?

Maria. If you will say it with me.

Goetz. It's lucky that for once advantage coincides for both of us. No need to blush! Your glances are proof enough. Well then, Weislingen! Clasp hands together and let me say Amen!—My friend and brother!—I thank you, sister! You know how to spin more than flax. You've twisted the thread that's snared this bird of paradise. You don't quite look free, Adelbert! What's the matter? Myself—I'm completely happy: what I could hope for only in dreams is now real, and I feel I'm dreaming. Ah! now my dream is over. It seemed this night as if I gave you my iron hand, my right one, and you held me so tightly that it came loose from my brassarts, as if it were broken off. It frightened me and woke me up. I should have kept on dreaming, then I'd have seen how you provided me with a new, living hand.—Now you must be gone to set your castle and estates in perfect order. The damned court made you neglect both. I must call my wife. Elisabeth!

MARIA. My brother is filled with joy.

WEISLINGEN. And yet I can challenge him for that distinction.

GOETZ. You'll have a charming place to live.

MARIA. Franconia is blessed land.

WEISLINGEN. And I may truly say, my castle stands in its most blessed and charming region.

GOETZ. That you may, and I will affirm it. Here flows the Main and there the hill rises gradually, clothed in tilled fields and vineyards and crowned by your castle, then the river quickly twists round the bend behind the rock of your castle. The windows of the great hall open on the steep drop to the water, a view to the distance many hours away.

Elisabeth enters.

ELISABETH. What are you up to?

GOETZ. You must join your hand with ours and wish God's blessing on these two. They're engaged.

ELISABETH. So quickly.

GOETZ. Yet not unexpectedly.

ELISABETH. May you always desire her as you have while wooing her! And more! May you be as happy as your love for her endures.

WEISLINGEN. Amen! I wish for no joy but on these terms.

GOETZ. The bridegroom, dear wife, must undertake a short journey; for a great change draws many smaller ones after. He must first withdraw from the Bishop's court, to allow that friendship gradually to grow cold. Then he must rescue his properties from the hands of self-serving tenants. And then—but come, sister, Elisabeth!, come away. We'll leave him alone. His page no doubt has private business to convey.

WEISLINGEN. Nothing that you may not know.

GOETZ. No need. Franconians and Swabians! You're more closely related now than ever. And how we'll keep a hold on those princes! (*The three leave.*)

WEISLINGEN. Dear God in Heaven! that you could provide such bliss for one so undeserving. It overwhelms me. How dependent I was on wretched people I thought I controlled, on favors from my prince, on the flattery of sycophants at court. Goetz, dear Goetz, you have restored me to myself, and Maria, you make my change of heart complete. I feel as free as if I breathed the open air. Bamberg I wish to see no more. I will cut loose from all those shameful bonds that kept me beneath my true self. My spirit soars, here is nothing of that ponderous struggle for a greatness denied. And so it's certain that he alone is joyful and great who needs neither to command nor to obey in order to be something.

Franz enters.

FRANZ. God's greeting, my noble Lord! I bring so many messages that I scarcely know how to begin. Bamberg and its environs for ten miles around send you a thousandfold: God's greeting!

WEISLINGEN. Welcome, Franz. What else do you bring?

FRANZ. Your place in the memory of the court and everywhere is beyond what I can say.

WEISLINGEN. That won't last long.

FRANZ. As long as you live! and after your death it will shine more brightly than the brass lettering on a tombstone. How they all took your misfortune to heart!

WEISLINGEN. What did the Bishop say?

FRANZ. He was so eager for news that with the busy speed of his questioning he prevented my answering. He already knew about it, since Faerber, who escaped from Haslach, brought him that message. But he wanted to know everything. He asked very anxiously whether you had been wounded. I said, "He's all right, from the hair on the top of his head to the toenails on his little toe."

WEISLINGEN. What did he say about the proposals?

FRANZ. He was ready to turn over everything at once, the squire and money as well, just so that you would be freed. But when he heard that you could be released without it, and your word alone would be weighed as equal to the boy, then he absolutely insisted that the struggle with Berlichingen be postponed. He told me a hundred things to say to you, I've forgotten them. It was a long sermon on a single text: "I can't do without Weislingen."

WEISLINGEN. He'll have to learn how!

FRANZ. What do you mean? He said, "Make him hurry, everything waits upon him."

WEISLINGEN. Let it wait. I am not returning to the court.

FRANZ. Not to the court? Lord! What makes you say that? If you only knew what I know. If you could but dream what I have seen.

WEISLINGEN. What happened to you?

FRANZ. Just the memory of it is enough to make me lose control. Bamberg is Bamberg no longer, an angel in woman's form has transformed it into the antechamber of heaven.

WEISLINGEN. Nothing more?

FRANZ. I'll turn priest if you see her and don't lose your mind.

WEISLINGEN. Who is she then?

FRANZ. Adelheid von Walldorf.

WEISLINGEN. Her! I've heard a lot about her beauty.

FRANZ. Heard! That's as much as saying, I've seen music. It is just as impossible for the tongue to express the line of her perfections, since the eye itself in her presence is not good enough.

WEISLINGEN. You're not making sense.

FRANZ. That may be. That last time I saw her I had no more control of my senses than a drunkard. Or rather, let me say, I felt at that moment the way the saints must feel in the presence of a heavenly vision. All my senses stronger, more exalted and more complete, and yet the use of none.

WEISLINGEN. That is strange.

FRANZ. When I took my leave from the Bishop, she was with him. They were playing chess. He was very gracious, gave me his hand to kiss and said a great deal to me, much of it I didn't hear. For I was gazing at the lady beside him, she had fixed her eyes on the chess board, as if she were planning a masterstroke. A fine, calculating expression upon her mouth and cheeks! I would have liked to be the ivory chess king. Nobility and friendliness were blended in her brow. And the blinding light of her face and breast, offset by her dark hair!

WEISLINGEN. The sight has turned you into a poet.

FRANZ. In that moment I can feel what makes a poet, a full heart, filled with one single emotion. When the Bishop had ended and I bowed to him, she looked at me and said: "From me, too—greetings from a stranger! Tell him he should come quickly. New friends are waiting for him, he should not despise them, even though he may be so rich in old ones."—I wanted to answer something, but the passage between heart and tongue was blocked. I bowed my head. I would have sacrificed all my possessions to be allowed to kiss the tip of her little finger! While I was standing there, the Bishop dropped a pawn, I reached down to pick it up and in doing so touched the hem of her dress; that sent shock waves all through my limbs, and I have no idea how I managed to get out through the door.

WEISLINGEN. Is her husband at court?

FRANZ. She has been a widow for four months. She is staying in Bamberg to be distracted. You will see her. When she looks at you, it's as if you were standing in the sunlight of spring.

WEISLINGEN. It would have a weaker effect on me.

FRANZ. I hear you are as good as married.

WEISLINGEN. Would that I already were. My gentle Maria will make my life a happiness. Her sweet soul is mirrored in her blue eyes. And like an angel from heaven, formed of innocence and love, wisely she guides my heart toward peace and happiness. Pack up my things! And then to my castle! I do not wish to see Bamberg, even if St. Vitus in person bid me to come. (*He leaves*.)

FRANZ. God forbid! We'll hope for the best! Maria is loving and beautiful, and I can't blame a prisoner and a sick man for falling in love with her. In her eyes there is solace, a congenial melancholy.—But surrounding you, Adelheid, there is life, fire, courage—What I would do!—I am a fool—One glance from her made me that way. My Lord must go there! I must go there! And then I'll gaze on her until I recover my senses again or else go quite mad.

ACT II

Bamberg
A Hall
The Bishop, Adelheid, playing chess. Liebetraut with a zither. Ladies and Courtiers gathered around them by the fireplace.

LIEBETRAUT (*plays and sings*).

Young Cupid flew hither
With bow and with quiver,
His torch like a brand,
To vaunt in the battle
His masculine mettle,
His conquering hand.
  Up! Up!
  On! On!
His weapons were clashing
His winglets were flashing,
His eyes, how they burned!

And here he found bosoms—
Alas, they were bare;
And laps here to sit on;
They welcomed him there.
He shook all his arrows
Right into the flames.
They cradled him, squeezed him,
And played loving games.
  Heigh, eigh, ho, popeio!

ADELHEID. You're not concentrating on the game. Check to your king!
BISHOP. There is still a way out.
ADELHEID. But not for long. Check to your king!
LIEBETRAUT. This is not a game I'd play, were I a great lord; I'd ban it in the court and in all the land.

ADELHEID. It's true, this game is a test for the brain.

LIEBETRAUT. Not for that! I'd rather hear the toll of the funeral bell and the cry of ominous birds, rather the barking of the angry watchdog Conscience, rather hear them even through a deep sleep, than to hear from your knights, your bishops and your other beasts that eternal: "Check to the king!"

BISHOP. Who could ever have thought that up!

LIEBETRAUT. Someone for example who was weak and had a strong conscience, as often they go together. They call it a royal game and claim it was invented for a king, who rewarded the inventor with an ocean of largess. If that is true, I feel that I see him before me. He was a minor in wits or in years, the ward of his mother or his wife, had baby hair in his beard and flax at his temples, he was as pliable as a willow-shoot and liked to play checkers and with the ladies, not out of passion—God forbid!—but to pass the time. His tutor, too active for a scholar, too inflexible for a man of the world, invented the game *in usum Delphini*, thus making it so like his Majesty—and so on.

ADELHEID. Checkmate! Liebetraut, you should fill in the gaps of our history books.

They stand up.

LIEBETRAUT. The gaps of our genealogies—that would be more profitable. Ever since the deeds of our ancestors have served the same purpose as their portraits, namely to decorate the empty walls of our rooms and our characters, there would be profit in it.

BISHOP. He won't come, you say!

ADELHEID. I beg you, put it out of your mind.

BISHOP. What could it be?

LIEBETRAUT. What? The causes can be prayed off like rosary beads. He has fallen into a kind of contrition, which I could cure him of in a hurry.

BISHOP. Do that, go to him.

LIEBETRAUT. My assignment?

BISHOP. No restrictions. Spare nothing, if you can bring him back.

LIEBETRAUT. May I also involve you, my Lady?

ADELHEID. With discretion.

LIEBETRAUT. That is a broad assignment.

ADELHEID. Do you know me so little, or are you too young to know the right tone for speaking to Weislingen about me?

LIEBETRAUT. With the tone of a bird-call, I should think.

ADELHEID. You'll never learn to be sensible.

LIEBETRAUT. Does one ever learn that, dear Lady?

BISHOP. Go on, go on. Take the best horse from my stable, choose your squires, and bring him here to me!

LIEBETRAUT. If I cannot conjure him hither, then say that an old woman who cures warts and freckles knows more about sympathetic magic than I.

BISHOP. What good will that do! Berlichingen has taken him in completely. If he comes to us, he will want to leave again.

LIEBETRAUT. Want to, no question, but whether he can. The handshake of a prince and the smile of a beautiful woman! No Weislingen will get free of those. I hasten to take my leave of your Grace.

BISHOP. A happy journey.

ADELHEID. Adieu. (*He leaves.*)

BISHOP. Once he is here I leave it to you.

ADELHEID. Do you want to use me as bird-bait?

BISHOP. Not at all.

ADELHEID. As a decoy then?

BISHOP. No, that's Liebetraut's role. I beg you, do not refuse me what no one else can grant.

ADELHEID. We'll see.

Jaxthausen
Hanns von Selbitz. Goetz.

SELBITZ. Everyone will praise you for proclaiming a feud against those Nurembergers.

GOETZ. It would have destroyed me if I had failed to repay them for very long. It's come to light, they betrayed my squire to the Bambergers. They'd better not forget me.

SELBITZ. They have an old grievance against you.

GOETZ. And I against them, I'm even pleased that they made the first move.

SELBITZ. The imperial cities and the clergy have already sided together.

GOETZ. They have a reason to.

SELBITZ. We'll try to make things hot for them in Hell.

GOETZ. I was counting on you. Would to God the burgomaster of Nuremberg with his golden chain around his neck might fall into our net; with all his wit he'd be in for a surprise.

SELBITZ. I hear Weislingen is on our side again. Will he join us?

GOETZ. Not yet, there's a reason why he can't yet openly give us his support; but for the while it's enough that he's not against us. Without him the priest is no better than the vestments are without the priest.

SELBITZ. When do we set out?

GOETZ. Tomorrow or the day after. Soon there'll be merchants from Bamberg and Nuremberg coming from the Frankfurt Fair. It will bring us a good catch.

SELBITZ. God willing. (*They leave.*)

Bamberg
Adelheid's Room
Adelheid. Lady-in-Waiting.

ADELHEID. He's here, you say! I hardly believe it.

LADY. If I had not seen him myself, I would say I doubted it.

ADELHEID. The Bishop should mount Liebetraut in gold, he has achieved a masterpiece.

LADY. I saw him as he was about to ride into the castle, he was mounted on a white horse. As it approached the bridge it shied and wouldn't budge from the spot. The people came running down all the streets to see him. They enjoyed the horse's bad behavior. On all sides he was greeted, and he thanked them all. He sat his mount with an easy indifference, and with flattery and threats he finally forced it into the gate, Liebetraut with him and just a few squires.

ADELHEID. How does he please you?

LADY. As few men have. He looked like the Emperor here (*points to a portrait of Maximilian*), as if he were his son. The nose a bit smaller, just such friendly, light-brown eyes, just such beautiful blond hair, and built like a statue. A bit of sadness in his face—I don't know—it was very attractive!

ADELHEID. I'm curious to see him.

LADY. That would be a Lord for you.

ADELHEID. Fool!

LADY. Children and fools—

Liebetraut enters.

LIEBETRAUT. Now, dear Lady, what have I earned?

ADELHEID. A cuckold's horns from your wife. For to judge by this you must have already cajoled many a neighbor's honest housewife away from her duty.

LIEBETRAUT. Not so, dear Lady! Into her duty, you mean to say; for if it ever happened, then I cajoled her into her husband's bed.

ADELHEID. How did you manage to bring him here?

LIEBETRAUT. You know only too well how to catch a woodcock; do I have to teach you my little tricks as well?—First, I acted as if I knew nothing, understood nothing about his conduct, and placed him at the disadvantage of having to tell the whole story. Right away, I saw it all from a different side than he, couldn't understand—couldn't see—and so forth. Then I spoke about Bamberg, everything all at once, great and small, awakened certain memories, and once I got his imagination working, I managed to connect a number of threads which I found torn. He did not know what was happening to him, felt a new longing toward Bamberg, he wanted to—without wanting to. When he turned to his own heart and tried to work it all out, when he was much too concerned with himself to take care for himself, I slipped a line around his neck woven with three powerful strands: women, princely favor, and flattery, and with that I dragged him here.

ADELHEID. What did you say about me?

LIEBETRAUT. The simple truth. That you were having difficulties with your estates—were hoping, since he counts for so much with the Emperor, that he could easily end that for you.

ADELHEID. Fine.

LIEBETRAUT. The Bishop will bring him to you.

ADELHEID. I shall await them. (*Liebetraut leaves.*) With feelings such as I've seldom felt, in awaiting a visit.

In the Spessart
Berlichingen. Selbitz. Georg as squire.

GOETZ. You didn't find him, Georg?

GEORG. The day before he had ridden with Liebetraut to Bamberg and two squires with him.

GOETZ. I can't see what that's all about.

SELBITZ. I can. Your reconciliation was a bit too hasty to last for long. Liebetraut is a clever fellow, he's let himself be hoodwinked by him.

GOETZ. Do you believe he'll break his bond?

SELBITZ. The first step has been taken.

GOETZ. I don't believe it. Who knows what need there was to go to court; they still are in his debt there; let's hope for the best.

SELBITZ. Would God he deserves it and might do what's best!

GOETZ. A plan occurs to me. We'll have Georg put on that captured cloak from the Bamberg trooper and give him the safe-conduct pass; let him ride to Bamberg and see how things stand.

GEORG. I've long hoped for that.

GOETZ. It's your first mission. Be careful, boy! I'd be sorry if you met with an accident.

GEORG. Don't worry, I don't care how many men I find crawling around me, to me it's only like rats and mice. (*He leaves.*)

Bamberg
The Bishop. Weislingen.

BISHOP. You do not wish to be kept here longer?

WEISLINGEN. You would not ask that I break my oath.

BISHOP. I could have asked that you not swear it. What sort of spirit possessed you? Could I not have set you free without that? Do I count for so little at the Imperial Court?

WEISLINGEN. It is done; forgive me if you can.

BISHOP. I do not comprehend at all what required you to take such a step! Why renounce me? Were there not a hundred other conditions by which to get free? Do we not hold his squire? Wouldn't I have given money enough to quiet him down again? Our operations against him and his companions would have gone on.—Ah, I forget that I am talking with his friend, who is now working against me and can easily defuse the mines which he himself put in place.

WEISLINGEN. Gracious Lord!

BISHOP. And yet—now that I see your face again, hear your voice. It's not possible, not possible!

WEISLINGEN. Farewell, gracious Lord.

BISHOP. I give you my blessing. Formerly, whenever we parted, I said: "Till we meet again." Now—God willing, we'll never see each other again.

WEISLINGEN. There's a lot that can change.

BISHOP. Alas, there's too much that has changed already. Perhaps I will see you once again, as an enemy before my walls, laying waste my fields, which now have you to thank that they are in full bloom.

WEISLINGEN. No, gracious Lord.

BISHOP. You cannot say No. The secular estates, my neighbors, all are out to get me. As long as I had you—Go, Weislingen! I have nothing more to say to you. You have undone a great deal. Go!

WEISLINGEN. And I do not know what to say. (*Bishop leaves.*)

Enter Franz.

FRANZ. Adelheid is waiting for you. She is not well. But she does not want to let you go without saying goodbye.

WEISLINGEN. Come.

FRANZ. Are we really leaving?

WEISLINGEN. This very evening.—

FRANZ. I feel as if I were taking leave of the world.

WEISLINGEN. So do I, and as if I didn't know where I was going either.

Adelheid's Room
Adelheid. Lady.

LADY. You're looking pale, dear Lady.

ADELHEID. —I don't love him, and yet I wish he would stay. You see, I could live with him, even if I do not yet want him as a husband.

LADY. Do you believe he's going?

ADELHEID. He's gone to the Bishop to take his leave.

LADY. After that he still has a hard stand to make.

ADELHEID. What do you mean?

LADY. How can you ask, dear Lady? You caught his heart on your hook, and if he wants to tear himself free, he'll bleed to death.

Adelheid. Weislingen.

WEISLINGEN. You are not well, dear Lady?

ADELHEID. That can be of little concern to you. You abandon us, abandon us forever. Why do you ask whether we live or die?

WEISLINGEN. You misjudge me.

ADELHEID. I take you as you seem to be.

WEISLINGEN. Appearances deceive.

ADELHEID. So you're a chameleon?

WEISLINGEN. If only you could see my heart!

ADELHEID. Pretty things would meet my eyes.

WEISLINGEN. Indeed! You would find your image there.

ADELHEID. In some forgotten corner alongside the portraits of extinct families. I beg you, Weislingen, remember with whom you speak. False words count most when they are masks for our deeds. A masquerader who is recognized plays a pathetic role. You do not deny your deeds and yet speak the reverse; what should anyone take you for?

WEISLINGEN. What you will. I am so plagued by what I am that it matters little to me what I am taken for.

ADELHEID. You come to take your leave.

WEISLINGEN. Allow me to kiss your hand, and I will say: Farewell. You remind me! I did not think.—I am a burden, dear Lady.

ADELHEID. You misinterpret: I wanted to assist your leaving, since you want to leave.

WEISLINGEN. Oh, say rather that I must. Were I not obliged by knightly duty, the sacred clasp of hands—

ADELHEID. Go on! go! Tell that tale to the girls who read the Emperor's *Theuerdank* and wish they might have such a husband. Knightly duty! Childish games!

WEISLINGEN. You do not believe that.

ADELHEID. Upon my oath, you're dissembling! What have you promised? and to whom? You pledge your allegiance to a man who denies his duty to the Emperor and the Empire, and at just the moment when through your capture he incurs the imperial ban as punishment. Obliged by your duty!—a duty which cannot be more valid than an illegal oath obtained by force. Do not our laws release us from such vows? Teach such wisdom to children who believe in hobgoblins. Other matters lie concealed here. To become an enemy of the Empire, an enemy of the civil peace and welfare! An enemy of the Emperor! Companion to a brigand! You, Weislingen, with your gentle soul!

WEISLINGEN. If you only knew him—

ADELHEID. I only wish that justice might be done him. He has an exalted, unfettered soul. And for that very reason, woe to you, Weislingen! Go and imagine that you're his companion. Go! and let yourself be ruled by him. You are friendly, congenial—

WEISLINGEN. And so is he.

ADELHEID. But you are yielding, and he is not! Without realizing it you'll be swept away by him, you'll be the slave of a nobleman, when you could be the master of princes.—But it is cruel to paint such a dark picture of your future status.

WEISLINGEN. If you could have felt how affectionately he received me.

ADELHEID. Affectionately! You credit him with that? It was what he owed you; and what would you have lost if he had been hostile? To me that would have been even more welcome. An arrogant man like that—

WEISLINGEN. You speak about your enemy.

ADELHEID. I speak for your freedom—And I have no idea at all why I should be interested in that. Farewell!

WEISLINGEN. Allow me just a moment more. (*He takes her hand and is silent.*)

ADELHEID. Have you anything further to say to me?

WEISLINGEN. ——I must leave.

ADELHEID. Then go.

WEISLINGEN. Dear Lady!—I cannot.

ADELHEID. You must.

WEISLINGEN. Is this to be my last sight of you?

ADELHEID. Go, I am ill, at a most inopportune time.

WEISLINGEN. Do not look at me so.

ADELHEID. Will you be our enemy and have us smile at you? Go!

WEISLINGEN. Adelheid!

ADELHEID. I hate you!

Franz enters.

FRANZ. Noble Lord! The Bishop is calling for you.

ADELHEID. Go! Go!

FRANZ. He bids you to come quickly.

ADELHEID. Go! Go!

WEISLINGEN. I will not say goodbye, I will see you again. (*He leaves.*)

ADELHEID. See me again? We shall tend to that. Margarete, if he comes, send him away! I am ill, I have a headache, I'm sleeping—Send him away! If he can still be won, then this is the way to do it. (*She leaves.*)

Antechamber
Weislingen. Franz.

WEISLINGEN. She won't see me?

FRANZ. Night's coming on; shall I saddle the horses?

WEISLINGEN. She won't see me!
FRANZ. When will your Grace order the horses?
WEISLINGEN. It is too late! We will stay here.
FRANZ. Thank God! (*He leaves.*)
WEISLINGEN. You'll stay? Be on your guard, the temptation is great. My horse shied as I tried to ride through the castle gate, my good angel stood in his way, he knew the dangers that awaited me here.—Still, it's wrong not to attend to the various matters which I left unfinished for the Bishop and at least arrange them in such a way that a successor can pick things up where I left them. That can all be done without damaging the bond between Berlichingen and me. For they won't keep me here.—Would have been better if I hadn't come. But I will be off—tomorrow, or the day after. (*He leaves.*)

In the Spessart
Goetz. Selbitz. Georg.

SELBITZ. You see, it went just as I said.
GOETZ. No! no! no!
GEORG. Believe me, I'm telling you the truth. I did as you commanded, took the cloak of the Bamberger and his pass, and in order to earn my food and drink, I escorted peasants from Reineck up to Bamberg.
SELBITZ. In disguise? That could have turned out badly for you.
GEORG. That's my thought, too, looking back. A rider who thinks ahead will not attempt any great leaps. I came to Bamberg and right away I heard the story at the inn: Weislingen and the Bishop are reconciled and they talked a lot about a marriage with the widow von Walldorf.
GOETZ. Just talk.
GEORG. I saw him when he was escorting her to table. She is beautiful, by my oath, she is beautiful. We all bowed, she thanked all of us, he nodded his head, looked very pleased with himself, they went on past, and the people murmured: a handsome pair!
GOETZ. That may be.
GEORG. Listen further! When he went to mass the next day, I watched for my chance. He was alone with a page. I stood below him on the stair and spoke softly to him: "A few words from your friend Berlichingen!" He was startled; I saw in his face a confession of his misdeed, he scarcely had the heart to look at me, at me: a mere squire.
SELBITZ. That's because his conscience was worse than your rank.
GEORG. "Are you a Bamberger?" said he. "I bring you greetings from the Knight of Berlichingen," said I, "and I'm to ask you—" "Come tomorrow morning," said he, "to my room, we will talk further."
GOETZ. Did you go?
GEORG. Indeed I did, and had to wait in the antechamber for a long,

long while. And those silken boys stared at me from front and back. "Go ahead and look," I thought.—Finally I was led in, he seemed angry, it was no matter to me. I stepped up to him and carried out my assignment. He acted hostile and angry, like someone who has no courage and doesn't want it to be noticed. He was amazed that you used a squire to take him to task. That upset me. I said, there were two kinds of people, brave ones and scoundrels, and I served Goetz von Berlichingen. Now he started in and spouted all kinds of confusing stuff, which came to this: You had rushed him, and he had no obligation to you, and wanted nothing to do with you.

GOETZ. You have that from his own mouth?

GEORG. That and still more—He threatened me.

GOETZ. That's enough! Now he is lost to us, too! Loyalty and trust, you've betrayed me once again. Poor Maria! How will I break this to you?

SELBITZ. I had rather lose my second leg than be such a dirty dog. (*They leave.*)

Bamberg
Adelheid. Weislingen.

ADELHEID. Time begins to drag unbearably for me; I don't want to talk and I'm ashamed to play with you. Boredom, you're more trouble than a cold fever.

WEISLINGEN. Have you already grown tired of me?

ADELHEID. Not of you so much as your company. I wish you were where you wanted to go, and we had not held you back.

WEISLINGEN. Such is woman's favor! First, with the warmth of a mother she broods over our dearest hopes; then like a fickle hen she leaves the nest and abandons her growing progeny to death and decay.

ADELHEID. Blame it on the woman! A reckless gambler tears up and tramples on the cards which were the innocent cause of his losing. But allow me to tell you something about men. Who are you to talk about being fickle? You, who are seldom what you claim to be, never what you ought to be. Monarchs in holiday robes, envied by the mob. What would the wife of a tailor give to wear a string of pearls about her neck from the hem of your cloak that is kicked aside contemptuously by your heels!

WEISLINGEN. You are bitter.

ADELHEID. That's the refrain to your song. Before I knew you, Weislingen, I was like the tailor's wife. Rumor with its hundred tongues, not speaking metaphorically either, had drawn you out as a tooth surgeon would, so I let myself be talked into wishing: "If only you could catch a glimpse of this quintessence of the male sex, this phoenix of a Weislingen!" My wish was granted to me.

WEISLINGEN. And this phoenix proved to be an ordinary cock-of-the-walk.

ADELHEID. No, Weislingen, I became interested in you.

WEISLINGEN. It seemed so—

ADELHEID. And was. For truly you even surpassed your reputation. The mob only respects the reflected light of merit. Just as I have a tendency not to think about the people I like, so we lived awhile side by side; I felt something was missing and I didn't know what it was that I found lacking in you. Finally my eyes were opened. Instead of the active man who enlivened the affairs of a principality, who did not forget himself and his reputation in doing so, who had scaled the heights of the clouds in a hundred good deeds, as over mountains heaped one on top of another—I suddenly saw this man whining like a sickly poet, melancholic as a healthy girl, and more idle than an aged bachelor. At first I attributed this to your misfortune, which still lay fresh upon your heart, and I excused you as well as I could. Now, since you seem to be getting worse from day to day, you'll have to forgive me if I withdraw my favor from you. You have no right to possess it, I gave it as a gift for life to another, who could not transfer it to you.

WEISLINGEN. Then set me free!

ADELHEID. Not before all hope is lost. Solitude in such circumstances is dangerous.—You poor man! You're as dejected as someone whose first girl has been unfaithful, and just for that reason I will not give you up. Give me your hand, forgive me for what my love has said to you.

WEISLINGEN. If you could love me, if you could grant me only one drop of relief for my ardent passion! Adelheid! your accusations are most unjust! If you could guess even a hundredth part of what has been going on in me all this time, you would not have torn me this way and that way so mercilessly, with condescension, indifference and contempt.—You smile!—To come to terms with myself again after taking such an overhasty step, cost me more than one day. To turn against the man whose memory is still so vividly new in my affections!

ADELHEID. Strange man, to love the one you envy! That's as if I were to provide provisions for my enemy.

WEISLINGEN. I know this matter brooks no delay. He has received the news that I am Weislingen again, and he will avail himself of his advantage over us. Besides, Adelheid, we're not so slow as you think. Our horsemen are reinforced and alert, our negotiations are going forward, and we hope the Imperial Diet in Augsburg will bring our projects to fulfillment.

ADELHEID. You're going there?

WEISLINGEN. If I could only take one hope along with me. (*He kisses her hand.*)

ADELHEID. Oh, you of little faith! Only signs and wonders! Go, Weislingen, and complete your work. The Bishop's advantage and yours and mine are so interwoven that even if only for the sake of politics—

WEISLINGEN. How can you joke about it?

ADELHEID. I'm not joking. My estates are being held by the haughty Duke, and yours will not long be left in place by Goetz; and if we do not keep together like our enemies and steer the Emperor to our side, we'll be lost.

WEISLINGEN. I'm not worried. The majority of the princes thinks as we do. The Emperor is demanding aid against the Turks and to get it he'll have to stand by us. What a pleasure it will be for me to liberate your estates from overbearing enemies, to get these unruly Swabian heads back down on their pillows and to restore peace to the Bishopric and to ourselves. And then?—

ADELHEID. One day follows another, and the future's in the hands of destiny.

WEISLINGEN. But we have to want it.

ADELHEID. And we do want it.

WEISLINGEN. Truly?

ADELHEID. Of course. Now go.

WEISLINGEN. You sorceress!

An Inn

A peasant wedding. Music and dancing outside.
The Bride's Father, Goetz, Selbitz at a table.

The Bridegroom comes up to them.

GOETZ. And the most clever thing of all is that you resolve your quarrel so happily, so congenially, with a marriage.

FATHER OF THE BRIDE. Better than I could have dreamed it. In peace and quiet with my neighbors and a daughter well taken care of in the bargain!

BRIDEGROOM. And I'm the owner of the lot at issue and besides have won the prettiest filly in the whole village. Would God that you had started your feud even sooner!

SELBITZ. How long have you been in court?

FATHER OF THE BRIDE. Almost eight years. I'd rather have the ague for as long again as have to start that up once more. That's all a hassle, you wouldn't believe, till you squeeze a verdict out of the hearts of those periwigs; and what have you got when all is done? May the devil fetch that Assessor Sapupi! He's a damned swarthy Italian!

BRIDEGROOM. Yes, that's a crazy fellow. Twice I was over there.

FATHER OF THE BRIDE. And I three times. And look you, my Lords: how are we finally going to get our verdict, where I've as much right as the other fellow, and he as much as me, and we just stand there with our mouths wide open, until the good Lord gives me the idea to let him have my daughter and the whole works as well.

GOETZ (*drinks*). Here's luck in future trials!

FATHER OF THE BRIDE. God willing! But however it may be, I'll not submit again to court procedures as long as I live. What that costs for a pretty penny! For every bow your attorney makes, it's you who has to pay up.

SELBITZ. Well, there are imperial visitations once a year.

FATHER OF THE BRIDE. Not a trace of them! And many a handsome thaler was squeezed out of me for extras. An unbelievable swindle!

GOETZ. How do you mean?

FATHER OF THE BRIDE. Ah, they all hold out their paws palms up! The Assessor alone, may God forgive him, took me for eighteen gold guilders.

BRIDEGROOM. Who?

FATHER OF THE BRIDE. Who else but this Sapupi!

GOETZ. That's a scandal.

FATHER OF THE BRIDE. Indeed it is. I had to put down twenty. And when I'd paid it all out to him, in his country house, which is a splendid place, in the great hall, I thought my heart would break for grief. For don't you see, a man's house and yard can stand secure, but where's he to find ready cash? There I stood, God knows how I felt. I didn't have so much as a red cent in my pocket for my travel expenses. Finally I summon up my courage and tell him so. Now when he saw I was about to go under, he threw back two of them and sent me away.

BRIDEGROOM. That's not possible! Sapupi?

FATHER OF THE BRIDE. Why are you acting surprised? Of course, it was him. No one else.

BRIDEGROOM. The devil take him, he also relieved me of fifteen gold guilders.

FATHER OF THE BRIDE. Damnation!

SELBITZ. Goetz! *We're* supposed to be the brigands!

FATHER OF THE BRIDE. So that's the reason the verdict came out so one-sided. You dog!

GOETZ. Don't let that go unpunished.

FATHER OF THE BRIDE. What should we do?

GOETZ. Get yourself to Speyer, it's just now the time for the visitation; lodge a complaint, they have to investigate it and then they'll help you to get what's yours.

BRIDEGROOM. Do you think we can get it through?

GOETZ. If I could get hold of him by the ears, I'd promise it to you.

SELBITZ. For that sum it's worth a try.

GOETZ. There were times when I'd ride out for a fourth that amount.
FATHER OF THE BRIDE. What do you think?
BRIDEGROOM. Let's try it, come what may.

Enter Georg.

GEORG. The Nurembergers are on the march.
GOETZ. Whereabouts?
GEORG. If we get moving right away, we'll catch them between Beerheim and Muehlbach, in the forest.
SELBITZ. Splendid!
GOETZ. Come on, children! God be with you all! and may he help us all to get what's ours!
PEASANT. Many thanks to you! Won't you stay for a late snack?
GOETZ. No time. Adieu.

ACT III

Augsburg
A Garden
Two Merchants from Nuremberg.

FIRST MERCHANT. Let's stand here, the Emperor has to come by there. He's just coming along the Allée.
SECOND MERCHANT. Who is that with him?
FIRST MERCHANT. Adelbert von Weislingen.
SECOND MERCHANT. Bamberg's friend! That's good.
FIRST MERCHANT. Let's kneel before him, and I'll do the talking.
SECOND MERCHANT. All right, here they come.

Emperor. Weislingen.

FIRST MERCHANT. He looks annoyed.
EMPEROR. I am disheartened, Weislingen, and when I look back over my past life, I might well despair, so many projects half complete, so many failed! and all that because there is no prince in the Empire so small but he's more concerned with his own whims than with my thoughts.

The Merchants throw themselves at his feet.

MERCHANT. Supreme Majesty! Allpowerful!
EMPEROR. Who are you? What's going on?
MERCHANT. Poor merchants from Nuremberg, your Majesty's servants,

and we appeal to you for help. Goetz von Berlichingen and Hans von Selbitz fell upon thirty of us who were coming from the Frankfurt Fair under escort from Bamberg and robbed us. We pray to your Imperial Majesty for help, for support, else we are all ruined, forced to beg for our bread.

EMPEROR. Dear God! Dear God! What is this? One of them has only one hand, the other only one leg, if they just had two hands and two legs, what would you do then?

MERCHANT. We beg your Majesty most humbly to cast a sympathetic eye upon our troubled circumstances.

EMPEROR. Is this the way it goes? If a merchant loses a sack of pepper, the whole Empire is expected to take arms, and if there is trouble at hand, where much is at stake for his Imperial Majesty and the Empire, involving kingdoms, principalities, duchies and what all else, then no human being can get you together.

WEISLINGEN. You come at an unsuitable time. Go and wait here for a few days.

MERCHANT. We commend us to your Grace. (*They leave.*)

EMPEROR. Still more troubles! They proliferate like the heads of Hydra.

WEISLINGEN. And will not be eliminated but by fire and sword, and by resolute action.

EMPEROR. Do you think so?

WEISLINGEN. I hold nothing more certain, providing your Majesty and the princes could reach accord about other, more insignificant conflicts. It is by no means all of Germany that complains of unrest. Only Franconia and Swabia still glow from the embers of civil war and its internal destruction. And even there many of the nobles and the freeborn yearn for peace and quiet. If we only could get rid of this Sickingen, this Selbitz—this Berlichingen, the rest would soon collapse of its own accord. Those are the ones whose spirit drives the rebellious crowd.

EMPEROR. I wish I could spare those people, they are brave and noble. If I were to fight a war, I would need them among my army.

WEISLINGEN. It could be wished that they had learned long since to obey their duty. And what's more it would be extremely dangerous to reward their rebellious undertakings with positions of honor. For just such imperial generosity and grace is what till now they have so mightily abused, and their followers, who place their trust and hope on this, will not be checked until we have reduced them to nothing in the eyes of the world and have cut them off from all prospects for the future.

EMPEROR. So you advise force.

WEISLINGEN. I see no other means to control this delusion that possesses entire regions. Do we not already hear in various places the most bitter complaints of the nobles, that their vassals, their bondsmen rebel against them and challenge them, threaten to diminish their traditional sovereignty, so that most dangerous consequences are to be feared?

EMPEROR. This would be an opportune moment to move against Berlichingen and Selbitz, only I would not wish that any harm be done to them. I'd like to have them captive, and then they'd have to swear an oath of truce, to stay peacefully in their castles, and not to stray outside their ban. At the next session I will propose it.

WEISLINGEN. A joyous acclamation will spare your Majesty the end of your speech. (*They leave.*)

Jaxthausen
Sickingen. Berlichingen.

SICKINGEN. Yes, I have come to ask your noble sister for her heart and her hand.

GOETZ. I could wish you had come earlier. I must tell you, during his captivity Weislingen won her love, sued for her hand, and I gave him my consent. I released him, that captive bird, and he scorns the generous hand which fed him in his need. He's winging about, looking for nourishment, God knows on what bush.

SICKINGEN. Is that true?

GOETZ. As I have said.

SICKINGEN. He has severed a twofold bond. Be grateful that you are not now more closely related to that traitor.

GOETZ. She sits there, the poor girl, and laments and prays her life away.

SICKINGEN. We shall try to make her sing.

GOETZ. What? Can you bring yourself to marry an abandoned woman?

SICKINGEN. It's an honor to both of you, being betrayed by him. Should the poor girl have to enter a convent just because the first man she met was worthless? Far from it! I hold to my commitment, that she become the queen of all my castles.

GOETZ. I'm telling you that she was not indifferent to him.

SICKINGEN. Don't you trust me to chase off the shadow of a scoundrel? Let us go to her. (*They leave.*)

Camp of the Imperial Legation
Captain. Officers.

CAPTAIN. We must move carefully and spare our people as much as possible. Our strict orders are to drive him into a corner and capture him alive. It won't be easy, for who will dare to lay hand on him?

First Officer. That's true! And he will defend himself like a wild boar. Besides, in all his life he has never done any harm to us, and everyone will pass up the opportunity to risk life and limb for the sake of the Emperor and the Empire.

Second Officer. It would be a disgrace if we don't capture him. If I can just latch on to his coattail, he'll not get loose.

First Officer. Just don't grab him with your teeth, he might dislocate your jaw. My dear fellow, such people are not to be captured like a thief in flight.

Second Officer. We'll see.

Captain. Our letter must have reached him by now. We must not delay sending out a patrol to observe him.

Second Officer. Let me lead them.

Captain. You are unfamiliar with the territory.

Second Officer. One of my men was born and raised here.

Captain. That's agreeable to me. (*They leave.*)

Jaxthausen
Sickingen.

Sickingen. It's all going as I hoped; she was a bit startled by my proposal and looked me over from head to foot; I bet she was comparing me to her Whitefish. Thank God I can stand the scrutiny. She answered little and in confusion, all the better! Let it simmer for a time. With girls who have been wounded by misfortune in love a proposal of marriage makes a good broth.

Goetz enters.

Sickingen. What news, brother?

Goetz. I've been proclaimed an outlaw.

Sickingen. What?

Goetz. There, read the edifying letter. The Emperor has ordered the ban to be executed against me, the ban that says to carve up my flesh to feed the birds beneath the sky and the beasts upon the field.

Sickingen. Let them have their turn first. I'm here at just the right time.

Goetz. No, Sickingen, you must be off. You would trample your great projects in thc bud if you became an enemy of the Empire at such an inopportune time. You can also be more valuable to me if you appear to be neutral. The Emperor loves you, and the worst that can happen to me is to be taken prisoner, then you can use your good word, to rescue me from the ruin into which your premature aid would plunge us both. For what would happen? Now things are going against me; if they learn you are with me, they'll send more forces and we would be in no way better off. The Emperor controls things at the source, and I would be irretrievably lost, if it were possible to blow bravery into men as quickly as you can blow trumpets to marshall them.

SICKINGEN. At least I can secretly assign you twenty knights or so.

GOETZ. Good. I've already sent Georg to Selbitz and my men around the countryside. Dear Brother, when my people are gathered, it will be a troop of men the likes of which few princes have seen in one place.

SICKINGEN. You will be few against many.

GOETZ. One wolf is too many for a whole herd of sheep.

SICKINGEN. But if they have a good shepherd?

GOETZ. Don't worry! They're only hirelings. And even the best knight can do nothing, if he is not lord of his own actions. For instance, once they got after me, when I had promised to serve the Count Palatine against Conrad Schott. He presented me a memo from the Chancellery, telling me how I was supposed to ride and how to behave. I threw the paper back at the magistrates and said I didn't know how to operate that way; I don't know what I may run into that's not written in that piece of paper; I must keep my own eyes open and see what I have to do.

SICKINGEN. Good luck, brother! I'll leave at once and send you what I can gather together in a hurry.

GOETZ. Come join the ladies once more, I left them together. I wish you might have her word before you leave. Then send me the horsemen and come in secret to take Maria away, for my castle, I fear, will soon be no place for women to stay.

SICKINGEN. We'll hope for the best. (*They leave.*)

Bamberg
Adelheid's Room
Adelheid. Franz.

ADELHEID. So both the expeditions have already set out?

FRANZ. Yes, and my Lord has the pleasure of taking the field against your enemies. I wanted right away to go along, as glad as I am to see you. And I also want to be off again, so I can return soon with good news. My Lord has given me permission.

ADELHEID. How are things with him?

FRANZ. He is in good spirits. He commanded me to kiss your hand.

ADELHEID. There—your lips are warm.

FRANZ (*aside, indicating his breast*). Here it's still warmer! (*Aloud:*) Dear Lady, your servants are the luckiest fellows under the sun.

ADELHEID. Who is the leader against Berlichingen?

FRANZ. Baron von Sirau. Farewell, dear Lady. I must be off again. Do not forget me.

ADELHEID. You must eat, and drink, and rest.

FRANZ. What for? I've seen you. I'm not tired and not hungry.
ADELHEID. I know how loyal you are.
FRANZ. Ah, dear Lady.
ADELHEID. You can't keep this up; have some rest and something to eat.
FRANZ. What good care you take for a poor young fellow! (*He leaves.*)
ADELHEID. There were tears in his eyes. I love him from my heart. No one was ever so truly and warmly devoted to me. (*She leaves.*)

Jaxthausen
Goetz. Georg.

GEORG. He wants to speak with you himself. I don't know him, he's a big man with black, fiery eyes.
GOETZ. Bring him in.

Lerse enters.

GOETZ. God be with you. What do you bring me?
LERSE. Only myself, that's not much, but all that it is I offer you.
GOETZ. You are welcome, doubly welcome, a brave man, and at this time, when I had no hopes for winning new friends, but feared with every passing hour to lose my old ones. Give me your name.
LERSE. Franz Lerse.
GOETZ. I thank you, Franz, for the privilege of meeting a brave man.
LERSE. I gave you that privilege once before, but then you did not thank me for it.
GOETZ. I don't remember you.
LERSE. I'd be sorry if you did. Do you still remember how you came to be enemies with Conrad Schott because of the Count Palatine and wanted to ride to Hassfurth for carnival?
GOETZ. Well do I remember.
LERSE. You remember how along the way near a village you met up with twenty-five horsemen?
GOETZ. That's right. At first I took them for only twelve and divided my group—we were sixteen—and stopped at the village, behind the barn, meaning to let them move past me. Then I was going to follow after them, as I had laid out the plan with the rest of the group.
LERSE. But we saw you and rode up a hill by the village. You rode past and stopped below. When we saw you weren't about to come up, we rode down.
GOETZ. That's when I first saw I'd stuck my hand into the fire. Twenty-five against eight! There was no time to dally there. Erhard Truchsess ran one of my fellows through, for which I charged him off his horse. If they'd all held out like him and one other fellow, it would have gone badly for me and my small band.
LERSE. The fellow you say—

GOETZ. He was the bravest of any I've ever seen. He made things hot for me. Whenever I thought I'd got rid of him and was about to deal with some others, he was at my side again, slashing furiously. He cut through to my arm, a bit of a flesh wound.

LERSE. Have you forgiven him?

GOETZ. I liked him all too well.

LERSE. Well, I hope you'll be satisfied with me, I gave you a sample of my work on your own self.

GOETZ. You're the one? Then welcome, welcome. Oh, Maximilian, can you say you ever recruited anyone in your service this way?

LERSE. I'm surprised you didn't think of me sooner.

GOETZ. How should it occur to me that someone would offer me his service who tried to defeat me like the worst of my enemies?

LERSE. Precisely that, my Lord! From my youth I served as squire and have even taken on many a knight. When we attacked you, I was glad. I knew your name and so got to know you. You remember that I gave way, you saw it wasn't fear, for I came on again. In short, I got to know you and from that hour I was determined to serve you.

GOETZ. How long will you stay with me?

LERSE. For a year. Without pay.

GOETZ. No, you'll be signed on like any other, and more so, like the one who gave me such a go of it at Remlin.

Georg enters.

GEORG. Hans von Selbitz sends you his greetings. He'll be here tomorrow with fifty men.

GOETZ. Good.

GEORG. There's a troop of Imperials coming along the Kocher, no doubt to observe you.

GOETZ. How many?

GEORG. Fifty of them.

GOETZ. No more? Come on, Lerse, we'll beat them up, so Selbitz, when he comes, will find one bit of work already done.

LERSE. That'll be a nice early harvest.

GOETZ. To horse! (*They leave.*)

Forest, at the Edge of a Swamp
Two Imperial Soldiers, meeting each other.

FIRST SOLDIER. What are you up to here?

SECOND SOLDIER. I got leave to take care of nature's call. Since all that wild fracas in the dark last night my bowels are acting up, so I have to get off my horse every other minute.

FIRST SOLDIER. Have the troops stopped near here?

SECOND SOLDIER. About an hour up through the woods.

FIRST SOLDIER. Then how have you wandered off this far?

SECOND SOLDIER. I beg you, don't betray me. I'm trying to get to the next village, to see if I can't relieve my troubles with warm compresses. Where are you coming from?

FIRST SOLDIER. From the next village. I'm bringing wine and bread to our officer.

SECOND SOLDIER. So, he gets something for himself right before our eyes, and we're supposed to fast! Fine example.

FIRST SOLDIER. Come back with me, you rogue.

SECOND SOLDIER. I'd be a fool to. There are many in the group who'd be glad to fast if they could get as far away from it as I have.

FIRST SOLDIER. Do you hear that? Horses!

SECOND SOLDIER. Oh Lord!

FIRST SOLDIER. I'll climb this tree.

SECOND SOLDIER. I'll hide in these reeds.

Goetz, Lerse, Georg, Soldiers on horseback.

GOETZ. Here past the pond and to the left into the woods, then we'll come around behind them. (*They ride on.*)

FIRST SOLDIER (*climbs down from the tree*). This is no good. Michel! He doesn't answer? Michel, they're gone. (*He goes to the swamp.*) Michel! Oh God, he's sunk into it. Michel! he doesn't hear me, he's suffocated. You're done for, you coward.—We're defeated. Enemy, enemy everywhere.

Goetz, Georg on horseback.

GOETZ. Stop, fellow, or you're a dead man.

SOLDIER. Spare my life!

GOETZ. Your sword! Georg, lead him to the other prisoners Lerse's holding down there by the woods. I've got to catch up with their leader, he's fleeing. (*He leaves.*)

SOLDIER. What's become of the knight who was leading us?

GEORG. My Master knocked him off his horse head over heels, so his helmet stuck in the mire. His troopers lifted him onto his horse and off they went like madmen. (*They leave.*)

Camp
Captain. First Officer.

FIRST OFFICER. They're fleeing toward camp from far off.

CAPTAIN. He must be at their heels. Have fifty men move out as far as the mill, if he extends himself too far perhaps we can catch him. (*Officer leaves.*)

Second Officer, led in.

CAPTAIN. How goes it, young man? Have they knocked a few points from your antlers?

OFFICER. A plague on you! If I had antlers, even the strongest would have splintered like glass. You devil! He set upon me so, I felt as if I'd been struck to earth by a thunderbolt.

CAPTAIN. Thank God you've come out of it.

OFFICER. There's nothing to be thankful for, a couple of my ribs are broken. Where's the field surgeon? (*They leave.*)

Jaxthausen
Goetz. Selbitz.

GOETZ. What do you say to this declaration of ban, Selbitz?

SELBITZ. It's a trick of Weislingen's.

GOETZ. You think so?

SELBITZ. I don't think so, I know so.

GOETZ. How's that?

SELBITZ. He was there at the Imperial Diet, I tell you, at the Emperor's side.

GOETZ. Well, we'll just have to undo another of his schemes.

SELBITZ. Hope so.

GOETZ. Let's be off! and the rabbit hunt can begin again.

Camp
Captain. Officers.

CAPTAIN. This way we accomplish nothing, my Lords. He defeats us one detachment after the other, and whoever isn't killed or captured runs off in God's name toward Turkey rather than back into camp, so every day we grow weaker. Once and for all, we must go after him, and that in earnest, I want to be there myself and let him see who he's got to deal with.

OFFICER. That's all right by us, only he has the hang of the land so, knows all the paths and trails in the hills so well that he's as tough to catch as a mouse on a granary floor.

CAPTAIN. We'll get him all right. First, on to Jaxthausen. Whether he will or no, he'll have to come back to defend his castle.

OFFICER. Is our whole group to march?

CAPTAIN. Of course! Do you know that we've melted away by about a hundred?

OFFICER. Then let's move fast, before the whole iceberg thaws, it's getting warmer around us and we sit here like butter in the sun.

Mountain and Forest
Goetz. Selbitz. Troops.

GOETZ. They come in full force. It was high time that Sickingen's troops joined up with us.

SELBITZ. Let's divide up. I'll move around the hill to the left.

GOETZ. Good. And you, Franz, lead your fifty to the right up through the woods, they'll come across the heath, I'll take a stand against them. Georg, you stay with me. And when you see that they're attacking me, then fall on both their flanks with no delay. We'll slap 'em down. They don't think we can face them. (*They leave.*)

Heath, on One Side a Hill, on the Other a Forest
Captain. Troops for the Imperial Legation.

CAPTAIN. He's stopping on the heath! That's an impertinence. He'll pay for it. What! Not to fear the torrent that's roaring down on him?

OFFICER. I wish you would not ride at the front of our column, he looks as if he means to take the first who comes at him and plant him head downward in the earth. Better to ride in the rear.

CAPTAIN. Not willingly.

OFFICER. I beg you. You're still the knot that binds this bundle of hazel-rods together, loosen it and he'll snap them one by one like reeds.

CAPTAIN. Blow, trumpeter! and, all of you, blow him away! (*They leave.*)

Selbitz at a gallop from behind the hill.

SELBITZ. Follow me! Let them call to their hands: Be fruitful and multiply. (*He leaves.*)

Lerse from the forest.

LERSE. To the aid of Goetz! He's almost surrounded. Brave Selbitz, you've already broken through. We'll sow the heath with their thistle-heads. (*Passes on. Tumult.*)

A Hill with a Watchtower
Selbitz, wounded. Soldiers.

SELBITZ. Set me down here and get back to Goetz.

FIRST SOLDIER. Let us stay, Sir, you need us.

SELBITZ. Climb up on the watchtower, one of you, and see how things are going.

FIRST SOLDIER. How can I get up?

SECOND SOLDIER. Climb on my shoulders, then you can reach the hole and boost yourself up to the opening. (*Climbs up.*)

FIRST SOLDIER. Oh, Sir!

SELBITZ. What do you see?

FIRST SOLDIER. Your horsemen in flight. Toward the hill.

SELBITZ. Damned cowards! I wish they were standing fast and I were hit in the head by a bullet. Ride down, someone, and curse them, drive them back. (*Soldier leaves.*)

SELBITZ. Can you see Goetz?

SOLDIER. I see his three black feathers in the midst of the melee.

SELBITZ. Swim, brave swimmer. And here I lie!

SOLDIER. A white plume, who is that?

SELBITZ. The Captain.

SOLDIER. Goetz is pushing his way toward him—bam! He's down.

SELBITZ. The Captain?

SOLDIER. Yes, Sir.

SELBITZ. Good! Good!

SOLDIER. Oh! Oh! I don't see Goetz any longer.

SELBITZ. Then Selbitz dies.

SOLDIER. A terrible milling about where he stood. Georg's blue plume has also disappeared.

SELBITZ. Come on down. Do you see Lerse?

SOLDIER. Nothing. Everything is all topsy turvy.

SELBITZ. No more! Come! How do Sickingen's horsemen hold?

SOLDIER. Well.—There's one in flight toward the forest. Another! A whole troop. Goetz is done for.

SELBITZ. Come down.

SOLDIER. I can't—Yes! Yes! I see Goetz! I see Georg!

SELBITZ. On horseback?

SOLDIER. High on horseback! Victory! Victory! They're fleeing.

SELBITZ. The Imperial troops?

SOLDIER. Their banner in the midst of them, Goetz after them from behind. They're scattering. Goetz has reached the standard bearer—He's got the banner—He's stopped. A handful of men around him. My comrade has reached him—They're moving up here.

Goetz. Georg. Lerse. Troop of soldiers.

SELBITZ. Goetz, good news! Victory! Victory!

GOETZ (*dismounts*). But at what cost! You're wounded, Selbitz.

SELBITZ. You're alive and have won the victory. I did little. And those dogs, my troopers! How did you get free?

GOETZ. This time it worked! And to Georg here I owe thanks for my life and here to Lerse also. I threw their Captain from his steed. They cut down my horse and threw themselves on me, Georg fought through to me and dismounted, I like lightning up on his steed, he like thunder mounted again as well. How did you get that horse?

GEORG. From one of them who was swinging at you; I thrust my dagger into his gut when his cuirass was lifted up a bit. Down he fell, and I helped you free of an enemy and myself to a horse.

GOETZ. Now, there we stuck, till Franz fought his way in to us, and then we mowed through them from inside.

LERSE. The dogs I was leading were supposed to mow their way in from the outside until our scythes could meet, but they all took flight like Imperial troops.

GOETZ. Friend and foe both fled. Only the small group of you kept my back free, I had enough to do with the fellows in front of me. The fall of their Captain helped me shake them up, and they fled. I have their banner and a few prisoners.

SELBITZ. Did the Captain escape you?

GOETZ. By then they had rescued him. Come, boys, come, Selbitz! Make a stretcher with branches, you won't be able to ride. Come along to my castle. They're scattered. But we are few, and I don't know whether they've got troops to send after us. I offer you my hospitality, my friends. A glass of wine tastes good after a scrap like this.

Camp
Captain.

CAPTAIN. I'd like to kill you all with my own hands, a thousand curses on you! What do you mean, running away! He had less than a handful of men left! To run away like dirty cowards, from one man! No one will believe it, except for those who want to ridicule us.—Ride around, you and you and you. Wherever you find any of our scattered troops, either bring them back or strike them down. We must grind these notches out of our swords, even if the blades get worn down completely in the process.

Jaxthausen
Goetz. Lerse. Georg.

GOETZ. We can't delay for a single moment! Poor fellows, I can't allow you any rest at all. Quickly hunt around and try to round up some horsemen. Send them all to Weilern, there they'll be safest. If we hesitate, then they'll march on my castle. (*Both of them leave.*) I need to send someone out for news. Things are beginning to get hot, and if there were only some brave fellows left, but that's the way it is with the mob. (*He leaves.*)

Sickingen. Maria.

MARIA. I beg you, dear Sickingen, do not leave my brother! His horsemen, Selbitz's, yours, are all scattered; he is alone, Selbitz is wounded and has been taken to his castle, and I fear the worst.

SICKINGEN. Be calm, I shall not leave you.

Goetz enters.

GOETZ. Come into the church, the priest is waiting. In a quarter hour you can be a married couple.

SICKINGEN. Let me stay here.

GOETZ. You must go to the church now.

SICKINGEN. Gladly—and after that?

GOETZ. After that you can be on your way.

SICKINGEN. Goetz!

GOETZ. Won't you go to the church?

SICKINGEN. Come, come.

Camp

Captain. Knight.

CAPTAIN. How many are they all together?

KNIGHT. Hundred and fifty.

CAPTAIN. Out of four hundred! That's bad. Up now, quick and straight toward Jaxthausen, before he's recovered and can put himself in our way again.

Jaxthausen

Goetz. Elisabeth. Maria. Sickingen.

GOETZ. God bless you, grant you happy days, and preserve those he takes from you for your children.

ELISABETH. And may he make them just like you: upright! And then let them be whatever they want.

SICKINGEN. I thank you. And thank you, Maria. I led you to the altar and you will lead me to happiness.

MARIA. Let's set out together on a pilgrimage to this strange and blessed land.

GOETZ. Good luck on the journey.

MARIA. I don't mean it that way, we won't abandon you.

GOETZ. You must do so, sister.

MARIA. You're very cruel, brother.

GOETZ. And you're more gentle than wise.

Georg enters.

GEORG (*secretly*). I can't scare up anybody. One fellow was willing, then he changed his mind and wouldn't.

GOETZ. All right, Georg. Luck is beginning to get moody with me. I felt it coming. (*Aloud:*) Sickingen, I beg you, leave this very evening. Persuade Maria. She is now your wife. Make her realize she is! When women get mixed up in our affairs, our foes are safer in the open field than they'd otherwise be in their castles.

Servant enters.

SERVANT (*quietly*). Lord, the Imperial column is on the march, straight for us, very fast.

GOETZ. I've prodded them awake with whips. How many are they?

SERVANT. About two hundred. They can't be more than two hours from here.

GOETZ. Still beyond the river?

SERVANT. Yes, Lord.

GOETZ. If I only had fifty men, I'd not let them across. Did you not see Lerse?

SERVANT. No, Lord.

GOETZ. Instruct everyone to keep themselves in readiness.—There must be a parting, my loved ones. Weep, my dear Maria, there will come times when you will rejoice. It's better for you to weep on your wedding day, than for excess of joy to be the herald of future misery. Farewell, Maria. Farewell, brother.

MARIA. I cannot leave you, sister. Dear brother, don't refuse us! Have you so little respect for my husband that you scorn his help in this extremity?

GOETZ. Yes, it's come a long way with me. Perhaps I'm close to the end. You two begin your life today, and you should not share my fate. I have ordered your horses saddled. You must leave at once.

MARIA. Brother! Brother!

ELISABETH (*to Sickingen*). Give in to him! Leave!

SICKINGEN. Dear Maria, we must go.

MARIA. You, too? My heart will break.

GOETZ. Then stay. In a few hours my castle will be surrounded.

MARIA. Woe! woe!

GOETZ. We will defend ourselves as best we can.

MARIA. Mother of God, have mercy upon us.

GOETZ. And at the last, we'll die or we'll surrender.—You will have wept your noble husband into a common fate with me.

MARIA. You torture me.

GOETZ. Stay! Stay! We will be taken prisoner together. Sickingen, you'll fall along with me into the pit! I would have hoped you'd be the one to help me out.

MARIA. We will have to leave. Sister, sister!

GOETZ. Bring her to safety and then remember my cause.

SICKINGEN. I shall not enter her bed until I know that you're out of danger.

GOETZ. Sister—dear sister! (*He kisses her.*)

SICKINGEN. Away from here! Away!

GOETZ. One moment more.—I shall see you again. Be assured. We shall all meet again. (*Sickingen and Maria leave.*)

GOETZ. I drove them away, and now that she leaves, I'd like to keep them here. Elisabeth, you will stay with me?

ELISABETH. Until death. (*She leaves.*)

GOETZ. If God loves a man, he'll give him a wife like that.

Georg enters.

GEORG. They're nearby, I saw them from the tower. The sun rose and I saw their pikes flashing. When I saw them I felt no more fear than a cat faced by an army of mice. Though it's we who play the rats.

GOETZ. Make sure the gates are bolted. Barricade the inside with beams and stones. (*Georg leaves.*) We'll make fools of their patience. And as for their bravery, let them chew it away on their fingernails. (*Herald outside.*) Aha! some redcoated scoundrel, to put the question to us, whether we want to hoist the white flag. (*He goes to the window.*) What is that? (*Talking is heard in the distance.*)

GOETZ (*into his beard*). A noose around your neck.

Herald keeps talking.

GOETZ. "An insult to his Majesty!"—A priest put up that challenge.

Herald concludes.

GOETZ (*answers*). I should surrender! Unconditionally! Who are you talking to! Am I some brigand! Tell your Captain: To his Imperial Majesty, as ever, I offer all due respect. But as for him, you tell him, he can kiss my arse! (*He slams the window shut.*)

Siege. Kitchen

Elisabeth. Goetz joins her.

GOETZ. You have so much work, dear wife.

ELISABETH. I only wish I might have it for a long time. We will hardly be able to hold out for long.

GOETZ. We had no time to equip ourselves.

ELISABETH. And all these people whom you're always feeding. Our supply of wine is already dwindling.

GOETZ. If we can only hold out up to a certain point, so they offer to bargain for surrender. We'll do them plenty of damage. They'll shoot at us all day long and wound our walls and chip our windows. Lerse is a brave fellow; he creeps about with his musket; wherever anyone dares get too close, bang! he's done for.

SERVANT. Coal, my Lady!

GOETZ. What's happening?

SERVANT. The bullets are all gone, we want to cast new ones.

GOETZ. How are we fixed for powder?

SERVANT. Not badly. We're saving our shots well.

Hall

Lerse with a bullet mold. Servant with coal.

LERSE. Put it over there and see where you can find lead in the house. Meanwhile, I'll help myself here. (*Lifts a window from its frame and smashes the panes.*) Every advantage counts.—That's the way of the world, no man knows what can come of a thing. The glazier who set these panes never dreamed that the lead might some day give one of his great-grandchildren a splitting headache! And when my father begot me, he wasn't thinking what bird in the sky, what worm in the earth might feed on me.

Georg enters with an eaves trough.

GEORG. Here's your lead. If you hit them with only half of it, there won't be a one who gets away to report to his Majesty: Lord, we made a poor showing.

LERSE (*cutting some off*). A nice piece.

GEORG. Let the rain water run off some other way! I'm not bothered by it; a bold rider and a proper rain will get through anywhere!

LERSE (*as he pours*). Hold the ladle. (*He goes to the window.*) There's an Imperial lad sneaking about with his gun; they think we're all shot out. Let him sample this bullet, hot from the pan. (*He loads.*)

GEORG (*places the ladle to the mold*). Let me see.

LERSE (*shoots*). One sparrow down!

GEORG. He was shooting at me before (*they pour*), as I was climbing out of the attic window and trying to reach the eaves trough. He hit a dove that was perched next to me, it fell into the eaves trough; I thanked him for the roast and climbed back in with double booty.

LERSE. Now let's load up and walk around the whole of the castle, to earn our noonday meal.

Goetz enters.

GOETZ. Wait, Lerse! I need to talk to you! You, Georg, I don't want to keep you from the hunt. (*Georg leaves.*)

GOETZ. They're offering to negotiate.

LERSE. Let me go out to them and hear what they propose.

GOETZ. I know what it will be: house arrest, with stipulations attached.

LERSE. That won't do. How would it be if they were to grant free withdrawal, since you're not expecting any relief from Sickingen. We could bury the gold and silver where no dowser could find it for them, abandon the castle to them and get away in style.

GOETZ. They'll not allow us.

LERSE. It's worth a try. We'll call for a safe conduct and I'll go out. (*He leaves.*)

Hall

Goetz, Elisabeth, Georg, Servants at table.

GOETZ. So we are brought together by danger. Eat heartily, my friends! Don't forget drinking! The bottle is empty. Another, dear wife. (*Elisabeth shrugs her shoulders.*) Is there no more?

ELISABETH (*quietly*). One more! I put it aside for you.

GOETZ. Oh no, my dear! Bring it out! They need the strength, not me; it's my affair after all.

ELISABETH. Go get it out there in the cupboard.

GOETZ. It's the last one. And I feel as if we had no need to hold back. I haven't felt so pleased in a long time. (*He pours.*) Long live the Emperor!

ALL. Long may he live!

GOETZ. Let that be our next-to-last word when we're dying. I love him, for we share the same destiny. And I am more fortunate than he. He has to catch the mice for the imperial estates, while the rats are gnawing away at his possessions. I know he wishes sometimes that he were dead, rather than serve any longer as the soul of so crippled a body. (*He pours.*) There's just enough for one more round. And when our blood begins to dwindle like the wine in this bottle, first flowing weakly, then drop by drop (*he pours the last drops into his glass*), what should our last word be?

GEORG. Long live freedom!

GOETZ. Long live freedom!

ALL. Long live freedom!

GOETZ. And if that survives us, we can die in peace. For we'll see in spirit our grandchildren happy and the Emperors of our grandchildren happy. If the servants of our princes serve them as nobly and freely as you serve me, if the princes serve the Emperor as I would serve him—

GEORG. Then a lot would have to change.

GOETZ. Not so much as it might seem. Have I not known splendid men among the princes, and should such a race have died out? Good men, who were fortunate in themselves and their subjects; who could tolerate a free and noble neighbor beside them and neither fear him nor envy him; whose hearts rejoiced when they could view a number of their equals as guests at table, and did not need to transform knights into court toadies in order to live with them.

GEORG. Have you known such lords?

GOETZ. Indeed. I'll remember as long as I live how the Landgrave of Hanau held a hunt and the princes and lords who attended took their food under an open sky and the people from the countryside all came running to see them. That was no masquerade that he had staged in honor of himself. But the full, round heads of the boys and girls, all those red cheeks, and the prosperous men and the dignified elders, and all those happy faces, and how they shared in the glory of their master, who enjoyed himself on God's ground among them!

GEORG. That was a nobleman as perfect as you.

GOETZ. Should we not hope that more such princes might rule all together? That homage to the Emperor, peace and friendship among neighbors, and love among subjects will be the most valuable family treasure, inherited by grandchildren and great-grandchildren? Every man would preserve what is his own and increase it within himself, instead of believing as now that there is no increase for them unless they ruin others.

GEORG. And after that would we still go riding?

GOETZ. Would to God there might be no uneasy minds in all of Germany! We would still find enough to do. We could clear the mountains of wolves, could bring a roast from the forest to our neighbor who plows the soil in peace, and in return we would share his supper with him. If that were not sufficient for us, we could take our place with our brothers, like Cherubim with flaming swords, at the boundaries of the Empire, to face the wolves, the Turks, and the foxes, the French, and at the same time protect the exposed lands of our Emperor and the tranquility of his realm. That would be a life, Georg! when a man could risk his skin for the well-being of all. (*Georg jumps up.*) Where are you going?

GEORG. Ah, I forgot that we are locked in—and that the Emperor has locked us in—and to escape with our skins we must risk our skins.

GOETZ. Be of good courage!

Lerse enters.

LERSE. Freedom! Freedom! These are wretched men, indecisive, cautious asses. You are to withdraw with weapons, horses and armor. Provisions must be left behind.

GOETZ. They will not get a toothache chewing on what we leave.

LERSE (*secretly*). Have you hidden the silver?

GOETZ. No! Wife, go with Franz, he has something to say to you. (*All leave.*)

Courtyard of the Castle
Georg, in the stable, sings.

Once a bird was caught by a boy,
Hum, Hum!
He laughed into the cage with joy,
Hum, Hum!
So! So!
H'm! H'm!

He trusts his joy, so foolishly,
Hum, Hum!
Thrusts in his paw so clumsily,
Hum, Hum!
So! So!
H'm! H'm!

Out flew the tom-tit onto a thorn,
Hum, Hum!
And laughed the stupid boy to scorn,
Hum, Hum!
So! So!
H'm! H'm!

GOETZ (*enters*). How do things stand?

GEORG (*leads his horse out*). All saddled up.

GOETZ. You're quick.

GEORG. Like the bird out of its cage.

All the besieged enter.

GOETZ. You've all got your guns? Not so! Go up and fetch the best ones from the gun rack, it's all the same now. We'll ride ahead.

GEORG.

Hum! Hum!
So! So!
H'm! H'm! (*They leave.*)

Hall
Two Servants at the Gun Rack.

FIRST SERVANT. I'll take this one.
SECOND SERVANT. And I'll have this. There's an even better one.
FIRST SERVANT. Not so! Hurry, get out of here!
SECOND SERVANT. Listen!
FIRST SERVANT (*jumps to the window*). Help, merciful God! They're murdering our master! He's thrown from his horse! Georg's down!
SECOND SERVANT. How can we escape? Along the wall, down the nut tree, into the field! (*He leaves.*)
FIRST SERVANT. Franz is still holding them off, I'll go help him. If they all die, I don't want to live. (*He leaves.*)

ACT IV

Inn at Heilbronn
Goetz.

GOETZ. I feel like the evil spirit conjured into a sack by the Capuchin. I wear myself out and it gets me nowhere. These perjurors!

Elisabeth enters.

GOETZ. What news, Elisabeth, about my loyal followers?
ELISABETH. Nothing definite. Some were cut down, some lie in prison. No one could or would tell me anything more about them by name.
GOETZ. Is that the reward of loyalty? of childlike obedience?—'That it may be well with thee, and thou mayest live long on the earth!'
ELISABETH. Dear husband, do not chide our heavenly Father! They have their reward, it was born with them, a free and noble heart. Let them be captives, they are still free! You pay heed to the deputation of Councilors, their great golden chains suit their faces—
GOETZ. As a jewel of gold in a swine's snout. I'd like to see them lock up Georg and Franz!
ELISABETH. It would be a sight to make the angels weep.
GOETZ. I would not weep. I would grit my teeth and chew the cud of my fury. In chains, the apples of my eye! You dear lads, if only you had not loved me!—I could never get my fill of gazing on them.—Not to keep their word, given in the Emperor's name!
ELISABETH. Put such thoughts out of your mind. Consider the fact that you must appear before their Councils. You are in no state to confront them effectively, and I fear the worst.

GOETZ. What will they do to me?
ELISABETH. The Sergeant-at-arms!
GOETZ. The Jackass-at-justice! Hauls their sacks to the mill and their dung to the field. What is it?

Sergeant-at-arms enters.

SERGEANT. The Lord Commissioners are assembled in the Courthouse and have sent me for you.
GOETZ. I will come.
SERGEANT. I will accompany you.
GOETZ. A great honor.
ELISABETH. Keep your temper.
GOETZ. Have no fear. (*They leave.*)

The Courthouse
Imperial Councilors. Captain. Magistrates of Heilbronn.

MAGISTRATE. We have, as you ordered, assembled the strongest and boldest citizens; they're waiting here for your signal, to overpower Berlichingen.
FIRST COUNCILOR. It will be a great pleasure to be able to inform his Imperial Majesty of your willingness to obey his highest command.—Are they laborers?
MAGISTRATE. Blacksmiths, drayers of wine, carpenters, men with well-practiced fists and well equipped here. (*Pointing to his chest.*)
COUNCILOR. Good.

Sergeant-at-arms enters.

SERGEANT. Goetz von Berlichingen is waiting at the door.
COUNCILOR. Let him in!

Goetz enters.

GOETZ. God's greeting to you, gentlemen. What do you want of me?
COUNCILOR. First, that you consider where you are and before whom.
GOETZ. By my oath, I know exactly who you are, my Lords.
COUNCILOR. You do as your duty requires.
GOETZ. With all my heart.
COUNCILOR. Take a seat.
GOETZ. Down below there? I can stand. The stool smells of poor sinners, as indeed the whole chamber does.
COUNCILOR. Then stand!
GOETZ. To the point, if you please.
COUNCILOR. We shall proceed in proper order.
GOETZ. I'm satisfied with that; I wish it had always been that way.

COUNCILOR. You know that you were delivered into our hands unconditionally.

GOETZ. What will you give me, if I forget?

COUNCILOR. If I could give you a sense of discretion, I'd be helping your case.

GOETZ. Helping it! If only you could! That of course would take more than it would to damage it.

CLERK. Should I put all this into the record?

COUNCILOR. Whatever pertains to the proceedings.

GOETZ. As far as I'm concerned, you can have it printed.

COUNCILOR. You were in the Emperor's power, whose sovereign justice was replaced by fatherly clemency, who instead of consigning you to a dungeon, lodged you rather in Heilbronn, one of his beloved cities. You promised under oath, as befits a knight, to present yourself and to await with humility whatever follows.

GOETZ. True, and I am here and waiting.

COUNCILOR. And we are here to announce to you the clemency and favor of his Imperial Majesty. He pardons you your transgressions, pronounces you free of the ban and of all well-deserved punishment, which you will acknowledge with submissive gratitude and in return will repeat the oath of fealty, which will here be read out to you.

GOETZ. I am his Majesty's loyal servant, as ever. Just one word before you go on: my people, where are they? What will happen to them?

COUNCILOR. That is no concern of yours.

GOETZ. Then may the Emperor turn his face away from you when you are in need! They were my comrades and still are. Where have you taken them?

COUNCILOR. We are not obliged to give you any account of that.

GOETZ. Aha! I forgot that you are not even bound by what you promise, let alone—

COUNCILOR. Our commission is to present you with the oath of fealty. Submit to the Emperor and you will find a way to plead for the life and liberty of your comrades.

GOETZ. Your piece of paper!

COUNCILOR. Clerk, read it!

CLERK. "I, Goetz von Berlichingen, acknowledge publicly by this letter that I did recently rise up against my Emperor and his Empire in a rebellious manner"—

GOETZ. That's not true! I am no rebel, I have committed no crime against his Imperial Majesty, and the Empire is no concern of mine.

COUNCILOR. Restrain yourself and listen to the rest.

GOETZ. I don't want to hear any more. Let anyone step forth and testify! Have I ever taken one step against the Emperor, against the House of Austria? Have I not proven at all times, in all my actions, that I know better than anyone what Germany owes its Regent? and especially what the lesser nobles, knights, and freemen owe their Emperor? I would have to be a scoundrel if I allowed myself to be persuaded to put my signature to that.

COUNCILOR. And yet we have explicit orders to persuade you amicably to do just that or, in the event of non-compliance, to throw you into prison.

GOETZ. In prison! Me!

COUNCILOR. And there you can await your destiny at the hands of justice, if you refuse to accept it from the hands of clemency.

GOETZ. In prison! You abuse the Imperial power. In prison! That is not his command. What! First to set a trap for me, those traitors, and then bait it with their oath, their knightly word! Then to promise me house arrest and break that promise again.

COUNCILOR. We are not obliged to keep faith with a brigand.

GOETZ. If you did not bear the image of the Emperor, which I venerate even in its meanest counterfeit, I'd force that word "brigand" down your throat until you choked on it! I am engaged in an honorable feud. You could give thanks to God and boast of it before all the world, if you ever in your life performed so noble a deed as that for which I now sit here captive.

The Councilor gestures to the Magistrate, who rings a bell.

GOETZ. Not for the sake of sorry gain, not to grab land and people away from those who are small and defenseless, did I go to war—no, to liberate my squire and to protect my skin! Do you see any wrong in that? Neither Emperor nor Empire would ever have lost any sleep over our need. Thank God, I still have *one* hand and I was right to use it.

Citizens march in, poles in their hands, weapons at their sides.

GOETZ. What's the meaning of this?

COUNCILOR. You won't listen. Seize him!

GOETZ. So that's the idea, is it? Unless you're a Hungarian ox, don't come too near me. This right hand of mine can give you such a box on the ear that will cure you once and for all of headache, toothache and all the aches of life. (*They make for him, he strikes one to the ground and rips the weapon from the side of another, they retreat.*) Come on! Come on! It'd be a pleasure to get to know the boldest of you.

COUNCILOR. Surrender!

GOETZ. With a sword in my hand? Do you know that all I have to do now is beat my way through these rabbit hunters and head for the open field? But I want to teach you all how to keep your word. Promise me a knight's house arrest and I'll yield up my sword and be your prisoner as before.

COUNCILOR. With a sword in your hand you want to bargain with the Emperor?

GOETZ. God forbid! Only with you and your noble company.—You can all go home, good people. You'll gain nothing for your time, and what you'll get here is nothing but bruises.

COUNCILORS. Grab him! Doesn't your love for your Emperor give you more courage than this?

GOETZ. No more than the Emperor will give them in the way of bandages to heal the wounds their courage might get for them.

Sergeant-at-arms enters.

SERGEANT. The tower watch has just called out: a troop of more than two hundred is marching toward the city. They advanced without warning from behind the vineyards and are threatening our walls.

COUNCILOR. Good God! what is this?

Guard enters.

GUARD. Franz von Sickingen stands at the gate and wishes you to know: he has heard how the oath given his brother-in-law has been broken, and how the men of Heilbronn have given support to it all. He demands an explanation or else within an hour he will set fire to the city at all four corners and open it up for plunder.

GOETZ. Bold brother!

COUNCILOR. Step out, Goetz!—What's to be done?

MAGISTRATE. Have mercy on us and on our citizens. Sickingen is boundless in his anger, he is man enough to do it.

COUNCILOR. Are we to abandon our rights and the Emperor's?

CAPTAIN. If we only had people to assert them. But this way we could all be killed, and the whole affair would be that much worse. We'll win by yielding.

MAGISTRATE. Let's appeal to Goetz to put in a good word for us. I feel as if I can already see the city in flames.

COUNCILOR. Bring Goetz in!

GOETZ. What now?

COUNCILOR. You would do well to dissuade your brother-in-law from his rebellious plan. Instead of rescuing you from destruction, he'll plunge you deeper down by taking your part.

GOETZ (*sees Elisabeth at the door, secretly to her*). Go and tell him: he should break in without delay and come up here, but not do any harm to the city. If these scoundrels oppose him, he should use force. It doesn't matter to me if I get killed, if only they all get cut down along with me.

A Great Hall in the Courthouse
Sickingen. Goetz.
The entire courthouse is occupied by Sickingen's troops.

GOETZ. That was rescue from heaven! How did you arrive so unexpectedly and just when you were needed, brother?

SICKINGEN. No magic in it. I had sent out two or three scouts to find how things were with you. At news of their perjury here I set out. Now we've got them.

GOETZ. I demand nothing more than a knight's house arrest.

SICKINGEN. You are too honorable. Not even to make use of the advantage that a just man possesses over perjurers! They're sitting there in the wrong, let's not put any pillows under them. They have shamefully abused the Emperor's orders. And if I know his Majesty, you can certainly demand more than that. It's not enough.

GOETZ. I have always been content with little.

SICKINGEN. And have always received too little. My opinion is: they should release your followers from prison and allow them to withdraw to your castle, along with yourself, upon your oath. You can promise not to go beyond your boundaries and you'll still be better off than here.

GOETZ. They will say that my estates are forfeit to the Emperor.

SICKINGEN. Then we'll say that you want to live there for rent until the Emperor grants them back to you again. Let them squirm like eels in a basket, they'll not slip away from us. They'll speak of Imperial Majesty, of their Commission. That won't matter to us, I know the Emperor, too, and count for something with him. He has always wanted to have you among his forces. You won't have to sit for long in your castle before you're called up.

GOETZ. Soon, God willing, before I forget how to use a sword.

SICKINGEN. Courage cannot be unlearned, just as it cannot be learned. Don't worry about a thing! When your affairs are all arranged I'll go to court, for my own plans are beginning to ripen. Favorable signs encourage me: "Get started!" There is nothing left for me to do but sound out the Emperor's mind. Trier and the Palatinate would sooner expect an attack from heaven than to have me fall upon them. And I will come like a hailstorm! And if we have any say in our destiny, you'll soon be brother-in-law to a Prince Elector. I hope I can count on your fist for this undertaking.

GOETZ (*looks at his hand*). Ah, this was the meaning of the dream I had the day after I promised Maria to Weislingen. He promised me his loyalty and grasped my hand so strongly that it pulled out of its socket as if broken off. Ah! I'm more defenseless at this moment than I was when it was first shot off. Weislingen! Weislingen!

SICKINGEN. Forget a traitor! We will annihilate his schemes, undermine his esteem, and both conscience and shame will devour him to death. I see them, in my mind I see my enemies, your enemies overthrown. Goetz, just one half year more!

GOETZ. Your soul is soaring high. I don't know, for some time now no joyful prospects have opened up for mine.—I have been in greater distress before and have been taken prisoner before, and I've never felt the way I feel now.

SICKINGEN. Good luck brings good courage. Come along to the periwigs! They have had the floor long enough, let's take over the job for once. (*They leave.*)

Adelheid's Castle
Adelheid. Weislingen.

ADELHEID. That's despicable!

WEISLINGEN. I gnashed my teeth! Such a good plan, so well executed, and in the end they let him withdraw to his castle! That damned Sickingen!

ADELHEID. They should not have done it.

WEISLINGEN. They were trapped. What could they do? Sickingen threatened them with fire and sword, that arrogant, hot-tempered man! I hate him. His prestige swells like a surging river; once it has gathered in a few streams the rest follow on their own.

ADELHEID. Did they not have the Emperor?

WEISLINGEN. Dear wife! He's only the merest shadow of one, he's grown old and cranky. When he heard what had happened, and that I was agitating along with the other governing councilors, he said: "Leave them in peace! I can well afford to allow old Goetz his little territory, and if he stays quiet there, how can you complain about him?" We discussed the welfare of the state. "Oh," said he, "if only I had always had councilors who had made me turn my restless mind more to the happiness of individual people!"

ADELHEID. He's losing his spirit as ruler.

WEISLINGEN. We went at it about Sickingen.—"That is one of my loyal servants," said he, "even if he did not act upon my command he performed my will far better than my official ministers, and I can give my approval, either before or after."

ADELHEID. It makes me want to tear myself apart.

WEISLINGEN. Despite that, I've not yet given up all hope. He has been left to himself in his castle on his word as a knight, to keep the peace there. For him that's impossible; soon enough we'll find cause against him.

ADELHEID. And all the sooner, since we have hopes that the Emperor will shortly depart this world, and Prince Charles, his admirable successor, promises more sovereign attitudes.

WEISLINGEN. Charles? He has neither been elected nor crowned.

ADELHEID. Yet who does not wish and hope for it?

WEISLINGEN. You have an exalted notion of his qualities; one might almost think you were looking at them with different eyes.

ADELHEID. You offend me, Weislingen. Do you take me to be that way?

WEISLINGEN. I said nothing intended to offend you. Yet I cannot keep silent on this. Charles's unusual interest in you worries me.

ADELHEID. And my behavior?

WEISLINGEN. You're a woman. You dislike no one who pays court to you.

ADELHEID. But you men?

WEISLINGEN. It gnaws at my heart, the very thought is terrible! Adelheid!

ADELHEID. Can I cure your folly?

WEISLINGEN. If you wanted to! You could remove yourself from the court.

ADELHEID. Tell me the way and the means. Are you not yourself at court? Should I abandon you and my friends, in order to converse with the hoot owls at my castle? No, Weislingen, nothing would come of that. Put your mind at ease, you know how I love you.

WEISLINGEN. A sacred anchor in this storm, as long as the line doesn't break. (*He leaves.*)

ADELHEID. So that's how you're going to be! It's all I needed. The ambitions of my heart are too important to allow you to stand in the way. Charles! A great man, a fine man, and someday Emperor! and why should he be the only man who is not flattered by the possession of my favors? Weislingen, don't try to stop me or you'll go down and my path will take me right over you.

Franz enters with a letter.

FRANZ. Here, dear Lady.

ADELHEID. Did Prince Charles himself give it to you?

FRANZ. Yes.

ADELHEID. What's the matter? You look distressed.

FRANZ. It is your wish that I should languish and die. In my years of hope you make me despair.

ADELHEID (*aside*). I'm sorry for him—and how little it costs to make him happy! (*Openly*:) Don't be discouraged, my boy! I feel your love and your loyalty and I shall never be ungrateful.

FRANZ (*overwhelmed*). If you were to be so, I would be devastated. By God, there's not a drop of blood in my veins which is not devoted to you, not a wish in my mind but to love you and to do what pleases you.

ADELHEID. Dear boy!

FRANZ. You are flattering me. (*Bursts into tears.*) If my devotion deserves no more than to see others preferred, to see how your thoughts turn toward this Charles—

ADELHEID. You have no idea what you want, still less what you say.

FRANZ (*stamping his foot in frustration and anger*). I do not want any more of this! I will no longer play your go-between.

ADELHEID. Franz! You forget yourself.

FRANZ. To sacrifice myself! And my dear master!

ADELHEID. Out of my sight!

FRANZ. Dear Lady!

ADELHEID. Go, reveal my secret to your dear master! I was a fool to take you for what you are not.

FRANZ. Dear, gentle Lady! You know that I adore you.

ADELHEID. And you used to be my friend, so close to my heart. Go, betray me!

FRANZ. I'd sooner tear the heart from my body! Forgive me, dear Lady! My heart is too full, my senses can't endure it.

ADELHEID. Dear, passionate youth! (*She takes his hands and draws him to her and they meet with kisses. He falls weeping upon her shoulder.*)

ADELHEID. Leave me, the walls are traitors. Leave me! (*She frees herself.*) Do not waver from your love and your loyalty, and yours will be the most beautiful reward. (*She leaves.*)

FRANZ. The most beautiful reward! Let me only live till then! I would murder my own father, if he challenged my place here.

Jaxthausen

Goetz at a table. Elisabeth near him with her work; there is a lamp on the table and writing materials.

GOETZ. This idleness is distasteful to me, and the limits imposed on me get narrower from day to day; I wish I could sleep, or at least deceive myself into thinking that peace and quiet were something pleasant.

ELISABETH. So keep on writing the history of your life which you've started. Put the evidence into the hands of your friends, with which to shame your enemies; create for a noble posterity the pleasure of not misunderstanding you.

GOETZ. Alas! Writing is a busy form of idleness; it does not bring pleasure. When I write about what I have done, I get angry about the loss of the time when I could still do something.

ELISABETH (*picks up the text*). Don't be difficult. You've just got to the first time you were imprisoned at Heilbronn.

GOETZ. That was a fatal place for me from the beginning.

ELISABETH (*reads*). "There were even some members of the League who said to me that I'd acted foolishly, to stand up to my worst enemies, since I could guess that they would not deal gently with me; so I answered:"—Well, what did you answer? Keep writing.

GOETZ. I said: "Don't I often stake my skin for the goods and gold of others? Why should I not stake it on my word?"

ELISABETH. That is your reputation.

GOETZ. And they can't take that away from me! They've taken everything else, property, freedom—

ELISABETH. That was the time at the inn when I met those people from Miltenberg and Singlingen who didn't recognize me. I enjoyed myself as if I had given birth to a son. They were praising you to each other and saying: "He is the model of a knight, bold and noble in his freedom and calm and loyal in his misfortunes."

GOETZ. Let them find only *one*, to whom I ever broke my word! And Lord knows, I've sweated harder to serve my neighbor than myself, and labored to achieve the name of a bold and loyal knight, not for riches and rank. And thank God, what I worked for, I won.

Lerse and Georg enter with game.

GOETZ. My greetings to you, brave huntsmen!

GEORG. We've been changed to this from brave horsemen. Riding boots are easily made into slippers.

LERSE. The hunt is still something—and a kind of warfare.

GEORG. If only we did not have to deal so much around here with imperial flunkies! Do you recall, my Lord, how you prophesied to us: if the world were turned around, we would be hunters. We've become that without its happening.

GOETZ. It's all the same in the end, we have been displaced from our own sphere.

GEORG. These are questionable times. For the past week a fearsome comet has been seen and all of Germany is afraid that it means the death of the Emperor, who is very ill.

GOETZ. Very ill! Our own path is coming to an end.

LERSE. And nearby there are even more terrible changes. The peasants have started an awful rebellion.

GOETZ. Whereabouts?

LERSE. In the heart of Swabia. They're destroying, burning, and murdering. I fear they'll make the whole region into a wasteland.

GEORG. There's a fearsome war going on. More than a hundred villages have already joined the rebellion and there are more every day. The winds of a storm recently tore up whole forests and shortly after that, in the region where the rebellion began, two fiery swords in the shape of a cross were seen in the sky.

GOETZ. Some of my good friends and knights must be suffering innocently with the others!

GEORG. Too bad we're not allowed to ride!

ACT V

Peasant's War
Tumult in a village and plundering.
Women and old men with children and baggage.
Flight.

OLD MAN. Away! away! We must escape from these murdering dogs.

WOMAN. Merciful God! the sky is so blood-red, the setting sun blood-red!

MOTHER. That means a fire.

WOMAN. My husband! My husband!

OLD MAN. Away! away! Into the forest! (*They move on.*)

Link enters.

LINK. Anyone who gets in your way, strike down! The village is ours. Just be sure nothing of the crops gets destroyed or left behind. Plunder everything and quickly! We'll set fire to everything right now!

Metzler, running down from the hill.

METZLER. How's it going, Link?

LINK. It's all a great mess, don't you see, you've come just in time for the wind-up. Where from?

METZLER. From Weinsberg. That was quite a party.

LINK. How so?

METZLER. We cut them all down, and it was great work!

LINK. Who all?

METZLER. Dietrich von Weiler led the dance. The fool! We got 'em all surrounded, with our whole raging mob, and up there in the church tower he wanted to make a nice deal with us. Pow! Someone shot him right through the head. We roared up like a storm and out the window with the fellow.

LINK. Ha!

METZLER (*to the peasants*). You dogs, do I have to kick you to make you go? The way they hold back and mill about, the asses!

LINK. Set fire! Let them roast inside! Let's go! Get a move on, you rogues!

METZLER. Then we led out the others, Helfenstein and Eltershofen, about thirteen nobles, altogether about eighty. Led them out into the plain towards Heilbronn. What a jubilation and a tumult by our people, as the long line of these poor rich sinners came along, staring at each other and earth and heaven! They were surrounded before they knew it and all cut down with pikes.

LINK. And I couldn't be there!

METZLER. In all my days I never had such a good time.

LINK. Keep moving! Get out!

PEASANT. Everything's empty.

LINK. Then set fire everywhere.

METZLER. That'll give us a nice little blaze. See how those guys tumbled all over each other and croaked like frogs! It made me feel good all over, like a glass of brandy. There was a Rixinger there who used to ride to the hunt with a great plume in his hat and flaring nostrils, driving us in front of him along with his hounds, *like* his hounds! I hadn't seen him all this time, his fool's face caught my eye right away. Bash! a pike right between the ribs, there he lay, all four limbs stretched out across his companions. They were like rabbits chased by hounds in the hunt, these fellows, lurching one over another.

LINK. It's already smoking nicely.

METZLER. Back there it's burning. So let's just move on out with the loot to the main force.

LINK. Where are they camped?

METZLER. This side of Heilbronn. They're lacking a commander that all the people would respect. We're only their own kind, they sense that and get difficult.

LINK. Who do they have in mind?

METZLER. Max Stumpf or Goetz von Berlichingen.

LINK. That would be good—give the whole business some polish if Goetz would do it; he always counted as an upright knight. Come on! come on! We're off toward Heilbronn. Pass the word!

METZLER. The fire will light us a good ways further on. Did you see the great comet?

LINK. Yes. That's an awful, terrible sign! If we march through the night, we can see it all right. It rises around one o'clock.

METZLER. And stays for only five quarter-hours. It looks like an arm flexed, with a sword, all blood-yellow-red.

LINK. Did you see the three stars at the point and side of the sword?

METZLER. And the broad cloud-colored tail with thousands and thousands of streamers like pikes and in between like little swords.

LINK. It gave me the shivers. The way it's all so pale red and under it so many bright fiery flames and, in between, the frightful faces with smoking heads and beards!

METZLER. Did you see them, too? And it keeps twinkling all about as if it were floating on a bloody sea and shifts back and forth—enough to make you lose your mind!

LINK. Come on! come on! (*They leave.*)

A Field

In the distance can be seen two villages burning and a cloister.
Kohl. Wild. Max Stumpf. A Mob.

MAX STUMPF. You can't expect me to be your commander. For me and for you it would be no use. I am a subject of the Count Palatine; how could I lead against my Lord? You would constantly suspect that I did not act from the heart.

KOHL. We knew you would find an excuse.

Goetz, Lerse, Georg enter.

GOETZ. What do you want with me?

KOHL. You are to be our commander.

GOETZ. Am I to break my knightly word to the Emperor and leave my ban?

WILD. That is no excuse.

GOETZ. And if I were totally free and you continued to behave as you did at Weinsberg toward the nobles and the lords and carry on this way, so that the country round about burns and bleeds, and I was meant to assist you in this shameful, raging business—you'd have to beat me to death like a mad dog before I'd become your chief!

KOHL. If that had not happened, perhaps it would never happen.

STUMPF. That was just the trouble, that they had no leader whom they respected and who could control their rage. Take on the command, I beg you, Goetz. The princes will be grateful to you, all of Germany will. It will be for the best and the advantage of all. People and lands will both be spared.

GOETZ. Why don't you take it on?

STUMPF. I've said I'd have nothing to do with them.

KOHL. We don't have time to hang up saddles and hold unnecessary discourse. Short and sweet: Goetz, be our commander, or look out for your castle and your skin. And you've two hours to think it over. Keep an eye on him!

GOETZ. What need for that? I can decide as well now as later. Why did you set out? To get back your rights and freedom? Why do you ravage and destroy the land? If you're willing to stop all your ill deeds and behave like responsible people who know what they want, then

I'll help you to get your demands and be your commander for a week.

WILD. What happened, happened in the first heat of it, and we don't need you to prevent it in the future.

KOHL. A quarter-year at least you've got to commit to us.

STUMPF. Make it four weeks, with that you can both be satisfied.

GOETZ. All right with me.

KOHL. Your hand!

GOETZ. And promise me to send this agreement you've made with me to all your troops, in writing, to be followed strictly under penalty.

WILD. Well, all right! It will be done.

GOETZ. Then I pledge myself to you for four weeks.

STUMPF. Good luck! Whatever you do, spare our gracious Lord, the Count Palatine.

KOHL (*softly*). Watch him. See that no one talks to him except in your presence.

GOETZ. Lerse! Return to my wife. Stay by her. She shall soon have news of me.

Goetz, Stumpf, Georg, Lerse, some of the peasants leave.
Metzler, Link enter.

METZLER. What's this we hear of a contract? What's a contract for?

LINK. It's an insult to accept such a contract.

KOHL. We know what we're to do as well as you, and we have free rein.

WILD. This ravaging and burning and murdering had to finally stop, today or tomorrow; this way we have won a brave commander besides.

METZLER. What do you mean stop? You traitor! Why are we here? To avenge ourselves on our enemies, to advance ourselves.—That advice was given to you by some prince's lackey.

KOHL. Come on, Wild, he's like an animal. (*They leave.*)

METZLER. Go ahead! There's not one group will stay with you. The scoundrels! Link, let's get the others riled up and set fire to Miltenberg over there, and if there is any trouble about this contract, we'll knock the heads off all the contractors together.

LINK. We've got the main force of troops on our side.

Mountain and Valley
A Mill Below
A Troop of Horsemen. Weistingen comes out of the mill with Franz and a Messenger.

WEISLINGEN. My horse!—You've also communicated this to the other lords?

MESSENGER. At least seven companies will meet up with you in the forest behind the town of Miltenberg. The peasants are moving toward it from below. Messengers have been sent in all directions, the entire League will shortly come together. It can't fail; it is reported that there's dissension among them.

WEISLINGEN. All the better!—Franz!

FRANZ. My Lord?

WEISLINGEN. Do this exactly as I say. I charge you upon your soul. Give her this letter. She should leave the Court for my castle! At once! You are to wait until you have seen her ride away and then report it to me.

FRANZ. It will be done as you command.

WEISLINGEN. Tell her, she has to. (*To the Messenger*:) Now take us by the shortest and best way.

MESSENGER. We must go around. All the rivers have overflowed from this terrible rain.

Jaxthausen
Elisabeth. Lerse.

LERSE. Be comforted, dear Lady!

ELISABETH. Ah, Lerse, there were tears in his eyes when he said goodbye to me. It is cruel, cruel!

LERSE. He will return.

ELISABETH. It's not that. Whenever he rode out to achieve an honorable victory I was never sad at heart. I rejoiced at his return, which now makes me so uneasy.

LERSE. Such a noble man.—

ELISABETH. Don't call him that, it only makes for more misery. These villains! They threatened to murder him and to burn down his castle.—If he comes back again.—I see him in deep gloom. His enemies will trump up false charges against him, and he will not be able to deny them!

LERSE. He will and he can.

ELISABETH. He has broken the ban under which he was placed. Deny it!

LERSE. No! He was forced; where are the grounds to condemn him?

ELISABETH. Malice seeks no grounds, only causes. He has associated himself with rebels, miscreants, murderers, he has taken their lead. Deny it!

LERSE. Stop torturing yourself and me. Have they not solemnly promised him not to undertake any more acts of violence like those at Weinsberg? Did I not myself hear them say: if it had not happened, perhaps it would never happen? Would not both princes and lords have to be grateful to him if he voluntarily became the leader of an unruly mob in order to put a stop to their raging and to spare so many people and so much property?

ELISABETH. You are a devoted advocate.—If they were to take him prisoner, treat him as a rebel, and his grey head—Lerse, I would lose my mind.

LERSE. Send gentle sleep to her body, dear Father of Mankind, if you will not grant any comfort to her soul!

ELISABETH. Georg promised to bring me any news. But he won't be allowed to do what he wants either. They are worse than prisoners. I know they are guarded like enemies. That good Georg! He did not wish to be separated from his Lord.

LERSE. My heart bled when he made me leave him. If *you* had not needed my help, all the dangers of the most shameful death could not have separated me from him.

ELISABETH. I don't know where Sickingen can be. If only I could send a messenger to Maria.

LERSE. Write to her, I will take care of it. (*Exit.*)

Near a Village
Goetz. Georg.

GOETZ. Quickly, to horse, Georg! I can see Miltenberg burning. This is the way they keep a contract! Ride there and give them a piece of my mind. Murderous arsonists! I declare myself free of them. Let them elect a gypsy as commander, not me. Quick, Georg! (*Georg leaves.*) Would that I were a thousand miles from here and lay in the deepest dungeon there is in all of Turkey. If only I could get away from them with honor. Every day I counter their plans, tell them the bitterest truths, so they'll tire of me and let me go.

A Stranger.

STRANGER. God's greeting, my noble Lord.

GOETZ. God thank you for it. What is it? Your name?

STRANGER. That's of no concern. I've come to tell you that your life is in danger. The leaders are tired of taking such harsh words from you, they've decided to get you out of the way. Keep your temper or else look for an escape, and may God guide you. (*He leaves.*)

GOETZ. What a way to end your life, Goetz, to die like this! Let it be! This way my death will signify most certainly to all the world that I have had nothing in common with these dogs.

Several Peasants.

FIRST PEASANT. Lord! Lord! They've been defeated, they're taken prisoner.

GOETZ. Who?

SECOND PEASANT. Those who burned Miltenberg. A troop of the League appeared from behind the hill and ambushed them all of a sudden.

GOETZ. They'll get their due reward.—Ah, Georg! Georg!—They'll have captured him along with those scoundrels.—My Georg! My Georg!

Enter the Leaders.

LINK. Away, Commander, away! There's no time to delay. Our enemy is close by and powerful.

GOETZ. Who set fire to Miltenberg?

METZLER. If you want to make trouble, you'll have to learn not to.

KOHL. Look to your skin and ours. Leave! Leave!

GOETZ (*to Metzler*). Are you threatening me? You wretch! Do you think that you can intimidate me just because the blood of Count von Helfenstein stains your clothes?

METZLER. Berlichingen!

GOETZ. You may well name me by name and my children will not be ashamed of it.

METZLER. You coward! Princes' lackey!

Goetz hits him over the head and fells him. The others separate them.

KOHL. You're all mad! The enemy is breaking through on all sides and you wrangle.

LINK. Out of here! (*Tumult and alarums.*)

Weislingen. Horsemen.

WEISLINGEN. After them! After them! They're fleeing. Don't let rain and darkness hold you back. Goetz is among them, I hear. Make a special effort to catch him. Our people say he's badly wounded. (*The horsemen leave.*) And once I've got you!—It will be a mercy if we secretly execute your death sentence in prison.—So his light will be extinguished from human memory and you can breathe more freely, foolish heart. (*He leaves.*)

Night. In the Wild Forest. Gypsy Camp
Gypsy Mother at her fire.

MOTHER. Mend the roof-thatch over the ditch, daughter, later tonight there'll be rain enough.

Boy enters.

BOY. A hamster, Mother. There! Two field mice.

MOTHER. I'll skin them for you and roast them, and you'll get a cap from the little pelts.—Are you bleeding?

BOY. Hamster bit me.

MOTHER. Fetch me dry kindling so the fire will be burning bright when your father gets here, he'll be all soaked through.

Another Gypsywoman enters, a child on her back.

FIRST GYPSYWOMAN. Did the begging go well?

SECOND GYPSYWOMAN. Not very. The country is all in a tumult, so you're not safe with your life. Two villages burning bright.

FIRST GYPSYWOMAN. Is that a fire down there, that glow? I've been watching it a long while. You get so used to the signs of fire in the sky lately.

Enter Gypsy Captain, three companions.

CAPTAIN. Do you hear the Wild Huntsman?

FIRST GYPSY. He's riding right over us.

CAPTAIN. How his hounds are barking! Bow! Wow!

SECOND GYPSY. His whip is cracking.

THIRD GYPSY. The huntsmen are shouting. Tally ho!

MOTHER. You've brought in a devil of a lot of baggage!

CAPTAIN. It's easy to fish in muddy waters. The peasants are robbing each other, it ought to be all right for us.

SECOND GYPSYWOMAN. What have you got, Wolf?

WOLF. A rabbit, there, and a rooster. A roasting spit. A bundle of linen. Three cooking spoons and a horse's bridle.

STICKS. A wool blanket I've got, a pair of boots and tinder and powder.

MOTHER. It's all soaking wet, we'll have to dry it, give it here.

CAPTAIN. Listen, a horse! Go, see what's up.

Goetz enters on horseback.

GOETZ. Thank God! I see a fire there, it's gypsies. I'm bleeding from my wounds, my enemies right behind me. Holy God, you bring me to a terrible end!

CAPTAIN. Is it in peace you come?

GOETZ. I beg you all for help. My wounds make me weak. Help me dismount!

CAPTAIN. Help him. A nobleman by his looks and his speech.

WOLF (*quietly*). It's Goetz von Berlichingen.

CAPTAIN. Welcome here! Whatever we have is yours.

GOETZ. My thanks!

CAPTAIN. Come into my tent.

Captain's Tent
Captain. Goetz.

CAPTAIN. Call mother, have her bring bloodroot and bandages.

Goetz takes off his armor.

CAPTAIN. Here's my Sunday jacket.
GOETZ. May God reward you!

The Mother binds his wounds.

CAPTAIN. It warms my heart to have you here.
GOETZ. Do you know me?
CAPTAIN. Who wouldn't know you! Goetz, we'd lay down our life and blood for you.

Enter Schricks.

SCHRICKS. Riders coming through the forest. They're Leaguers.
CAPTAIN. Your pursuers! They mustn't get to you. Up, Schricks! Call out the others! We know the trails better than they do, we'll shoot them down before they know we're there. (*They leave.*)
GOETZ (*alone*). Ah, Emperor! Emperor! Robbers protect your children. (*Heavy shooting is heard.*) These wild fellows, straight and true!

Gypsywoman enters.

GYPSYWOMAN. Save yourself! The enemy is overpowering us.
GOETZ. Where is my horse?
GYPSYWOMAN. Right out here.
GOETZ (*buckles on his sword and mounts without his armor*). For one last time let them feel my arm. I'm not so weak yet. (*He leaves.*)
GYPSYWOMAN. He's riding to our people. (*Flight.*)
WOLF. Away! away! All is lost. Our Captain's been shot. Goetz is captured. (*Wailing of women and flight.*)

Adelheid's Bedroom
Adelheid with a letter.

ADELHEID. He or I! What insolence! To threaten me!—We'll outwit him. What's that sneaking through my hall? (*A knocking.*) Who's out there?

Franz, softly.

FRANZ. Open the door, my Lady.
ADELHEID. Franz! He's earned the favor of an open door. (*She lets him in.*)
FRANZ (*rushes to embrace her*). Dear gentle Lady!
ADELHEID. Are you shameless! What if anyone had heard you!
FRANZ. Oh, everyone's asleep, everyone!
ADELHEID. What do you want?

FRANZ. It gives me no peace. The threats of my Lord, your fate, my heart.

ADELHEID. Was he very angry when you left him?

FRANZ. As I never saw him before. "Let her go to her estates," said he, "she *must* do so."

ADELHEID. And we obey?

FRANZ. I know nothing, dear Lady.

ADELHEID. Betrayed and foolish boy, you do not see where this will lead. Here he knows I am in safety. For a long time he has been troubled by my freedom. He wants to have me on his estates. There he has the force to deal with me however his hatred may dictate.

FRANZ. He must not!

ADELHEID. Will you prevent him?

FRANZ. He must not!

ADELHEID. I can foresee the whole of my misery. He will tear me away from my castle by force, lock me up in a convent.

FRANZ. Hell and Death!

ADELHEID. Will you rescue me?

FRANZ. I'll do anything, anything!

ADELHEID (*weeping, embraces him*). Franz, ah, to rescue us!

FRANZ. Down with him! I'll set my foot upon his neck.

ADELHEID. No raging. I'll give you a letter to him, full of humility, saying that I'll obey him. And you pour this little bottle into his drink.

FRANZ. Give it to me! You will be free!

ADELHEID. Free! When you will no longer have to sneak on tiptoe to visit me.—When I no longer have to whisper in fear to you: "Leave me, Franz, the morning is near."

Heilbronn, in front of the Prison
Elisabeth. Lerse.

LERSE. May God relieve you of your misery, dear Lady. Maria is here.

ELISABETH. Thank God! Lerse, we've sunk into terrible misery. It's all going just as I had feared! Captured, thrown into the deepest dungeon as a mutineer, a miscreant—

LERSE. I know everything.

ELISABETH. Nothing, you know nothing, our wretchedness is too extreme! His age, his wounds, a creeping fever and, worse than all that, the darkness in his soul, that he should come to such an end.

LERSE. And that Weislingen should be the Commissioner.

ELISABETH. Weislingen?

LERSE. They have proceeded with unheard-of executions. Metzler was burned alive, hundreds have been broken on the wheel, impaled on pikes, beheaded, drawn and quartered. The countryside all around is like a butchershop where human flesh is cheap.

ELISABETH. Weislingen Commissioner! Oh, God! a ray of hope! Let Maria go to him for my sake, he cannot refuse her anything. He always had a soft heart, and when he sees her, whom he once loved so, who is so miserable because of him—Where is she?

LERSE. Still in the inn.

ELISABETH. Take me to her! She must go at once. I fear the worst.

Weislingen's Castle
Weislingen.

WEISLINGEN. I feel so sick, so weak. All my limbs are hollow. A wretched fever has devoured the marrow. No peace and quiet, neither day nor night. Poisonous dreams in a half-slumber. Last night I met Goetz in a forest. He drew his sword and challenged me. I reached for mine and my hand failed me. Then he thrust his back into its sheath, looked at me contemptuously and walked behind me.—He is captured and I quake before him. Wretched man! Your word condemned him to death, and you tremble before his figure in a dream, like some sinner!—And should he die?—Goetz! Goetz!—We humans do not guide ourselves; evil spirits are given power over us, so that they may exert their hellish purposes for our destruction. (*He sits down.*) Pale! Pale! How blue my nails are!—A cold, cold and devouring sweat cripples me in every limb. Everything is spinning before my eyes. If I could only sleep! Ah—

Enter Maria.

WEISLINGEN. Jesus and Mary!—Leave me in peace! Leave me in peace!—That's all I needed: the image of her! She must be dying, Maria's dying and so reveals herself to me.—Leave me, blessed Spirit, I am in misery enough!

MARIA. Weislingen, I am not a ghost. I am Maria.

WEISLINGEN. That is her voice.

MARIA. I have come to beg you for my brother's life. He is innocent, however deserving of punishment he may appear.

WEISLINGEN. Be silent, Maria! You angel of Heaven bring with you the torments of Hell. Speak no more.

MARIA. And my brother shall die? Weislingen, it is terrible that I should need to say this to you: he is innocent; that I should have to speak my grief in order to prevent you from committing such a despicable murder. Your soul is possessed by pernicious powers to its inmost depths. And this is Adelbert!

WEISLINGEN. You see how the consuming breath of Death has touched me, my strength is fading toward the grave. I would die in misery, and you come to plunge me into despair. If I could speak, your strongest hatred would be melted to pity and lamentation. Ah! Maria! Maria!

MARIA. My brother, Weislingen, is wasting away in prison. His grave wounds, his age. And his grey head—if you were capable of—Weislingen, we would despair!

WEISLINGEN. Enough! (*He pulls a bellcord.*)

Enter Franz in extreme agitation.

FRANZ. My Lord?

WEISLINGEN. Those papers there, Franz!

Franz brings them.

WEISLINGEN (*tears open a package and shows it to Maria*). Here is your brother's death warrant signed and sealed.

MARIA. Dear God in Heaven!

WEISLINGEN. And thus I tear it up! He will live. But can I make amends for what I have destroyed? Do not weep so, Franz! Good lad, my misery affects your heart too deeply.

Franz throws himself down before him and grasps his knees.

MARIA (*to herself*). He is very ill. The sight of him tears at my heart. How I loved him! and now, coming near him, I feel just how intensely.

WEISLINGEN. Franz, stand up and stop weeping! I can still recover. Where there's life there's hope.

FRANZ. No, you won't. You must die.

WEISLINGEN. I must?

FRANZ (*beside himself*). Poison! poison! From your wife!—It was me! me! (*He runs out.*)

WEISLINGEN. Maria, go after him. He is distraught. (*Maria leaves.*) Poisoned by my wife! Woe! woe! I feel it. Torment and death!

MARIA (*within*). Help! help!

WEISLINGEN (*tries to stand up*). God, I can't!

MAIRA (*enters*). He is dead. In his frenzy he plunged down from the hallway window into the river Main.

WEISLINGEN. He is better off.—And your brother is out of danger. The other commissioners, Seckendorf especially, are his friends. They'll grant him knightly imprisonment, on the pledge of his word. Farewell, Maria, now go.

MARIA. Let me stay with you, poor abandoned man.

WEISLINGEN. Abandoned indeed and destitute! You are a fearful avenger, God!—My wife.—

MARIA. Rid yourself of such thoughts! Turn your heart toward the Allmerciful.

WEISLINGEN. Leave, dear Soul, surrender me to my misery.—Horrible! Even your presence, Maria, my final solace, is torture.

MARIA (*to herself*). Give me strength, dear God! My soul will succumb along with his.

WEISLINGEN. Woe! woe! Poisoned by my wife!—My Franz seduced by that vile woman! How she must be waiting, listening for the messenger who will bring her the news: "He is dead." And you, Maria! Maria, why did you come, and reawaken every sleeping memory of my sins! Abandon me! Abandon me, that I may die.

MARIA. Let me stay! You are alone. Think of me as your attendant. Forget everything. May God forget everything you have done, as I forget everything you have done.

WEISLINGEN. You're a soul full of love, pray for me, pray for me! My heart is frozen.

MARIA. He will take pity on you.—You are pale.

WEISLINGEN. I am dying, dying, and cannot die. And in this terrible struggle between life and death are the torments of Hell.

MARIA. Merciful Father, have mercy on him! But one glance of Your love upon his heart so that it may open itself to Your solace and his spirit may carry hope, hope of life, across into death!

In a Dark, Narrow Vault
The Judges of the Secret Tribunal. All are hooded.

THE ELDEST JUDGE. Judges of the Secret Tribunal, sworn by the word and the sword to be blameless, to judge in secret and to avenge in secret, like God! If your hands are clean and your hearts are pure, raise your arms to Heaven and cry upon misdoers: "Woe! woe!"

ALL. Woe! woe!

THE ELDEST JUDGE. Summoner, commence the session of the Court.

THE SUMMONER. I, the Summoner, summon accusation against the misdoer. Whose heart is pure, whose hands are clean to swear by the word and by the sword, let him accuse by the word and by the sword, accuse! accuse!

THE ACCUSER (*steps forth*). My heart is pure of misdoing, my hands clean of innocent blood. May God forgive me evil thoughts and hinder the way to the will! I raise my hand aloft and accuse! accuse! accuse!

THE ELDEST JUDGE. Whom do you accuse?

THE ACCUSER. Upon the word and upon the sword, I accuse Adelheid von Weislingen. She is guilty of adultery, she poisoned her husband through her page. The boy executed himself, the husband is dead.

THE ELDEST JUDGE. Do you swear by the God of Truth that your accusation is true?

THE ACCUSER. I swear.

THE ELDEST JUDGE. Should it be found false, would you take upon your own neck the punishment for murder and adultery?

THE ACCUSER. I would do so.

THE ELDEST JUDGE. Your verdict.

They speak secretly to him.

THE ACCUSER. Judges of the Secret Tribunal, what is your judgment on Adelheid von Weislingen, accused of adultery and murder?

THE ELDEST JUDGE. She shall die! Die the bitter double death. With rope and dagger atone doubly for a double misdeed. Raise your hands on high and cry out: "Woe upon her! Woe! Woe!" Into the hands of her avenger!

ALL. Woe! woe! woe!

THE ELDEST JUDGE. Avenger! Avenger! Step forth!

The Avenger steps forth.

THE ELDEST JUDGE. Here grasp the cord and the sword, to eliminate her from the face of Heaven within one week's time. Wherever you may find her, down with her into the dust.—Judges, you who judge in secret and punish in secret, like God, preserve your hearts from misdeeds and your hands from innocent blood.

Courtyard of an Inn
Maria. Lerse.

MARIA. The horses have rested long enough. We must leave, Lerse.

LERSE. Just rest until tomorrow. The night is far too unfriendly.

MARIA. Lerse, I shall know no peace until I have seen my brother. Let us leave. The weather is clearing, we may expect a beautiful day.

LERSE. As you command.

Heilbronn. In the Prison
Goetz. Elisabeth.

ELISABETH. I beg you, dear husband, speak to me! Your silence frightens me. You're burning up inside. Come, let's look to your wounds; they are much improved. In such dispirited gloom I no longer recognize you.

GOETZ. You were looking for Goetz? He's long since gone. Gradually they have crippled me more and more, my hand, my freedom, my goods and good name. My head, what's that amount to?—What do you hear from Georg? Has Lerse gone for Georg?

ELISABETH. Yes, my dear. Raise yourself up, many things can turn for the better.

GOETZ. Whomever God strikes down, does not rise up again. I know best what burden lies upon my shoulders. I am used to bearing misfortune. And now it's not only Weislingen, not only the peasants, not only the death of the Emperor and not my wounds—it is all of them together. My hour is come. I had hoped it would be like my life. May *His* will be done!

ELISABETH. Won't you eat something?

GOETZ. Nothing, dear wife. Look how the sun is shining outside.

ELISABETH. A beautiful spring day.

GOETZ. My dear, if you could persuade the guard to allow me into his little garden for half an hour, so that I could enjoy the dear sun, the bright sky and the pure air.

ELISABETH. At once, and he will surely do it.

Little Garden in the Prison
Maria. Lerse.

MARIA. Go inside and see how things stand. (*Lerse leaves.*)

Elisabeth. Guard.

ELISABETH. God reward you for your love and loyalty to my lord. (*Guard leaves.*) Maria, what have you brought?

MARIA. My brother's safety. Ah, but my heart is torn in two. Weislingen is dead, poisoned by his wife. My husband is in danger. The princes are becoming too powerful for him, it is said that he is surrounded and under siege.

ELISABETH. Don't believe that rumor! And don't let Goetz notice anything.

MARIA. How are things going with him?

ELISABETH. I was afraid he would not live till your return. The hand of the Lord lies heavy upon him. And Georg is dead.

MARIA. Georg! That golden youth!

ELISABETH. When those worthless rebels were burning Miltenberg, his master sent him to make them stop. Just then a troop of the League overran them.—Georg! If they had all held out as he did, they would all have a right to a good conscience.

MARIA. Does Goetz know this?

ELISABETH. We've been concealing it from him. He asks me ten times a day and sends me out ten times a day to find out what Georg is doing. I am afraid to give his heart this one last shock.

MARIA. Oh, God, what use is hope upon this earth?

Enter Goetz, Lerse, Guard.

GOETZ. Almighty God! How blissful it is for a man to be beneath your sky! How free!—The trees are putting forth buds and the world is full of hope. Farewell, my loved ones; my roots have all been cut off, my strength is sinking toward the grave.

ELISABETH. May I send Lerse to the monastery for your son, so you may see him once again and bless him?

GOETZ. Leave him, he is holier than I, he needs no blessing from me.—On our wedding day, Elisabeth, I never thought that I might die this way.—My aged father blessed us, and a posterity of brave and noble sons flowed from his prayer.—You did not hear him, and I am the last.—Lerse, your face gives me joy at the hour of my death more than in the boldest fight. Then it was my spirit that guided yours, now it's you who hold me upright. Ah, if only I might see Georg once more, might warm myself on his gaze.—You all look to the ground and weep.—He is dead—Georg is dead.—Then die, Goetz.—You have outlived yourself, outlived the noble ones.—How did he die?—Ah, they captured him among those murderous incendiaries, and he was executed?

ELISABETH. No, he was cut down near Miltenberg. He defended himself like a lion, fighting for his freedom.

GOETZ. God be thanked! He was the best youth under the sun and brave.—Let my soul be released now.—Poor wife. I leave you behind in a corrupted world. Lerse, do not forsake her.—Close your hearts more carefully than your doors. The time of betrayal is coming, it will have free rein. The worthless ones will rule with deceit, and the noble man will fall into their nets. Maria, God give you back your husband once again! May he not fall so low as he has now climbed high! Selbitz died, and the dear Emperor, and my Georg.—Give me a drink of water!—Heavenly breezes—Freedom! Freedom! (*He dies.*)

ELISABETH. Only on high, on high with you. The world is a prison.

MARIA. Noble man! Noble man! Woe to the century that spurned you!

LERSE. Woe to coming generations that fail to understand you!

EGMONT

A Tragedy

Translated by Michael Hamburger

Characters

MARGARET OF PARMA, daughter of Charles V and Regent of the Netherlands
COUNT EGMONT, Prince of Gavre
WILLIAM OF ORANGE
DUKE OF ALBA
FERDINAND, his natural son
MACHIAVELLI, in the Regent's service
RICHARD, Egmont's private secretary
SILVA, GOMEZ } in Alba's service
CLARE, Egmont's mistress
HER MOTHER
BRACKENBURG, a burgess
SOEST, grocer; JETTER, tailor; CARPENTER; SOAPBOILER } citizens of Brussels
BUYCK, soldier under Egmont
RUYSUM, disabled soldier, hard of hearing
VANSEN, a clerk
People, attendants, guards, etc.

The scene is Brussels.
The year is 1568.

Act I

Crossbow Target Shooting

Soldiers and Citizens with crossbows. Jetter, citizen of Brussels, a tailor, steps forward and prepares to shoot. Soest, citizen of Brussels, a grocer.

Soest. Well, go ahead and shoot so there'll be an end to it. You won't beat me, anyway. Three in the black is more than you ever got in all your life. That means I'm champion for the year.

Jetter. Champion, indeed, and king as well. Who would begrudge you the honour? But you'll have to pay for two rounds; you'll have to pay for your skill as every champion does.

Buyck, a Dutchman, soldier serving under Egmont.

Buyck. Jetter, I'll buy those shots off you, share the prize, pay for the gentlemen's drinks: I've been here so very long and feel indebted to them for so much courtesy. If I miss, the turn shall count as yours.

Soest. I should really protest, for your bargain makes *me* the loser. But never mind, Buyck, shoot ahead.

Buyck (*shoots*). Well, here goes—One, two, three, four.

Soest. What, four in the black? You're the winner, then.

All. Three cheers for the king. Hip, hip, hurray, hurray, hurray.

Buyck. Thank you, gentlemen. But even "Champion" would be too much. Thank you for the honour.

Jetter. You've yourself to thank for it.

Ruysum, a Frisian, disabled soldier, hard of hearing.

Ruysum. Let me tell you!

Soest. Tell us what, old man?

Ruysum. Let me tell you: he shoots like his master, like Egmont.

Buyck. Compared to him I'm only a poor bungler. You should see him on the musket range; he hits the mark like no one else in the world. I don't mean when he's lucky or in the right mood. No: every time, he's no sooner taken aim than he's got the bull's-eye. It's he who taught me. I'd like to see the fellow who's served with him and not learnt anything from him! But I haven't forgotten, gentlemen. A king looks after his people; so let's have some wine, at the king's expense.

Jetter. It was agreed between us that each of us—

Buyck. I'm a stranger here, and king, and I pay no attention to your laws and customs.

Jetter. Why, you're worse than the Spaniards; they've had to leave our laws and customs alone, till now, anyway.

Ruysum. What do you say?

SOEST (*loudly*). He wants to stand all the drinks; he doesn't want us to put our money together and let the king only pay double.

RUYSUM. Let him, then. But no offence. That's his master's way too—to be lavish and never leave money to burn a hole in his pocket.

They bring wine.

ALL. Good health, your Majesty, and a prosperous life!

JETTER, *to* BUYCK. That's right: your Majesty. You deserve the honour.

BUYCK. Well, if it must be, thank you with all my heart.

SOEST. It must be; for no true citizen of the Low Countries will easily drink the health of our Spanish Majesty—not with all his heart.

RUYSUM. Whose health, did you say?

SOEST (*loudly*). Philip the Second, King of Spain.

RUYSUM. Our most gracious King and Lord! May God grant him a long reign.

SOEST. Didn't you prefer his father of blessed memory, Charles the Fifth?

RUYSUM. God have mercy on his soul. He was a great gentleman. He had the whole earth to take care of, but he was a father and brother to us all. And if he met you in the street, he greeted you as one neighbour greets another, and if that gave you a start, he was gracious enough to—Don't misunderstand me. I mean: he went out, rode out just as the fancy took him, with only a few men. There wasn't a dry eye to be seen when he abdicated and made his son governor of these parts. Don't misunderstand me, I say. But Philip's different, you'll admit; more majestic, if you like.

JETTER. No man ever saw him, when he was here, but in royal pomp and ceremony. He doesn't talk much, people say.

SOEST. He's not the man for us of the Low Countries. Our princes must be light-hearted like ourselves, live and let live. We won't be despised or pressed, good-natured fools though we are.

JETTER. The King would be gracious enough, I think, if only he had better advisers.

SOEST. No. Never. He doesn't take to our sort, he has no sympathy for us, he doesn't love us. How, then, can we love him in our turn? Why is every single one of us so fond of Count Egmont? Why would we gladly carry him about on our hands? Because you can see that he wishes us well; because you can read his cheerfulness, the free life he lives, the good opinion he has of us, in his eyes; because he hasn't a single possession that he wouldn't give away to a needy man, even to a man who didn't need it. Let's drink to Count Egmont! Buyck, it's your privilege to propose the first toast. Propose the health of your master!

BUYCK. With the greatest pleasure: Count Egmont.

RUYSUM. Victor at St. Quentin!

BUYCK. To the hero of Gravelingen!

ALL. To his health!

RUYSUM. St. Quentin was my last battle. I could hardly move another inch, hardly drag my heavy musket any further. And yet! I gave the Frenchman one last thing to remember me by, and got something too, though it only grazed my right leg.

BUYCK. But Gravelingen, friends, that was a pretty lively affair. There victory was ours alone. Hadn't those French dogs been burning and laying waste the whole length and breadth of Flanders? But, there's no doubt about it, we gave them what they deserved. Their old, tried soldiers held out for a long time, but we pressed and shot and slashed at them till they pulled faces and their lines began to give way. Then Egmont's horse was shot away from under him, and there was a long uncertain struggle, man to man, horse against horse, troop against troop, on the broad flat sand of the seashore. Then suddenly it came as if down from heaven, from the river mouth—the "bow, bow" of the big cannons firing right into the midst of the French. It was the English, who just happened to be passing on their way from Dunkirk under Admiral Malin. They didn't help us much, it's true; they could only get in with their smallest ships, and not close enough at that; and sometimes they shot at us by mistake. But it did us good, all the same. It broke the Frenchmen's spirit and gave us new courage. So now we made short work of them. Killed the whole lot or drove them into the water. And those fellows drowned as soon as they tasted water. As for us Dutchmen, we went in after them. Amphibians that we are, we didn't feel happy till we were in the water, like frogs, and we just went on fighting the enemy in the river, shot them down as if they were ducks. The few that got away after that—well, the peasant women saw to them: beat them down as they ran with pitchforks and pick-axes. So his French Majesty had no choice but to come to heel and make peace. So it's to us you owe that peace, to our great Egmont!

ALL. To our great Egmont! And again! And again! And yet again!

JETTER. If only he'd been appointed our Regent in Margaret of Parma's place!

SOEST. No, that's going too far. Honour where honour is due. I won't hear Margaret's name abused. Now it's my turn. Long live our gracious lady!

ALL. Long live Margaret!

SOEST. It's true, there's no denying the excellence of the women in the ruling house. Long live the Regent!

JETTER. She's clever and moderate in everything she does. If only she didn't stick to the parsons through thick and thin. It's partly her fault that we have those fourteen new bishoprics in our country. What can they be for? Only to push a lot of strangers into the best positions, where they used to put abbots elected by the chapter. And they want us to believe it's all for religion's sake. That's the root of the trouble. Three bishops were enough for us; honesty and decency were the rule in those days. Now everyone has to pretend that they're really necessary, and so there's no end to the trouble and bickering. And the more you look into the thing, the more murky it seems.

They drink.

SOEST. That was simply the King's will; she can do nothing about it either way.

JETTER. And now they tell us we mustn't sing those new psalms. And yet they're beautifully versified, and their tunes couldn't be more uplifting. We mustn't sing those, but as many profane and scurrilous ditties as we please. Why, do you think? They say those psalms contain heresies and goodness knows what else. And yet I've sung them before now and I couldn't see anything bad in them. It's a new idea.

BUYCK. I shouldn't dream of asking their permission. In our province we sing what we like. That's because Count Egmont is our governor; he doesn't interfere with things of that kind—in Ghent, in Ypres, in the whole of Flanders, whoever wants to, sings them.

Loudly:

Surely there's nothing more innocent than a spiritual song? Isn't that so, Father?

RUYSUM. Indeed. For it's a form of devotion and it purifies the heart.

JETTER. But they say it doesn't do so in the right way—not in *their* way. And it's always dangerous, so one leaves it alone. The servants of the Inquisition creep and snoop about everywhere. Many an honest man has come to grief already. To suppress our freedom of conscience—that was the last straw. If I can't do what I please, they might at least let me think and sing what I please.

SOEST. The Inquisition won't get the better of us. We're not like the Spaniards and will never let anyone tyrannize over our conscience. And the nobility too will have to start resisting it soon.

JETTER. We're in a very awkward position. If those fine people take it into their heads to come rushing into my house, and I'm sitting down, doing my work, and just happen to be humming a French psalm, without a thought in my head, whether virtuous or wicked, but I simply hum it because the tune is there inside me—well, that makes me a heretic, and they put me in jail. Or I'm out for a walk and stop when I see a crowd of people listening to some new preacher—one of those who've come from Germany—that makes me a rebel, no less, and they'll chop off my head as likely as not. Have you ever heard one of them preach?

SOEST. Very fine preachers, if you ask me. The other day I heard one speak to thousands and thousands of people. That was a different kettle of fish—not like ours, always beating about the bush, stuffing Latin tags down the people's throats. That one made no bones about it. He told us straight how they've been leading us by the nose till now, keeping us ignorant, and how we could have more light for the asking. And he proved it all from the Bible.

JETTER. I'm sure there is something in that. I've often said so myself and pondered on those matters. It's been troubling my head for a long time.

BUYCK. I suppose that's why they're so popular.

SOEST. And no wonder. Who wouldn't go to hear something that's good and new?

JETTER. What's the matter, then? Why can't any man be allowed to preach in his own way?

BUYCK. Drink up, gentlemen. All this chatter is making you forget your wine—and William of Orange too.

JETTER. Oh, we mustn't forget him. He's a real tower of strength: you've only to think of him to feel that you can hide behind him, and the devil himself wouldn't be able to get you out. To William of Orange, then!

ALL. To his health!

SOEST. Now, old man, propose your own health too!

RUYSUM. Old soldiers! All soldiers! Long live war!

BUYCK. Well said, old man. All soldiers! Long live war!

JETTER. War, war! Do you know what you're saying? That word comes to you easily enough, and I suppose that's natural, but I can't tell you how wretched it sounds to those of my kind. To hear nothing but drumbeats the whole year round; and hear nothing but one troop marching in here, another there; how they came over a hill and stopped by a windmill, how many were left there, how many in another place, and how they fight, and how one wins, the other loses, though for the life of me I can't understand who's won anything, who's lost. How a town is captured, the citizens murdered, and what becomes of the poor women, the innocent children. Affliction and terror, that's what it means to us, and every moment one thinks: "Look, they're coming! And they'll do the same to us."

SOEST. That's why a citizen too should always be trained to use arms.

JETTER. Yes, whoever has a wife and children learns to defend them. But I'd still rather hear about soldiers than see them.

BUYCK. I should take offence at that remark.

JETTER. It isn't aimed at you, friend. We were all relieved when we'd got rid of the Spanish occupation forces.

SOEST. Yes, indeed. You found those most irksome of all, didn't you?

JETTER. Don't try to make a fool of me.

SOEST. They were sorry to leave your house.

JETTER. Shut your mouth.

SOEST. They'd driven him out of his kitchen, his cellar, his sitting-room—and his bed.

Laughter.

JETTER. You're a fool.

BUYCK. Peace, gentlemen! Do you need a soldier to make peace between you? Well, since you don't want to have anything to do with our sort, you'd better propose a toast to yourselves, a civil toast.

JETTER. That we'll do gladly. Security and quiet!

SOEST. Order and freedom!

BUYCK. Bravo! That suits us too.

They clink glasses and cheerfully repeat these words, but in such a way that each calls out a different word and a kind of canon results. The old man listens and finally joins in also.

ALL. Security and quiet! Order and freedom!

The Regent's Palace
Margaret of Parma in hunting attire. Courtiers. Pages. Servants.

REGENT. You will cancel the hunt; I shall not ride today. Tell Machiavelli to come to me.

Exeunt all.

The thought of these terrible happenings gives me no peace. Nothing pleases me, nothing distracts me; always these misgivings, these cares torment me. The King will say that these are the fruits of my kindness, my consideration; and yet my conscience tells me that at every moment I did what was most advisable, that my only purpose was to do the right thing at the right time. Should I, then, have fanned these flames even sooner and made them spread, by exposing them to a tempest of wrath? It was my hope to set limits to their progress and stifle them by driving them back upon themselves. I know that this is the truth and by reminding myself of it I can absolve myself from all self-reproach. But how will my brother receive the news? For there is no denying it: the insolence of the new preachers has been growing daily. They have blasphemed against our most sacred tenets, subverted the dull minds of the common people, and released the spirit of confusion in their midst. Arrant rogues have joined the ranks of the insurgents and caused dreadful atrocities to be committed. Only to think of them makes me shudder, and now I must report them one by one to the Court, one by one and speedily, so that the general rumour will not forestall our account, so that the King will not suspect us of trying to conceal the rest. I can see no means, whether stern or gentle, of opposing this evil. Oh, what are we, then, the great on the crest of humanity's wave? We think that we rule its fury, but it bears us up and down, to and fro.

Enter Machiavelli.

REGENT. Have those letters to the King been drafted?

MACHIAVELLI. They will be ready for your signature in an hour's time.

REGENT. Have you made the report sufficiently detailed?

MACHIAVELLI. Detailed and elaborate, as the King likes them to be. I recount how the iconoclastic fury first broke out at St. Omer. How a raging mob, furnished with staves, axes, hammers, ladders, and ropes, accompanied by a few armed men, began by attacking chapels, churches, and monasteries, driving out the worshippers, breaking open the doors, throwing everything into disorder, tearing down the altars, breaking the statues of saints, destroying every painting, shattering, ripping up, stamping to pieces every consecrated and holy thing they could lay hands upon. How this rabble grew in numbers as it proceeded, how the inhabitants of Ypres opened the gates to them. How they laid waste the cathedral there with incredible speed, how they burnt the bishop's library. How a great mob of common folk, seized with the same frenzy, poured into Menin, Comines, Verwich, Lille, encountered no resistance anywhere, and how, in the twinkling of an eye, the conspiracy declared itself and struck almost throughout the whole of Flanders.

REGENT. Oh, the repetition of it renews my pain. And now there is the added fear that the evil will only grow and grow. Tell me what you think, Machiavelli?

MACHIAVELLI. Forgive me, your Highness, if my thoughts are more like whims; and though you have always been satisfied with my services, you have rarely chosen to take my advice. Often you have said in jest: "You're too farsighted, Machiavelli! You should be a historian: the man who acts should keep his eyes on what is nearest to him." And yet, didn't I predict this whole story? Did I not foresee it all?

REGENT. I too foresee a great deal without having the power to forestall it.

MACHIAVELLI. Briefly, then, and to the point: you will not suppress the new doctrine. Let them have their way but separate them from the orthodox. Give them churches, integrate them in the framework of society, restrict their influence: then you will have silenced the rebels at a single stroke. Every other measure will be in vain, and you will lay waste the country.

REGENT. Have you forgotten with what repugnance my brother condemned the very suggestion that the new doctrine might be tolerated? Don't you know how in every letter he reminds me most emphatically of my duty to maintain the true faith? That he will not hear of a peace and a unity established at the expense of religion? Even in the Provinces does he not keep spies unknown to us, so as to observe who is likely to go over to the new creed? Did he not amaze us by naming more than one person close to us who has become guilty of heresy, though in secret? Does he not command us to practise severity and ruthless justice? And you want me to be merciful? To make proposals to him that call on him to be considerate and tolerant? Should I not lose all his confidence, all his trust?

MACHIAVELLI. Well I know it; the King gives orders, he lets you know his intentions. You are to establish peace and quiet once more by a measure that will only increase the general embitterment, that will inevitably fan the fires of war from every direction. Consider what you are doing. The most powerful merchants have been infected, the nobility, the people, the soldiers. What is the use of adhering to his ideas, when everything around us is changing? If only some benevolent spirit would make it clear to Philip that it is more fitting for a king to rule citizens of two different creeds than to incite one party against the other.

REGENT. I forbid you to speak in that way. I know very well that in politics one can rarely keep faith or troth, but must ban frankness, kindness, and indulgence from one's heart. In worldly affairs that is only too true, but are we to toy with God, as we toy with one another? Are we to be indifferent to our proven doctrine, for which so many have offered up their lives? Should we yield even that to an upstart, uncertain, and self-contradictory fad?

MACHIAVELLI. Please don't think ill of me on that account.

REGENT. I know you to be a loyal servant, and I know that a man can be honest and prudent even though he has missed the nearest, straightest way to his soul's salvation. You are not the only one, Machiavelli, not the only man whom I must both respect and reproach.

MACHIAVELLI. To whom are you alluding?

REGENT. I will confess to you that Egmont aroused my deep and acute displeasure today.

MACHIAVELLI. By what kind of conduct?

REGENT. By his usual conduct, by his nonchalance and recklessness. I received the terrible news just as I was coming out of church in his and many others' company. I could not contain my grief, voiced my complaint and, turning to him, cried out: "Look what is happening in your province! And you put up with it, Count, you of whom the King expected so much?"

MACHIAVELLI. And what did he reply?

REGENT. As if it were nothing, a mere irrelevance, he retorted: "If only the people of the Netherlands were assured that the Constitution is safe, the rest could easily be settled."

MACHIAVELLI. Perhaps he spoke with more truth than prudence or piety. How can confidence be established and preserved when the people of the Netherlands see that we are more concerned with their possessions than with their well-being or the good of their souls? Have the new bishops saved more souls than they've swallowed rich benefices, and are not most of them foreigners? Still all the town governorships are held by Netherlanders: do the Spaniards trouble to conceal their irresistible covetousness for these places? Does not a people prefer to be ruled by its own kind, in its own fashion, rather than by strangers who begin by endeavouring to acquire property in the country at everyone's expense, who apply strange standards, and who rule harshly and without sympathy?

REGENT. You are placing yourself on the opposing side.

MACHIAVELLI. Not in my heart, certainly, and I wish that my head could be wholly on ours.

REGENT. If that is your view, it would be necessary for me to abdicate from the Regency; for Egmont and Orange once lived in high hopes of occupying that place. At that time they were rivals; now they are in league against me and have become friends, inseparable friends.

MACHIAVELLI. A dangerous couple!

REGENT. To be frank, I fear Orange, and I fear for Egmont. Orange is up to no good, his thoughts reach out to the distant future, he is secretive, seems to accept everything, never contradicts, and with the deepest reverence, with the greatest caution, he does what he pleases.

MACHIAVELLI. Quite the contrary of Egmont, who walks about as freely as if the world belonged to him.

REGENT. He wears his head as high as if the hand of Majesty were not suspended over it.

MACHIAVELLI. The people's eyes are all fixed on him, and all their hearts.

REGENT. He has never troubled about appearances—as if there were no one to call him to account. Still he bears the name of Egmont; is glad to hear himself called "Count Egmont," as if loath to forget that his ancestors were the lords of Geldern. Why doesn't he call himself Prince of Gavre, as he is entitled to? Why does he do it? Does he want to re-establish obsolete rights?

MACHIAVELLI. I look upon him as a loyal servant of the King.

REGENT. If he only wanted to, what indispensable services he could render the Government, instead of causing us endless annoyance without any profit to himself, as he's already done! His receptions, banquets, and carousals have done more to unify the nobility than the most dangerous secret conferences. From his toasts the guests have drawn a lasting intoxication, a chronic giddiness. How often his jests and jibes have stirred up the people's minds, and how the populace gaped at his new liveries, at the foolish badges of his servants!

MACHIAVELLI. I'm sure this was not his intention.

REGENT. So much the worse for us all. As I was saying: he harms us and does himself no good. He turns serious things into a joke, and we, so as not to appear idle and careless, must take his jokes seriously. So one worries the other, and what we try to avert is all the more certain to occur. He is more dangerous than the declared head of a conspiracy, and I should be very much surprised if at Court they don't keep a record of all his misdeeds. There's no denying it: hardly a week passes without his causing me grave discomfort, the very gravest discomfort.

MACHIAVELLI. It seems to me that in all things he acts according to his conscience.

REGENT. His conscience has a flattering mirror; his conduct is often offensive. Often he looks as if he were firmly convinced that he is really our master, though out of kindness he's obliging enough not to make us feel it, to refrain from simply driving us out of the country—with the assumption that we'll go in any case, all in good time.

MACHIAVELLI. I beg of you, don't put such a dangerous construction upon his frankness, his happy disposition, that takes important things lightly. You will only harm him and yourself.

REGENT. I put no construction on anything. I am merely speaking of the inevitable consequences and I know him well. His Netherlandish nobility and the Order of the Golden Fleece strengthen his confidence, his boldness. Both can guard him against the King's sudden, arbitrary displeasure. Just examine the matter precisely and you must agree that he alone is responsible for all the misfortunes that have descended on Flanders. He was the first to tolerate the new teachers, easy-going as he is, and perhaps secretly pleased that they gave us something to reckon with. No, don't interrupt me: I am taking the opportunity to tell you all that is on my mind. And I don't wish to discharge my arrows in vain; I know where he is vulnerable. Yes, Egmont too is vulnerable.

MACHIAVELLI. Have you summoned the Council? Is Orange coming too?

REGENT. I've sent to Antwerp for him. I propose to move the burden of responsibility very close to them; they must join me in seriously resisting the evil or else declare themselves rebels. Lose no time in finishing the letters and bring them to me for signature! Then quickly send off the experienced Vasca to Madrid—he is indefatigable and loyal—so that he shall be the first to convey the news to my brother, so that the rumour will not precede him. I will speak to him myself before he leaves.

MACHIAVELLI. Your commands will be executed both speedily and exactly.

Citizen's House
Clare. Clare's Mother. Brackenburg.

CLARE. Won't you hold the thread for me, Brackenburg?

BRACKENBURG. I beg you to spare me, my dear.

CLARE. What's the matter with you tonight? Why do you refuse me this little attention?

BRACKENBURG. Your thread keeps me so spell-bound that I can't avoid your eyes.

CLARE. Nonsense! Come and hold it!

MOTHER (*knitting in her arm-chair*). Why don't you sing? Brackenburg makes such a good second. You used to be so cheerful, both of you, and I never stopped laughing at your pranks.

BRACKENBURG. We used to be.

CLARE. Let's sing, then.

BRACKENBURG. Whatever you wish.

CLARE. Well, then, sing up; and make it lively. It's a military song and my favourite.

She winds the thread and sings with Brackenburg.

Strike up! To your drumming!
And blow the fife loud.
My sweetheart in armour
Commands the whole crowd.
His lance held aloft rules
Their going and coming.
Now faster my blood flows
My heart goes pit-pat.
O, would I wore doublet
And breeches and hat!

Then marching I'd follow
Him out through the gate
And roam with him fighting

Through province and state.
Our enemy's fleeing.
We shoot them as they run!
There's nothing like being
A man with a gun!

As they sing Brackenburg looks at Clare repeatedly; at the end his voice fails him, tears come into his eyes, he drops the thread, and goes to the window. Clare finishes the song by herself, her mother signals to her half-angrily, Clare rises, takes a few steps towards him, turns back irresolutely, and sits down.

MOTHER. What's going on outside, Brackenburg? I hear the sound of marching.

BRACKENBURG. It's the Regent's Life Guards.

CLARE. At this hour? What's the meaning of that?

She gets up and goes to the window with Brackenburg.

That's not the ordinary guard, there are many more of them, nearly the whole regiment. Oh, Brackenburg, do go and find out what's happening. It must be something special. Please go, my dear. Do me this favour!

BRACKENBURG. I'm going. I shall be with you again in a moment.

He holds out his hand to her as he leaves; she clasps it.

MOTHER. There you go again, sending him off!

CLARE. I'm curious; and besides—don't be angry with me—his presence pains me. I never know how to behave towards him. I'm in the wrong where he's concerned, and it grieves me to see him suffer so much because of it. When there's nothing I can do about it.

MOTHER. He's such a loyal fellow.

CLARE. That's why I can't help being kind to him. Often my hand seems to close of its own accord when his hand touches me in that tender, loving way. I reproach myself for deceiving him, for keeping a vain hope alive in his heart. I'm in a terrible quandary. God knows I'm not deceiving him. I don't want him to hope and yet I can't let him despair.

MOTHER. That's not right of you.

CLARE. I used to be fond of him and still wish him well with all my soul. I could have married him, and yet I think I was never in love with him.

MOTHER. But you would have been happy with him if you had.

CLARE. I'd have been well provided for and led a quiet life.

MOTHER. And you've lost all that through your own fault.

CLARE. I'm in a very strange position. When I ask myself how it came about, I know the answer and I don't know it. And then I've only to look at Egmont again to understand everything that's happened—and *more* than what's happened. What a man! All the Provinces idolize him; so how could I help being the happiest creature in the world when he holds me in his arms?

MOTHER. But what will become of us? What of the future?

CLARE. Oh, all I ask is whether he loves me; and would you call that a question?

MOTHER. Distress and anxiety, that's all one gets from one's children. How will it end, I ask you? Worry and grief all the time. No good will come of it. You've made yourself unhappy and made me unhappy.

CLARE (*nonchalantly*). You raised no objection at first.

MOTHER. Unfortunately not. I was too kind, too easy-going. I always am.

CLARE. When Egmont rode past and I went to the window, did you tell me off? Didn't you go to the window too? When he looked up, smiled, nodded, and called to me: did you mind? Didn't you feel that he honoured you by honouring your daughter?

MOTHER. Now you're reproaching me!

CLARE (*moved*). And then when he came more often to our street and it was clear to us that he came this way because of me, weren't you pleased in secret? Did you call me away when I stood behind the panes, waiting for him?

MOTHER. Could I know that it would go so far?

CLARE (*in a halting voice, restraining her tears*). And when he surprised us in the evening, wrapped in his cloak, and we were working by lamplight, who was it that hurried to receive him, since I remained seated, amazed, and glued to the chair?

MOTHER. And had I any reason to fear that this unhappy love would knock my clever little Clare off her feet and so quickly too? Now I have to accept the fact that my daughter——

CLARE (*breaking into tears*). Mother! There's no need to put it like that. Anyone would think you enjoy frightening me.

MOTHER (*weeping*). Yes, go on and cry on top of everything! Make me even more miserable by being sad! Isn't it bad enough that my only daughter is a fallen creature?

CLARE (*rising coldly*). Fallen? Egmont's mistress a fallen creature? There isn't a duchess who wouldn't envy little Clare her place in his heart. Oh, Mother, you've never used such words till now. Be patient with me, dear. . . . Leave other people to think *that* of me, leave the neighbours to whisper what they please. This room, this little house have been heaven to me since Egmont's love first crossed the threshold.

MOTHER. Well, it's true one can't help liking him. He's always so amiable and frank and easy.

CLARE. There's no strain of falsehood in him at all. And yet, Mother, he's the great Egmont. And when he comes to see me, he's all kindness and goodness. Why he even does his best to conceal his rank and his courage, he's so concerned about me. Here he's simply a man, a friend, and my dearest love.

MOTHER. Do you think he will come today?

CLARE. Didn't you notice how often I've been to the window? Didn't you notice how I listen when there's a noise at the door? Though I know that he won't come before nightfall, I still expect him every moment from the instant I get up in the morning. If only I were a boy and could go about with him all the time, to Court and everywhere! If only I could carry his standard for him in battle!

MOTHER. You've always been a sort of tomboy, even when you were a small child, now wild, now pensive. Don't you think you should put on something a little better?

CLARE. Maybe, Mother—if I feel bored. You know, yesterday some of his men passed by, singing songs in his praise. At least his name was part of the songs; I couldn't catch the rest. I could feel my heartbeats right up in my throat. I should have liked to call them back, if I hadn't been afraid of drawing attention to myself.

MOTHER. You be careful! Or your impulsive nature will spoil everything. You'll give yourself away. Just as you did the other day at your cousin's, when you found that woodcut and the inscription and exclaimed with a cry: "Count Egmont!" I turned crimson with shame.

CLARE. How could I not cry out? It was the battle of Gravelingen, and I found the letter C at the top of the picture, so I looked for C in the description. There I read: "Count Egmont, when his horse was shot dead under him." I felt my blood rise—and later I had to laugh at the woodcut Egmont, who was as tall as the tower of Gravelingen just next to him and the English ships on one side. What a strange idea I used to have of what a battle is like and what Count Egmont himself is like, when I was a girl, when they told stories about him, and of every Count and Duke—and how different they all seem now!

Re-enter Brackenburg.

CLARE. What's happening?

BRACKENBURG. No one is sure. They say that a new riot has broken out in Flanders, that the Regent is afraid it may spread to our parts. The Palace Guard has been strongly reinforced, there are crowds of citizens at the gates, the streets are full of people. . . . I think I should call on my old father.

As if about to leave.

CLARE. Shall we see you tomorrow? I'm just going to dress. We're expecting my cousin, and I look too slovenly for words. Will you help me, Mother? Take that book, Brackenburg, and bring me another of those histories!

MOTHER. Good-bye.
BRACKENBURG (*holding out his hand*). Won't you give me your hand?
CLARE (*refusing the hand*). When you come again.

Exeunt mother and daughter.

BRACKENBURG (*alone*). I had intended to leave at once, and now that she accepts the gesture and lets me go, I can hardly bear it. Oh, what a wretch I am! Not even moved by the fate of my country, the growing unrest. My own kind or the Spaniards, it's all the same to me, who's in power and who's in the right. How very different I was when I was a schoolboy! When they set us a piece called "Brutus's Speech on Liberty, an Exercise in Oratory," it was always Fritz who came first, and the headmaster said: "If only it were more tidy, not such a jumble of enthusiasms." I was all drive and ferment then! Now I drag myself along, hanging on that girl's eyes. Since I can't leave her alone, and she can't love me. Oh, she can't have rejected me entirely—can't have, yes or no, but half her love is no love. I'll not put up with it a moment longer! . . . Could it be true, then, what a friend whispered in my ear the other day? That she secretly receives a man at night, since she always drives me out so respectably before the evening? No, it's not true, it's a lie, a shameful, slanderous lie! Clare is as innocent as I'm unhappy. She's rejected me, cast me out of her heart. And can I go on like that? I'll not put up with it. . . . Already my country is divided against itself—more violently each day—and I simply languish away in the midst of all that turmoil! No, I'll not put up with it. When the bugle sounds, when a shot rings out it pierces me to the marrow. Yet it doesn't provoke me, doesn't challenge me to enter the fray, to save and dare with the rest. . . . Oh, wretched, despicable state. Better to put an end to it once and for all. Already once I threw myself into the water and sank—but my terrified nature was stronger. I felt that I could swim and reluctantly saved myself. . . . If only I could forget the time when she loved me or seemed to love me! . . . Why did that happiness pervade every bone of my body? Why have these hopes deprived me of all pleasure in life by showing me a paradise from afar? And that first kiss, the only one! Here (*resting his head on the table*) at this very place we were alone together—she had always been kind and pleasant to me—then she seemed to soften, she looked at me, all my senses were in a whirl, and I felt her lips on mine. And now? There's only death. Why do I hesitate?

He takes a small bottle out of his pocket.

This time it must not be in vain; not in vain that I stole this poison out of my brother's medicine chest. It shall rid me once and for all of this anguish, this uncertainty, this fever worse than death.

Act II

Square in Brussels
Jetter and a Carpenter meet.

CARPENTER. Didn't I predict it? Only a week ago, at the Guild meeting, I said there would be serious clashes.

JETTER. Is it true, then, that they've robbed the churches in Flanders?

CARPENTER. Plundered them, ruined them completely, both churches and chapels. Left nothing but the four bare walls. A lot of hooligans, every one of them. And that put a bad face on our good cause. We should rather have pleaded our just cause to the Regent in an orderly and firm manner and insisted on it. If we make speeches now or meet, they accuse us of joining the rebels.

JETTER. Yes. And so everyone thinks: why should I stick out my face—since my neck is all too close to it?

CARPENTER. I feel very uncomfortable, now that this turmoil has taken possession of the mob, the people who have nothing to lose. They make a mere pretext of what we too profess and will plunge our country into misfortune.

Soest joins them.

SOEST. Good morning, gentlemen. What's the news? Is it true that the iconoclasts are on their way here?

CARPENTER. They'd better keep their hands off here.

SOEST. A soldier came into my shop to buy tobacco. I questioned him. The Regent, clever, brave woman though she remains, has lost her head this time. Things must be very bad for her to hide like this behind her Guard. The Palace Guard has been heavily reinforced. It's even rumoured that she intends to flee from the town.

CARPENTER. She mustn't leave. Her presence protects us, and we shall give her more security than her clipped beards. And if she maintains our rights and liberties, we shall carry her aloft.

Soapboiler joins them.

SOAPBOILER. A nasty, filthy roughhouse! There's more and more trouble, and it will come to a bad end. . . . Be careful, now, and keep quiet, so that they won't take you for rebel agents.

SOEST. Look! There are the seven sages from Greece!

SOAPBOILER. I know there are many who secretly support the Calvinists, slander the bishops, and have no respect for the King. But a loyal subject, a true Catholic——

One by one various people join them, listening. Vansen joins them.

VANSEN. Greetings, gentlemen! What's been happening?

CARPENTER. Have nothing to do with that one. He's a scoundrel.

JETTER. Isn't he Dr. Wiet's clerk?

CARPENTER. He's had a good many masters. First he was a clerk and, when one employer after another had kicked him out for his knaveries, he began to botch the briefs of solicitors and barristers, and he's too fond of the brandy bottle.

More and more people gather and stand about in groups.

VANSEN. Why, you've got quite a crowd collected here and, what's more, you're putting your heads together. Quite an interesting occasion.

SOEST. I think so too.

VANSEN. Now, if one or the other of you had the heart, and one or the other had the head as well, we could break the Spanish chains with one blow.

SOEST. Sir, you must not speak like that! We have sworn loyalty to the King.

VANSEN. And the King to us! Don't forget that!

JETTER. Very true! Tell us your views!

SOME OTHERS. Listen to him! He knows what he's talking about.

VANSEN. I had an old employer once, who owned documents and letters about the most ancient decrees, contracts, and laws. He collected the rarest books. In one of them our whole constitution was set out: how we Netherlanders were ruled at first by single princes, all according to traditional rights, privileges, and customs; how our ancestors had every kind of respect for their Prince, as long as he ruled them as he must; and how they sat up as soon as he looked like being too big for his boots. Our deputies were after him at once; for every Province, however small, had its parliament and deputies.

CARPENTER. Shut your mouth! We've known all that for a long time. Every decent citizen knows as much about the constitution as he needs to know.

JETTER. Let him speak; there's always something new to be learnt.

SOEST. He's quite right.

SEVERAL OTHERS. Go on, tell us more. We don't hear that kind of thing every day.

VANSEN. That's what you're like, citizens. You just drift along from day to day and, just as you took over your trades from your parents, you let the government rule you as it pleases. You ask no questions about tradition, about history, about the rights of a Regent; and because you have failed in that, the Spaniards have pulled tight the net right over your heads.

SOEST. Who worries about that? If only a man has enough to eat.

JETTER. Damnation! Why didn't somebody get up in time and tell us these things?

VANSEN. I'm telling you now. The King in Spain, who happens to own all our provinces, has no right, all the same, to rule them any differently from the little princes who once owned them separately. Do you understand that?

JETTER. Explain it to us.

VANSEN. It's as clear as daylight. Should you not be judged according to the laws of your country? How could it be otherwise?

A CITIZEN. True enough!

VANSEN. Hasn't the citizen of Brussels other laws than the citizen of Antwerp? And the citizen of Antwerp than the citizen of Ghent? How could it be otherwise?

OTHER CITIZENS. By God, it's true.

VANSEN. But if you let things go on as they are, they'll soon show you a very different picture. Shame on it! What Charles the Bold, Frederick the Warrior, Charles V could not do, Philip does through a woman!

SOEST. Indeed. The old princes too tried to get away with it.

VANSEN. Naturally. . . . Our ancestors were on their guard. When they had a grudge against one of their masters, they would capture his son and heir, keep him prisoner, and only release him when all their conditions had been met—or something of that kind. Our ancestors were real men! They knew what was good for them. They knew how to get hold of things and keep them. Real men, I say. And that's why our privileges are so clearly outlined, our liberties so securely guarded.

SOAPBOILER. What's that you're saying about our liberties?

THE CROWD. Yes, our liberties, our privileges! Tell us more about our privileges!

VANSEN. We men of Brabant especially, though all Provinces have their advantages, we have the most splendid rights. I've read about them all.

SOEST. Tell us what they are.

JETTER. Let's have them all.

A CITIZEN. I beg you.

VANSEN. Firstly, it is written: The Duke of Brabant shall be a good and loyal master to us.

SOEST. Good, was that the word? Is that what it says?

JETTER. Loyal? Is that so?

VANSEN. That's what I'm telling you. He's bound to us by oath, as we are to him. Secondly: he must not impose on us, make felt, or propose to apply to us any power or expression of his will in whatever manner.

JETTER. Excellent. Must not impose on us.

SOEST. Not make felt.

ANOTHER. And propose to apply. That's the crux of it. Apply to no one, in whatever manner.

VANSEN. Most emphatically.

JETTER. Bring in the book.

A CITIZEN. Yes, we must see it.

OTHERS. The book, the book!

ANOTHER. Let's go to the Regent and show her the book.

ANOTHER. And you, Doctor, shall be our spokesman.

SOAPBOILER. Oh, the poor fools!

OTHERS. Give us another extract from the book.

SOAPBOILER. Another word out of him, and I'll make him swallow his teeth!

THE CROWD. Just let anyone try to do that! Tell us more about the privileges! Haven't we any more privileges?

VANSEN. Quite a number, friends, and very good and wholesome ones they are. It is written there too: The ruler must neither improve nor increase the status of the clergy without the consent of the nobles and the commons. Mark that, my friends! Nor alter the constitution of the Province in any way.

SOEST. Is that so?

VANSEN. I'll show it to you in writing, as set down two, three centuries ago.

CITIZENS. And we put up with the new bishops? The nobles must protect us, we must make trouble at once.

OTHERS. And we allow the Inquisition to terrorize us?

VANSEN. That's your fault.

THE PEOPLE. We still have Egmont! And Orange! They will see to it.

VANSEN. Your brothers in Flanders have begun the good work.

SOAPBOILER. You rat!

He hits him.

OTHERS (*resist and cry out*). Are you a Spaniard too?

ANOTHER. What? Strike that honourable gentleman?

ANOTHER. Strike a man of such erudition?

They fall upon the Soapboiler.

CARPENTER. For heaven's sake, stop it.

Others join in the brawl.

Citizens! Are you out of your senses?

Boys whistle, throw stones, incite dogs to attack. Citizens stand and gape, new people arrive, others walk about calmly, others again play all sorts of clownish tricks, shriek, and cheer.

OTHERS. Freedom and privileges! Privileges and freedom!

Enter Egmont with retinue.

EGMONT. Steady, steady now, all of you. What's going on? Silence! Separate them!

CARPENTER. Your lordship, you come like an angel from heaven. Quiet, all of you! Can't you see it's Count Egmont? Pay your respects to Count Egmont!

EGMONT. You here too? What do you think you are doing? Citizen against citizen. Doesn't even the proximity of our royal Regent restrain you from this folly? Disperse, all of you. Go back to your work. It's a bad sign when you start celebrating on working days. What was it all about?

The tumult dies down gradually, they all surround Egmont.

CARPENTER. They're brawling for their privileges.

EGMONT. Which they will recklessly destroy in the end. And who are you? You seem honest people to me.

CARPENTER. That is our endeavour.

EGMONT. Your trades?

CARPENTER. Carpenter, and master of the Guild.

EGMONT. And you?

SOEST. Grocer.

EGMONT. You?

JETTER. Tailor?

EGMONT. I remember, you worked at the liveries of my men. Your name is Jetter.

JETTER. It is gracious of you to recall it.

EGMONT. I don't easily forget anyone I have seen and spoken to. . . . Now do what you can to restore order, all of you, and to maintain it. Your position is awkward enough as it is. Do not provoke the King even more, for it is he who is in power, and will show it too. A decent citizen, who earns an honest and industrious living, will always have as much freedom as he needs.

CARPENTER. Very true, sir. And that's the rub. The pickpockets, the drunkards, the idlers, by your lordship's leave, those are the ones who make trouble out of boredom and root for privileges out of hunger, and tell lies to the inquisitive and credulous, and start brawls for the sake of a tankard of beer that someone will stand them, though many thousands will suffer because of it. That's just what they want. We keep our houses and cupboards too well locked, so they'd like to drive us out with fire-brands.

EGMONT. You can rely on every kind of help. Measures have been taken to resist this evil in the most effective way. Stand fast against the alien doctrine, and never think that privileges can be secured by riots. Stay at home. Do not allow them to create disturbances in the streets. A few sensible people can do much.

Meanwhile the great crowd has dispersed.

CARPENTER. Thank you, Your Excellency, thank you for your good opinion of us. We shall do all we can.

Exit Egmont.

A gracious gentleman! A true Netherlander! Nothing Spanish about him.

JETTER. If only he were our Regent! It would be a pleasure to obey him.

SOEST. The King takes good care to prevent that. He always puts one of his people in that place.

JETTER. Did you notice his dress? It was in the latest fashion, the Spanish cut.

CARPENTER. A handsome gentleman.

JETTER. His neck would be a real feast to the executioner.

SOEST. Are you mad? What's got into your head?

JETTER. Yes, it's silly enough, the things that get into one's head. It's just what I happen to feel. When I see a fine, long neck, I can't help thinking at once: that's a good one for the axe. . . . All these cursed executions! One can't get them out of one's mind. When the young fellows go swimming and I see a bare back, at once I remember dozens that I've seen lashed by the cat-o'-nine-tails. If I meet a really fat paunch I can already see it roast on the stake. At night in my dreams I feel pinches in all my limbs. It's simply that one can't be carefree for one hour. Every sort of pleasure or jollity is soon forgotten; but the horrible apparitions might be branded on my forehead, they never leave me alone.

Egmont's House

Secretary at a table covered with papers; he rises restlessly.

SECRETARY. He still doesn't come, and I've been waiting these two hours pen in hand, papers in front of me; and it's the very day when I want to leave early. My feet itch to be gone; I can hardly bear the delay. "Be there on the stroke of the clock," he commanded before he went out. And now he doesn't come. There's so much to be done, I shan't be finished before midnight. True, he's quite capable of closing an eye. But I should still prefer him to be strict and then let me go at the proper time. One could arrange things in that case. It's two whole hours since he left the Regent; I wonder who it is he's button-holed on the way.

Enter Egmont.

EGMONT. Well, how is it?

SECRETARY. I am ready, and three messengers are waiting.

EGMONT. It seems I was out too long for your liking—to judge by the face you're making.

SECRETARY. I have been waiting for some considerable time to execute your orders. Here are the papers!

EGMONT. Donna Elvira will be angry with me when she hears that I've kept you.

SECRETARY. You are joking.

EGMONT. No, my dear fellow. There's no need to feel ashamed. You have shown the best taste. She's pretty enough, and I'm very glad that you have a lady friend in the Palace. What do the dispatches say?

SECRETARY. All kinds of things, but little that is pleasing.

EGMONT. In that case it's a good thing that we have no lack of pleasantness in our own house and needn't wait for it to come to us from outside. Are there many letters?

SECRETARY. Quite enough, and three messengers are waiting.

EGMONT. Tell me, then! Only what's essential.

SECRETARY. It's all essential.

EGMONT. One thing after another, then, but be quick about it.

SECRETARY. Captain Breda sends a report on the latest occurrences in Ghent and the surrounding district. Things are more quiet there, on the whole.

EGMONT. I suppose he mentions certain isolated cases of insolence and insubordination?

SECRETARY. Yes, there are incidents of that sort.

EGMONT. Well, spare me the particulars.

SECRETARY. They've arrested six more persons who tore down the statue of Our Lady at Verwich. He asks whether they are to be hanged like the others.

EGMONT. I'm tired of hangings. Let them be soundly whipped and released.

SECRETARY. There are two women among them. Are they to be whipped as well?

EGMONT. As for them, he is to let them off with a warning.

SECRETARY. Brink, of Breda's company, wants to marry. The captain hopes you will forbid it. There are so many women hanging around the regiment, he writes, that when we're on the march it looks less like a body of soldiers than a troop of gipsies.

EGMONT. Let it pass in Brink's case. He's a fine young fellow. He begged me most urgently before I left. But after him no one is to receive permission, much as it grieves me to refuse the poor devils their best amusement—and they've troubles enough as it is.

SECRETARY. Two of your men, Seter and Hart, have behaved abominably towards a girl, an innkeeper's daughter. They caught her when she was alone, and the girl had no means of defending herself.

EGMONT. If she's an honest girl, and they used force, they are to be birched for three days in succession, and if they have any possessions, Captain Breda is to confiscate enough of them to make provision for the girl.

SECRETARY. One of the foreign preachers entered Comines in secret, and was apprehended. He swears that he was on his way to France. According to orders he is to be beheaded.

EGMONT. They are to take him to the frontier quietly and assure him that he won't get away with it a second time.

SECRETARY. A dispatch from your Receiver-General. He writes that too little money is coming in, that he can hardly send the required sum within a week, that the disturbances have thrown everything into the greatest disorder.

EGMONT. The money must be sent. Let him find it how and where he can.

SECRETARY. He says he will do his best and will at last take action against Raymond, who has been your debtor for so long, and have him arrested.

EGMONT. But Raymond has promised to repay the money.

SECRETARY. Last time he gave himself a fortnight to do so.

EGMONT. Well, let him have another fortnight; after that they may go ahead and sue him.

SECRETARY. You are right. It's not incapacity, but ill will on his part. He will certainly take notice as soon as he sees that you're in earnest. . . . The Receiver-General goes on to say that he proposes to withhold half a month's pay from the old soldiers, widows, and some others to whom you have granted pensions. That would give him time to make arrangements, and they would have to manage as best they can.

EGMONT. How does he think they will manage? Those people need the money more than I do. He will refrain from withholding the pensions.

SECRETARY. What are your orders then? Where is he to obtain the funds?

EGMONT. That's his business, and I told him so in my previous dispatch.

SECRETARY. That's why he makes these proposals.

EGMONT. They are not good enough. He must think of other measures. He is to make other proposals, acceptable ones, and above all, he must find the money.

SECRETARY. I have left Count Olivat's letter here for you once more. Forgive me for drawing your attention to it again. More than anyone, the old gentleman deserves a full reply. It was your wish to write to him in person. Without doubt, he loves you like a father.

EGMONT. I haven't the time. And of all odious things, writing is the most odious to me. You're so good at imitating my handwriting, write it in my name. I'm expecting Orange. I haven't the time—and I would like his doubts to be answered by something truly comforting.

SECRETARY. Only tell me roughly what you think; I can then draft the reply and submit it to you. It shall be penned in such a way that it could pass for your handwriting in a court of law.

EGMONT. Give me the letter.

After glancing at it:

The dear, honest old man! I wonder were you as cautious as that when you were young? Did you never climb a fortress wall? In battle, did you remain at the back, as prudence demands? The loyal, solicitous old man! He wants me to live and be happy and does not feel that to live for safety's sake is to be dead already. Tell him not to be anxious; I shall act as I must and shall know how to protect myself. Let him use his influence at Court in my favour and be assured of my wholehearted gratitude.

SECRETARY. Is that all? He expects a great deal more.

EGMONT. What more should I say? If you want to be more long-winded, be so by all means. The crux is always the same: they want me to live in a way that is not my way. It's my good fortune to be cheerful, to take life easy, to travel light and fast, and I will not exchange these for the security of a tomb. It happens that I haven't a drop of blood in my veins that accords with the Spanish way of life; nor any desire to adapt my gait to the measured courtly cadence. Do I live only to take thought for my life? Should I forbid myself to enjoy the present moment, so as to be certain of the next? And consume the next moment too with cares and apprehensions?

SECRETARY. I beg you, sir, don't be so hard on the good gentleman. You are kind to everyone else. Only tell me a few agreeable words that will calm your noble friend. You see how careful he is, how delicately he touches you.

EGMONT. And yet he always touches this same string. He has long known how I hate these incessant admonitions. They serve only to unnerve me, never to help. And if I were a sleepwalker, balanced on the knife-edge of a roof top, would it be a friendly act to call out my name to warn me, wake me, and kill me? Let every man go his own way and look after himself.

SECRETARY. It is fitting for you not to be worried. But someone who knows and loves you——

EGMONT (*reading the letter*). There he goes again, repeating the old tales of what we did and said one evening in the easy expansiveness of sociability and wine! And of all the consequences and proofs drawn and dragged from them the whole length and breadth of the kingdom. Very well, we had cap and bells embroidered on the arms of our servants, and later had this badge of folly changed to a sheaf of arrows—an even more dangerous symbol to all those who looked for significance where there was none. There was this folly and that, conceived and born within a single moment of merriment; we were responsible for sending off a most noble band, furnished with beggars' scrips and a self-chosen sobriquet to remind the King of his duty with mock humility; are responsible for—what else? Is a carnival charade to be accounted high treason? Are we to be grudged the small coloured rags which our youthful exuberance, our excited imagination may wrap around the wretched bareness of our lives? If you take life too seriously, what is it worth? If the mornings do not rouse us to new pleasures, if the evenings leave us without the comfort of hope, is it worth while to dress and undress at all? Does the sun shine for me today so that I may ponder on what happened yesterday? So that I may fathom and link that which is not to be fathomed or linked—the destiny of a future day? Spare me these considerations, leave them to scholars and courtiers. Let these reflect and make plans, creep and crawl, arrive where they may, creep their way into what positions they can. If any of this is of any use to you, without turning your epistle into a book, you are welcome to it. The dear old man takes everything too seriously. His letter makes me think of a friend who has long held my hand in his and presses it once more before releasing it.

SECRETARY. Forgive me, but it makes a pedestrian dizzy to watch a traveller rush past him with such speed.

EGMONT. Enough, my dear fellow! Not another word! As though whipped by invisible spirits, the horses of the sun, Time's horses, run away with the light chariot of our destinies; and we have no choice but to grip the reins with resolute courage and, now to the right, now to the left, avert the wheels from a stone here, a precipice there. As for the end of the journey, who knows what it is? When we hardly remember where it began.

SECRETARY. Oh, sir!

EGMONT. I stand in a high and prominent place and must rise still higher. I have hope, courage, and strength. I have not yet attained the crest of my growth and when I *have* attained the highest point, I shall stand there unwavering, without fear. If I must fall, let a thunderbolt, a gale, even a false step hurl me down into the depths; I shall not be alone there but with thousands of good men. I have never disdained to stake my all in war for the slightest gain, like any decent soldier; and do you expect me to turn niggard when the prize is nothing less than the entire worth of a free life?

SECRETARY. Oh, sir! You do not know what you are saying. May God preserve you!

EGMONT. Collect your papers now. Orange is coming. Complete whatever is most urgent, so that the couriers can leave before the gates are shut. Other things can wait. Leave the letter to the Count till tomorrow. Don't fail to visit Elvira and give her my regards. Find out how the Regent is keeping; they say that she's not well, though she conceals it.

Exit secretary. Enter Orange.

EGMONT. Welcome, Orange. You seem somewhat constrained.

ORANGE. What do you say to our conversation with the Regent?

EGMONT. I saw nothing extraordinary in her manner of receiving us. It wasn't the first time I have seen her in that state. I had the impression that she was unwell.

ORANGE. Didn't you observe that she was more reticent? At first, she wanted to be calm and express her approval of our conduct during the new uprising of the mob. Later, she hinted that this could easily appear in a false light, then diverted the conversation to her usual topic: that her amiable, benevolent disposition, her friendship for us Netherlanders have never been duly appreciated, that we have taken it too much for granted, that none of her efforts seemed to lead to the desired results, that she might well grow weary in the end and the King resort to very different measures. Did you note all this?

EGMONT. No, not all of it; I was thinking of something different at the time. She is a woman, dear Orange, and women always wish that everyone will meekly creep under their gentle yoke, that every Hercules will doff his lion's skin and join their knitting group; that, because they desire peace, the ferment that seizes a people, the tempest that mighty rivals raise among themselves, can be soothed by a kind word, and that the most hostile elements will lie down together at their feet in gentle concord. That is the case with her also. And since she cannot bring about this state, she has no alternative but to become ill-tempered, to complain of ingratitude and lack of wisdom, to threaten us with terrible consequences and to threaten—that she will leave us!

ORANGE. And don't you believe that this time she will carry out her threat?

EGMONT. Never! How often I've seen her in her travelling clothes! Where could she go? Here she is Governor, Queen. Do you suppose that she relishes the thought of going into insignificant retirement at her brother's court? Or of going to Italy and burdening herself with the old family matters?

ORANGE. People think her incapable of such a decision because they have seen her hesitate and withdraw. And yet she has it in her; new circumstances drive her to the long-delayed resolution. What if she did go? And the King sent someone else?

EGMONT. Well, he would come, and would find plenty of things to occupy him. He would come with great plans, projects, and ideas of how to arrange, control, and hold together all things; and would be struggling with this trifle today, that trifle tomorrow, would come up against this obstruction the day after, spend a month on preparations and schemes, another on being disappointed with undertakings that have failed, half a year on the troubles caused by a single Province. For him too time would pass, his head would grow giddy, and one thing follow another as before, so that he would have cause to thank God if he succeeded in keeping his ship off the rocks instead of navigating great oceans along a charted course.

ORANGE. But what if someone advised the King to make an experiment?

EGMONT. And what might that be?

ORANGE. To see what the torso would do without a head.

EGMONT. What do you mean?

ORANGE. Egmont, for many years now I have been deeply concerned with all our affairs, my head always bent over them as over a chessboard, and I do not regard any move on the other side as insignificant. And just as idle persons enquire with the greatest care into the secrets of nature, so I consider it the duty, the vocation, of a prince to know the views and strategy of all parties. I have cause to fear an eruption. The King has long acted according to certain principles; he sees that these are inadequate; what can be more likely than that he will try other means?

EGMONT. That's not my opinion. When one grows old and has tried so many things and the world still refuses to become a tidy place, surely one puts up with it in the end.

ORANGE. There's one thing he hasn't tried.

EGMONT. Well?

ORANGE. To spare the people and destroy the princes.

EGMONT. An old fear, and widespread. It's not worth worrying about.

ORANGE. Once it was a worry; gradually it became a probability to me; finally, it's become a certainty.

EGMONT. And has the King any subjects more loyal than ourselves?

ORANGE. We serve him in our fashion; and we can admit to each other that we know well how to balance the King's rights against ours.

EGMONT. Who wouldn't? We are his subjects and pay him such tribute as is due to him.

ORANGE. But what if he claimed *more*, and called disloyalty what we call insisting on our rights?

EGMONT. We shall be able to defend ourselves. Let him convoke the Knights of the Golden Fleece; we shall submit to their judgement.

ORANGE. And what if the verdict precedes the trial, the punishment precedes the verdict?

EGMONT. That would be an injustice of which Philip could never be guilty, and an act of folly of which, in my view, both he and his counsellors are incapable——

ORANGE. And what if they did prove to be unjust and foolish?

EGMONT. No, Orange, it's impossible. Who would dare to lay hands on us? . . . To arrest us would be a vain and useless act. No, they do not dare to raise the banner of tyranny so high. The gust of wind that would bear this news across the country would fan an enormous blaze. And what would be the point of it? It is not the King alone who has the right to judge and condemn. And would they destroy us in secret, like a band of vulgar assassins? They cannot even think of such a thing. A terrible pact would unite the whole people at once. Undying hatred and eternal separation from the Spanish name would violently declare themselves.

ORANGE. In that case the fire would rage over our graves, and the blood of our enemies would flow as an idle expiatory offering. Let us take thought to prevent it, Egmont.

EGMONT. But how can we?

ORANGE. Alba is on his way.

EGMONT. I don't believe it.

ORANGE. I know it.

EGMONT. The Regent would not hear of it.

ORANGE. Another reason for my conviction. The Regent will yield her place to him. I know his murderous disposition, and he will bring an army with him.

EGMONT. To harass the Provinces once more? The people will grow most unruly.

ORANGE. They will take care of the people's heads.

EGMONT. No, no, I say.

ORANGE. Let us leave, each for his Province. There we shall reinforce ourselves. He will not begin with a show of brute force.

EGMONT. Must we not be there to welcome him when he comes?

ORANGE. We shall procrastinate.

EGMONT. And if he demands our presence at his arrival, in the King's name?

ORANGE. We shall look for evasions.

EGMONT. And if he presses us?

ORANGE. We shall excuse ourselves.

EGMONT. And if he insists on it?

ORANGE. We shall refuse all the more firmly.

EGMONT. And war will have been declared, and we shall be rebels. Orange, don't let your cleverness mislead you; I know that it isn't fear that moves you to retreat. Consider the implications of this step.

ORANGE. I have considered them.

EGMONT. Consider what you will be guilty of, if you are wrong: of the most ruinous war that has ever laid waste a country. Your refusal will be the signal which calls all the provinces to arms at once; it will serve to justify every act of cruelty for which Spain has never lacked anything but a pretext. What we have long kept down with the utmost difficulty, you will rouse up with a single call to the most frightful turmoil. Think of the cities, the nobles, the people; of commerce, agriculture, the trades. And think of the destruction, the slaughter! . . . True, in the field the soldier looks calmly upon his dying comrade; but it is the corpses of citizens, children, young women which will float down the rivers to where you stand. So that you will be filled with horror, no longer knowing whose cause you are defending, since those are perishing for whose freedom you took arms. And how will you feel when you have to tell yourself: it was for my safety that I took them?

ORANGE. We are not individual men, Egmont. If it is fitting for us to sacrifice ourselves for the sake of thousands, it is fitting too to spare ourselves for the sake of thousands.

EGMONT. The man who spares himself must become suspicious of himself.

ORANGE. The man who knows himself can advance or retreat with confidence.

EGMONT. The evil which you fear becomes a certainty by your deed.

ORANGE. It is prudent and bold to meet the inevitable disaster.

EGMONT. In a peril so great the slightest hope should be fostered.

ORANGE. There is no room left for the lightest manoeuvre on our part; the abyss lies right in front of us.

EGMONT. Is the King's favour so narrow a ledge?

ORANGE. Not so narrow, but slippery.

EGMONT. By God! You do him an injustice. I will not suffer anyone to think ill of him. He is Charles's son and incapable of baseness.

ORANGE. Kings are never guilty of baseness.

EGMONT. You should get to know him better.

ORANGE. It is that very knowledge which advises us not to await the outcome of this dangerous test.

EGMONT. No test is dangerous if one has the necessary courage.

ORANGE. You are getting excited, Egmont.

EGMONT. I must see with my own eyes.

ORANGE. Oh, if only you would see with mine for once! My dear friend, because your eyes are open you think that you see. I am going! Wait for Alba's arrival if you must, and God be with you! Perhaps my refusal will save you. Perhaps the dragon will think it has caught nothing if it cannot devour both of us at once. Perhaps it will hesitate, so as to be more sure of success, and perhaps by then you will see the matter in its true light. But be quick then! Quick as lightning! Save yourself. Save yourself, my friend. Farewell. Let nothing escape your watchfulness: the size of his army, how he occupies the city, how much power the Regent retains, how well your friends are prepared. Keep me informed. . . . Egmont——

EGMONT. Well?

ORANGE (*taking his hand*). Let me persuade you. Come with me!

EGMONT. What, Orange, tears in *your* eyes?

ORANGE. To weep for one who is lost is not unmanly.

EGMONT. You regard me as lost?

ORANGE. You are. Think again! You have only the briefest of respites. Farewell.

Exit.

EGMONT (*alone*). Strange that other people's thoughts have such influence on us! It would never have occurred to me, and this man's apprehensions have infected me . . . Away! It's an alien drop in my blood. Let my sound nature throw it out again! And there's one kind remedy still to bathe away the pensive wrinkles on my brow.

ACT III

The Regent's Palace
Margaret of Parma.

REGENT. I should have guessed it. Oh, if one's days are spent in toil and stress, one always thinks one is doing one's utmost; and the person who looks on from afar and gives orders believes he demands only what is possible. . . . Oh, these Kings! . . . I should never have thought that it could grieve me so. It is so pleasant to rule! . . . And to abdicate? . . . I cannot think how my father could do it; and yet I shall do it also.

Machiavelli appears in the background.

REGENT. Come closer, Machiavelli! I am just thinking about my brother's letter.

MACHIAVELLI. And may I know what it contains?

REGENT. As much tender attention to me as solicitude for his states. He commends the steadfastness, industry, and loyalty with which I have hitherto upheld the rights of His Majesty in these Provinces. He pities me because the unruly people is causing me so much trouble now.

He is so entirely convinced of the profundity of my insight, so extraordinarily pleased with the prudence of my conduct, that I must almost say: the letter is too well written for a King, certainly for a brother.

MACHIAVELLI. This is not the first time he has informed you of his well-deserved satisfaction.

REGENT. But the first time it is a mere figure of rhetoric.

MACHIAVELLI. I don't follow you.

REGENT. You will. For after this induction, he expresses the opinion that without a bodyguard, without a small army, I shall always cut a bad figure here. We were wrong, he says, to withdraw our soldiers from the Provinces because the population complained. An occupation force, he believes, which loads down the citizen's neck prevents him by its weight from indulging in high leaps.

MACHIAVELLI. It would have a most unsettling effect on the people's state of mind.

REGENT. The King, however, is of the opinion——Are you listening? He is of the opinion that an efficient general, one who does not listen to reason, would very soon put the people and nobility, citizens and peasantry, in their place; and is therefore sending a powerful force commanded—by the Duke of Alba.

MACHIAVELLI. Alba?

REGENT. That surprises you?

MACHIAVELLI. You say he is sending. I suppose he asks you whether he should send.

REGENT. The King does not ask, he sends.

MACHIAVELLI. In that case you will have an experienced military man in your service.

REGENT. In my service? Speak your mind, Machiavelli!

MACHIAVELLI. I am anxious not to anticipate, madam.

REGENT. And I am anxious to disguise the truth! It is very painful to me, very painful. I wish my brother had said what he thinks instead of sending formal epistles which a Secretary of State has drawn up.

MACHIAVELLI. Should we not try to understand . . .

REGENT. But I know them by heart. They want the place cleaned and swept; and since they do not act themselves, they lend their trust to any man who appears broom in hand. Oh, I can see the King and his Council as clearly as if they were embroidered on this tapestry.

MACHIAVELLI. So vividly?

REGENT. Not a single feature is missing. There are good men among them. Honest Rodrick, who is so experienced and moderate, does not aim too high and yet lets nothing fall too low. Honest Alonzo, hard-working Freneda, solid Las Vagas and a few others who will cooperate when the good party comes into power. But on the other side there sits the hollow-eyed Toledan with the brazen brow and the deep, fiery glance, mumbling between his teeth of female softheartedness, misplaced indulgence, and that women may sit a horse already broken, but make poor equerries themselves, and other such pleasantries to which I once had to listen in the company of the political gentlemen.

MACHIAVELLI. You have chosen a good palette for the portrait.

REGENT. Admit it, Machiavelli, of all the colours and shades with which I could choose to paint no tone is as yellow-brown, as gall-black as the colour of Alba's face or as the colour with which he paints. To him, everyone is a blasphemer, a traitor to the King; for on that score he can have them all racked, burnt, hanged, drawn and quartered. . . . The good I have done here probably looks like nothing from a distance, simply because it is good. So he will seize on every caprice long past, recall every disturbance long ago put down; and the King will have such a vision of mutiny, rebellion, and recklessness that he will think the people here devour one another, when we have long forgotten some fleeting, passing misconduct of a nation still rough. Then he will conceive a deep, heartfelt hatred for these poor people; they will seem repulsive to him, indeed like beasts and monsters; he will look around for fire and sword, imagining that that is how to tame men.

MACHIAVELLI. I think you exaggerate a little and take the whole matter too seriously. After all, you will be Regent still.

REGENT. Oh, I know all about that. He will bring a royal directive. I have grown old enough in affairs of state to know how one displaces a person without depriving him of his rank and title. First he will bring a royal directive, which will be twisted and vague; he will make changes all around him, for he has the power, and if I complain he will use the pretext of a secret directive; if I ask to see it, he will prevaricate; if I insist, he will show me a document that contains something quite different; and if I am still not satisfied, he will do no more than he would if I were speaking. Meanwhile he will have done what I fear and irrevocably averted what I wish.

MACHIAVELLI. I wish I could contradict you.

REGENT. What I have calmed with unspeakable patience, he will stir up again by hardheartedness and cruelty. I shall see my work perish before my very eyes and bear the blame for his acts into the bargain.

MACHIAVELLI. Do not anticipate, Your Highness.

REGENT. Well, I still have enough self-control to be quiet. Let him come, I shall make way for him with good grace before he pushes me out.

MACHIAVELLI. And you will take this grave step with such alacrity?

REGENT. It's more difficult for me than you think. If one is accustomed to rule, if it was given to one in youth to hold the fate of thousands daily in one's hand, one descends from the throne as into a grave. But sooner that than remain like a spectre among the living and with hollow gestures lay claim to a place which another has inherited, possesses, and enjoys.

Clare's House
Clare and Mother.

MOTHER. Never have I seen such love as Brackenburg's; I thought it was only to be found in legends about heroes.

CLARE (*walks up and down the room, humming a song with closed lips*).

Happy alone
Is whom love has in thrall.

MOTHER. He suspects how you stand with Egmont. And I think that if you gave him a little encouragement, if you wanted him to, he would still marry you.

CLARE (*sings*).

Gladdened
And saddened
And troubled in vain,
Longing
And thronging
With wavering pain,
Raised up to heaven,
The deeper to fall,
Happy alone
Is whom love has in thrall.

MOTHER. Oh, leave off the "by-low, lie-low."

CLARE. No, don't say anything against it. It's a powerful song. More than once I've lulled a big child to sleep with it.

MOTHER. You can't think of anything except your love. If only you wouldn't forget everything because of that *one* thing. You should have some respect for Brackenburg, I tell you. He might still make you happy one day.

CLARE. Brackenburg?

MOTHER. Oh yes, there will come a time. . . . You children foresee nothing and will not listen to our experience. Youth and true love, it all comes to an end; and there comes a time when one gives thanks to God for somewhere to lay one's head.

CLARE (*shudders, keeps silent, and then bursts out*). Mother, let the time come then, like death. To think of it in advance is horrible! And what if it does come! If we must—then—then we shall face up to it as best we can. To think of losing Egmont!

In tears.

No, it's impossible, quite impossible.

Enter Egmont in a riding cloak, his hat pressed down onto his face.

EGMONT. Clare!

CLARE (*utters a scream, totters*). Egmont!

She runs to him.

Egmont!

She embraces him and rests her head on his shoulder.

Oh, my dear, good, darling Egmont! So you've come. You're here!

EGMONT. Good evening, Mother.

MOTHER. Welcome to our house, Your Lordship. My little girl nearly pined away because of your long absence; she spent the whole day, as usual, talking and singing about you.

EGMONT. You'll give me some supper, won't you?

MOTHER. You do us too much honour. If only we had something to offer you.

CLARE. Of course we have. Don't worry about it, Mother; I've made all the arrangements already and prepared something. But don't let me down, Mother.

MOTHER. It's paltry enough.

CLARE. Just be patient. And besides, I say to myself: when he's with me, I'm not in the least hungry, so he shouldn't have too big an appetite when I'm with him.

EGMONT. Do you think so?

Clare stamps her foot and turns her back on him in a pique.

EGMONT. What's the matter with you?

CLARE. Oh, you're so chilly today. You haven't offered to kiss me yet. Why do you keep your arms wrapped in your cloak like a new-born baby? It isn't right for a soldier or a lover to keep his arms wrapped up.

EGMONT. At times it is, sweetheart, at times. When the soldier is on his guard and trying to get the better of his enemy by stealth, he pulls himself together, puts his arms around himself, and waits till his plan of action has matured. And a lover . . .

MOTHER. Won't you sit down, make yourself comfortable? I must go to the kitchen. Clare forgets everything when you're here. You will have to make do with what we have to offer.

EGMONT. Your good will is the best spice.

Exit Mother.

CLARE. And what would you call my love?

EGMONT. Anything you like.

CLARE. Compare it to something, if you have the heart.

EGMONT. Well, first of all . . .

He throws off his cloak and stands there splendidly dressed.

CLARE. Goodness!

EGMONT. Now my arms are free.

He hugs her.

CLARE. Stop it! You'll spoil your appearance.

She steps back.

How splendid it is! Now I mustn't touch you.

EGMONT. Are you satisfied? I promised I'd come dressed in Spanish fashion one day.

CLARE. I never asked you again. I thought you didn't want to. . . . Oh, and the Golden Fleece!

EGMONT. Well, there it is for you.

CLARE. And did the Emperor hang it around your neck?

EGMONT. Yes, child. And the chain and the pendant grant the most noble liberties to the man who wears them. There is no one on earth who has the right to judge my actions other than the Grand Master of the Order, together with the assembled company of Knights.

CLARE. Oh, you could let the whole world stand in judgement over you! The velvet is too lovely for words, and the gold thread! And the embroidery! . . . One doesn't know where to begin.

EGMONT. Look your fill.

CLARE. And the Golden Fleece! You told me the story and said it was a symbol of all that is great and precious, only to be earned and won by the most strenuous endeavours. It is very precious—I can compare it to your love. I wear it next to my heart as well—and then . . .

EGMONT. What were you going to say?

CLARE. And then the comparison doesn't apply.

EGMONT. How do you mean?

CLARE. Because I haven't won your love by strenuous endeavours; I haven't earned it.

EGMONT. In love it's different. You have earned it because you don't try to win it, and usually only those people get it who don't chase after it.

CLARE. Did you derive that conclusion from yourself? Did you make this proud observation about yourself? You, whom all the people loves?

EGMONT. If only I'd done something for them! If only I could do something for them. It is their kind will to love me.

CLARE. I suppose you saw the Regent today?

EGMONT. I did.

CLARE. Are you on good terms with her?

EGMONT. It looks that way. We are amiable and helpful to each other.

CLARE. And in your heart?

EGMONT. I wish her well. Each of us has his own aims. But that is neither here nor there. She's an excellent woman, knows her men, and would see deep enough even if she weren't suspicious. I cause her a great deal of trouble because she is always looking for secret motives behind my conduct, and I have none.

CLARE. None at all?

EGMONT. Well, yes. A few little reservations. Every wine leaves a deposit of tartar if it's left long enough in the barrel. But Orange provides better entertainment for her all the same, and sets her new puzzles incessantly. He has made people believe that he always harbours some secret project; and so now she is always looking at his forehead wondering what he's thinking, or at his steps, wondering where he may be directing them.

CLARE. Does she conceal her motives?

EGMONT. She's the Regent. What do you expect?

CLARE. Forgive me. What I meant to ask was: is she deceitful?

EGMONT. No more and no less than anyone who wishes to attain his ends.

CLARE. I could never be at home in the great world. But then she has a masculine mind; she's a different kind of woman from us seamstresses and cooks. She is noble, brave, resolute.

EGMONT. Yes, as long as things are not too topsy-turvy. This time she's not so sure of herself.

CLARE. How so?

EGMONT. She has a little moustache too, on her upper lip, and occasional attacks of gout. A real Amazon.

CLARE. A majestic woman! I should be afraid to enter her presence.

EGMONT. You're not usually so shy. But then it wouldn't be fear, only girlish modesty.

Clare casts down her eyes, takes his hand, and nestles against him.

EGMONT. I understand you, my dear. You can raise your eyes.

CLARE. Let me be silent. Let me hold you. Let me look into your eyes: find everything in them, comfort and hope and joy and grief.

She puts her arms around him and looks at him.

Tell me. Tell me. I don't understand. Are you Egmont? Count

Egmont, the great Egmont who raises such an ado, whom the newspapers write about, whom the Provinces adore?

EGMONT. No, my little Clare, I am not.

CLARE. What?

EGMONT. You see——Clare! Let me sit down.

He sits down, she kneels in front of him on a stool, puts her arms on his knees, and looks at him.

That Egmont is an ill-tempered, stiff, cold Egmont, who has to keep up appearances, now make this face, now that; who is tormented, misunderstood, entangled, while other people think he is gay and carefree; loved by a people that does not know its own mind, honoured and carried aloft by a mob for which there is no help; surrounded by friends on whom he must not rely; closely watched by men who desire to harm him in every possible way; toiling and striving, often aimlessly, nearly always unrewarded. . . . Oh, let me say no more about him! How he fares, how he feels! But this one, Clare, this one is calm, candid, happy, beloved and understood by the best of hearts, which he too understands wholly and presses to him with complete love and trust.

He embraces her.

That is *your* Egmont.

CLARE. Then let me die. The world has no joys beyond these!

ACT IV

A Street

Jetter. Carpenter.

JETTER. Hey, there. Hush. Hey, there, neighbour, a word with you!

CARPENTER. Be on your way and keep quiet.

JETTER. Only one word. No news?

CARPENTER. None, except that we've been forbidden to talk of the news.

JETTER. What do you mean?

CARPENTER. Come close to the wall of this house. Keep your eyes and ears open. As soon as he arrived the Duke of Alba issued an order to the effect that if two or three are found talking together in the street they will be declared guilty of high treason without examination or trial.

JETTER. Oh, dreadful!

CARPENTER. The penalty for discussing affairs of state is life imprisonment.

JETTER. All our liberty lost!

CARPENTER. And on pain of death no one is to express disapproval of the government's actions.

JETTER. And our heads likely to be lost as well!

CARPENTER. And great rewards will be promised to induce fathers, mothers, children, relations, friends, servants to reveal what is going on in the home to a special court appointed for that purpose.

JETTER. Let's go home.

CARPENTER. And those who obey are promised that they will suffer no harm in their persons or property.

JETTER. How gracious of them! Didn't I feel aggrieved as soon as the Duke entered our city? Ever since, I've felt as though the sky were covered with black crêpe and hung down so low that one has to bend down to avoid knocking one's head against it.

CARPENTER. And how did you like his soldiers? They're a different kettle of fish to the ones we're used to. Don't you agree?

JETTER. Disgusting! It freezes your marrow to see a body of them march down the street. Straight as posts, their eyes glued on the next man's back, not a single man out of step. And when they're on guard duty and you pass by, you feel as though they could see right into your head, and they look so stiff and grumpy that you seem to see a taskmaster at every corner. They made me feel ill. Our militia, at least, was a gay lot. They took liberties, stood about with legs straddled, wore their hats over one eye, lived, and let live; but those fellows are like machines with a devil inside.

CARPENTER. If one of them calls out "Halt!" and jumps to the alert, do you think one would stop?

JETTER. It would be the death of me at once!

CARPENTER. Let's go home.

JETTER. No good will come of this. Good-bye.

Enter Soest.

SOEST. Friends! Comrades!

CARPENTER. Quiet. Don't detain us.

SOEST. Have you heard?

JETTER. Only too much!

SOEST. The Regent has left.

JETTER. Now God have mercy on us!

CARPENTER. She was our only hope.

SOEST. Suddenly, and in secret. She didn't get on with the Duke; she sent a message to the nobles to say she will return. No one believes it.

CARPENTER. May God forgive the nobles for allowing this new scourge to descend on our backs. They could have prevented it. All our privileges are lost.

JETTER. Not a word about privileges, for God's sake. I can smell the powder of a firing squad. The sun refuses to rise, the mists reek of rotten flesh.

SOEST. Orange is gone too.

CARPENTER. That means we've been left to our fate.

SOEST. Count Egmont is still with us.

JETTER. Thank God for that. May all the saints give him strength, so that he'll do his best; he is the only one who can help us.

Enter Vansen.

VANSEN. Well, fancy that. A few citizens who haven't yet crept away into their dens!

JETTER. Do us a favour: be on your way.

VANSEN. You're not very polite.

CARPENTER. This isn't the time for fine phrases. Are you looking for trouble again? Has your back healed already?

VANSEN. Never ask a soldier about his wounds. If I couldn't take a hiding at times, I shouldn't have got anywhere.

JETTER. Things may become more serious.

VANSEN. It seems that the approaching thunderstorm is making all your limbs feel miserably tired.

CARPENTER. If you don't keep quiet your limbs will soon start moving in a different direction.

VANSEN. Poor little mice, to fall into despair, just because the master of the house has got himself a new cat! Things have changed a bit, that's all; but we shall go about our business just as we did before, never you worry!

CARPENTER. You're a loud-mouthed good-for-nothing.

VANSEN. As for you, brother nitwit, let the Duke do his worst. The old tomcat looks as if he's been eating devils instead of mice, and now he's got indigestion as a result. Just let him get on with it; he has to eat, drink, and sleep like the rest of us. I'm not at all anxious about us, if only we take our time. At the start all goes easily; but later he too will find out that it's more pleasant to live in the larder where the bacon is stored, and to rest at night than to stalk a few mice in the loft, with nothing but fruit all around. Just keep calm. I know what governors are like.

CARPENTER. There's no telling what a fellow like that will blurt out. If I'd ever said anything like it, I shouldn't feel safe for a minute.

VANSEN. Don't you worry, God in heaven doesn't hear anything about worms of your sort, let alone the Regent.

JETTER. Filthy blasphemer!

VANSEN. I know of some people for whom it would be a lot better if they acted the hero less and had a little more discretion instead.

CARPENTER. What do you mean by that?

VANSEN. Hmm! The Count is what I mean.

JETTER. Egmont? What has he got to fear?

VANSEN. I'm a poor devil and could live a whole year on what he loses in one night. And yet he'd do well to give me his income for a whole year if he could have my head for a quarter of an hour.

JETTER. That's what you think. Egmont's got more sense in his hair than you have in your brain.

VANSEN. Say what you like. But he hasn't got more subtlety. It's the great lords who're the first to deceive themselves. He shouldn't be so trusting.

JETTER. Stuff and nonsense. A nobleman like Egmont?

VANSEN. That's just it. Just because he isn't a tailor.

JETTER. Dirty slanderer!

VANSEN. What I wish him is to have your courage just for an hour, so that it could trouble him and make him itch till it drives him out of town.

JETTER. You speak like a fool; he's as safe as a star in the sky.

VANSEN. Have you never seen one shoot off? . . . Gone in a jiffy.

CARPENTER. Who could harm him?

VANSEN. Who could harm him? Why, do you think you could prevent it? Are you going to start a rebellion when they arrest him?

JETTER. Oh!

VANSEN. Would you risk your skin for his sake?

SOEST. Eh!

VANSEN (*imitating them*). Ee, ah, oo! Run through the whole alphabet to express your surprise! That's how it is and how it will be. God have mercy on him.

JETTER. I'm shocked by your impudence. Such a noble, righteous man— —And you talk of danger?

VANSEN. It's the knave who does well for himself everywhere. On the stool of repentance he makes a fool of the judge; on the judgement seat he delights in making a criminal out of the prosecutor. I once had to copy one of those documents, when the Chief of Police received a load of praise and money from Court because he'd made a self-confessed rascal out of some honest soul they wanted out of the way.

CARPENTER. That's another arrant lie! How can they find any evidence, if the man is innocent?

VANSEN. Oh, my poor sparrow-brain! When there's nothing to be read out of the evidence, they read something into it. Honesty makes you rash—it can make you stubborn too. So they start by asking harmless questions, and the accused is proud of his innocence, as they call it, so he blurts out everything which a sensible man would conceal. Then the prosecutor makes new questions out of the answers and carefully notes any little contradiction that may appear. That's where he attaches his rope, and if the poor fool allows himself to be convinced that he's said too much here, too little there, and perhaps withheld some piece of evidence for no reason at all; or if, in the end, he allows them to frighten him—well, in that case, they're well on the way. And I assure you that the beggar women who pick rags out of the rubbish bins are not more thorough than one of those rogue-makers when he's set his heart on patching together a straw-and-rag scarecrow out of every little crooked, twisted, rumpled, hidden, familiar, denied indication and circumstance, if only to be able to hang his victim in effigy. And the poor fellow has cause to be thankful if he lives to see himself hanged.

JETTER. No one can say he hasn't a fluent tongue in his head.

CARPENTER. That kind of talk may work with flies. But wasps laugh at the yarns you spin.

VANSEN. After the spiders have gone. Look, that tall Duke looks just like one of your garden spiders; not one of the fat-bellied ones—they're less dangerous—but one of the long-legged kind with small bodies that don't get fat with eating and spin very fine threads, though all the tougher for that.

JETTER. Egmont is a Knight of the Golden Fleece: who would dare to lay hands on him? He can only be judged by those of his own kind, by the entire Order. It's your foul mouth and your bad conscience that make you talk such gibberish.

VANSEN. What makes you think I don't wish him well? I've nothing against him. He's an excellent gentleman. He let off a couple of my best friends, who would otherwise have been hanged by now, with a sound whipping. Now, off with you! Get along! That's my advice to you now. I can see a new patrol just starting their rounds over there, and they don't look as if they're going to drink our health. We mustn't be in too much of a hurry, but stand and look on for a while. I've a couple of nieces and an old crony who keeps a tavern; if those men aren't tame by the time they've tasted their wares, they must be as tough as wolves.

Culenburg Palace. The Duke of Alba's Residence
Silva and Gomez meet.

SILVA. Have you carried out the Duke's instructions?

GOMEZ. Punctiliously. All the daily patrols have been ordered to appear at the appointed time at the different places I have detailed to them;

meanwhile, they will patrol the town as usual to maintain the peace. None knows about any of the others; each patrol thinks that the order concerns only its own men, and the cordon can be closed in a moment when necessary so that every approach to the Palace will be cut off. Do you know the reason for this order?

SILVA. I am accustomed to obey orders without questioning them. And who is easier to obey than the Duke, since the outcome will soon prove that his instructions were judicious?

GOMEZ. Oh yes, of course. And I am not surprised to find that you're growing as uncommunicative and monosyllabic as he is since you have to attend him all the time. It seems strange to me, since I am used to the lighter Italian etiquette. My loyalty and obedience are the same as ever; but I have got into the habit of chattering and arguing. As for you people, you keep silent all the time and never relax. The Duke seems to me like an iron tower without any door to which his staff have the key. The other day I heard him remark at table about some carefree, affable fellow that he was like a bad tavern with a sign advertising brandy to attract idlers, beggars, and thieves.

SILVA. And did he not lead us in silence to this place?

GOMEZ. There's no denying that. Certainly, anyone who witnessed his skill in moving the army here from Italy has seen something worth remembering. How he twined his way, as it were, through friend and foe, through the French, the King's men, and the heretics, through the Swiss and their confederates, maintained the strictest discipline and succeeded in conducting so potentially dangerous a movement with such ease and without giving offence to anyone. We have certainly seen something and learnt something.

SILVA. And here too. Isn't everything peaceful and quiet, as though there had never been any uprising?

GOMEZ. Well, it was quiet in most places when we arrived.

SILVA. The Provinces are a great deal calmer than they were; and if anyone does move now, it's in order to flee. But he will soon put an end to that as well, if I'm not mistaken.

GOMEZ. The King will be pleased with him as never before.

SILVA. And nothing remains more urgent for us than to be sure of *his* pleasure. If the King should come here, the Duke and anyone whom he commends will doubtless be generously rewarded.

GOMEZ. Do you think that the King will come?

SILVA. The many preparations that are being made would suggest that it is very likely.

GOMEZ. They don't convince me.

SILVA. In that case, at least refrain from evincing an opinion on the matter. For if it is not the King's intention to come, what is certain is that we are intended to believe so.

Enter Ferdinand, Alba's natural son.

FERDINAND. Has my father not come out?
SILVA. We are waiting for him.
FERDINAND. The princes will soon be here.
GOMEZ. Are they expected today?
FERDINAND. Orange and Egmont.
GOMEZ (*softly to Silva*). Something has dawned on me.
SILVA. Then keep it to yourself!

Enter the Duke of Alba. As he enters and comes forward, the others step back.

ALBA. Gomez!
GOMEZ (*comes forward*). My Lord!
ALBA. You have instructed and detailed the guards?
GOMEZ. With the utmost precision. The daily patrols——
ALBA. Very well. You will wait in the gallery. Silva will inform you of the exact moment when you will call them in and occupy the approaches to the Palace. You know the rest.
GOMEZ. Yes.

Exit.

ALBA. Silva!
SILVA. Here I am.
ALBA. Everything I have valued in you—courage, determination, promptness in the execution of orders—all these you must show today.
SILVA. I thank you for giving me the opportunity to prove that I am unchanged.
ALBA. As soon as the princes have entered my cabinet, lose no time in arresting Egmont's private secretary. You have made all the necessary arrangements to seize the other persons who have been indicated?
SILVA. Rely on us! Their fate, like a well-calculated eclipse of the sun, will meet them punctually and terribly.
ALBA. You have kept all their movements under observation?
SILVA. Not one has escaped me. Especially not Egmont's. He is the only one whose conduct has not changed since your arrival. Spends the whole day trying out one horse after another, invites guests, is always merry and amusing at table, plays at dice, shoots, and creeps to his sweetheart at night. Whereas the others have made a distinct break in their way of life. They stay at home; the fronts of their houses look like those of men who are ill in bed.
ALBA. Hurry, therefore, before they recover against our will.

SILVA. I shall catch them. At your command we shall overwhelm them with official honours. Panic will seize them. Diplomatically they offer us cautious thanks and feel that it would be wisest to flee; not one of them dares to move one step; they hesitate, cannot get together; and his social sense prevents each one from acting boldly for himself. They would like to avoid all suspicion and yet they become more and more suspect. With the greatest pleasure I foresee the complete success of your stratagem.

ALBA. I take pleasure only in the accomplished act . . . and not easily even in that, for there always remains something to give us cause for thought and anxiety. Fortune, in her obstinate way, may insist on conferring glory on what is base and worthless, and on dishonouring well-considered deeds with a base outcome. Wait here till the princes come, then give Gomez the order to occupy the streets and at once proceed in person to arrest Egmont's secretary and the others that have been indicated to you. When you have done so, come here and report it to my son, so that he may convey the news to me in the cabinet.

SILVA. I hope to have the honour of attending on you tonight.

Alba goes to his son, who has been standing on the gallery.

SILVA. I dare not tell him, but I am losing hope. I fear it will not be as he thinks. I see spirits who, silent and pensive, weigh the destiny of princes and many thousands of men on black scales. Slowly the pointer vacillates, the judges seem deep in thought. At last this scale goes down, that one rises at the breath of obstinate Fortune, and the verdict has been pronounced.

Exit.

ALBA (*stepping forward with Ferdinand*). What was you impression of the city?

FERDINAND. Everything has become very quiet. As though to pass the time of day I rode up and down the streets. Your well-distributed patrols keep their fear so tense that no one dares to breathe a word. The city looks like a field when a thunderstorm flashes in the distance: one doesn't see a bird or an animal that isn't scurrying off to seek shelter.

ALBA. Is that all you saw and encountered?

FERDINAND. Egmont came riding into the market-place with some men. We exchanged greetings; he had an unruly horse, which I was compelled to praise. "Let us lose no time in breaking in horses, we shall need them soon!" he called out to me. He said we should meet again this very day, as he was coming at your request to confer with you.

ALBA. He will meet you again.

FERDINAND. Of all the noblemen I know here I like him best. It seems that we shall be friends.

ALBA. You are still too impetuous and incautious; you always remind me of your mother's fecklessness which drove her unconditionally into my arms. More than once appearances have led you to enter into dangerous relationships precipitately.

FERDINAND. You will find me flexible.

ALBA. Because of your young blood I forgive these impulsive affections, this heedless gaiety. Only never forget what is the work I was called to accomplish, nor what part in it I wish to entrust to you.

FERDINAND. Admonish me and do not spare me, where you think it necessary.

ALBA (*after a pause*). My son!

FERDINAND. My father!

ALBA. The princes will soon be here. Orange and Egmont are coming. It is not out of mistrust that I now reveal to you what will happen. They will not leave this Palace.

FERDINAND. What is your plan?

ALBA. It has been decided to hold them here. . . . You are astonished! Now, hear what you are to do. As for the reasons, you will know them when it is done; there is no time now to go into them. You are the one with whom I would wish to discuss the greatest, most secret issues. A strong bond unites us. You are dear and close to me. I should like to confide everything to you. It is not the habit of obedience alone that I wish to inculcate in you, but also the capacity to plan, to command, to execute—these too I should like to perpetuate in you. To leave you a great inheritance and the King the most useful of servants; to provide you with the best that I have, so that you need not be ashamed to take your place among your brothers.

FERDINAND. How can I ever repay the debt of this love that you bestow on me alone, while a whole Empire trembles with awe of you?

ALBA. Now listen: this is what I want you to do. As soon as the princes have entered, every point of access to the Palace will be occupied. Gomez will see to this. Silva will hasten to arrest Egmont's secretary and other highly suspicious persons. You will supervise the guards at the gate and in the courts. Above all, put your most reliable men into the rooms adjoining this one, then wait in the gallery till Silva returns to bring me some insignificant paper as a sign that his commission has been executed. Then stay in the antechamber till Orange leaves. Follow him; I shall detain Egmont here, as if there were something else I wished to discuss with him. At the end of the gallery demand Orange's sword, call the guard, quickly put away the dangerous fellow; and I shall seize Egmont here.

FERDINAND. I shall obey you, Father. For the first time with a heavy heart and with anxiety.

ALBA. I forgive you; it's the first great day you have known.

Enter Silva.

SILVA. A messenger from Antwerp. Here is Orange's letter! He is not coming.

ALBA. Is that what the messenger tells you?

SILVA. No, it's my heart that tells me.

ALBA. My evil genius speaks in you.

After reading the letter he waves his hand at both of them, and they withdraw to the gallery. He remains alone in the front.

He is not coming! And he puts off his explanation till the last moment. He dares *not* to come. So this time, contrary to my expectations, the prudent man was prudent enough not to be prudent. Time presses. Only a little turn more of the minute hand and a great work will have been done or missed, irrevocably missed; for it can neither be repeated not kept secret. Long ago I had considered every possibility, even this one, and determined what was to be done in this case. And now that it has to be done I can hardly prevent the *pro* and *contra* from vacillating once more in my mind. . . . Is it wise to catch the others if he escapes me? Should I postpone it and let Egmont go with his men, with so many of them, who now, perhaps only today, are in my power? Thus Fate compels me, who was invincible. How long I pondered it! How well I prepared it! How fine and great was my plan! How close my hope to its aim! And now, at the moment of decision, I am placed between two evils. As into a lottery urn, I plunge my hand into the dark future: what I draw out is still tightly folded, unknown to me, perhaps a winner, perhaps a blank.

He grows alert, as if he can hear something, and steps to the window.

It's he! Egmont! Did your horse carry you in so easily, without sensing the smell of blood or the spirit with drawn sword who received you at the gate? . . . Dismount! . . . Now you have one foot in the grave; and now both feet! Yes, go on and stroke it, pat its neck for serving you so bravely—for the last time—and to me no choice remains. Never could Egmont hand himself over a second time as dazzled as he is now. . . . Listen!

Ferdinand and Silva approach hurriedly.

ALBA. You will do as I commanded; I do not change my mind. I shall detain Egmont as best I can until you, Ferdinand, have brought me news about Silva. Then remain close to me! You, also, Fate deprives of this great merit, to have caught the King's greatest enemy with your own hands.

To Silva.

Make haste!

To Ferdinand.

Go to meet him!

Alba, left alone for a few moments, paces the room in silence.
Enter Egmont.

EGMONT. I come to hear the King's will, to discover what service he asks of our loyalty which remains eternally devoted to him.

ALBA. What he desires above all is to know your opinion.

EGMONT. On what matter? Is Orange coming too? I expected to find him here.

ALBA. I much regret his absence at this important hour. The King desires your opinion, your advice, as to how these States can be pacified. Indeed he hopes that you will effectively collaborate in the task of curbing the unrest and establishing complete and lasting order in the Provinces.

EGMONT. You must know better than I that everything is quiet enough already, and indeed was more quiet still before the appearance of the new soldiers filled the people with fear and anxiety.

ALBA. If I am not mistaken, you wish to imply that it would have been most advisable on the King's part never to have placed me in the position of asking your advice.

EGMONT. I beg your pardon. It is not for me to judge whether the King should have sent the army, whether the power of his royal presence alone would not have proved more effective. The army is here; he is not. But we should be very ungrateful, very unmindful, if we did not remember what we owe to the Regent. Let us admit it: by her conduct, as wise as it was brave, she succeeded in quelling the insurgents by force and by esteem, by cunning and persuasion; and, to the astonishment of the whole world, in the space of a few months she recalled a rebellious people to its duty.

ALBA. I don't deny it. The riot has been put down, and everyone seems to have been driven back into the bonds of obedience. But does it not depend on each one's arbitrary whim whether or not he chooses to remain in them? Who will prevent the people from breaking out again? Where is the power that will restrain them? Who guarantees to us that they will continue to prove loyal subjects? Their good will is all the security we have.

EGMONT. And is not the good will of a people the safest and noblest of securities? By God! When can a King feel more secure than when all of them stand by one, and one stands by all? More secure, I mean, from internal and external enemies?

ALBA. Surely we are not going to persuade ourselves that this is the case in these Provinces at present?

EGMONT. Let the King issue a general amnesty, let him set their minds at rest, and we shall soon see loyalty and love return in the train of trust.

ALBA. And let everyone who has profaned the King's majesty, the sanctity of religion, go about scot-free where he pleases? To serve as a walking proof to others that atrocious crimes go unpunished?

EGMONT. But should not a crime of folly, of drunkenness, be excused rather than cruelly punished? Especially where there is well-founded hope, if not certainty, that these evils will not recur? Were kings any less secure, are they not praised by contemporaries and by posterity alike for finding it in them to pardon, pity, or despise an affront to their dignity? Is it not for that very reason that they are likened to God, who is far too great to be affected by every blasphemy?

ALBA. And for that very reason the King must fight for the dignity of God and religion, and we for the King's honour. What the One Above disdains to parry, it is our duty to avenge. Where I am judge, no guilty man shall rejoice in his impunity.

EGMONT. Do you think, then, that you will reach them all? Don't we hear daily that terror is driving them from one place to another, and out of the country? The richest will remove their wealth, themselves, their children, and their friends; the poor will place their hands at their neighbours' service.

ALBA. They will, if we cannot prevent them. That is why the King demands advice and help of all the princes, seriousness of every governor; not only tales about how things are and how they might be if we allowed everything to go on as it is. To look upon a great evil, flatter oneself with hope, put one's trust in time, at the most to deliver one blow, as in a carnival farce so that one can hear the smack and appear to be doing something when one's desire is to do nothing—might not this arouse the suspicion that one is watching the rebellion with pleasure, unwilling to incite it, yet glad to encourage it?

EGMONT (*about to lose his temper, restrains himself and, after a short pause, says calmly*). Not every intention is manifest, and the intentions of many are early misinterpreted. Thus we are told everywhere that the King's intention is not so much to rule the Provinces in accordance with clear and unambiguous laws, to protect the majesty of religion and grant general peace to his people, as to enslave them absolutely, deprive them of their ancient rights, grasp their possessions, curtail the fine privileges of the aristocracy, for whose sake alone the noble man would dedicate body and soul to his service.

Religion, they say, is only a splendid screen behind which every dangerous scheme can be more easily hatched. The people are on their knees and worship the holy embroidered emblems, but behind the screen the bird catcher lurks and listens, waiting to ensnare them.

ALBA. Must I hear this from *you?*

EGMONT. These are not my views. Only what is said and rumoured abroad by great and small, foolish and wise alike. The Netherlanders fear a double yoke; and who has pledged to maintain their freedom?

ALBA. Freedom? A fine word, if only one could understand it! What kind of freedom do they want? What is the freedom of the most free? To do what is right! . . . And in this the King will not hinder them. No, no! They do not feel free if they cannot harm themselves and others. Would it not be better to abdicate than to rule such a people? When foreign enemies press us, of whom no citizen is aware because he is concerned with the most immediate things, and the King asks for help, they will quarrel among themselves and make common cause with their enemies. Far better to hedge them in, to treat them like children, so that one can lead them to their own welfare like children. Believe me, a people does not grow up, or grow wise; a people remains perpetually childish.

EGMONT. How rarely a King attains discretion! And should not the many put their trust in the many rather than in one? And not even in one, but in the few that surround the one, the clan that grows old under its master's gaze? I suppose this clan alone has the right to grow wise.

ALBA. Perhaps it has, just because it is not left to its own devices.

EGMONT. And for that reason is reluctant to leave anyone else to his own devices. Do what you please. I've replied to your question and repeat: it will not work. It cannot work. I know my compatriots. They are men worthy to walk on God's earth; each one a world to himself, a little king, steadfast, active, capable, loyal, attached to old customs. It is hard to win their confidence, easy to keep it. Stubborn and steadfast! Pressure they will bear; oppression never.

ALBA (*who meanwhile has turned his head several times*). Would you repeat all that in the presence of the King?

EGMONT. All the worse, if his presence made me afraid! All the better for him, for his people if he inspired me with courage, gave me confidence to say a great deal more!

ALBA. If what you have to say is useful, I can listen to it as well as he can.

EGMONT. I should say to him: the shepherd can easily drive a whole herd of sheep along, the ox draws its plough without resisting. But if you wish to ride a thoroughbred horse, you must learn to read its thoughts, you must demand nothing foolish nor demand it foolishly. That is why the citizens wish to retain their old constitution, to be ruled by their compatriots, for they know how they will be led and can expect these leaders to be both disinterested and concerned with the people's fate.

ALBA. But shouldn't the Regent be empowered to change these old traditions? And could not this be the most precious of his privileges? What is permanent in this world? And should one expect a political institution to be permanent? Must not the circumstances change in time, and, for that very reason, must not an old constitution become the cause of a thousand evils, because it takes no account of the present state of the people? I fear that these old rights are so acceptable because they offer dark recesses in which the cunning and the mighty can hide and hold out at the people's cost, at the expense of the whole.

EGMONT. And these arbitrary changes, these unrestricted interferences on the part of the highest authority, do they not forebode that one desires to do what thousands must not do? He desires to liberate himself alone, so that he may gratify every whim, translate every thought into action. And if we were to put all our trust in him, a good wise King, can he speak for his successors? Can he assure us that none will rule without mercy and consideration? Who then would save us from absolute despotism, when he sends us his servants and minions to rule and dispose as they please, without knowledge of our country or of its needs, meet no resistance, and feel free of all responsibility?

ALBA (*who has looked behind him again*). Nothing is more natural than that a King should seek to rule by his own means and prefer to entrust his orders to those who understand him best, endeavour to understand him, and obey his will unconditionally.

EGMONT. And it is just as natural that the citizen should wish to be ruled by those who were born and bred where he was, who were imbued with the same ideas of right and wrong, whom he can look upon as brothers.

ALBA. And yet the aristocracy can hardly be said to have shared equally with these brothers?

EGMONT. This occurred centuries ago and is now accepted without envy. But if new men were sent to us gratuitously to enrich themselves once more at the nation's expense, if the people knew themselves to be at the mercy of a severe, bold, and unlimited avarice, it would cause a ferment that would not easily subside into itself.

ALBA. You tell me what I ought not to hear; I too am a foreigner.

EGMONT. My telling it to you shows that I don't mean you.

ALBA. Even so I would rather not hear it from you. The King sent me in the hope that I should receive the support of the nobility. The King *wills* his will. The King, after long reflection, has seen what the people requires; things cannot go on, cannot remain as they were. It is the

King's intention to restrict them for their own good, if need be to thrust their own welfare upon them, to sacrifice the harmful citizens so that the best may live in peace and enjoy the blessing of wise government. This is his resolve. To convey it to the nobility is my charge; and what I demand in his name is advice as to how it is to be done, not what is to be done, for this he has decided.

EGMONT. Unfortunately your words justify the people's apprehension, the general apprehension. For he has decided what no prince has the right to decide. His will is to weaken, oppress, destroy the strength of his people—their self-confidence, their own conception of themselves—so as to be able to rule them without effort. His will is to corrupt the very core of their individuality; doubtless with the intention to make them happier. His will is to annihilate them so that they will become something, a different something. Oh, if his intention is good, it is being misguided. It is not the King whom this people resists; what it opposes is only the King who is taking the first unfortunate steps in a direction utterly wrong.

ALBA. In your state of mind it seems useless for us to try to come to an understanding. You belittle the King and hold his advisers in contempt if you doubt that all this has already been considered, investigated, and weighed up. It is not my business to go into every *pro* and *contra* once more. Obedience is what I ask of the people—and of you, the foremost and greatest, I ask counsel and action as pledges for this absolute duty.

EGMONT. Demand our heads and have done with it! Whether his neck will bend under this yoke or bow to the axe is all one to a noble soul. It was in vain that I spoke at such length. I have shaken the air, and gained nothing more.

Enter Ferdinand.

FERDINAND. Forgive me for interrupting your conversation. The bearer of this letter requires an urgent reply.

ALBA. Excuse me while I see what it contains.

Steps aside.

FERDINAND, *to* EGMONT. That's a fine horse your men have brought to fetch you.

EGMONT. It's not the worst. I've had it for a while; I'm thinking of parting with it. If you like it, perhaps we can come to terms.

FERDINAND. Good. Let's discuss the matter.

Alba motions to his son, who withdraws to the back.

EGMONT. Good-bye. Dismiss me now, for, by God, I can think of nothing more to say.

ALBA. A happy chance has prevented you from betraying your thoughts farther. Recklessly you opened the very folds of your heart and have accused yourself much more severely than any opponent could have done in his malice.

EGMONT. The rebuke does not touch me; I know myself well enough, and am aware how devoted I am to the King—much more than many who serve their own interests in his service. It is with reluctance that I leave this quarrel without seeing it resolved, and only wish that our service of one master, the welfare of a country, will soon unite us. Perhaps a second conference and the presence of the other princes, who are absent today, will bring about at some happier moment what today seems impossible. With that hope I leave you.

ALBA (*giving a sign to Ferdinand*). Stop, Egmont! Your sword!

The middle door opens; one catches a glimpse of the gallery occupied by guards, who remain immobile.

EGMONT (*after a brief, astonished silence*). So that was your purpose! It was for that you called me?

Clutching his sword, as if to defend himself.

Did you think I'm defenceless?

ALBA. It is the King's order; you are my prisoner.

At the same moment armed men enter from both sides.

EGMONT (*after a silence*). The King? Oh, Orange, Orange!

After a pause, handing over his sword.

Well, take it, then. It has served me more often to defend the King's cause than to protect this body.

Exit through the middle door. The armed men follow him out; also Alba's son. Alba remains standing.

ACT V

Street at Dusk
Clare. Brackenburg. Citizens.

BRACKENBURG. Darling. For heaven's sake! What are you doing?

CLARE. Come with me, Brackenburg. You can't know much about people or you wouldn't doubt that we shall free him. For don't they love him dearly? I swear that every one of them is filled with a burning desire to save him, to avert this danger from a precious life and give back freedom to the most free of all. Come on! All that's lacking is a voice to call them together. They haven't forgotten what they owe to him and they know that it's his mighty arm alone that protects them from disaster. On his account and their own they must stake all they have. And what is it we stake? Our lives, at the most, and those are not worth preserving if he dies.

BRACKENBURG. Poor, foolish girl! You don't see the power that fetters us hopelessly!

CLARE. They don't seem unbreakable to me. But let's not waste time on idle words! Here come some of those honest, brave fellows of the old sort. Listen, friends. Listen, neighbours. . . . Tell me, what news of Egmont?

CARPENTER. What does the child want? Tell her to be quiet.

CLARE. Come closer, so that we can talk softly till we're in agreement, and stronger. We haven't a moment to lose. The insolent tyranny that dares to put him in chains is drawing its dagger to murder him. Oh, friends, every minute of the gathering dusk makes me more anxious. I fear this night. Come on! Let's divide into small groups and run through every district, calling the citizens out into the street. Each will take his old weapons. We shall meet again in the marketplace, and our stream will sweep everyone along with it. Our enemies will find themselves surrounded and flooded, and will know that they are defeated. How can a handful of slaves resist us? And he, back in our midst, will turn about, know that he's free, and thank us all one day, thank us who were so deeply in his debt. Perhaps he'll see—no, certainly he'll see—another dawn break in an open sky.

CARPENTER. What's the matter with you, girl?

CLARE. Don't you understand me? I'm speaking of the Count! I'm speaking of Egmont.

JETTER. Don't mention that name. It's deadly.

CLARE. Not that name. What? Not mention his name? Who doesn't mention it at every possible opportunity? Who can escape it anywhere? Often I've read it in these stars, every letter of it. And you ask me not to mention it? What can you mean? Oh, friends, dear good neighbours, you're dreaming, come to your senses. Don't stare at me so blankly and timidly. Nor glance about you in that furtive way! I'm only calling out to you what every one of you wants. Isn't my voice the very voice of your own hearts? Who, in this ominous night, before retiring to a restless bed, would not fall on his knees in earnest prayer imploring Heaven for his safety? Ask one another; let each of you ask himself! And who will not say after me: Egmont's freedom or death!

JETTER. God preserve us! This will end in disaster.

CLARE. Don't go. Stay here instead of cringing from his name, which once you welcomed, happily applauded. When rumour announced him, when the news spread: "Egmont is coming! He is coming back from Ghent!" the inhabitants of those streets through which he must pass thought themselves lucky. And when you heard the clatter of his horses each one threw down his work at once, and over all the care-worn faces which you thrust out of the windows there passed a gleam of joy and hope like a ray of sunlight cast by his face. Then you lifted up your children on the threshold and pointed out to them: "Look, that's Count Egmont, the tallest, there! That's Egmont! The one from whom you can expect better times than ever your poor fathers knew!" Don't wait to let your children ask one day: "Where is he gone? Where are the times you promised us?" . . . And here we stand chattering! Wasting idle words, betraying him!

SOEST. You should be ashamed of yourself, Brackenburg. Don't let her go on. Stop her before it's too late.

BRACKENBURG. Clare, my dearest, let's go. What will your mother say? It could be . . .

CLARE. Do you take me for a child, or a madwoman? What could be? You won't drag me away from this terrible certainty with any hope you can invent. You must listen to me and you shall: for I can see you're deeply troubled and can find no guidance in your own hearts. Just let a single glance pierce through the present danger, back to the past, the recent past. Or turn your thoughts to the future! Can you live at all, *will* you live if he perishes? With his last breath our freedom too expires. What was he to you? For whose sake did he deliver himself up to the most pressing danger? Only for you his wounds bled and healed. The great spirit that supported you all languishes in a cell, and treacherous murder lurks in the dark corners. Perhaps he is thinking of you, placing his hopes in you, though accustomed only to give and to fulfil.

CARPENTER. Come along; let's be off.

CLARE. And I have no strength, no muscles like yours; but I have what all of you lack—courage and contempt for danger! If only my breath could infuse you with some of it! If only I could lend you human warmth and vigour by pressing you to my breast! Come with me! I shall walk in your midst! Just as a floating banner, in itself defenceless, leads a band of noble warriors on, so, flaring over all your heads, my spirit hovers, and love and courage will weld this wavering, scattered people into a terrible army.

JETTER. Get her away from here! I feel sorry for her.

Exeunt Citizens.

BRACKENBURG. Clare, my dear. Can't you see where we are?

CLARE. Yes: under the sky that so often seemed to expand more gloriously when noble Egmont walked under it. It's from these windows they looked out, four or five heads, one above the other. In front of these doors they bowed and scraped when he looked down at the lily-livered wretches. Oh, how I loved them then, because they honoured him. Had he been a tyrant, they would have every right to sneak away from him now. But they loved him! Oh, those hands that could raise hats are too feeble to lift a sword. . . . Brackenburg, what about us? Can we reproach them? These arms, that so often held him fast, what are they doing for him? Cunning has always succeeded so well in this world. You know the ins and outs, you know the old Palace. Nothing is impossible. But tell me what to do!

BRACKENBURG. What if we went home?

CLARE. A good idea!

BRACKENBURG. There's one of Alba's patrols on that corner; do listen to the voice of reason. Do you think I'm a coward? Don't you think me capable of dying for you? But we're both out of our senses, I no less than you. Can't you see what's impossible? Try to pull yourself together. You're beside yourself.

CLARE. Beside myself? That's disgusting, Brackenburg. It's you who're beside yourself. When you were loud in your reverence for the hero, called him your friend, your protector, your hope, and cheered him when he appeared—then I stood in my corner of the room, half raised the window, listened, and hid myself, and yet my heart beat faster than the hearts of all you men. And now again it beats faster than all your hearts! You hide yourselves because it's good for you, deny him and don't even feel that you will perish if he dies.

BRACKENBURG. Let's go home.

CLARE. Home?

BRACKENBURG. Only try to think! Look about you. These are the streets where you walked only on Sundays, through which you passed modestly on your way to church, where, with excessive respectability, you were angry with me if I joined you with a friendly word of greeting. Here you stand and talk and act in full view of the public. Only try to think, my dearest. What's the use of it all?

CLARE. Home! Oh yes, I remember. I'm thinking, Brackenburg. Let's go home! Do you know where my home is?

Exeunt.

Prison

Lighted by a lamp, a bunk in the background. Egmont, alone.

EGMONT. Old friend, ever-faithful sleep, do you forsake me too, like my other friends? How willingly once you descended upon my free head and, like a lovely myrtle wreath of love, cooled my temples. In the midst of battle, on the wave of love, lightly breathing I rested in your arms like a burgeoning boy. When gales roared through trees and foliage, branch and crest creaked as they bent, yet deep within the heart's core remained unmoving. What is it that shakes you now? What is it that shivers your steadfast loyal will? I feel it, it is the sound of the murderous axe that nibbles at my root. Still I stand fast and upright, but an inward shudder runs through me. Yes, treacherous power prevails, it is stronger than I. It undermines the high, solid trunk; before the bark has withered, roaring and shattering, the crest will fall.

Why, now, you that so often blew away mighty cares from your head like soap-bubbles, why now can you not drive off the thousand-limbed forebodings that stir within your heart? Since when has Death assumed a fearful appearance for you, who once lived calmly with this changing image as with all the other shapes of the familiar world? But then, it is not he, the swift enemy, whom the healthy man longs to meet in close combat; the prison cell it is, prefiguring the grave, repulsive to the hero and the coward alike. I found it insufferable enough to sit on my padded chair when in solemn council the princes endlessly and repetitively debated what could have been decided in a moment, and when between the gloomy walls of a great hall the beams of the ceiling seemed to throttle me! Then I would hurry out as soon as possible and leap upon my horse's back with a deep breath! Then quickly out where we belong! Out to the fields, where from the earth all Nature's most immediate remedies, vaporous, rise, and through the heavens, wafting all the blessings of the planets, enwrapping us, descend upon our heads; where, like the earthborn giant, strengthened by our mother's touch, we rise to our full height; where we feel wholly human, one with all that's human, human desire pulsing through every vein; where the urge to press forward, to be victorious, to seize, to use one's fists, to possess, to conquer glows in the young huntsman's soul; where the soldier is quick to arrogate to himself his inborn claim to all the world and in his terrible freedom rages like a hailstorm through meadow, field, and forest, wreaking destruction, and knows no bounds that human hands have set. A mere phantasm, this, this dream of remembered bliss that so long was mine. What has treacherous Fortune done with it? Does Fortune now refuse to grant you that quick death you never shunned in the full glare of the sun, to offer you instead a foretaste of the grave in nauseous mustiness? How vilely now it breathes upon me from these stones! Already life congeals; and from my bed, as from the grave, my foot recoils.

O Care, you that begin your murderous work before the event, leave off! Since when has Egmont been alone, utterly alone in this world? It's doubt that makes you helpless now, not Fortune. Has the

King's justice, in which you trusted all your life, has the Regent's friendship which—why not admit it now?—was almost love, have these vanished like a shining, fiery mirage of the night? And do they leave you lonely now, plunged into darkness, on a dangerous track? Will not Orange venture out scheming at the head of your assembled friends? Will not a crowd collect and, with growing force, go out to rescue an old friend?

O walls that now enclose me, do not halt the kindly progress of so many spirits. And that courage which once poured out of my eyes into theirs, let it now flow back from their hearts into mine. Oh yes, they stir in their thousands, they are coming, to stand by me now. Their pious wishes wing their way to Heaven and beg for a miracle. And if no angel comes to my aid from above, I see them take up their swords and lances. The gates split in two, the bars burst asunder, the wall comes crashing down with their impact, and gladly Egmont steps out towards the freedom of approaching day. How many familiar faces receive me jubilantly. Oh, Clare, if you were a man, I should surely see you here, the very first to welcome me, and I should owe you what it is hard to owe to a King, freedom.

Clare's House

Clare comes out of her bedroom with a lamp and a glass of water. She sets down the glass on the table and goes to the window.

CLARE. Brackenburg? Is that you? What was that noise? No one yet? It was no one. I shall put the lamp on the window-sill so that he can see that I'm still awake, that I'm still waiting for him. He promised to bring me news. News? No, horrible certainty. Egmont condemned! What court of law has the right to summon him? And yet they condemn him. Does the King condemn him, or the Duke? And the Regent washes her hands of it. Orange dilly-dallies, and all his friends. . . . Is this the world of whose inconstancy and unreliability I have heard much, but experienced nothing? Is this the world? Who would be so wicked as to be an enemy to him? Could malice be powerful enough to cause the sudden downfall of one so generally loved and esteemed? And yet it *is* so. It is. . . . Oh, Egmont, both from God and men I thought you safe as in my arms! What was I to you? You called me yours, and I was truly yours, wholly devoted and dedicated to you. . . . What am I now? In vain I stretch out my arms towards the noose that grips you. You helpless, and I free! Here is the key to my door. My coming and going depend on my own free will, and yet I am nothing to you. Oh, fetter me to keep me from despair! And cast me down into the deepest dungeon to beat my head against damp walls, to whimper for freedom, dream of how I would help him if I weren't fettered and chained—how I should help him then! But now I'm free, and in that freedom lies the fear of impotence. Fully conscious, yet incapable of moving a finger to help him. Oh, even the smaller part of you, your Clare, is a prisoner as you are and, separated from you, wastes her last strength in a deathly convulsion. . . . I hear someone creeping in—a cough, Brackenburg—yes, he's come. Poor, honest Brackenburg, your fate is always the same. Your sweetheart opens the door to you at night, but oh, for how unhappy, ill-omened a meeting!

Enter Brackenburg.

CLARE. You look so pale and harassed, Brackenburg. What is it?

BRACKENBURG. I've passed through dangers and detours to see you. All the main streets are guarded. I stole my way to you through alleys and dark nooks.

CLARE. Tell me what's happening.

BRACKENBURG (*taking a seat*). Oh, Clare, I feel like weeping. I had no love for him. He was the rich man who lured away the poor man's only sheep to a better pasture. I've never cursed him. God made me loyal and softhearted. But all my life dissolved in pain and flowed out of me, and my daily hope was that I should languish away.

CLARE. Forget it, Brackenburg! Forget yourself. Tell me about him. Is it true? He's been condemned?

BRACKENBURG. He has. I know it beyond doubt.

CLARE. And he's still alive?

BRACKENBURG. Yes, he's still alive.

CLARE. How can you be sure about it? Tyranny murders the glorious man overnight. His blood flows where no one can see him. The people lies drugged in anxious sleep and dreams of rescue, dreams the fulfilment of its impotent wish. Meanwhile, dissatisfied with us, his soul forsakes this world. He's gone! Don't deceive me. Don't deceive yourself.

BRACKENBURG. No, he's alive, I assure you. . . . But the Spaniard is preparing a terrible spectacle for the people whom he wants to tread underfoot violently and forever; he will crush every heart that stirs for freedom.

CLARE. Carry on and calmly pronounce my death sentence also. Already I am walking closer and closer to the fields of the blessed and can feel the comfort wafted over from those regions of everlasting peace. Tell me all.

BRACKENBURG. I could tell by the patrol and gather from stray remarks that something gruesome is being prepared in secret in the market-place. Through byways, through familiar passages, I crept to my cousin's house and looked down on the market-place from a back window. Torches flickered in a wide circle of Spanish soldiers. I strained my eyes, unaccustomed to such sights, and out of the night a black scaffold loomed up at me, spacious and high. I felt faint with horror. A great many men were busy around it, draping black cloth around any of the woodwork that was still white and visible. Last of all they covered the steps as well; I saw them do it. They seemed to be dedicating the site for an abominable sacrifice. A white crucifix, which shone in the night like silver, had been erected high up on one side. I looked on and grew more and more certain of the terrible certainty. Still torches swayed about here and there; gradually they vanished or went out. All at once this monstrous progeny of the night had returned to its mother's womb.

CLARE. Quiet, Brackenburg. Be silent now. Let this veil cover my soul. The spectres are gone, and you, lovely night, lend your cloak to the earth that's in ferment inwardly; no longer Earth will bear her loathsome burden but opens her deep jaws and, grating, swallows down the murderous scaffold. And surely an angel will be sent by that God whom they have blasphemously made a witness to their fury; bolts and fetters will break at the messenger's holy touch, and he will surround our friend with a mild radiance; gently and silently he'll lead him through the night to freedom. And my way too leads through that darkness secretly, and I go to meet him.

BRACKENBURG (*detaining her*). Where, child, where? What are you going to do?

CLARE. Quiet, my dear, so that no one will wake up; so that we shan't wake ourselves. Do you know this little bottle, Brackenburg? I took it away from you for a joke, when you used to threaten suicide in your impatience. . . . And now, my friend——

BRACKENBURG. By all the saints!

CLARE. You won't prevent it. Death is my part. And don't begrudge me this quick, gentle death, which for yourself you held in readiness. Give me your hand! At the very moment when I open the dark door which permits no going back, I could tell you by the pressure of this hand how much I loved you and how much I pitied you. My brother died young, it was you I chose to take his place. Your heart protested, tormented itself and me—more and more hotly you demanded what was not meant for you. Forgive me, and farewell. Let me call you brother; it is a name in which a host of other names are contained. And faithfully treasure my last parting gift—accept this kiss. Death unites all things, Brackenburg, and it unites us too.

BRACKENBURG. Then let me die with you. Share it with me, share it! There is enough of it to put out two lives.

CLARE. No, you shall live, you can live. Help my mother, who but for you would die of poverty. Be to her what I can no longer be; live together and weep for me. Weep for your country and for him who alone could have preserved it. The present generation will not recover from this shame, even the fury of revenge will not blot it out. Poor people, drag out your lives through this age that is no age at all. Today the world comes to a sudden stop; its turning ceases, and my pulse will beat but a few minutes longer. Farewell.

BRACKENBURG. Oh, live with us, as we for you alone! You murder us in you. Oh, live and suffer! Inseparable we shall support you at either side, and always considerate, love shall grant you the utmost comfort, two living arms. Be ours, because I may not say, be mine.

CLARE. Quiet, Brackenburg, you're not aware how you touch me. What is hope to you is despair to me.

BRACKENBURG. Share that hope with the living. Stay on the brink of the abyss; glance down it once and look back at us.

CLARE. I have conquered; don't call me back into the battle.

BRACKENBURG. You're in a daze; wrapped up in night you seek the depth. But even now not every light is out, still many a day will dawn.

CLARE. Woe to you, woe! Cruelly you tear up the curtain before my eyes. Yes, that day will break! In vain pull all the mists about itself and break against its will. Anxiously the citizen will look out of his window, the night leave behind a black stain; he looks, and, horribly, the murderous scaffold grows in daylight. In renewed anguish the profaned image of Christ will raise an imploring eye to the Father above. The sun will not dare to shine, refusing to mark the hour at which he is to die. Wearily the hands of the clock move on their way, one hour after another strikes. Stop! Now it is time! The premonition of morning drives me to my grave.

She goes to the window as if to look out and secretly drinks.

BRACKENBURG. Clare! Clare!

CLARE (*goes to the table and drinks the water*). Here is the rest. I do not ask you to follow. Do what you may, farewell. Put out this lamp quietly and without delay. I am going to lie down. Creep away softly, close the door behind you. Quietly! Don't wake my mother. Go, save yourself! Save yourself! If you don't want to be taken for my murderer.

Exit.

BRACKENBURG. She leaves me, as usual, for the last time. Oh, if a human soul could know its power to rend a loving heart! She leaves me standing here, left by myself, and death and life are equally loathsome to me now. To die alone! Weep, you lovers, there is no harder fate than mine. She shares the poison with me and dismisses me. Sends me away from her! She drags me after her and pushes me back into life.

Oh, Egmont, what a praiseworthy lot is yours! She is the first to set out, you'll take the wreath of victory from her hand; bringing all heaven with her she meets you on your way. . . . And shall I follow? To stand aside again? And carry inextinguishable envy into those celestial realms? On earth there is no staying now for me, and hell and heaven offer equal anguish. How welcome the dreadful hand of annihilation would be to this wretch!

Exit Brackenburg. The stage remains unchanged for a while. Then music, signifying the death of Clare, strikes up; the lamp, which Brackenburg forgot to extinguish, flares up a few times more, then goes out. Soon the scene changes to

Prison

Egmont lies sleeping on his berth. There is a rattling of keys, and the door opens. Servants enter with torches, followed by Ferdinand, Alba's son, and Silva, accompanied by armed men. Egmont wakes up with a start.

EGMONT. Who are you, who so roughly shake away sleep from my eyes? What do your defiant, uncertain glances betoken to me? Why this dreadful procession? What lying nightmare have you come to present to my half-awakened spirit?

SILVA. The Duke sends us to announce your sentence to you.

EGMONT. Have you brought the hangman too to execute it?

SILVA. Listen to it, then you will know what awaits you.

EGMONT. This befits you well and befits your shameful undertaking. Hatched out at night and carried out at night. So this insolent deed of injustice may remain hidden. Step forward boldly, you who keep the sword concealed beneath your cloak. Here is my head, the freest that ever tyranny severed from its socket.

SILVA. You are mistaken. What fair judges have resolved they will not conceal from the face of day.

EGMONT. In that case their insolence exceeds all measure and conception.

SILVA (*takes the verdict from one of the attendants, unfolds it, and reads*). "In the name of the King, and by authority of a special power bestowed on us by His Majesty to judge all his subjects, of whatever station, not excluding Knights of the Golden Fleece, after due . . ."

EGMONT. Can the King bestow that power?

SILVA. "After due, lawful, and exact examination of the evidence we declare you, Henry, Count Egmont, Prince of Gavre, guilty of High Treason, and pronounce the sentence: that at the first break of day you be led from your cell to the marketplace and that there, in the full view of the people, as a warning to all traitors, you suffer death by the sword. Signed in Brussels on . . ."

Date and year are read out indistinctly, so that audience do not catch them.

". . . by Ferdinand, Duke of Alba, President of the Court of the Twelve."
Now you know your fate; you have little time left to reconcile yourself to it, put your house in order, and take leave of your nearest and dearest.

Exeunt Silva and attendants. Ferdinand remains with two torch bearers. The stage is dimly lit.

EGMONT (*has remained standing, deep in thought, and allowed Silva to leave without looking up. He thinks he is alone and as he raises his eyes he sees Alba's son*). You stay behind? Is it your wish to add to my astonishment, my horror, by your presence? Are you perhaps waiting to bring your father the welcome news of my unmanly despair? Go, then! Tell him. Tell him that he deceives neither me nor the world with his lies. At first they will whisper it behind his back, then tell it to him, the ambitious seeker of fame, aloud and more loudly still; and when one day he descends from this peak, thousands of voices will cry it out at him! Not the welfare of the state, not the dignity of the King, not the peace of the Provinces brought him here. For his own sake he counselled war, so that the warrior might prove himself in war! It was he who created this monstrous confusion, so that he would be needed! And I fall as a victim to his vile hatred, his mean jealousy. Yes, I know it and have the right to say it: the dying man, the mortally wounded, may say it. The conceited man envied me; to destroy me was his dear and long-deliberated plan. Even when we were younger and played at dice together, and piles of gold, one after another, speedily moved from his side to mine, he stood there grimly, pretending indifference but inwardly consumed with anger, more at my gain than at his loss. I still recall the glowering gaze, the significant pallor when, at a public festivity, in front of many thousands of people, we competed in a shooting match. He challenged me, and both nations, Spaniards and Netherlanders, stood there betting and wishing. I beat him; his bullet missed, mine hit the mark. A loud cheer broke from my supporters and resounded in the air. Now his shot hits me. Tell him that I know it, that I know him, that the world despises every sign of victory which a petty mind erects for itself by base wiles. As for you, if it is possible for a son to forsake the ways of his father, practise shame in time, by feeling ashamed for him whom you would like to revere with all your heart.

FERDINAND. I listen to you without interrupting. Your reproaches weigh on me like the blows of a club on a helmet. I feel the impact but I am armed. You strike home but you do not wound me. All I feel is the pain that rends my heart. Woe is me that I should have grown up to look on such a sight, that I was destined to act in such a play!

EGMONT. What am I to make of that lamentation? Why should you be moved or troubled? Is it belated remorse at your part in the shameful conspiracy? You are so young, and your appearance promises well. You were so candid, so friendly towards me. As long as I looked at you, I was reconciled to your father. And just as false, more false than he, you lured me into the snare. You are the hideous one! Whoever trusts *him* does so at his peril; but who would suspect any peril in trusting you? Be off with you. Don't rob me of these last moments! Be off, so that I may collect my thoughts, forget the world, and you before all else! . . .

FERDINAND. What can I say to you? I stand and look at you and yet I do not see you nor feel that I am myself. Shall I excuse myself? Shall I assure you that I did not discover my father's intentions till late, till right at the end; that I acted as a passive, inanimate instrument of his will? What can it matter now what you may think of me? You are lost; and I, wretch that I am, only stand here to convince you of it and to bewail you.

EGMONT. What a strange voice, what unexpected comfort to meet on my way to the grave! You, the son of my first, almost my only enemy, you feel sorry for me, you are not on the side of my murderers? Speak up. Tell me! In what light am I to regard you?

FERDINAND. Cruel father! Oh yes, I recognize you in that command. You knew my feelings, my disposition, which so often you rebuked as the inheritance of a tender mother. To mould me in your image you sent me here. To see this man on the edge of his yawning grave, in the grip of a violent death, you compel me; no matter what becomes of me, no matter that I suffer the deepest anguish. If only I become deaf and blind to every kind of plight. If only I become insensitive!

EGMONT. You astonish me! Control yourself! Stand up and speak like a man!

FERDINAND. Oh, that I were a woman! So that one could say to me: what's moving you? What disturbs you so? Tell me of a greater, a more monstrous evil—make me the witness to a more abominable deed. I shall thank you, I shall say: it was nothing.

EGMONT. You forget yourself. Remember where you are!

FERDINAND. Let this passion rage, let me lament unrestrained! I have no wish to appear firm, when all is collapsing inside me. To think that I must see you here! You of all men! Oh, it's horrible. You don't understand me. And should you understand me? . . . Egmont! Egmont!

Falling on Egmont's neck.

EGMONT. Solve me this riddle!

FERDINAND. No riddle.

EGMONT. How can you be so deeply moved by the fate of a stranger?

FERDINAND. No stranger. You're no stranger to me. It was your name that in my first youth shone to me like a star of heaven. How often I listened to tales about you, asked about you! The child's hope is the youth, the youth's hope the man. That is how you strode in front of me, always ahead of me, and always unenvious I saw you in front and followed you, step by step. Then at last I hoped to see you and did see you, and my heart went out to you. You I had chosen for myself, and confirmed my choice when I saw you. Now, only now, I hoped to be with you, to live with you, to grasp you, to——Well, all that has been cut off now, and I see you here.

EGMONT. My friend, if it is of any help to you, accept my assurance that from the first moment I felt drawn to you. And listen to me. Let's exchange a few calm words. Tell me: is it the strict, serious intention of your father to kill me?

FERDINAND. It is.

EGMONT. This sentence, then, is not an idle show devised to frighten me, to punish me by fear and threats, to humiliate me, only to raise me up again by royal grace?

FERDINAND. No, alas, it is not. At first I consoled myself with this remote hope: and already then I felt pained and troubled to see you in this state. Now it is real, definite. No, I shall not control myself. Who will help me, advise me, how to escape the inevitable?

EGMONT. Then listen to me! If you are possessed by such a mighty urge to save me, if you abhor the superior strength of those who keep me fettered, save me then. Every moment is precious. You are the son of the all-powerful and powerful enough yourself. . . . Let us escape! I know the ways; the means cannot be unknown to you. Only these walls, only a few miles divide me from my friends. Loosen these fetters, take me to them, and be one of us. You can be sure the King will thank you one day for rescuing me. At present he is surprised, and perhaps he hasn't been informed of anything. Your father dares and decides; and His Majesty must approve what has been done, even if he is horrified by it. You are thinking? Oh, think out my way to freedom! Speak, and feed the last hope of my living soul!

FERDINAND. No more, I beg you. Every word you speak adds to my despair. There is no way out, no help, no refuge. . . . This torments me, it lacerates my heart. I myself helped to pull the net tight; I know how strongly and tightly it is knitted; I know how the way has been barred to every bold or ingenious resort. I feel that I share your fetters and those of all the others. Should I be lamenting now if I hadn't tried everything? I have lain at his feet, argued and implored. He sent me here to destroy in one moment all the joy and zest that still remained in me.

EGMONT. And there's no escape?

FERDINAND. None.

EGMONT (*stamping his foot*). No escape! Sweet life, dear lovely habit of living and of being active! I must part from you! And so indifferently too! Not in the tumult of battle, in the uproar of arms, in the scattering of a teeming crowd, do you grant me a brief farewell; you take no brusque leave of me, do not shorten the moment of parting. I am to seize your hand, look into your eyes once more, feel your beauty and worth intensely, poignantly as never before, then resolutely tear myself away and say: Good-bye!

FERDINAND. And I am to stand beside you, looking on, unable to hold or hinder you. Oh, what voice would suffice for this complaint? What heart would not break its bonds at this misery!

EGMONT. Calm yourself!

FERDINAND. You can be calm, you can renounce and take this difficult step like a hero, since Necessity holds you by the hand. What can I do? What should I do? You conquer yourself and us; you have come through. As for me, I survive both you and myself. In the banquet's merriment I shall have lost my light, in the tumult of battle my banner. Dreary, confused, and flat the future seems to me.

EGMONT. Young friend, whom by a strange twist of fortune I win and lose at the same time, who feel my death agony, suffer it on my behalf, look at me now; you do not lose me. If my life to you was a mirror in which you liked to contemplate yourself, let my death be the same. Men are not together only when they meet; even the most distant, the departed lives in us. I live for you and have lived long enough for myself. Every day of my life I was glad to be alive, every day of my life I did my duty with quick efficiency, as my conscience demanded. Now life comes to its end, as it could have done sooner, much sooner, even on the sands of Gravelingen. I cease to live; but at least I *have* lived. Now live as I did, my friend, gladly and with zest, and do not shun death!

FERDINAND. You might have preserved yourself for our sake; you should have done. You killed yourself. Often I've heard people talk about you—wise men, both hostile to you and well-disposed, and heard them debate your worth at great length. But in the end they agreed, no one dared to deny, everyone admitted: yes, he treads a dangerous path. How often I wished I could warn you! Did you have no friends, then?

EGMONT. I was warned.

FERDINAND. And, point by point, I found all these accusations set down once more in the present charge—and your replies! Good enough to excuse you; not pertinent enough to exculpate you——

EGMONT. That is as it may be. Men think that they direct their lives and are in control of themselves; yet their inmost selves are irresistibly pulled towards their destinies. Let's not reflect on it; I can easily rid myself of such thoughts—but not of my concern for this country. Yet even this will be taken care of. If my blood can flow for many and buy peace for my people, it flows willingly. I fear it won't be so. But men should cease to fret where they may no longer act. If you can limit or divert your father's nefarious power, do so! Who will be able to do it? . . . Farewell.

FERDINAND. I can't go.

EGMONT. I heartily commend my servants to you. I have good men and women in my service; see that they are not dispersed or made unhappy! What's become of Richard, my secretary?

FERDINAND. He preceded you. They beheaded him as your abettor in High Treason.

EGMONT. Poor soul! . . . One thing more, and then good-bye. My strength is exhausted. Whatever may preoccupy our minds, in the end Nature exacts her dues and that most insistently; and as a child entwined by a snake enjoys refreshing sleep, so the tired man lies down once more on the very threshold of death and deeply rests, as if a long day's journey lay ahead of him. . . . And one thing more—I know a girl; you will not despise her, since she was mine. Now that I have entrusted her to your care, I die at peace. You are a noble-minded man; a woman who finds such a man is safe from harm. Is my old William alive? Is he at liberty?

FERDINAND. The vigorous old man who always rides out with you?

EGMONT. That's the one.

FERDINAND. He's alive and at liberty.

EGMONT. He knows where she lives; let him take you there and pay him to the end of his days for showing you the way to that treasure. Farewell!

FERDINAND. I am not going.

EGMONT (*pushing him to the door*). Farewell!

FERDINAND. Oh, let me stay!

EGMONT. No leave-taking, friend.

He escorts Ferdinand to the door and tears himself away from him there. Ferdinand, in a daze, hurries away.

EGMONT (*alone*). Malevolent man! You never thought to render me this favour through your son. Through him I have been relieved of my cares and pain, of fear and every anxious feeling. Gently, yet urgently, Nature demands her last tribute. All is resolved; and all concluded. And that which in the previous night kept me awake on my uncertain bed now lulls my senses with unalterable certainty.

He sits down on his berth. Music.

Sweet sleep! Like purest happiness most willingly you come unbidden, unimplored! You loosen every knot of strenuous thought, consuming all the images of joy and pain; unobstructed flows the circle of inner harmonies and swathed in agreeable delirium, we sink and cease to be.

He falls asleep; the music accompanies his sleep. Behind his bed the wall seems to open, a radiant apparition enters. Liberty in heavenly raiment, shining, rests upon a cloud. She has Clare's features and bows down towards the sleeping hero. She expresses a feeling of compassion, she seems to commiserate with him. Soon she calms herself and, with an enlivening gesture, shows him the quiver of arrows, then her staff and helmet. She invites him to be of good cheer and, by indicating to him that his death will win freedom for the Provinces, acclaims him victor and hands him a laurel wreath. As she approaches his head with the wreath, Egmont moves, like one stirring in his sleep, so that he comes to lie with his face turned up to her. She holds the wreath suspended over his head; from the distance one hears the warlike music of drums and fifes. At the first, soft sound of this the apparition vanishes. The music grows louder. Egmont awakes; the prison is dimly lit by the dawn. His first movement is to put his hand to his head: he rises and looks about, keeping his hand on his head.

Gone is the wreath! Beautiful image, the light of day has driven you away! But it was they! Truly it was, combined, the two most treasured comforts of my heart. Divine Liberty, borrowing my beloved's features and shape; the sweet girl dressed in the heavenly raiment of her friend. In one solemn moment they appear united, more solemn than charming. With blood-stained soles she came before me, the billowing folds of her garment stained with blood. My blood it was, and that of many noble men. No, it was not shed in vain. Press on, brave people! The goddess of Victory leads you. And as the sea bursts through the dykes you build, so you shall burst and tumble down the mound of tyranny and, flooding all, wash it away from the dear site it has usurped.

Drumbeats come nearer.

Listen! Listen! How often this sound called me to stride freely towards the field of battle and victory! How blithely the companions trod that dangerous, honourable course! I too go from this cell to meet an honourable death; I die for freedom, for which I lived and fought and for which I now passively offer up myself.

The background is filled with a line of Spanish soldiers, carrying halberds.

Yes, go on and summon them! Close your ranks, you won't frighten me. I am accustomed to stand in front of spears, facing spears, and surrounded on all sides by the threat of death, to feel brave life flow through me with redoubled speed.

Drumbeats.

The enemy encircles you! His swords are flashing! Courage, friends, more courage! Behind you parents, wives, and children wait!

Pointing at the guards.

And these, the ruler's hollow words impel, not their true feelings. Protect your property! And to preserve your dearest ones, willingly, gladly fall as my example shows you.

Drumbeats. As he walks towards the guards, towards the back exit, the curtain falls; the music strikes up and concludes in a victorious strain.

CLAVIGO

A Tragedy

Translated by Robert M. Browning

Characters

Clavigo, director of the royal archives
Carlos, his friend
Beaumarchais
Marie Beaumarchais
Sophie Guilbert, *née* Beaumarchais
Guilbert, her husband
Buenco
Saint George

The scene is in Madrid.

Act I

Clavigo's Apartments
Clavigo. Carlos.

Clavigo (*getting up from his writing table*). This piece will have wide appeal. The women are all bound to be crazy about it. What do you say, Carlos, don't you think my weekly is now one of the leading periodicals in Europe?

Carlos. We don't have another author in Spain today who unites such depth of thought and luxuriant imagination with such a brilliant, relaxed style.

Clavigo. Just watch me! I'm going to become the creator of good taste among the Spaniards. We are a very impressionable people. My fellow citizens know and trust me, and, between you and me, I'm learning more every day, my sensibilities are expanding and my style is becoming more and more exact and more expressive.

Carlos. Fine, Clavigo! But if you don't mind my saying so, I liked your things better when you were still writing them at Marie's feet, when that dear, happy creature still exerted an influence on you. Somehow it all had a more youthful, fresher air.

Clavigo. Those good times are gone now, Carlos. I'll gladly admit that I wrote with a more open heart then, and it's true that from the very start she was in good measure responsible for my early public appeal. But in the long run, Carlos, one soon tires of women. Weren't you the first to approve my decision to break with her?

Carlos. You'd have gone stale. Women are much too monotonous. Still, it seems to me it's about time you looked around for a new project. It's no good just sitting on a sandbank.

Clavigo. My project is the court and I've no time to lose. Haven't I done pretty well for a foreigner who came here without family connections, with no reputation, without wealth? And that at a court where it's so hard to attract notice among all that pushing crowd! I feel very good when I look back on the road I've traveled. A favorite of the first men of the realm! Honored for my learning, my rank! Director of the royal archives! Carlos, all that spurs me on. I'd be nothing if I remained what I am! Excelsior! What if it does cost effort and cunning! You need to keep all your wits about you. But women! bah! With women you fritter away too much time.

Carlos. You fool, that's your problem. I can't live without women, and they don't hinder me in the slightest. Of course, I don't whisper so many sweet nothings in their ear, don't let myself be turned on a spit for months at a time for sentimental reasons and that sort of thing.

And nice girls are not at all to my taste. You've soon talked about everything you can think of; and afterwards you trail around for a while, and they've hardly begun to warm up to you, when they want to get married. I hate that like poison.—What's on your mind, Clavigo?

CLAVIGO. I can't forget that I deserted Marie—deceived her—Call it what you like.

CARLOS. You're a strange one! It seems to me you only live once in this world, have all these powers, these prospects only *once*, and if you don't take advantage of them to the full extent of your abilities, don't push things as far as they will go, you're a fool. Get married? get married just when life's starting to roll? Settle down to domesticity, pull in your horns, when you still have half your career ahead of you, when you still have worlds to conquer? It was natural for you to love her; but to promise her marriage was folly, and if you had kept your word, it would have been pure madness.

CLAVIGO. I don't understand the human heart. I truly loved her, she attracted me, held me, and when I sat at her feet, I swore to her, swore to myself, that it would be that way forever, that I would be hers as soon as I got an appointment, had a position—And now—oh, Carlos!

CARLOS. When you are established and have reached the goal you've set there'll still be time enough to crown and confirm your good fortune by seeking an advantageous marriage into a rich and respected family.

CLAVIGO. She's gone! Completely gone out of my heart, and if from time to time I didn't remember how unfortunate she is—How can one be so changeable!

CARLOS. If we were constant, I'd be surprised. Look, doesn't everything in the world change? Why should our passions be constant? Don't worry, she's not the first girl that's been jilted, and not the first one to get over it. If you want my advice, there's a young widow across the way—

CLAVIGO. You know I don't think much of such advice. A love affair that's not spontaneous doesn't interest me.

CARLOS. Mighty particular, aren't you?

CLAVIGO. Never mind about that. And don't forget that our main business at present is to make ourselves indispensable to the new minister. The fact that Whal has resigned as governor of the Indies is rather a blow for us, but I'm not too alarmed—he still has influence. He and Grimaldi are friends, and we can flatter and bow—

CARLOS. And think and do what we please.

CLAVIGO. That's always the main thing. (*Rings for the servant.*) Take this to the printer!

CARLOS. Will I see you this evening?

CLAVIGO. Probably not. You can send someone around to inquire.

CARLOS. I'd dearly love to do something tonight that would cheer me up. I have to sit at my desk all afternoon and write. No end to it.

CLAVIGO. Never mind! If we didn't work for so many people, we wouldn't have outstripped so many. (*Exit.*)

Guilbert's House
Sophie Guilbert. Marie Beaumarchais. Buenco.

BUENCO (*to Marie*). You had a bad night?

SOPHIE. I warned her yesterday evening. She was so gay and exuberant and stayed up talking until eleven o'clock, then she was feverish, couldn't sleep, and now she's having trouble breathing again and has been crying all morning.

MARIE. Why doesn't our brother come! He's two days overdue.

SOPHIE. Be patient, he'll come.

MARIE (*getting up*). I'm so curious to see this brother, my savior and my judge. I can scarcely remember him.

SOPHIE. Oh, I remember him very well—he was a spirited, frank, well-behaved lad of thirteen when our father sent us here.

MARIE. A great, noble soul. You saw the letter he wrote when he heard of my misfortune. Every word of it is engraved on my heart. "If you are to blame," he wrote, "expect no forgiveness. You'll only have the further burden of a brother's scorn and a father's curse. But if you are blameless, oh, then let every vengeance, every burning vengeance fall upon your betrayer!"—It makes me tremble! He will come. I do not tremble for myself, God knows I'm innocent.—My friends, you must—I don't know what I want! O Clavigo!

SOPHIE. You won't listen! You'll kill yourself.

MARIE. I'll be quiet. I won't cry. It seems to me I just don't have any more tears. Why tears anyway? I'm only sorry I'm making your lives hard for you. Because, after all, what am I complaining about? I had so much joy as long as our old friend was living. Clavigo's love gave me such joy, perhaps more than mine gave him. And now—but what difference does it make? What difference does it make if a girl's heart breaks—if she pines away and ends her youthful days in torment?

BUENCO. For God's sake, Mademoiselle!

MARIE. Or if it's all the same to her—that he doesn't love me any more? Oh, why am I no longer lovable?—But he ought to pity me, pity the poor girl he made himself indispensable to, the girl who's now supposed to creep into a corner for the rest of her life and cry her heart out.—Pity! I don't want pity from that creature.

SOPHIE. If only I could teach you to despise that worthless, hateful man!

MARIE. No, sister, he's not worthless; and do I have to despise the one I hate?—Hate! Yes, sometimes I *do* hate him, sometimes, when the

Spanish spirit comes over me. Lately, oh—lately, when we happened to meet him, the sight of him filled me with warm love! And then when I got home and recalled his behavior and the calm, cold way he looked at me as he walked past beside his brilliant lady—then I became a Spaniard at heart, and reached for my poniard, provided myself with poison, and disguised myself. You're surprised, Buenco? All in my imagination of course!

SOPHIE. Foolish girl!

MARIE. I followed him in my imagination. I saw him at the feet of his new mistress, displaying all the tenderness and humility with which he poisoned me—I took aim at the heart of that traitor! Oh Buenco!—Then suddenly I was once more the soft-hearted French girl who knows no love potions and no avenging dagger. We're in a bad way! Songs and dances to entertain our lovers, fans to punish them with—and if they're unfaithful?—Tell me, sister, what do they do in France when lovers are unfaithful?

SOPHIE. They put a spell on them.

MARIE. And then?

SOPHIE. They let them go.

MARIE. Let them go! Well, then, why shouldn't I let Clavigo go? If that's the style in France, why not in Spain too? Why should a Frenchwoman in Spain not be a Frenchwoman? We'll just let him go and find ourselves someone else. That's the way it's done in France, it seems.

BUENCO. What he broke off was his solemn promise, not a frivolous affair or a mere social attachment. Mademoiselle, you have been deeply injured and insulted. My rank as an insignificant, peaceful citizen of Madrid has never seemed to me so onerous, so anxiety-ridden as now, when I feel so weak and incapable of procuring justice for you against that blackguard of a courtier!

MARIE. When he was still Clavigo and not yet director of the King's archives, when he was a stranger, a newcomer in our house, how charming he was, how kind! All his ambitions, all his aspirations seemed born of love. It was for me that he strove for fame, position, wealth: now he has it, and I!——

Enter Guilbert.

GUILBERT (*in an undertone, to his wife*). Your brother's coming.

MARIE. Our brother! (*She is trembling, they lead her to an armchair.*) Where? Where? Bring him to me! Bring me to him!

Enter Beaumarchais.

BEAUMARCHAIS. Sister! (*He embraces Sophie, then runs to embrace Marie.*) Sister! Friends! O Sister!

MARIE. You're here? Thank God you're here!

BEAUMARCHAIS. Let me pull myself together.

MARIE. My heart, my poor heart!

SOPHIE. Calm yourselves. Brother, I was hoping to see you more composed.

BEAUMARCHAIS. More composed! Are you composed? Can't I tell by that dear girl's unhappy features, by your eyes red with weeping, your worried pallor, by the deathly silence of your friends that you are as miserable as I had imagined you to be all the while I was on my way here? More miserable—for now I see you, take you in my arms, and feel everything twice as strongly. O my sister!

SOPHIE. What about our father?

BEAUMARCHAIS. He'll bless both you and me if I can save you.

BUENCO. Permit me, sir, as a stranger who recognizes in you at first glance an upright, noble man, to express my fervent sympathy in this whole matter. Sir! You've made this long, arduous journey to save your sister, to avenge her. Welcome! You are as welcome as an angel, even though you put us all to shame!

BEAUMARCHAIS. I had hoped to find hearts like yours in Spain, sir. That spurred me on to take this step. Nowhere, nowhere in the world is there a dearth of sympathetic, encouraging souls, if only someone comes along whose circumstances give him full freedom to do what he is determined to do. And, my friends, I am full of hope: there are always admirable men among the great and mighty, and the King's ear is seldom deaf, though our voice is usually too weak to carry to such heights.

SOPHIE. Come, sister, come! Lie down a bit! She's quite beside herself. (*They lead Marie away.*)

MARIE. My brother!

BEAUMARCHAIS. Let's hope to God you're blameless! If you are, every, every vengeance on that traitor! (*Exeunt Marie and Sophie.*) Brother! Friends! For that's what you are, I can tell by your looks. Let me collect my wits. And then: a clear, impartial account of this whole affair. That will guide my actions. The feeling that I'm in the right will strengthen my determination, and, believe me, if our cause is just, we'll find justice.

ACT II

Clavigo's Apartments
Clavigo.

CLAVIGO. Who can those Frenchmen be who sent word they would call?—Frenchmen! I used to like the race!—And now, why not now?

Strange how a person who can rise above so many scruples is still held at some point by a single thread.—Forget it!—Why should I owe Marie more than I owe myself? Is it my duty to make myself unhappy because a girl loves me?

A servant.

SERVANT. The foreigners, sir.

CLAVIGO. Show them in. You told their man I was expecting them for breakfast?

SERVANT. As you ordered.

CLAVIGO. I'll be right back.

Beaumarchais. Saint George.
Servant places chairs for them and leaves.

BEAUMARCHAIS. I'm so relieved finally to be here, to have him at last—he'll not escape me. Just be calm, or at least show a calm exterior! My sister! My sister! Who would have believed that you could be as blameless as you are unfortunate? It will all come out, you shall be fearfully avenged. And oh, dear God, let my soul remain as calm as it is at this moment, that in my terrible pain I may act with restraint and as wisely as possible!

SAINT GEORGE. Yes, my friend, I call upon all the wisdom and deliberateness that you have ever shown. Promise me once more that you'll remember where you are—in a foreign land where all your influence and all your money won't protect you against the machinations of a base enemy.

BEAUMARCHAIS. Don't worry! You play your role well, he won't know which of us he has to deal with. I'll put him on the rack. Oh, I'm in a fine enough humor to roast him over a slow fire.

Clavigo returns.

CLAVIGO. Gentlemen, I'm delighted to see men of your nationality in my house. I've always esteemed the French.

BEAUMARCHAIS. I hope, sir, that we may be worthy of the honor you are so kind as to do our countrymen.

SAINT GEORGE. The pleasure of making your acquaintance has dispelled our fears that we might be intruding upon you.

CLAVIGO. Those whom the first glance recommends should not carry modesty to such lengths.

BEAUMARCHAIS. I am sure you can't be surprised to receive a visit from foreigners, since the excellence of your writings has made you as well known abroad as the eminent offices entrusted to you by your King distinguish you in your fatherland.

CLAVIGO. The King has been most gracious to me for my modest services, and the public has received very kindly the insignificant products of my pen. I hope to contribute in some measure to the improvement of taste and the dissemination of learning in my country. For it is that alone which binds nations together, that alone that makes friends of the most distant spirits and maintains such a delightful union among them, a union unfortunately often broken by affairs of state.

BEAUMARCHAIS. I am delighted to hear such words from a man who has equal influence on the state and on learning. I must admit you took the words out of my mouth, and that brings me straightway to the business I came to see you about. A society of worthy learned men has commissioned me, wherever I might travel, to institute a correspondence between them and the best minds of this kingdom. And since no Spaniard writes better than the author of those pages so well known under the name of "The Thinker," a man with whom I have the honor to be speaking—

Clavigo bows politely.

And who is a particular ornament to learning, knowing, as he does, how to combine with his talents such a degree of wordly wisdom; a man who cannot fail to ascend those brilliant heights of which his character and his learning make him worthy—all this being the case, I believe I could do my friends no more gratifying service than to introduce them to such a man.

CLAVIGO. No proposal in the world could be more welcome to me, gentlemen. It would fulfill the most beguiling hopes that have often occupied my heart without prospect of gratification. Not that I think I could satisfy the wishes of your learned friends through my correspondence—my vanity does not go *that* far. But since I have the good fortune to be associated with the best minds in Spain, since nothing that is accomplished in our great kingdom in the arts and sciences even by more obscure individuals escapes my attention, I have regarded myself up to now as a kind of intermediary who has the modest merit of making the discoveries of others useful to the commonality. But now, through your intervention, I shall become a merchant who is happily able to spread the fame of his fatherland abroad by distributing its native products and in turn to enrich his own land with foreign treasures. And so you will permit me, sir, not to treat a gentleman who so generously brings me such a welcome message as a stranger. Allow me to ask: What business, what pressing affair has led you to undertake this long journey? Not that I am indiscreet enough to want to satisfy an idle curiosity; no, believe me, I ask only with the purest intention of placing all the power, all the influence I may possess at your disposal; for I can tell you immediately that you have come to a place where a foreigner meets with innumerable difficulties in the conduct of his business, especially at court.

BEAUMARCHAIS. I accept your generous offer with many thanks. I have no secrets to keep from you, sir; and my friend can hear what I have to say; he's well informed of the matter.

Clavigo looks at Saint George attentively.

A French merchant with many children and of modest fortune had a number of business associates in Spain. One of the wealthiest of them came to Paris fifteen years ago and made this proposal: "Give me two of your daughters, I'll take them with me to Madrid and care for them. I'm unmarried, along in years, without relatives. They will comfort my old age and upon my death inherit one of the most prosperous businesses in Spain." He was entrusted with the eldest and one of the younger daughters. The father undertook to provide the Spaniard with all the French merchandise he might ask for, and all seemed to be going well until the associate died, leaving not a cent to the two young Frenchwomen, who now found themselves in the difficult situation of having to run the business alone.

In the meantime the eldest had married and despite their slender resources they were able through their social charm and lively spirits to keep a large number of friends, who vied with each other in enhancing both their credit and their business opportunities.

Clavigo is becoming more and more attentive.

Just about this time a young man, a native of the Canary Islands, had gained an introduction to their house.

Clavigo's jaw drops, his serious air gradually turns into ever more visible embarrassment.

Despite his lowly station and small fortune, he is received graciously. The young women, noticing that he is keen on learning French, give him every opportunity to perfect his skill in a short time.

Eager to make a name for himself, he hits upon the idea of providing the city of Madrid with a refinement still unknown in Spain, namely, a moral weekly in the style of the English "Spectator." The two Frenchwomen encourage him in every way; no one doubts that such an undertaking will gain wide public acclaim. In short, cheered by the prospect of becoming a person of some consequence, he ventures to propose marriage to the younger sister.

His hopes are encouraged. "Try to make your fortune," the elder sister tells him, "and if some office, some favor at court gives you the right to think of marrying my sister, and if she prefers you to other suitors, I won't withhold my consent."

Clavigo squirms in most painful confusion.

The younger sister refuses various acceptable offers; her liking for the man in question grows and helps her to bear the concern she feels about her uncertain future. She is as interested in his fortunes as if they were her own and urges him to publish the first issue of his journal, which now appears under a very promising title.

Clavigo is in the throes of the most frightful embarrassment.

(*Coldy*:) The paper is an astounding success. The King himself, delighted by this charming production, publicly bestows upon the author signs of his favor. He is promised the first considerable appointment that falls vacant. From that moment on he allows no rival to approach his beloved and courts her openly. The marriage is postponed only in expectation of the promised appointment.—Finally, after six years of patient waiting, of unbroken affection, devotion and love on the part of the girl; after six years of gratitude, struggle and sacred promises on the part of the man, the appointment comes—and the man disappears.

Clavigo involuntarily heaves a deep sigh, which he tries to suppress. He is quite beside himself.

The affair had attracted too much attention for people to be indifferent to the outcome. A house for two families had been rented. The whole town was buzzing. The friends of the two sisters were up in arms and sought vengeance. They turned to persons in powerful positions, but the base fellow, now skilled in court intrigue, is able to foil all their efforts and is even so insolent as to threaten the unfortunate sisters, daring to tell their friends when they approach him: the Frenchwomen had better be careful, he would challenge them to try to hurt him, and if they should make bold to take steps against him, it would be easy for him to ruin them, living as they did in a foreign country, where they are without help and protection.

When the younger sister heard this, she fell into convulsions that almost cost her her life. In her desperation the elder sister writes to France, describing the public disgrace inflicted upon them. Their brother in France is horribly agitated by this news and obtains permission to leave the country in order to give aid and counsel in this confused affair. Like an arrow he flies from Paris to Madrid, and the brother—is me! I am the one who has left everything behind: country, family, position, pleasures, in order to avenge an innocent, despairing sister in Spain.

I come, armed with a just cause and firm determination, to unmask a traitor, to paint his true soul on his face with the point of my sword, and the traitor—is you!

CLAVIGO. Listen to me, sir—I am—I have—I don't doubt—

BEAUMARCHAIS. Don't interrupt me. You have nothing to tell me and a lot to hear from me.

Now, for a start, be so good as to declare in the presence of this gentleman who has come with me from France for this express purpose, whether my sister, through any kind of unfaithfulness, frivolous action, weakness, misbehavior or any other fault has deserved this public disgrace at your hands.

CLAVIGO. No, sir; your sister, Doña Maria, is a young woman of great sense, charm and virtue.

BEAUMARCHAIS. Has she ever given you occasion to complain about her or to lose respect for her?

CLAVIGO. No! Never!

BEAUMARCHAIS (*standing up*). Then why, you brute! did you have the cruelty to torment the poor girl to death? Just because her heart preferred you to ten others, who were all more honorable and wealthier than you.

CLAVIGO. Oh sir! If you only knew how I've been put upon, how all kinds of advisers and circumstances—

BEAUMARCHAIS. That will do. (*To Saint George*:) You've heard my sister's justification—go and spread the word! What I still have to tell this gentleman needs no witnesses.

Clavigo gets up. Saint George leaves.

BEAUMARCHAIS. Stay right where you are. (*They sit down again.*) Since we've got this far, I'm going to make you a proposal I hope you will approve.

It's to your advantage and to mine that you should not marry Marie. I'm sure you're aware that I haven't come to play the stage brother who merely wants to advance the plot and find a husband for his sister. You have insulted an honorable girl in cold blood because you thought she was in a foreign country without support and protection. Only a scoundrel would act that way, a scoundrel! And so, first of all, you are to write a declaration in your own hand, voluntarily, with the doors open, in the presence of your servants: that you are a despicable human being who has deceived and betrayed my sister, demeaning her without the slightest reason. I shall take this declaration to Aranjuez, where our ambassador is staying, show it to him, have it printed, and by the day after tomorrow it will be all over court and on every street corner in Madrid. I have powerful friends here, I have time and money, and I'll employ every means to persecute you in the cruelest way possible, until my sister's wrath is laid, she is satisfied and herself bids me stop.

CLAVIGO. I won't write any such declaration.

BEAUMARCHAIS. I can believe that; I might not either, if I were in your place. But here's the next thing: If you do not write it, I'll dog your footsteps from this moment on, I'll follow you everywhere until you are weary of my company and try to get rid of me behind the Buen Retiro. If I'm luckier than you, then, without having seen the ambassador or spoken to a soul, I'll take my dying sister in my arms, lift her into a carriage and return with her to France. If fate favors you, at least I shall have done what I could, and you can have the last laugh. Meanwhile, let's eat breakfast!

Beaumarchais rings. A servant brings chocolate. Beaumarchais takes his cup and walks up and down in the adjoining gallery, examining the paintings.

CLAVIGO. Air! Air!—That surprised you, eh? to be shaken like a schoolboy—Where are you, Clavigo? How are you going to get out of this? How *can* you get out of it?—A terrible mess your foolishness, your treachery has plunged you into! (*He reaches for a dagger lying on the table.*) Ha! Once and for all!—(*He leaves the dagger where it is.*)—No other way, no remedy but death? or murder? Repulsive thought! To deprive the unhappy girl of her only comfort, her only support, her brother!—And to have to see the blood of a brave and noble man! To burden myself with the double, insupportable curse of a ruined family!—Oh, that wasn't the prospect you glimpsed when that lovable creature so charmed you in the first hours of your acquaintanceship! And when you left her you were blind to the horrible consequences of your shameful action!—What bliss awaited you in her arms! in the friendship of such a brother!—Marie! Marie! Oh, if you could forgive me! If I could wash everything away in tears at your feet!—And why can't I?—My heart's overflowing; my soul opens in hope!—Monsieur Beaumarchais!

BEAUMARCHAIS. What is your decision?

CLAVIGO. Listen to me! My behavior toward your sister is inexcusable. My vanity led me astray, I was afraid I would ruin my prospects for life by this marriage. Had I known that she had such a brother as you, she would not have been in my eyes an insignificant foreigner—I would have hoped for the most eminent advantages from such a union. You inspire me, sir, with the greatest esteem, and by making me feel most keenly how much in the wrong I have been, you give me the strength and the desire to make amends. I throw myself at your feet! Help me, help me if you can to erase my guilt and put an end to this misfortune! Give me back your sister, give me *to her*! How happy I would be to receive from your hands a wife and the forgiveness of my transgressions!

BEAUMARCHAIS. It's too late! My sister no longer loves you, and I despise you. Write the declaration I demand, that's all I ask, and leave it to me to execute an exquisite revenge!

CLAVIGO. Your stubbornness is neither just nor wise. I'll admit that it does not depend on me whether or not I want to make amends for such an exacerbated evil. Whether I *can* make amends depends on your admirable sister and whether she is willing to look at a wretch like me, who does not deserve to see the light of day. But it is your duty, sir, to find that out and to conduct yourself accordingly, if the step you're taking is not to look like some thoughtless, juvenile prank undertaken in the heat of the moment. If Doña Maria can't be moved—oh, I know her heart, her kindness! Her heavenly soul is vividly present to me! If she cannot be moved, then the time will have come.

BEAUMARCHAIS. I still demand the declaration.

CLAVIGO (*going to the table*). And suppose I have recourse to this?

Takes up the dagger.

BEAUMARCHAIS (*leaving*). Oh, very well, sir! Very well indeed!

CLAVIGO (*detaining him*). One more word. You have right on your side; let me supply you with wisdom. Consider what you are doing! In either instance, we are all irreparably lost. Wouldn't I perish of remorse and anxiety if your blood colored my blade, if, in addition to all her misfortune, I were to deprive Maria of a brother? And then: the murderer of Clavigo would never get back across the Pyrenees.

BEAUMARCHAIS. Your declaration, sir, your declaration!

CLAVIGO. So be it. I'll do everything in my power to convince you of the honest intentions with which your presence inspires me. I'll write the declaration. I'll write it from your dictation. Only promise me not to make use of it until I have been able to convince Maria of my changed and contrite heart, until I have spoken with your eldest sister and she has put in a kind word for me with my beloved. Wait until then, sir!

BEAUMARCHAIS. I am going to Aranjuez.

CLAVIGO. Very well, then; until you return, my declaration shall remain in your pocket. If she has not forgiven me by then, give your vengeance free rein! My proposal is just, decent, and wise; if you will not accept it, let there be war to the death between us! And the victims of your excessive haste will always be you and your poor sister.

BEAUMARCHAIS. It becomes you to pity those you have ruined.

CLAVIGO (*seating himself*.) Do you agree to my condition?

BEAUMARCHAIS. Very well, I'll yield! But no reprieve. I return from Aranjuez, make inquiries, learn the truth! And if you have not been forgiven—as indeed I hope you won't be—off to the printer with your declaration!

CLAVIGO (*taking writing paper*). What is your wish?

BEAUMARCHAIS. In the presence of the servants, if you please!

CLAVIGO. What's the point of that?

BEAUMARCHAIS. Just tell them to go into the adjoining gallery. It shall not be said that I have forced you.

CLAVIGO. What scruples!

BEAUMARCHAIS. I am in Spain, and have you to deal with.

CLAVIGO. Very well! (*He rings. Servant.*) Call the servants together, and all of you go into the gallery. (*Servant leaves, the others come and occupy the gallery.*)

CLAVIGO. Leave it to me to write the declaration.

BEAUMARCHAIS. Sorry! You will please write what I tell you. "I, the undersigned Joseph Clavigo, director of the royal archives—"

CLAVIGO. Archives.

BEAUMARCHAIS. "do hereby confess that, after having been kindly received in the house of Madame Guilbert,—"

CLAVIGO. Guilbert.

BEAUMARCHAIS. "I willfully deceived, by frequent promises of marriage, her sister, Mademoiselle Marie de Beaumarchais." Have you got that?

CLAVIGO. But sir!

BEAUMARCHAIS. Do you have another word for it?

CLAVIGO. Well, I should think—

BEAUMARCHAIS. Deceive is the word. What you did, you can write, can't you?—"I deserted her, without any kind of fault or failing on her part which might have served as pretext or excuse for my mendacious behavior."

CLAVIGO. I must say!

BEAUMARCHAIS. "On the contrary, the conduct of the young woman was always blameless, pure, and worthy of all respect."

CLAVIGO. All respect.

BEAUMARCHAIS. "I confess that through my actions, my frivolous language, and the interpretation to which it was subject I have publicly demeaned this virtuous woman, for which I hereby beg her forgiveness, although I do not deem myself worthy of receiving it."

Clavigo pauses.

Write! Write!—"In witness whereof I, without duress and of my own free will, indite this document and give my solemn promise that, if this should not suffice to satisfy the injured party, I stand ready to satisfy her in any way she may demand. Madrid."

CLAVIGO (*rises, signals the servants to leave and hands Beaumarchais the paper*). I know I'm dealing with an injured but generous man. You will keep your word and postpone your revenge. Only in hope and expectation of that have I written this disgraceful document. Otherwise, nothing would have brought me to do it. But before I venture to appear before Doña Maria, I am determined to delegate someone to put in a good word for me—and that someone is you.

Beaumarchais. I wouldn't dream of it!

Clavigo. Tell her at least of the bitter, heartfelt remorse you have seen me exhibit. That is all I ask. Don't refuse me that, else I'll have to choose a less convincing advocate, and you owe her a truthful account of what you have seen. Tell her how you found me!

Beaumarchais. Very well, I can do that and I will. And now, adieu.

Clavigo. Farewell. (*He tries to shake hands, but Beaumarchais refuses.*)

Clavigo (*alone*). From one frame of mind to another before you know it. I'm reeling, dreaming!—That declaration, I should never have written it.—Everything came so fast—a bolt from the blue!

Enter Carlos.

Carlos. Who was here? The whole house is in an uproar.

Clavigo. Marie's brother.

Carlos. That's what I thought. That old dog of a servant that used to be with the Guilberts tells me all the gossip; he knew yesterday that he was expected—I saw him just a moment ago. So he was here?

Clavigo. An excellent chap.

Carlos. We'll soon get rid of him. I've been thinking about it on my way over.—What happened? Did he challenge you? Demand a declaration clearing the family honor? Was he in a fine frenzy, the fellow?

Clavigo. He demanded a declaration that his sister had given me no grounds for changing my mind.

Carlos. And you composed one for him?

Clavigo. It seemed the best thing to do.

Carlos. Fine, splendid! Nothing else happened?

Clavigo. He insisted on a duel or a declaration.

Carlos. You were smart to give him the declaration. Who wants to risk his life against such a romantic windbag? Was he vehement in demanding the document?

Clavigo. He dictated it to me, and I had to call the servants into the gallery.

Carlos. I see! Ha! Now I have you, my fine-feathered friend! That'll break his neck. Call me a pen-pusher, if I don't have that rascal in jail in two days, and on a transport to the Indies the next.

Clavigo. No, Carlos. Things are not the way you think.

Carlos. How's that?

Clavigo. Through his intervention and my own efforts I hope to obtain forgiveness from that unhappy girl.

Carlos. Clavigo!

Clavigo. I hope to erase the past, restore our shattered relationship, and regain my honor in my own eyes and in the eyes of the world.

Carlos. What the devil! Has your brain gone soft? I can see you're still a bookworm. Let yourself be led around by the nose like that! Don't you see it's nothing but a simple-minded scheme to tie you hand and foot?

CLAVIGO. No, Carlos. He doesn't want the marriage; they don't want it; she wants nothing to do with me.

CARLOS. That's the tune! No, my friend, don't be peeved, but on the stage I've seen country squires fooled that way.

CLAVIGO. You're insulting me. Please save your humor for my wedding. I'm determined to marry Marie. Voluntarily, because it's my desire. All my hope and all my happiness lie in the thought of obtaining her forgiveness. Then good-bye, pride! Heaven lies on the bosom of that dear girl as it always did. All the renown I attain, all the greatness to which I rise will make me twice as happy; for my darling will share it with me and she'll make me twice the man. Farewell! I must go speak to the Guilberts.

CARLOS. At least wait until we've eaten!

CLAVIGO. Not a moment longer.

CARLOS (*watches him leave and stands for a moment in silence*). There's someone who's out to make a fool of himself. (*Exit.*)

ACT III

Guilbert's House
Sophie Guilbert. Marie Beaumarchais.

MARIE. You saw him? I'm trembling in every limb! You saw him? I almost fainted when I heard that he was coming, and you saw him? No, I cannot, will not, cannot ever see him again.

SOPHIE. I was quite beside myself when he came in; for didn't I love him as you did, with the fullest, purest, most sisterly love? Didn't his absence offend and torture me too? And then, to see him back again, lying at my feet full of remorse!—O Sister, there's something so enchanting in his look, the tone of his voice. He—

MARIE. No, never, never again!

SOPHIE. He's still the same, still the same good, gentle, feeling heart, still the same impetuosity and passion. Still the same eagerness to be loved, and the same sense of torment if he isn't. Everything, everything! And he speaks of you, Marie, as he did in those happy days of his most fervent devotion. It's as though your guardian angel had placed this interval of faithlessness and absence between you, to break the dragging monotony of your long acquaintanceship and rejuvenate your feeling for each other.

MARIE. Are you pleading his case?

SOPHIE. No, sister, and I didn't promise that I would. But look, my dear, I see things as they are. You and our brother, you see them in a much too romantic light. Your lover was untrue to you and left you—you have that in common with many another decent girl! But now he comes back full of repentance and wants to make amends for his trespasses, renew all the old hopes—and that's a piece of luck others wouldn't be so likely to spurn.

MARIE. My heart would break!

SOPHIE. That I believe. The first sight of him is bound to affect you deeply. But I beg you, my darling, this anxiety, this embarrassment that seems to be overpowering all your senses—don't take it for hatred or disgust. Your heart speaks for him more than you think, and you don't dare see him again just because you long to so much.

MARIE. Have pity!

SOPHIE. I want you to be happy. If I felt that you despised him, that you were indifferent to him, I'd not say another word, and he'd never see my face again. But the way things are, my love,—you'll thank me for having helped you to overcome this anxious uncertainty, which is only a sign of how fervently you love him.

Enter Guilbert, Buenco.

SOPHIE. Ah, welcome, friends, Guilbert, Buenco! Come help me inspire this girl with a bit of courage and determination, there's pressing need.

BUENCO. I wish I could say: Don't take him back!

SOPHIE. Buenco!

BUENCO. It makes my heart sink to think that he is after all to possess this angel, whom he insulted so shamelessly and almost dragged to the grave. Possess her? Why? How is he going to make amends for all he's done?—So he comes back—suddenly it suits his whim—and says: "Now I like her, now I want her!"—Just as though this splendid soul were a shoddy piece of goods you finally throw into the bargain after the buyer has tortured you by making the lowest possible offers and by running back and forth like a Jewish used clothes dealer. No, he'll not get my vote, even if Marie's heart should speak for him.—Comes back? And why just at this point? Why now? Did he have to wait until the bold-hearted brother arrived, whose vengeance he has a right to fear, before crawling back like a schoolboy to beg forgiveness?—Bah! He's as cowardly as he is contemptible!

GUILBERT. You're talking like a Spaniard, and as though you didn't know the Spanish. We're in greater danger at this moment than any of you realize.

MARIE. But Guilbert!

GUILBERT. I have all respect for our brother's enterprising spirit, I've been quietly watching his heroic actions and hope that all may turn out well, hope that Marie may decide to give Clavigo her hand, for (*smiling*) he already has her heart.—

MARIE. How cruel you are.

SOPHIE. Oh, listen to him, please do!

GUILBERT. Your brother has wrung a declaration from him that is to clear your name in the eyes of the whole world, and that will be our ruin.

BUENCO. What?

MARIE. O God!

GUILBERT. He wrote it in the hope of making you change your mind. If he is unsuccessful, then he must do all in his power to destroy the document. He can and he will. Your brother means to have it printed and distributed right after he returns from Aranjuez. I'm afraid that if you *don't* change your mind, your brother will never return.

SOPHIE. O my dear husband!

MARIE. I'm in despair!

GUILBERT. Clavigo can't let the document be made public. If you refuse his offer, and he is a man of honor, he will challenge your brother, and one or the other will be left dead. Whether your brother dies or is victorious, he's lost. A foreigner in Spain! Murderer of a court favorite! Sister, it's all very well to have noble feelings and high sentiments, but to cause your own ruin and that of your family—

MARIE. Help me, Sophie, tell me what to do —

GUILBERT. Refute me if you can, Buenco!

BUENCO. He won't dare, he fears for his life—otherwise, he wouldn't have written it at all; nor would he be offering his hand to Marie.

GUILBERT. All the worse. Now he'll find a hundred to lend him their arm, a hundred who are willing to waylay and kill our brother. Hey, Buenco! Are you so naive? A courtier doesn't have any bravos in his pay?

BUENCO. The King is mighty and he is good.

GUILBERT. Then let's be on our way! Break through all the walls, the guards, the ceremonial and everything with which sycophantic courtiers fence him off from his people! Go ahead and save us!—Who's that coming?

Enter Clavigo.

CLAVIGO. I must! I must!

Marie cries out and falls into Sophie's arms.

SOPHIE. You cruel man! Don't you see what you're doing?

Guilbert and Buenco come and stand near her.

CLAVIGO. Yes, it's her, it's her! And I am Clavigo. Listen to me, please, even if you won't look at me! When Guilbert was first kind enough to receive me in his house, when I was still an impoverished, callow youth and felt an irrepressible passion for you, was that to my credit? Or wasn't it rather an inner harmony of our natures, a secret inclination of our feelings that made you not insensitive to me, so that after a time I began to flatter myself that your heart belonged to me? And now—am I not the same person? Aren't you the same? Why shouldn't I dare hope? Why shouldn't I plead? Wouldn't you take back to your bosom a friend, a lover, whom you had thought lost on a long, perilous voyage, if he were to return unexpectedly and lay his life, now saved, at your feet? And haven't *I* been tossed on just such a stormy sea all this time? Are not the passions with which we must eternally contend more terrible, more unconquerable than the waves that carry an unfortunate man far from his native shores?

Marie! Marie! How can you hate me when I have never ceased to love you? In the midst of all the worldly frenzy, through all the siren songs of vanity and pride, I have never forgotten those serene, openhearted hours I spent in blissful contentment at your feet, when we saw life's fair prospects ready to unfold like flowers before us.

And now, why don't you want to fulfill with me all the hopes we had? Do you mean to refuse life's joys because a dismal episode intruded upon our hopes? No, my dear, believe me, the best friends in the world are not wholly pure; the highest bliss must suffer interference from our passions, from fate. Are we to complain because our lot is no better than that of others? And do we want to be guilty of rejecting this opportunity of healing past injuries, of restoring a shattered family, of rewarding the heroic action of your noble brother and of forever confirming our own happiness?

My friends, though I am not deserving of you, you must be my friends because you are friends of the virtuous life to which I now return, join your prayers with mine! Marie! (*He casts himself at her feet.*) Marie, don't you still know my voice? Can you no longer understand the language of my heart? Marie! Marie!

MARIE. O Clavigo!

CLAVIGO (*springs up, seizes her hand and covers it with ecstatic kisses*). She forgives me! She loves me! (*He embraces Guilbert and Buenco.*) She still loves me! O Marie, my heart told me you did! Oh, had I thrown myself at your feet, not voiced my pain, only wept out my repentance, you would have understood me without words, even as you now forgive me wordlessly. That intimate relationship of our souls has not been blotted out; they still understand each other as they did before, when no word, no outward sign was needed to communicate our inmost feelings. Marie—Marie—Marie!—

Enter Beaumarchais.

BEAUMARCHAIS. Ha!

CLAVIGO (*flying toward him*). Brother!

BEAUMARCHAIS. You forgive him?

MARIE. Leave me alone! I feel faint. (*They lead her away.*)

BEAUMARCHAIS. Did she forgive him?

BUENCO. It looks that way.

BEAUMARCHAIS. You don't deserve your good fortune.

CLAVIGO. Believe me, I know that.

SOPHIE (*returns*). She forgives him. Her eyes were streaming. She sobbed and cried out: "He should leave and let me recover! I forgive him." Then she fell about my neck and cried: "O sister! How does he know I love him so much?"

CLAVIGO (*kissing her hand*). I'm the happiest man under the sun. Brother!

BEAUMARCHAIS (*embraces him*). Good then, from the heart. Although I must tell you: I still can't be your friend, can't love you yet. But now you're one of us and we'll let by-gones be by-gones. Here is the document you gave me. (*He takes it out of his portfolio, tears it in two and hands it to him.*)

CLAVIGO. I am yours, forever yours.

SOPHIE. Please go, Clavigo, so that she doesn't hear your voice and can calm down.

CLAVIGO (*embracing each in turn*). Farewell! Farewell!—A thousand kisses to my angel! (*Exit.*)

BEAUMARCHAIS. So that's the way it is, though I wish it were otherwise. (*Smiling*:) She is really a kindhearted creature. And, my friends, I must admit: it was also exactly what the ambassador had in mind. It was his wish that Marie should forgive him and a happy marriage put an end to this distasteful business.

GUILBERT. I too feel much relieved.

BUENCO. He's now your brother-in-law, so good-bye! You won't see me in your house again.

BEAUMARCHAIS. But sir!

GUILBERT. Buenco!

BUENCO. I'll hate him till the Judgment Day. And you'll soon find out what kind of person you're dealing with. (*Exit.*)

GUILBERT. A melancholy bird of ill omen, Buenco. But he'll come round when he sees that all's well.

BEAUMARCHAIS. Just the same, I was a bit hasty in giving him back that declaration.

GUILBERT. Never mind! Never mind! No far-fetched ideas, please! (*Exit.*)

ACT IV

Clavigo's Apartments
Carlos alone.

CARLOS. It is praiseworthy that the state appoints guardians for persons that have shown themselves by excessive extravagance or other irresponsible acts not to be in possession of all their faculties. And if the authorities, who otherwise take small notice of our well-being, do this, why shouldn't we do it for a friend? Clavigo, you're in a bad way! But I still have hope. And if you're only halfway as amenable as you used to be, there's still just time enough to save you from a piece of idiocy that, given your vivacious, sensitive nature, is bound to make you miserable and lead you to an early grave. There he comes.

Enter Clavigo, pensive.

CLAVIGO. Good day, Carlos.

CARLOS. What a melancholy, constrained "good day"! Is *that* the humor your fiancée puts you in?

CLAVIGO. She's an angel! They are fine people!

CARLOS. You won't be in such a rush with the wedding that one can't have some gala clothes embroidered?

CLAVIGO. Whether you're serious or joking, at our wedding there'll be no parading about in embroidered clothes.

CARLOS. I can believe that.

CLAVIGO. Our pleasure in each other, harmonious friendliness is to be the splendor of this wedding.

CARLOS. So it's going to be a small, quiet affair?

CLAVIGO. As becomes people who feel that their happiness rests entirely in themselves.

CARLOS. In *those* circumstances it's a good idea.

CLAVIGO. Circumstances! What do you mean by "those circumstances"?

CARLOS. As the matter stands, lies, and shows itself to be.

CLAVIGO. Listen, Carlos, I can't stand this carping tone with friends. I know you're not for this marriage. But if you've something to say against it, then say it! How does the matter stand, how does it "show itself to be"?

CARLOS. Plenty of strange and unexpected things happen in this life, and it would be too bad if everything were entirely predictable. One would have nothing to marvel at, nothing to knock people's heads together about, nothing to gossip about.

CLAVIGO. It'll cause a stir all right.

CARLOS. Clavigo's wedding! Indeed it will. How many girls there must be in Madrid who have their caps set for you, who are hoping to catch you, and now you play this trick on them!

CLAVIGO. That can't be helped.

CARLOS. It's strange though. I've not known many men who made such a deep impression on women as you. In every class and condition there are nice girls busy with plans and hopes of catching you. Some have their beauty to offer, others their wealth, their position, their wit, their family connections. You should hear the compliments I'm paid on your account! For you can be sure neither my snub nose, nor my curly hair, nor my well-known scorn for women can be the reason.

CLAVIGO. You're joking.

CARLOS. I tell you I've had proposals and propositions in my hands, written by the tenderest, scrawliest little paws, as misspelt as a genuine love letter from a girl can be. How many duennas have I got my hands on that way!

CLAVIGO. And you told me nothing about all this?

CARLOS. I didn't want to bother you with empty fantasies. Besides, I never supposed that you would seriously confine yourself to *one*. O Clavigo, I've had your best interests at heart as though they were my own! I have no friend but you; I can't stand other people, and now it's getting so I can't stand you either.

CLAVIGO. For pity's sake, calm down!

CARLOS. Burn down a fellow's house after he's spent ten years building it, and send him a confessor who counsels Christian patience!—One shouldn't take an interest in anyone but oneself—people aren't worth—

CLAVIGO. Your old misanthropic tune again?

CARLOS. If I completely succumb to misanthropy, who's to blame but you? I asked myself: What good's the most advantageous marriage to him now? He's got far enough for the run-of-the-mill person, but with his brains and his gifts it's irresponsible—he can't remain where he is.—I laid my plans. There aren't many who are so enterprising and adaptable, and at the same time so brainy and energetic. He's at home in any field; as archive director he can quickly acquire the most important information, he'll make himself necessary, and if some cabinet change occurs, presto! he's a minister.

CLAVIGO. I'll admit that was often my dream.

CARLOS. Dream! Just as sure as I can climb that tower, if I set about it with the firm resolve to reach the top, just as surely would you have overcome all difficulties. And then I wouldn't have worried about the rest. You have no inheritance—all the better. That would have made you all the more eager to acquire a fortune and hold on to it. A tax-gatherer who doesn't get rich is a simpleton. Besides, I don't see why the country doesn't owe taxes to a minister just as well as to the King. The King lends the authority of his name, the minister the power to enforce it. And when I had finished with all that, *then* I'd look around for a match for you. I know many a proud house that would have closed its eyes to your origins. Some of the wealthiest would have been glad to foot the bill so that you could live as befits your station, merely to be able to bask in the reflected glory of the second King—but now—

CLAVIGO. That's not fair, you demean my present station too much. And do you think I can't climb any higher, take still mightier steps?

CARLOS. My friend, if you break the heart out of a plant, it may still grow and grow, put out hundreds of shoots, and you may get a heavy bush, but the proud royal growth of its first impulse is gone forever. And don't think the court will view this marriage with indifference. Have you forgotten what kind of men advised you against your association with Marie? Have you forgotten who first gave you the prudent idea of leaving her? Shall I count them off on my fingers?

CLAVIGO. The thought that so few will approve this step has already been tormenting me.

CARLOS. No one! And won't your highly placed friends have a right to be indignant if you, without consulting them, go and throw yourself away like an impulsive boy at a fair throwing his money away on a bag of wormy nuts?

CLAVIGO. That's rude, Carlos, and exaggerated.

CARLOS. Not a bit. If someone commits an extravagant piece of foolishness out of passion, I don't object. Marries the chambermaid because she's beautiful as an angel! People may blame the fellow, but they'll envy him too.

CLAVIGO. What people will think! Always what people will think!

CARLOS. You know I'm not a man who always seeks the approval of others; nonetheless, it's eternally true: he who does nothing for others, does nothing for himself. And if people don't admire or envy you, *you're* not happy either.

CLAVIGO. The world judges by appearances. But the man who gets Marie, ah, he's the one to be envied!

CARLOS. What a thing is, is also what it seems. But I'll admit there must be hidden qualities that make your happiness enviable; for what one sees with his own eyes and can comprehend with one's God-given wits—

CLAVIGO. You want to ruin me.

CARLOS. How did *that* happen? That's what the town will be asking. How did that happen? That's what they'll ask at court. For God's sake, how did that happen? She's poor, has no position. If Clavigo hadn't once had an affair with her, no one would even know she existed. They say she's cultivated, pleasant, witty!—Who marries a woman for that reason? That evaporates after two months of marriage. Oh, someone says, she's supposed to be beautiful, charming, ravishingly beautiful.—Then one can understand it, says another—

CLAVIGO (*becomes confused, heaves a sigh*). Oh!

CARLOS. Beautiful? one woman says. Oh, not bad. I haven't seen her in six years, she may have changed, says another. Just keep your eyes open, says a third, he'll soon be introducing her into society. And so people ask, gape, go to balls, grow impatient, always remembering the proud Clavigo who never used to appear in public without leading in triumph a handsome, queenly Spanish woman on his arm, whose full bosom, glowing cheeks, flashing eyes seemed to be asking the world: am I not worthy of my escort? And meanwhile in her haughty pride she would let her silken train sail as far out in the wind as possible to make herself appear the more imposing and dignified.—And now this gentleman finally appears and everyone is speechless; for he comes on the scene leading his hollow-eyed French girl, mincing along, short of stature, consumption written in every feature, though she's tried to cover up her deathly pallor with powder and rouge. It drives one to distraction, brother of mine; I take to my heels when people start to buttonhole me, question and cross-examine me and simply cannot understand—

CLAVIGO (*seizing his hand*). My friend, my brother. I'm in a desperate situation. I'll tell you, I'll confess to you: I nearly fainted when I saw Marie again! Her features were so changed—she's so pale, emaciated! Oh, that's my fault! The result of my treachery.

CARLOS. Nonsense! That's all in your head. She had consumption when you were still courting her. I told you a hundred times, but you lovers can neither see nor smell. Clavigo, it's shameful! To forget everything, everything for a sickly woman, who will bear you sickly children that will politely go out like a beggar's lantern when they reach a certain age.—A man who could found a family that perhaps one day—No, I'm going out of my wits, my head's swimming!

CLAVIGO. Carlos, what can I say? When I first saw her again, in the intoxication of the moment my heart rushed towards her—but oh! when that was past—pity, deep pity took possession of me. But love? It was as though in the midst of my joy I felt death's cold hand touching my neck. I tried to be gay, to play my old cheerful self for the benefit of those around me—but it was no use. I was stiff, constrained. If they had not been beside themselves, they would certainly have noticed.

CARLOS. Hell, death and damnation! And you mean to marry her?—

Clavigo stands sunk in thought without answering.

You're lost, irretrievably lost! Farewell, brother, let me forget it all and spend the rest of my days grinding my teeth at your fateful blindness! Yes, all of it! Make yourself a laughing-stock in the eyes of the world and not even satisfy one passion, one desire in return! Pigheadedly infect yourself with a disease that, while it undermines your inward powers, at the same time makes you an object of revulsion.

CLAVIGO. Carlos! Carlos!

CARLOS. Better never to have risen than to fall so far! How they'll look at you! There's the girl's brother, they'll say. Must be quite a fellow to have buffaloed him that way. Didn't have the nerve to face him down. Ho! our braggart courtiers will say, you can see he's no *caballero*. Bah! cries one of them and pulls his hat down over his eyes, that Frenchman should have tried that on *me*! Then he slaps his belly, the rogue, though he's not fit to be your stable boy.

CLAVIGO (*in an attack of violent anxiety bursts into tears and falls about Carlos's neck*). Save me! Friend, brother! Save me! Save me from perjuring myself again, from boundless disgrace, from myself—I can't bear it!

CARLOS. You poor, miserable creature! I was hoping this immature raving, these stormy tears, this melting melancholy was a thing of the past. I was hoping to find in you a man unshaken, no longer in the grip of that dejection that so often made you weep on my shoulder. Get hold of yourself, Clavigo, get hold of yourself!

CLAVIGO. No, let me weep! (*He throws himself into an armchair.*)

CARLOS. Woe unto you that you have entered upon a career you won't finish! With your sensibilities, your principles, which would delight an ordinary citizen, you had to combine an accursed longing for greatness! But what is greatness, Clavigo? To rise above others in rank and esteem? Don't you believe it! If your heart is not greater than the hearts of others, if you are not capable of calmly disregarding circumstances that would arouse fear in an ordinary man, then with all your ribbons and crosses, with the crown itself, you're nothing but an ordinary man yourself. Take yourself in hand, calm down!

Clavigo straightens up, looks at Carlos and extends his hand. Carlos grasps it eagerly.

Up, up, my friend! And come to a decision! Look, I'll drop all other arguments, I'll merely say: Here are two proposals, equally balanced on the pans of the scales. Either you marry Marie and find your happiness in a quiet bourgeois existence with its calm domestic joys, or you continue on your glorious course until you reach the not too distant goal.—I'll set aside all else and merely say: The tongue of the scales is steady, it depends on your decision which of the two pans will rise, which fall. Good. Only make up your mind!—There's nothing more pitiable than a man who can't make up his mind, who hovers between two sentiments, wants to unite them both, unable to understand that nothing *can* unite them except the doubt and uncertainty that are torturing him. Come, give Marie your hand, act like an honorable chap who sacrifices his life's happiness to his given word, who regards it as his duty to make good what he has ruined and who has never extended the range of his passions and influence so far that he isn't able to make it good. Then enjoy the happiness of calm limitation, the approval of a prudent conscience, and all the bliss allotted to those who are capable of creating their own happiness and that of those who belong to them—Make up your mind, then I'll say: you're a true man—

CLAVIGO. If I only had a spark of your strength, Carlos, your courage.

CARLOS. It's sleeping within you, that spark. I'll blow on it till it bursts into flames. But now look at the other side and behold the good fortune and greatness that await you. I won't depict your prospects in bright poetic colors; you can imagine them for yourself as they were present to your mind's eye in all their clarity before that French hothead confused you. But there too, Clavigo, you must be a true man and pursue your goal without looking right or left. Let your soul expand and be filled with the certainty that extraordinary men are extraordinary precisely because, among other reasons, their duties differ from those of ordinary men: he whose task it is to survey a great whole, to govern and preserve it, need not reproach himself if he neglects petty details and sacrifices trivial things to the welfare of the whole. If the Creator does that in nature and the King in the state, why shouldn't we do it in order to become like them?

CLAVIGO. Carlos, I am a little man.

CARLOS. We are not little because circumstances trouble us, only if we let them overwhelm us. One more breath, and you'll be your old self again. Rid yourself of the remains of this pitiable passion which suits you in these times no more than would the grey jacket and modest air you wore when you first came to Madrid. What the girl has done for you, you've long since repaid. And as for your being indebted to her for being the first to receive you kindly—ha! don't you think that another would have done just as much and more for the pleasure of your company, without making such pretensions? Would it occur to you to give a schoolmaster half your fortune because he taught you your ABC's thirty years ago? Well, Clavigo?

CLAVIGO. All well and good; on the whole you may be right; the only thing is, how to get out of this mess we're in? Give me some concrete advice about that, do something useful, then talk!

CARLOS. Good! Then you'll do it?

CLAVIGO. Make me able to and I will. My brain's a blank. Think for me!

CARLOS. Very well then. First you make an appointment with the gentleman to meet you in a safe spot. Then, at sword's point, you demand back the declaration you wrote without due consideration and under duress.

CLAVIGO. I already have it; he tore it up and gave it to me.

CARLOS. Excellent! Excellent! The first step is already accomplished!—Why did you let me go on talking all this time?—Now, to be brief: You calmly write to him that you don't consider it a good idea to marry his sister; he can learn the reason if he will meet you this evening, accompanied by a friend and armed as he sees fit, at this or that spot. And your signature.—Come, Clavigo, write that! I'll be your second, and the devil would have to have his finger in the pie, if—

Clavigo goes to the table.

Wait a minute! Just a word. When I consider the matter, it's a simple-minded idea. Who are we to risk our skin against this hothead? Besides, his conduct and his position do not make him deserving of being regarded as our equal. Listen to this! If I accuse him on a capital charge, alleging that he came secretly to Madrid, announced himself and his accomplice to you under an assumed name, first gained your confidence with kindly words and then took you by surprise, forced you to write a declaration, which he then went away to distribute—that will break his neck. He'll find out what it means to feud with a Spaniard in the midst of the peace and security of his own house.

CLAVIGO. You're right.

CARLOS. But suppose that in the meanwhile, before the trial begins and the gentleman has a chance to play all kinds of tricks on us, we took the safe course and made short work of him?

CLAVIGO. I see what you mean and I know you're man enough to do it.

CARLOS. You may be sure of that! I've been playing this game for twenty-five years and I've seen the best of men with beads of sweat standing on their brow from fear—if I can't bring off a stunt like this! Just give me a free hand; you don't need to do or write anything. If you put the brother in prison, it's a pretty good sign you don't care for his sister.

CLAVIGO. No, Carlos. Whatever the situation, I can't and won't stand for that! Beaumarchais is a decent man and he's not going to languish in some disgraceful prison for the sake of his just cause. Let's hear another proposal, Carlos, another one!

CARLOS. Bah! Don't be childish! We're not going to eat him, he'll be well taken care of, and it can't last long. Because, when he sees we mean business, he's going to repent of his theatrical zeal; he'll go back to France and thank us most graciously if we give his sister a yearly allowance—in fact, that may have been all he wanted in the first place.

CLAVIGO. So be it then! But don't mistreat him!

CARLOS. Don't worry!—One more precautionary measure. One can never know whether some gossip may not reach his ears. He might ambush you and spoil everything. So move out of your house at once and be sure that none of your servants knows where you're going. Pack only what you absolutely need. I'll send a boy to pick it up and to take you to a place where the *santa hermandad* itself can't find you. I always have a few such ratholes available. Adieu.

CLAVIGO. Farewell!

CARLOS. Courage, brother! When this is over, we'll take our royal ease.

Guilbert's House
Sophie. Marie, with sewing.

MARIE. Buenco left in such a huff?

SOPHIE. That was only natural. He loves you and how could he bear the sight of a man he must hate twice over?

MARIE. He's the best, most virtuous man of our class that I know. (*Showing her sewing*:) Is this the way to do it? I pull it in here and tuck in the end? It will look lovely.

SOPHIE. Yes, fine. I'm going to put a straw band on my bonnet. Nothing suits me so well. Why are you smiling?

MARIE. I'm laughing at myself. We girls are a strange race: scarcely have we lifted up our heads again, and right away it's ribbons and finery!

SOPHIE. You can't say that of yourself. From the moment Clavigo left you, nothing gave you any joy.

Marie starts and looks toward the door.

SOPHIE. What's the matter?

MARIE (*uneasily*). I thought someone was coming. Oh my poor heart! It will be the death of me yet. Just feel how it's pounding—from fear of nothing!

SOPHIE. Be calm. You look pale. Please, dear!

MARIE (*pointing to her breast*). I feel such pressure here. Sharp pains. It will kill me.

SOPHIE. Take care of yourself!

MARIE. I'm a foolish, unhappy girl. Pain and joy have undermined my life with equal force. I tell you, it's but half a joy to have him back. I'll not have much pleasure from the happiness that awaits me in his arms. Maybe none at all.

SOPHIE. Sister, my dear, only one! You plague yourself with such strange notions!

MARIE. Why should I deceive myself?

SOPHIE. You're young, fortunate and have everything to hope for.

MARIE. Hope! That dear, sweet balm of life often charms my soul. Bold youthful dreams hover before me and accompany the beloved figure of that incomparable man who will now again be mine. O Sophie, how charming he is! During the time we were apart he has—how can I express it?—all the great qualities his modesty used to hide have now unfolded. He's become a man, and with this pure sense of himself that is so without pride, without vanity, he's bound to carry every heart before him.—And he is to be my husband?—No, sister, I was never worthy of him—and now less than ever!

SOPHIE. Take him and be happy!—I hear your brother!

Enter Beaumarchais.

BEAUMARCHAIS. Where's Guilbert?

SOPHIE. He's been gone quite a while; he should be back soon.

MARIE. What's the matter, brother? (*She jumps up and embraces him.*) My dear brother, what's the matter?

BEAUMARCHAIS. Nothing, my Marie. Leave me alone.

MARIE. If I'm your Marie, tell me what's bothering you!

SOPHIE. Let him be! Men often make faces without anything bothering them.

MARIE. No, no. I've known this face of yours only a short time, but it already expresses for me all your feelings. I can read on your brow all that goes on in your frank, pure soul. Something's happened that oppresses you. Tell me, what is it?

BEAUMARCHAIS. It's nothing, my dears; I hope, at bottom it's nothing. Clavigo—

MARIE. What?

BEAUMARCHAIS. I went to see Clavigo. He was not at home.

SOPHIE. And that perturbs you?

BEAUMARCHAIS. His servant said he'd gone on a journey; where, he didn't know. No one knew how long he'd be away. Suppose he was just refusing to see me. Suppose he really has gone away. What's the object? Why?

MARIE. We'll wait and see.

BEAUMARCHAIS. Your tongue's a liar. Ha! The pallor of your cheeks, your trembling limbs—everything shows that you can't "wait and see." (*He takes her in his arms.*) I swear to you by your pounding, trembling heart. Hear me, just God! Hear me, all you saints! You shall be avenged, if he—my senses reel at the thought—if he has gone back on his word, if he should twice be guilty of such horrible perjury, if he should be making a jest of our misery—No, it's not possible, it's not possible—You shall be avenged!

SOPHIE. You're too hasty, brother. Spare her, I beg you!

Marie sits down.

What's the matter? You're growing faint.

MARIE. No, no; you always get so worried.

SOPHIE (*offering her a glass*). Here, drink some water!

MARIE. Never mind! What's the use? Oh, very well, give it to me.

BEAUMARCHAIS. Where's Guilbert? Where's Buenco? Please send for them. (*Exit Sophie.*) How do you feel, Marie?

MARIE. Well, quite well. What do you think, brother?

BEAUMARCHAIS. What, my dear?

MARIE. Oh!

BEAUMARCHAIS. Is it hard for you to breathe?

MARIE. This ceaseless pounding of my heart takes my breath away.

BEAUMARCHAIS. Haven't you any remedy? Don't you need a sedative?

MARIE. I know one remedy—I've long been praying to God for it.

BEAUMARCHAIS. You shall have it, and I hope from me.

MARIE. It's all right.

Sophie returns.

SOPHIE. A courier just delivered this letter. He came from Aranjuez.

BEAUMARCHAIS. That's the seal and hand of our ambassador.

SOPHIE. I asked him to dismount and take some refreshment, but he had other dispatches to deliver.

MARIE. Sophie, would you send the maid for a doctor?

SOPHIE. Is something the matter with you? Dear God! What's the matter?

MARIE. You frighten me so that finally I'll hardly dare ask for a glass of water—Sophie!—Brother!—What's in the letter? Look how he's trembling! How downcast he looks!

SOPHIE. Brother, my brother!

Beaumarchais, speechless, throws himself in an armchair and lets the letter fall from his hand.

Brother! (*She picks up the letter and reads it.*)

MARIE. Let me see it! I must—(*She starts to get up.*) Oh! I feel it—it's the end. Sister, I beg you, be merciful, put me out of my misery at once. He's betrayed us!

BEAUMARCHAIS (*springing up*). He's betrayed us! (*Beating his brow and breast.*) Here! here! everything hollow, dead to all feeling, as though a lightning stoke had lamed my senses. Marie! Marie, you are betrayed!—And I'm standing here! Where shall I go? What shall I do?—I see nothing, no way, no salvation! (*He throws himself into the chair.*)

Enter Guilbert.

SOPHIE. Guilbert! Tell us what to do! Help us! We're lost!

GUILBERT. Woman!

SOPHIE. Read it! Read! The ambassador informs our brother that Clavigo has accused him on a capital charge, claiming he stole into his house under a false name, threatened him with a pistol while he was still in bed, and forced him to sign a shameful declaration. And if he doesn't leave Spain immediately they're going to drag him to prison, and the ambassador himself won't be able to obtain his release.

BEAUMARCHAIS (*leaping up*). Let them! Let them drag me to prison. But only away from his corpse, away from the spot where I shall have slaked my thirst. Terrible, raging thirst for his blood possesses every fiber of my body. God in heaven, I thank thee for sending me relief in my unbearable, burning anguish! Refreshment! What a thirst for revenge I feel in my breast! How this glorious feeling, this lust for his blood snatches me away from self-destruction, carries me beyond myself! Revenge! How wonderful I feel! Everything in me longs to seize him, destroy him!

SOPHIE. Brother, you are frightful.

BEAUMARCHAIS. All the better.—No sword, no firearm! I'll throttle him with my bare hands, then the bliss will be all mine! Then I will know that I destroyed him myself.

MARIE. My heart, oh my heart!

BEAUMARCHAIS. I couldn't save you, but you shall be avenged. I'm baying on his trail, my teeth yearn for his flesh, my palate for the taste of his blood. Have I become a raging beast? My pulse is leaping, greed for him makes every muscle in my body twitch. I would eternally hate anyone who poisoned him now and treacherously put him out of the way. Help me find him, Guilbert! Where's Buenco? Help me find him, all of you!

GUILBERT. Save yourself! You're out of your mind.

MARIE. Try to flee, brother!

BEAUMARCHAIS. Not till I catch him! I've got to catch him! Ah, if I only had him there beyond the seas! I'd take him alive and tie him to a stake and dismember him limb by limb. Then I'd roast his limbs before his eyes and eat them with gusto. And I'd serve you women a portion too!

SOPHIE. Take him away, he'll kill his sister.

Enter Buenco.

BUENCO. You must leave at once, sir! I saw it coming. I had my eye on everything. And now they're out after you. You're lost if you don't get out of Madrid at once.

BEAUMARCHAIS. Never! Where's Clavigo?

BUENCO. I don't know.

BEAUMARCHAIS. You do know. I beg you on bended knee: tell me!

SOPHIE. For God's sake, Buenco!

MARIE. Oh! Air! Give me air! (*She sinks down.*) Clavigo!

BUENCO. Help, she's dying!

SOPHIE. Oh God in heaven, do not abandon her! Go, brother, go!

BEAUMARCHAIS (*kneels beside Marie, who in spite of all their efforts does not regain consciousness*). Leave you? How can I leave you?

SOPHIE. Then stay and ruin us all. You've already killed Marie. Oh my poor sister! You're gone, and it's all on account of your brother's rashness.

BEAUMARCHAIS. Stop, sister!

SOPHIE (*mockingly*). Rescuer! Avenger! Save yourself!

BEAUMARCHAIS. Do I deserve that?

SOPHIE. Give her back to me! And then go to prison, go to your martyr's scaffold, shed your blood, and give her back to me!

BEAUMARCHAIS. Sophie!

SOPHIE. Oh, she's gone, she's dead—so preserve yourself for our sake! (*Falling on his neck.*) Brother, my brother, save yourself for us! for our father! Hurry, hurry! It was her fate! She has fulfilled it. There's a God in heaven, leave vengeance to him.

BUENCO. Go, go! Come along with me, I'll hide you until we find a way to get you out of the kingdom.

BEAUMARCHAIS (*falls down beside Marie and kisses her*). Sister!

They tear him away, he grasps Sophie, she frees herself. Marie is carried away, Buenco leaves with Beaumarchais.
Guilbert. A doctor.

SOPHIE (*returning from the next room, where they have taken Marie*). Too late! She's gone, dead!

GUILBERT. Come with me, doctor. See for yourself. It can't be possible.

ACT V

A Street in Front of Guilbert's House. Night
The house door stands open. In front of the door stand three men dressed in black cloaks, with torches. Enter Clavigo wrapped in a cloak, a sword under his arm. A Servant precedes him with a torch.

CLAVIGO. I told you to avoid this street.

SERVANT. We would have had to go a long way around, and you're in such a hurry. It's not far from here that Don Carlos is staying.

CLAVIGO. Torches over there?

SERVANT. Someone's funeral. Come along, sir!

CLAVIGO. Marie's house! A funeral! It makes me shudder in every limb. Go and ask who's being buried.

SERVANT (*goes to the men*). Who is it you're burying?

THE MEN. Marie Beaumarchais.

Clavigo sits down on a curbstone and covers his face.

SERVANT (*returns*). They're burying Marie Beaumarchais.

CLAVIGO (*leaps up*). Did you have to repeat it, you traitor! Repeat that awful word that chills me to the marrow of my bones!

SERVANT. Quiet, sir, come along! Remember the danger you're in!

CLAVIGO. Go to hell! I'm staying here.

SERVANT. O Carlos! If I could only find you! He's out of his mind! (*Exit.*)

Clavigo. The funeral guard in the distance.

CLAVIGO. Dead! Marie is dead! Those torches! her companions in mourning!—It's some trick of magic, a nocturnal vision that's frightening me, holding a mirror before me in which I'm to have a premonition of the result of my treachery.—There's still time! Still time!—I'm trembling, my heart's dissolved in terror. No! No! you mustn't die. I'm coming! I'm coming! Out of my sight, you spirits of night, blocking my path with your terrifying images! (*He runs at them.*) Out of my sight!—They don't move! They're looking around at me! Woe, o woe! They're men like me.—So it's true. True? Can you grasp it?—She's dead—With all the terror of darkness the feeling seizes me: she's dead! There she lies, the flower, at your feet—and you—Have mercy on me, God in heaven—I didn't kill her! Hide yourselves, you stars, don't look down, you who so often saw the miscreant leave this threshold, filled with deepest happiness, walking on air along this very street, his golden dreams set to music, while his sweetheart secretly watched him from behind her grating, filled with blissful expectations! And now you fill this house with grief and lamentation, this scene of your happiness with funeral chants!—Marie! Marie! Take me with you! Take me with you! (*Strains of a funeral march within.*) They're starting out for the grave!—Wait! Wait! Don't close the coffin! Let me look once more! (*He starts toward the house.*) But whom, whom would I dare face? Whom would I dare confront in their frightful pain?—Her friends? Her brother, whose heart is filled with raging grief? (*The music begins again.*) She's calling me! She's calling me! I'm coming!—What fear possesses me? What trembling holds me back?

The music begins again for a third time and continues. The torch-bearers before the door move, three more join them. They form a column to surround the funeral procession now coming out of the house. Six men carry the bier, on which rests a coffin covered by a pall.
Guilbert, Buenco, in deep mourning.

CLAVIGO (*stepping forward*). Halt!

GUILBERT. What voice was that?

CLAVIGO. Halt! (*The bearers stop.*)

BUENCO. Who dares disturb this solemn ceremony?

CLAVIGO. Set it down!

GUILBERT. Ha!

BUENCO. Wretch! Is there no end to your shameless deeds? Isn't your victim safe from you in her coffin?

CLAVIGO. Leave me alone! Don't enrage me! Desperate men are dangerous! I have to see her! (*He throws back the pall. Marie lies dressed in white with folded hands in the casket. Clavigo steps back and hides his face.*)

BUENCO. Do you want to raise her from the dead, so you can kill her again?

CLAVIGO. Miserable mocker!—Marie! (*He falls on his knees beside the bier.*)

Enter Beaumarchais.

BEAUMARCHAIS. Buenco has left me. She's not dead, they say. I've got to see for myself, in spite of the devil! I've got to see her. Torch-bearers! A funeral procession! (*He runs toward them, sees the coffin and falls upon it, speechless. They raise him up, he is faint. Guilbert supports him.*)

CLAVIGO (*rising up on the other side of the bier*). Marie! Marie!

BEAUMARCHAIS. That's his voice! Who's calling Marie? How rage boils in my veins at the sound of that voice!

CLAVIGO. It is I.

Beaumarchais, looking at him wildly and reaching for his sword. Guilbert restrains him.

I'm not afraid of your burning eyes, nor of the point of your sword. Look upon these closed eyes, these folded hands!

BEAUMARCHAIS. *You* show me that? (*He tears himself loose, comes at Clavigo, who draws; they fight, Beaumarchais plunges his sword in Clavigo's breast.*)

CLAVIGO (*sinking*). I thank you, brother! You have married us. (*He sinks down on the coffin.*)

BEAUMARCHAIS (*tearing him away*). Away from that saint, you damned soul!

CLAVIGO. God help me! (*The pall-bearers hold him.*)

BEAUMARCHAIS. Blood! Look up, Marie, look at your wedding gift, then close your eyes forever. See how I have consecrated your resting place with blood, the blood of your murderer! How beautiful! How lovely!

Enter Sophie.

SOPHIE. My God, brother, what's going on?

BEAUMARCHAIS. Come nearer, my dear, and look! I had hoped to strew her bridal bed with roses—see the roses with which I adorn her now on her way to heaven.

SOPHIE. We're lost!

CLAVIGO. Save yourself, you rash man! Get away from here before daybreak. May God, who sent you as avenger, guide your steps!—Sophie, forgive me! Brother—friends—forgive me!

BEAUMARCHAIS. How his streaming blood quenches all the burning vengeance in my heart! How my rage diminishes with his fleeting life! (*Going up to him.*) Die, I forgive you!

CLAVIGO. Give me your hand! And you, Sophie! You too, Buenco!

Buenco hesitates.

SOPHIE. Give him your hand, Buenco!

CLAVIGO. I thank, you, Sophie. You haven't changed. I thank all of you. And if you still hover here about this spot, spirit of my beloved, look down upon us, behold this heavenly kindness, give us your blessing—I'm coming! I'm coming!—Save yourself, brother! Tell me, did she forgive me? How was her dying?

SOPHIE. Her last word was your unfortunate name. She died without bidding us farewell.

CLAVIGO. I'll follow her and bring her your farewell.

Enter Carlos accompanied by Clavigo's servant.

CARLOS. Clavigo? Murderer!

CLAVIGO. Listen to me, Carlos! Here you see the victims of your worldly wisdom—And now, for the sake of the blood with which my life's fast fleeting—save my brother—

CARLOS. My friend! (*To servant:*) Don't stand there! Run for a doctor! (*Exit servant.*)

CLAVIGO. It's no use. Save this unfortunate man, my brother!—Give me your hand, promise me! They have forgiven me, and so I forgive *you.* Bring him to the border and—ah!

CARLOS (*stamping the ground*). Clavigo! Clavigo!

CLAVIGO (*staggering toward the bier, on which they let him down*).

Marie! Your hand! (*He unclasps her fingers and grasps her right hand.*)

SOPHIE (*to Beaumarchais*). Go, you unfortunate man, go!

CLAVIGO. I have her hand! Her cold, dead hand! You are mine—and here's the bridegroom's kiss. Ah!

SOPHIE. He's dying! Save yourself, brother!

Beaumarchais falls about Sophie's neck.
Sophie embraces him, at the same time gesturing for him to go.

STELLA

A Play for Lovers

Translated by Robert M. Browning
and Frank Ryder

Characters

STELLA
CECILIA (at first under the name of MADAME SOMMER)
FERNANDO
LUCY
STEWARD
POSTMISTRESS
ANNIE
CARL
SERVANTS
POSTILLION

Act I

Station on a Postroad
The sound of a posthorn is heard. Postmistress.

POSTMISTRESS. Carl! Carl!

A boy enters.

BOY. What's going on?

POSTMISTRESS. Where the devil were you? Get out there, the stagecoach is coming. Show the passengers in, carry their luggage, get a move on! Making faces again? (*Boy leaves. She calls after him.*) Just you wait, I'll teach you to pout. A tavern-boy has to be cheerful, on his toes. When a rascal like you gets to be master, everything goes to wrack and ruin. If I married again, it would only be to keep that pack of servants in line—it's too much for a woman to manage by herself!

Enter Madame Sommer, Lucy, in traveling costume. Carl.

LUCY (*carrying a portmanteau, to Carl*). Never mind, it's not heavy. Take my mother's package.

POSTMISTRESS. At your service, ladies! You're arriving early. The coach isn't usually ahead of time like this.

LUCY. We had a happy, good-looking young postillion. I'd like to travel all over the world with him. Anyway, there are only two of us and we haven't much luggage.

POSTMISTRESS. If you're looking for a meal, I'm afraid you'll have to wait a bit. Dinner's not ready yet.

MADAME SOMMER. Could I have just a bowl of soup?

LUCY. I'm in no hurry. Meanwhile would you take care of my mother?

POSTMISTRESS. Right away.

LUCY. Be sure it's a good hearty broth!

POSTMISTRESS. The best I have. (*Exit.*)

MADAME SOMMER. You can't stop giving people orders, can you? I should think you would have learned something during this trip. We've always paid for more than we could eat—and in our circumstances—!

LUCY. We've never had to go without.

MADAME SOMMER. But we were close to it.

Enter Postillion.

LUCY. Well, friend, how goes it? Looking for your tip, I suppose.

POSTILLION. Didn't I drive like an express coach?

LUCY. And that means you expressly deserve a big tip, right? I'd make you my private coachman, if only I had horses.

POSTILLION. Horses or no horses, I'm at your service.

LUCY. Here you are!

POSTILLION. Thank you, miss! Not going any farther?

LUCY. We're staying here for the time being.

POSTILLION. Goodbye, then! (*Exit.*)

MADAME SOMMER. I could tell by the look on his face that you gave him too much.

LUCY. Should we send him away grumbling? He was always so friendly. You keep saying I'm self-willed, Mother, but at least I'm not self-seeking.

MADAME SOMMER. Please don't misunderstand me, Lucy. I respect your frankness, as well as your good humor and generosity, but there's a place for those virtues—they don't belong everywhere.

LUCY. Mama, I really like this little town. And the house across the way—does that belong to the lady whose companion I'm to be?

MADAME SOMMER. I'm glad if you like the place that fate has assigned you.

LUCY. It's a bit quiet perhaps. I can tell that already. It's like the marketplace on Sunday. But the lady has a lovely garden, and they say she's a fine woman. We'll see how we get along. What are you looking around for, Mother?

MADAME SOMMER. Never mind, Lucy! You're a lucky girl, not to be reminded of anything! Oh, it used to be so different! Nothing is more painful to me than to enter one of these posthouses.

LUCY. No matter where you are you find something to torment yourself with!

MADAME SOMMER. And reason to do so too. How very different it was, my dear, when your father used to travel with me. That was the best time of our lives, with the whole world open to us, the first years of our marriage. Everything had the charm of newness for me then. Oh, to lie in his arms, to fly past all those thousands of sights and sounds! Every little detail interested me, because of *his* spirit, *his* love——

LUCY. I like traveling too.

MADAME SOMMER. And after a hot day's journey, when we found some tavern even poorer than this one, after annoying breakdowns and bad roads in winter, and when we enjoyed the simplest comforts together, sitting on a wooden bench, eating an omelet and boiled potatoes—it was different then!

LUCY. I think it's really time to forget him.

MADAME SOMMER. Have you any idea what that means: to forget? Dear girl, thank God you haven't yet lost anything that can't be replaced. From the moment I knew that he had left me, all my joy in life was gone. I was in the grip of despair. I had lost my sense of self; I had lost my god. I can scarcely recall the state I was in.

LUCY. I only remember that I used to sit on your bed and cry, because you were crying. It was in the green room, on the little bed. Losing that room was what grieved me most, when we had to sell the house.

MADAME SOMMER. You were only seven. You couldn't know what you were losing.

Enter Annie, with the soup. Postmistress. Carl.

ANNIE. Here's your soup, m'am.

MADAME SOMMER. Thank you, my dear! (*To Postmistress*:) Is that your daughter?

POSTMISTRESS. My stepdaughter, m'am. But she's a good girl and makes up for not having children of my own.

MADAME SOMMER. You're in mourning?

POSTMISTRESS. For my husband. He died three months ago. We didn't even have three years together.

MADAME SOMMER. You seem to be bearing up fairly well.

POSTMISTRESS. Oh, m'am, people like us have as little time to weep as we do to pray, unfortunately. Weekdays or Sundays, it's all the same. Unless the preacher just happens to hit on a certain text or you hear a funeral hymn. Carl, bring some napkins! Set this end of the table.

LUCY. Who owns the house across the way?

POSTMISTRESS. Our baroness. A lovely, friendly lady.

MADAME SOMMER. I'm glad to hear a neighbor confirm the assurances we were given long before we arrived here. My daughter is to stay with her and be her companion.

POSTMISTRESS. Then I wish you the very best.

LUCY. I hope I like her.

POSTMISTRESS. You'd be a strange person indeed if you didn't enjoy her company.

LUCY. So much the better. If I have to defer to someone else's wishes, my heart and will have to be in it, otherwise it won't work out.

POSTMISTRESS. Well, well! We'll have occasion to talk about that again before long, and you can tell me whether I was right or not. Anyone who lives in the company of our dear lady is fortunate. When my own daughter is a bit older she must enter her service at least for a few years; it will stand the girl in good stead all her life.

ANNIE. Just wait till you see her! She's so sweet! You can't believe how anxious she is to see you. She is quite fond of me too. Don't you want to call on her? I'll go with you.

LUCY. I have to freshen up first, and eat something.

ANNIE. May I go over, Mama? I want to tell the baroness that her young lady has arrived.

POSTMISTRESS. Yes, go ahead!

MADAME SOMMER. And tell her, my dear, that we'll call as soon as we have eaten. (*Annie leaves*.)

POSTMISTRESS. The girl's extremely fond of her. And she *is* the best soul in the world. She loves children. She teaches them how to sing and make all kinds of things. She takes peasant girls as servants until they've acquired some skill, then she looks for a good position for them. That's the way she spends her time since her husband left. I can't understand how she can be so unhappy and still so friendly, so kind.

MADAME SOMMER. Isn't she a widow?

POSTMISTRESS. Heaven only knows! Her husband, the baron, left three years ago and no one has seen or heard of him since. She loved him more than anything in the world. My own husband couldn't stop talking about them, once he got started. And he was right. I say myself there's not a loving spirit like that left in the world. Every year, on the day she last saw him, she receives no one, just shuts herself up in the house. Whenever she speaks of him it pierces your heart.

MADAME SOMMER. Poor, unhappy woman!

POSTMISTRESS. There's a lot more that could be said about it, too.

MADAME SOMMER. What do you mean?

POSTMISTRESS. I don't like to discuss it.

MADAME SOMMER. Yes, please tell me.

POSTMISTRESS. If you promise not to mention my name, I suppose I can. They moved here over eight years ago and bought the manor. No one knew them. We all called them the lord and lady and took him for an officer who had got rich in foreign service and now wanted to retire. She was still very young, no more than sixteen, and beautiful as an angel.

LUCY. So now she's not more than twenty-four?

POSTMISTRESS. She's had trouble enough for her age. She had a child that died in infancy. It's buried in the garden; no stone, just a grassy mound. Since the master left she's set up a kind of hermitage there and ordered her own grave at the same spot. My departed husband was well along in years and no great one for sentiment, but there was nothing he would rather talk about than the bliss of that pair, as long as they were living together. It changed a person completely, he used to say, just to see how they loved each other.

MADAME SOMMER. My heart goes out to her.

POSTMISTRESS. But you know how things are. They say the baron had strange principles. At any rate, he never went to church, and people who have no religion have no God and conform to no kind of order. Suddenly we heard the baron had left. He'd gone on a journey and simply didn't return.

MADAME SOMMER (*to herself*). The very image of my own fate.

POSTMISTRESS. Of course everyone was talking about it. Just at that time, three years ago last September, I came here as a young wife. Everyone had a different story. Some even whispered that they'd never been married. But don't give me away. They say he's a fine gentleman, that he eloped with her, and all kinds of things. Well, if a girl takes a step like that, she'll regret it all her life.

Enter Annie.

ANNIE. The baroness is anxious for you to come over, miss. She only wants to see you and speak to you for a moment.

LUCY. I can't go in these clothes.

POSTMISTRESS. Yes, go ahead. I give you my word, she won't mind.

LUCY. Will you go with me, Annie?

ANNIE. I'd love to!

MADAME SOMMER. Just a word, Lucy! (*The Postmistress withdraws.*) See to it that you don't give us away! Say nothing about our social position, about our circumstances. And treat her with respect.

LUCY. Oh, I know. My father was a merchant, went to America, died there, and for that reason our circumstances—I know, I've told that fairy tale often enough. (*Aloud:*) Didn't you want to take a little rest? You should. I'm sure our hostess can give you a room with a bed.

POSTMISTRESS. I have a nice quiet room facing the garden. (*To Lucy:*) I hope you like the baroness. (*Lucy leaves with Annie.*)

MADAME SOMMER. My daughter's a bit forward.

POSTMISTRESS. That's her age. Those proud seas will run low in time.

MADAME SOMMER. More's the pity.

POSTMISTRESS. I'll show you to your room, madame, if I may. (*Both leave.*)

Sound of a posthorn. Fernando, in officer's uniform. Servant.

SERVANT. Shall I have them hitch up again right away and load your baggage?

FERNANDO. Bring it in here, I told you. We're not going any farther.

SERVANT. No farther? But you said—

FERNANDO. I say, get me a room and take my things to it.

Exit Servant.

FERNANDO (*stepping to the window*). So I see it all again? This heavenly prospect! So I see it again? The scene of all my bliss! How still the house lies! Not a window open. The verandah where we sat so often, deserted! Mark this, Fernando, the cloistered atmosphere of her dwelling-place and how it bodes well for your hopes! Could it be that Fernando is the theme of her thoughts, the occupation of her solitude? Has he deserved that?

Oh, it seems to me as though I were awaking to life again after a long, cold, joyless sleep of death—everything is so new to me, so full of meaning. The trees, the spring, everything, everything! The fountains flowed in the very same way when we used to look out of the window together, lost in thought, thousands of times, both of us watching the flowing water. For me, its sound is a melody, a melody of reminiscence.

And she? She will be just as she was. No, Stella, you haven't changed; my heart tells me so. How it beats for you! But I won't, I mustn't! I must come to my senses first, convince myself that I am really here, not the victim of that dream that has so often led me, asleep and awake, from distant lands to this very spot. Stella! Stella! I'm coming! Do you feel my presence? Oh to be in your arms, to forget everything!

And if you are hovering near me, dear shade of my unhappy wife, forgive me, leave me! You are gone, so let me forget you, in the arms of this angel let me forget everything, my fate, all I have lost, my sorrows, my remorse.—I am so close to her and yet so far—And in one moment—No, I can't, I can't! I must come to my senses first, or I'll lie at her feet, unable to breathe.

Enter Postmistress.

POSTMISTRESS. Would you care to dine, sir?

FERNANDO. Is there anything ready?

POSTMISTRESS. Oh yes, we're only waiting for a young lady who has gone over to call on the baroness.

FERNANDO. And how is the baroness?

POSTMISTRESS. Do you know her?

FERNANDO. Years ago I went there occasionally. What is her husband doing?

POSTMISTRESS. Heaven knows. He left and didn't come back.

FERNANDO. He left?

POSTMISTRESS. That's right. Abandoned the dear soul. God forgive him!

FERNANDO. She'll have found comfort elsewhere.

POSTMISTRESS. Do you think so? Then you can't know her very well. She's been living like a nun, quite withdrawn, ever since I've known her. Almost no one comes to see her, neither strangers nor neighbors. She lives with her servants, befriends the village children, and is always kind and cheerful, in spite of her inward sorrow.

FERNANDO. I'd like to call on her.

POSTMISTRESS. Yes, do. Sometimes she invites us, the mayor's wife, the wife of the pastor and myself, and discusses all kinds of things with us. Of course we are careful never to mention her husband. But it did happen just once. God knows how we felt when she began to speak of him, to praise him, to weep. I tell you, sir, we all wept like babies and could hardly stop.

FERNANDO (*to himself*). Did you deserve so much from her?—(*Aloud:*) Has my servant been shown a room?

POSTMISTRESS. One flight up. Carl, show the gentleman the room!

Fernando leaves with the boy.
Enter Lucy and Annie.

POSTMISTRESS. Well, what do you say?

LUCY. A dear little woman. I'll get along well with her; you didn't praise her too highly. She would hardly let me leave. I had to give her my solemn promise to return right after our meal and bring my mother and our things.

POSTMISTRESS. Just as I thought! Would you like to eat now? A tall, handsome officer has just arrived and will join you, if you're not afraid of him.

LUCY. Not at all. I like soldiers better than other men. At least they don't pretend—you can tell the good ones from the bad right from the very beginning. Is my mother sleeping?

POSTMISTRESS. I don't know.

LUCY. I must go and look after her. (*Exit.*)

POSTMISTRESS. Carl! You've forgotten the salt-cellar again. Do you call that rinsed? Look at those glasses! I'd break them over your head if you were worth as much as they are!

Enter Fernando.

POSTMISTRESS. The young lady is back. She'll come to the table right away.

FERNANDO. Who is she?

POSTMISTRESS. I don't know. She seems to be a person of quality, but without means. She is to be the companion of the baroness.

FERNANDO. Is she young?

POSTMISTRESS. Very young. And saucy. Her mother is also here, upstairs.

Enter Lucy.

LUCY. How do you do!

FERNANDO. I'm charmed to find such a beautiful table companion.

Lucy bows.

POSTMISTRESS. Sit here, miss. And you here, sir.

FERNANDO. Aren't we to have the honor of your company?

POSTMISTRESS. If I stop, everything stops. (*Exit.*)

FERNANDO. Good then, a tête-à-tête!

LUCY. The table's between us, which is the way I like it.

FERNANDO. So you have made up your mind to live with the baroness?

LUCY. I had to!

FERNANDO. It seems to me you should be able to find a companion more entertaining than she is.

LUCY. For me, that's not the point.

FERNANDO. Am I to believe that just because of your honest face?

LUCY. Sir, I see you're like all men!

FERNANDO. That is to say?

LUCY. Arrogant from the start. You men think you're indispensable, but I don't know about that—I've managed to get along so far without men.

FERNANDO. Your father is no longer living?

LUCY. I can hardly remember that I had one. I was young when he left us to go to America. His ship sank, so we heard.

FERNANDO. And you seem so indifferent?

LUCY. What else can I be? He scarcely did me any favors, and though I forgive him for leaving us—what is dearer to a man than his freedom?—still I wouldn't want to be in my mother's place, dying of grief.

FERNANDO. So you are left without help and protection?

LUCY. We don't need it. True, our means are getting smaller every day, but on the other hand, I'm getting bigger every day, and I'm not afraid of being unable to support my mother.

FERNANDO. I'm amazed at your courage!

LUCY. It grows on one, my dear sir. When one so often fears the end has come and then finds oneself rescued again, that gives you confidence!

FERNANDO. And you can't impart any of that to your mother?

LUCY. Unfortunately, she's the loser, not I. I'm grateful to my father for having put me in the world. I love life and take pleasure in living. But she placed all her hopes in him and sacrificed to him the flower of her youth and now finds herself abandoned, suddenly abandoned—Oh, it must be terrible to feel abandoned!—I haven't lost anything yet; I can't really say.—You seem thoughtful.

FERNANDO. Yes, my dear, to live is to lose. (*Getting up*:) But one gains too. God keep you in good spirits! (*He takes her hand.*) You truly astonish me. Oh, my child, how happy——My hopes, my joys, the world has often—It's always—Then—

LUCY. What do you mean?

FERNANDO. All the best! My best, my warmest wishes for your happiness! (*Leaves.*)

LUCY. What a strange person! But he seems nice enough.

Act II

Stella. Servant.

Stella. Run over, quickly! Tell her I'm expecting her.

Servant. She promised she'd come right away.

Stella. But you see she hasn't. I like the girl very much. Go! And tell her to bring her mother with her.

Exit servant.

Stella. I can hardly wait till she comes. It's like waiting and hoping for a new dress to arrive. Stella, what a child you are! But why shouldn't I love someone?—I need a lot, a lot, to fill my heart! A lot? Poor Stella! A lot? —When he still loved you, when he still lay with his head in your lap, and the look in his eyes filled your soul, and—Oh God in heaven, mysterious are Thy ways! I used to lift my eyes from him as he kissed me, lift them up to you, oh Lord, my heart burning on his, drinking in his soul with trembling lips, and I would look up to You with tears of bliss and say with a full heart: Grant that we remain happy, Father! You have made us so happy!—But, it was not Your will—(*She falls into thought for a moment, then starts and presses her hands to her heart.*) No, Fernando, no, that was not a reproach!

Enter Lucy and Madame Sommer.

Stella. There she is! Dear girl, now you are mine.—Madame, I thank you for the confidence with which you entrust this treasure to my keeping. This willful little creature, this free spirit. Oh, I've already learned something from you, Lucy!

Madame Sommer. I see you realize what I am bringing you and leaving in your care.

Stella (*after looking at Madame Sommer for a moment*). Forgive me! I have learned your story. I know you are of good family. But I am surprised when I see you in person. From the first moment I feel trust and respect for you.

Madame Sommer. My dear lady—

Stella. Say nothing. What my heart feels, my tongue gladly confesses. I hear you're not well. How are you feeling? Please sit down!

Madame Sommer. Don't worry, my dear lady. This springtime journey with its changing sights, this blessed pure air that has so often renewed my soul, all this has had such a soothing effect on me that I welcome even the memory of past joys, and I see a reflection of the golden days of youth and love dawning within me.

Stella. Ah, those days! the first days of love!—No, you've not fled back to heaven, golden age! You still enclose every heart in those moments when the first flower of love unfolds.

MADAME SOMMER (*grasping Stella's hand*). How splendid! How sweet!

STELLA. Your face is gleaming like an angel's, your cheeks are aglow.

MADAME SOMMER. Oh, and my heart! How it opens! How it swells in your presence!

STELLA. You have loved. Thank God! a creature who understands me! Who can sympathize with me! Who does not gaze coldly on my sorrow.—We can't help it if this is the way we are. I have done everything! I have tried everything!—But what good did it do?—I wanted only one thing, not the world, just that one thing. Oh, the one we love is everywhere, and everything's for the one we love.

MADAME SOMMER. Your heaven is in your heart.

STELLA. Before I realize what I am doing, I picture him in my mind. The way he would turn and look at me, whatever company we were in. The way he came running across the meadow and threw himself into my arms at the garden gate.—And yes, I saw him there as he left—but he came back, came back to my arms——If I turn my thoughts to the busy world outside, there he is! When I used to sit in my box at the theater I was sure, wherever he might be, whether I could see him or not, that he noticed my every movement and loved me: the way I stood up, the way I sat down! I felt that the nodding of the plumes on my hat attracted him more than all the shining eyes around him, that all the music was only the tune to the eternal song in his heart: "Stella! Stella! How dear to me you are!"

LUCY. Can people really love each other so much?

STELLA. You ask, child? I can't give you an answer.—But what have I been talking to you about? Trifles, weighty trifles.—It's true, one's only a grown-up child, and yet it's so sweet—just the way children hide behind their pinafores and cry peek-a-boo so that you will look for them.——How it fills our heart when we have been hurt and are quite determined to leave the one we love, and what contortions of spiritual strength we must exert when we return to his presence! How resolve rises and falls in our bosoms! And then it all collapses at *one* look, at *one* touch of his hand!

MADAME SOMMER. How happy you are! Your life is still filled with a sensc of pure and pristine youth.

STELLA. A thousand years of tears and grief could not cancel out the joys of those first glances, of that trembling and stammering, of drawing close and turning away, of the first fleeting, fiery kiss, the first calming embrace—Madame, you're growing faint! My dear, what is it?

MADAME SOMMER. Men! Men!

STELLA. They make us happy and they make us miserable. They fill our hearts with premonitions of bliss, with new feelings and hopes we've never known before; they make our souls swell when their burning desire communicates itself to our every nerve. How everything in me responded, trembling, when he would pour out a world of suffering on my bosom, weeping uncontrollably! I begged him to spare himself—and me. In vain. He persisted until my very marrow was afire with the flames that were consuming him. I was a mere girl, and that girl became pure heart from top to toe, pure feeling. And where in the world, I ask you, is there a place now for such a creature, a place where she can live and breathe?

MADAME SOMMER. We believe what men tell us! In moments of passion they deceive themselves—is it any wonder they deceive *us*?

STELLA. Dear lady, an idea has suddenly occurred to me: Let us be for each other what they should have been for us! Let us remain together! Give me your hand!—From this moment onward I will not leave you!

LUCY. That's impossible.

STELLA. And why, Lucy?

MADAME SOMMER. My daughter feels—

STELLA. Surely not that I would be doing this as a favor to her? Oh, think what a favor you'd be doing *me* if you stayed! I mustn't be alone! My dear, I've tried everything—I raise poultry, I have dogs and a pet deer, I teach little girls to knit and embroider, just so I won't be alone, just to see someone besides myself, something alive and growing. And then sometimes, when I'm lucky, when on a fine spring morning a kindly deity seems to have lifted the burden from my bosom, when I wake up peacefully and see the sun shining on my blossoming trees, and feel the energy and the inclination to undertake the day's tasks, then I regain my courage, then I whisk about a while, doing this and arranging that, giving orders to the servants, and in my heart's joy I thank heaven aloud for those happy hours.

MADAME SOMMER. Oh yes, my dear lady, I know what you mean! To be busy and useful is a gift from heaven, a remedy for hearts unlucky in love.

STELLA. Remedy? Compensation, perhaps, but not a remedy. Something instead of what one has lost, but not the thing itself. Lost love! where is there a remedy for that?—Oh, sometimes when I am lost in thought, conjuring up sweet dreams of times gone by, picturing a future filled with hope, walking up and down in my garden in the dim moonlight, then I suddenly remember! remember that I am alone. I stretch out my arms in vain to the four winds, pronounce in vain love's magic charm with such urgency, such overflowing intensity, that it seems I should draw the moon from the sky—but I'm alone, no voice answers from the flowers and the stars shine down cold and gentle on my torment! And then, suddenly, my child's grave at my feet—

MADAME SOMMER. You had a child?

STELLA. Yes, my dear. This happiness too God gave me, the briefest taste of it, only to prepare me for a cup of lifelong bitterness.—When some barefoot country child comes running up to me with big innocent eyes and wants to kiss my hand, it hurts me to the marrow of my bones! My Minna would be just that age, I think to myself. Anxiously and lovingly I lift the child up, kiss it again and again; my heart is torn, tears pour from my eyes, and I take flight!

LUCY. But you've also been spared a great deal of trouble.

STELLA (*smiles and pats her on the shoulder*). How can I still be capable of feeling? How is it possible that those terrible moments did not kill me?—There my child lay, in front of me, nipped in the bud! I stood there, my heart turned to stone, without pain, without consciousness—just stood there! Then the nurse picked her up, pressed her to her bosom, and suddenly cried: She's alive!—I fell about her neck, bent over the child with streaming tears—knelt at the nurse's feet—But the woman was mistaken! She lay there dead and I lay beside her in utter, raving despair. (*Stella throws herself into an armchair.*)

MADAME SOMMER. You mustn't think about those scenes of sadness.

STELLA. No! It does me good, such good, to open my heart again, to talk freely of all that oppresses me.—Oh, and when I start to talk about *him*, the one who meant everything to me! He—you should see his portrait!—his portrait—I always think a person's image is the best text for anything one can feel or say about him.

LUCY. I'm curious.

STELLA (*opens her boudoir and shows them in*). Here, my dears, here!

MADAME SOMMER. Oh God!

STELLA. Yes! Yes! And still not the thousandth part of what he was. This brow, these black eyes, these brown locks, this earnestness—But the painter did not know how to express the love, the friendliness that poured forth when he opened his soul! My heart alone knows that!

LUCY. Madame, I'm amazed!

STELLA. A true man!

LUCY. I must tell you, m'am, that today over in the posthouse I dined with an officer who resembles this gentleman. It must be the same man! I'd bet my life on it.

STELLA. Today? You must be mistaken!

LUCY. Yes, today. Except that he was older, and burned darker from the sun. It's the same man, the very same!

STELLA (*pulling the bellcord*). Lucy, my heart's bursting! I'm going over!

LUCY. It wouldn't be proper.

STELLA. Proper? O my heart!—

Enter servant.

STELLA. William, go over to the posthouse right away! There's an officer there who's supposed to be—who is—Lucy, you tell him—He's to come over here.

LUCY. Did you know the master?

SERVANT. As well as I know myself.

LUCY. Then go to the posthouse; there's an officer there who looks remarkably like him. See if I'm mistaken. I'll swear it's him.

STELLA. Tell him to come, come at once! at once!—Oh, if I had all that behind me!—If only I had him in my—in—But of course you're deceiving yourself, Stella. It's not possible.—Leave me, my dears, leave my alone! (*She closes herself into the boudoir.*)

LUCY. Mother! What's the matter? You're so pale!

MADAME SOMMER. This is the last day of my life! My heart can't stand it. Everything, everything at once.

LUCY. Good God!

MADAME SOMMER. Her husband—the picture—the one she's waiting for—her beloved—That's *my* husband! Your father!

LUCY. Mother, o Mother!

MADAME SOMMER. And he's here! In a few minutes he'll sink into her arms! And we? Lucy, we must leave.

LUCY. We'll go wherever you say.

MADAME SOMMER. At once!

LUCY. Come into the garden. I'll go over to the posthouse. If the coach hasn't left, we can slip away—while she, drunk with joy—

MADAME SOMMER. —Is embracing him in the bliss of reunion—him! And I, at the very moment I find him again—forever, forever!

Enter Fernando, Servant.

SERVANT. This way! Don't you remember her boudoir? She's beside herself! Oh, to think that you're back!

Fernando goes past Lucy and Madame Sommer without noticing them.

MADAME SOMMER. It's him! It's him!—I'm lost!

ACT III

Stella, entering joyously with Fernando.

STELLA (*speaking to the walls*). He's here again! Do you see him? He's here again! (*Stepping in front of a picture of Venus.*) Do you see him, my Goddess? He's here again! How often I have paced up and down before you, fool that I am, and wept and moaned. He's here again! I can't believe my senses. I've so often looked at you, Goddess, and he was not here. Now you are here and he is here.—O my dear, my dear, you were gone such a long time! But now you're here! (*She throws her arms about his neck.*) You're here! I don't want to feel anything, see anything, know anything but that you're here!

FERNANDO. Stella, my Stella! (*Embracing her.*) God in heaven, you've given me back my tears!

STELLA. My only love!

FERNANDO. Stella, let me drink in your dear breath again, your breath—all the airs of the heavens were empty and stale in comparison!

STELLA. Dear man!

FERNANDO. Breathe new life and love of life into this parched, storm-torn, ravaged breast again! Breathe into me out of the fullness of your heart! (*Kisses her passionately.*)

STELLA. Dear Fernando!

FERNANDO. Revive me! Refresh me!—Here, where you breathe, everything hovers in youthful abundance. Here, love and lasting faithfulness would bind the thirsting wanderer.

STELLA. Dreamer!

FERNANDO. You cannot imagine what heaven's dew means to him who thirsts, to him who has returned from drear, sandy wastes to your bosom.

STELLA. And the bliss of the poor soul who has found again her one lost lamb and presses it to her breast?

FERNANDO (*at her feet*). My Stella!

STELLA. Get up, Fernando, get up! I can't bear to see you kneeling.

FERNANDO. Don't forbid me! Do I not always kneel before you? Does not my heart always bow to you? You, who are infinite love and kindness!

STELLA. I have you again!—I don't recognize myself anymore. I don't understand myself. But what difference does it make?

FERNANDO. I feel as I did in the first moments of our rapture. I hold you in my arms, I draw certainty of love from your lips; I reel, I ask myself, amazed, whether I'm awake or dreaming.

STELLA. Ah, Fernando, I can tell: you've not become a whit more sensible.

FERNANDO. God forbid!—But these moments of happiness in your arms make me a good person again, make me devout again. Stella, I can pray because I'm happy.

STELLA. God forgive you for being such a deceiver and yet so good—God forgive you; He made you that way—so fickle and so faithful! The moment I hear the sound of your voice again, I immediately think: that's Fernando, and he loves nothing in the world but me!

FERNANDO. And when I gaze into your dear blue eyes, and looking at them lose myself in thought, then I think that all the time I was away no image dwelt there but mine.

STELLA. And you are not wrong.

FERNANDO. No?

STELLA. I would tell you if you were! Didn't I confess to you in the first days of my full love all the little passions that had moved my heart? And didn't you love me all the more for it?

FERNANDO. Angel!

STELLA. Why do you look at me like that? I've gotten older, haven't I? Suffering has brushed the bloom from my cheeks, hasn't it?

FERNANDO. My rose! Sweet flower! Stella!—Why do you shake your head?

STELLA. That we can love you men so much!—That we do not blame you for the grief you cause us!

FERNANDO (*stroking her hair*). Has it given you grey hair, I wonder? Anyway, you are lucky to be so blond. I'd say you haven't lost any. (*He pulls the comb out of her hair; it tumbles down on her shoulders.*)

STELLA. You're bold, aren't you?

FERNANDO (*wrapping his arm in her hair*). Rinaldo back in his old chains again!

Enter Servant.

SERVANT. My lady!

STELLA. What's the matter? You look so cold and cross. You know I hate such looks when I'm in a good mood.

SERVANT. I'm sorry, m'am.—The two visitors are about to leave.

STELLA. What? Leave?

SERVANT. Yes, m'am. I saw the daughter go to the posthouse, then come back and speak to her mother. I went over and asked the postmistress. She said they had ordered a special carriage, because the mail coach had already left. I talked with them. The mother begged me with tears in her eyes to bring their baggage secretly, and to wish your ladyship a thousand blessings. She said they couldn't stay.

FERNANDO. Is it the lady who arrived today with her daughter?

STELLA. I meant to take the daughter as my companion and keep her mother here too.—Oh, why do they have to cause confusion at such a moment?

FERNANDO. What can be the matter with them?

STELLA. Heaven knows, I don't—and I don't want to! I would hate to lose them—just when I have you back, Fernando! It would kill me at a moment like this! You talk to them, Fernando. Now, right away!—Have the mother come over here, William. (*Exit servant.*) Talk to her, tell her she's free to choose—I'm going out in the garden, Fernando. Follow me! Soon!—Sing for him, you nightingales!

FERNANDO. My dearest love!

STELLA (*embracing him*). You'll come soon?

FERNANDO. Right away. (*Stella leaves.*)

FERNANDO (*alone*). Ye angels in heaven! How serene and free everything becomes in her presence!—Fernando, can you recognize yourself? Everything that oppressed my heart is gone, every care, every anxious recollection of what was—and what is to be—. Or—are you already stealing back?—And yet, when I look at you, Stella, hold your hand, all else flees, every other memory is blotted out!

Enter Steward.

STEWARD (*kissing Fernando's hand*). You're back again?

FERNANDO (*withdrawing his hand*). I am.

STEWARD. Please, don't stop me, don't stop me! Oh my dear master!

FERNANDO. Are you happy?

STEWARD. My wife's alive, I have two children—and you are back.

FERNANDO. How well have you been managing things?

STEWARD. So well that I'm ready to account to you at once. You'll be amazed at the way we've improved the estate.—But may I ask, how you have been getting along?

FERNANDO. Hush!—Or shall I tell you everything? Don't I owe that to you, old accomplice of my follies?

STEWARD. Thank the stars you weren't the leader of a band of gypsies. At a word from you I would have set fire to whole villages.

FERNANDO. You shall hear everything!

STEWARD. Your wife? Your daughter?

FERNANDO. I never found them. I didn't dare enter the city but I know from reliable sources that she put her trust in a merchant, a false friend, who talked her out of the investments I left to her, promising her a better return, and cheated her of everything. Under the pretext of moving to the country she left the area and disappeared, probably to eke out a meager existence by her own handiwork and that of her daughter. As you know, she had character and courage enough to undertake something like that.

STEWARD. And now you are back! We'll forgive you for staying away so long.

FERNANDO. I have been all over.

STEWARD. If I hadn't felt so comfortable at home with my wife and my two children, I would envy you the way you ventured back into the world again. Now are you going to stay with us?

FERNANDO. God willing!

STEWARD. When all's said and done, everything's still the same, no different, no better.

FERNANDO. Is there anyone who could forget the old days!

STEWARD. That brought us such joy but also such pain. I remember it all so clearly: how we found Cecilia so charming, paid such court to her, couldn't get rid of our youthful freedom quickly enough.

FERNANDO. It really was a beautiful, happy time!

STEWARD. And how she presented us with a lively vivacious little girl but at the same time lost some of her own vivacity and charm.

FERNANDO. Spare me this biography.

STEWARD. And how we looked around here and there, back and forth, until we finally met this angel, how there was no more talk, then, of coming and going but rather of having to decide which one we were going to make unhappy; how convenient we found it when an opportunity arose to sell the property, how we left after many losses, took the angel away with us, and sent her into exile here, a young thing unaware of the world and of herself.

FERNANDO. You're still as much of a moralizer and gossip as ever, it seems.

STEWARD. Didn't I have plenty of opportunity to learn? Was I not the confidant of your conscience? When you yearned to get away from here in turn, I don't know whether from sheer longing to find your wife and daughter again or partly from some secret unrest, and when I had to be of assistance to you in more than one way—

FERNANDO. That's enough for now.

STEWARD. Just stay with us, then all will be well. (*Exit.*)

Enter Servant.

SERVANT. Madame Sommer!

FERNANDO. Show her in. (*Exit servant.*)

FERNANDO (*alone*). This woman depresses me. There's never any pure happiness in the world, ever. This woman! Her daughter's show of bravery was disturbing enough; how will the mother's grief affect me?

Enter Madame Sommer.

FERNANDO (*to himself*). My God! Just to see her reminds me of my trespasses! Oh heart, my heart! Why, if you are capable of feeling and acting thus, do you not also have the strength to forgive yourself for what has happened?—A shadow cast by the figure of my wife! Oh, is there any place where I don't see it? (*Aloud*:) Madame!

MADAME SOMMER. What do you want of me, sir?

FERNANDO. I hoped you would be willing to become the companion of Stella and myself. Please sit down!

MADAME SOMMER. The presence of a miserable person is a burden to the happy, and alas! a happy person is even more of a burden to the miserable.

FERNANDO. I don't understand. Can you have failed to see what Stella is? Pure love, divine?

MADAME SOMMER. Sir, I intended to leave in secret. Let me go—I must. Believe me, I have my reasons! Please, let me go!

FERNANDO (*to himself*). That voice! That figure! (*Aloud*:) Madame! (*He turns aside.*) God, it's my wife! (*Aloud*:) Excuse me! (*He hurries away.*)

MADAME SOMMER (*alone*). He recognized me! God, I thank Thee for giving me strength in such a moment! Is this me, a woman defeated and torn asunder, who displays such quiet courage in a crisis? Kind, eternal Provider, You deprive our heart of nothing without keeping it for us in our hour of need.

Fernando returns.

FERNANDO (*to himself*). Does she recognize me? (*Aloud*:) I beg you, Madame, I implore you, be frank with me, open your heart!

MADAME SOMMER. I would have to tell you my whole sad story, and how could you be in the mood for grief and sorrows on a day when all the joys of life have been restored to you? And when you have restored all the joys of life to the worthiest of women! No, please, sir, do not insist!

FERNANDO. I beg you!

MADAME SOMMER. I would gladly spare you and myself! The memory of the first happy days of my life are a source of mortal anguish to me.

FERNANDO. You have not always been unhappy?

MADAME SOMMER. No. Otherwise I wouldn't be so unhappy now. (*After a pause, more freely*:) The days of my youth were bright and gay. I don't know what it was about me that so fascinated men; many courted me. For a few I felt friendship, attraction, but there was none I thought I wanted to spend my life with. And so those happy days went by like a rose chain of delights, one day joining friendly hands with the next. Still, I felt that something was lacking. When I looked more deeply into life, dimly foreseeing the joy and sorrow that lie in store for us, then I wanted a husband whose hand would always guide me, who, in exchange for the love my youthful heart could give him, would be my friend and protector when I grew old, taking the place of my parents, whom I had forsaken for him.

FERNANDO. And then?

MADAME SOMMER. I found the man! I found the one on whom from the first days of our acquaintance I set all my hopes! His vivacity of spirit seemed united with such loyalty of heart that my own heart soon disclosed itself to him. I gave him my friendship and, alas, how quickly then, my love. Dear Lord, when he rested on my bosom how grateful he seemed to be for the place You had made for him to lay his head! How he fled from the demands of business and the whirl of social distractions back to my arms, and in times of sadness what comfort I found on his breast!

FERNANDO. And what could it be that disturbed this sweet relationship?

MADAME SOMMER. Nothing endures. Oh, he loved me, loved me just as surely as I loved him. There was a time when his sole thought was to see me happy, to make me happy. It was the freest time of life, the first years of a relationship when one may now and then be troubled, but more by a little pettishness, a little boredom than by anything really wrong. Oh, he led me along that pleasant path and then he left me alone in a dreary, fearful wilderness.

FERNANDO (*growing more and more uneasy*). But how could he? His principles, his heart?

MADAME SOMMER. Can women know what beats in the breast of men?—I did not notice that for him everything was gradually becoming—what can I say?—not indifferent! one can't call it that. He still loved me! But he needed more than my love. I saw that I would have to share his desires, perhaps with another woman. I did not withhold my reproaches, and finally—

FERNANDO. You mean, he was capable of—

MADAME SOMMER. He left me. There is no name for my misery. All my hopes dashed in a moment! And in the very moment when I hoped to harvest the fruit of the bloom I had sacrificed—abandoned! abandoned! All the human heart depends on: love, trust, honor, position, increasing wealth, the prospect of a numerous, lovingly nurtured family, everything collapsed before my eyes, and I—and the unfortunate pledge of our love, our daughter—Numbing grief followed upon raging pain and my heart, worn out with weeping and despair, sank down exhausted. The financial misfortunes that struck me, deserted as I was, I hardly heeded or felt, until finally—

FERNANDO. He is a guilty man!

MADAME SOMMER (*with suppressed melancholy*). No, he is not—I feel sorry for a man who gives himself up to a girl.

FERNANDO. Madame!

MADAME SOMMER (*speaking with gentle irony, to conceal her emotion*). It's true! I regard him as a captive. Men say so themselves. A man is drawn from his world over into ours, a world with which he really has nothing in common. He deceives himself for a while, but woe unto us when his eyes are opened!—In the end, all I could be for him was a good housewife. One, to be sure, who made every effort to please him and care for him, who devoted all her days to the well-being of her house, her child, but had to deal with so many petty details that her heart and head were often distracted and she could not be an entertaining companion—a man with his vivacity and spirit was bound to find me shallow. He is not guilty.

FERNANDO (*at her feet*). I am!

MADAME SOMMER (*throwing herself upon him weeping*). My own!

FERNANDO. Cecilia! My wife!

CECILIA (*turning away*). No, not mine—My heart, you are deserting me!—(*Embracing him again*:) Fernando—whoever you are—let the tears of a miserable woman flow on your bosom—Hold me up for this one moment, then leave me forever!—I am not your wife!—Don't push me away!

FERNANDO. God!—Cecilia, your tears on my cheek—your heart trembling on mine! Spare me, spare me!

CECILIA. I want nothing, Fernando!—Only this moment! Let my heart pour itself out just this one time—it will become free and strong! You'll be rid of me—

FERNANDO. I'll part from life before I part from you!

CECILIA. I shall see you again, but not in this world. You belong to another and I cannot take you from her.—Oh, open up the heavens for me! One glimpse of that distant, blessed land, that eternal rest—In such a glimpse alone lies comfort in this fearful moment.

FERNANDO (*grasps her hand, gazes at her, embraces her*). Nothing, nothing in the world shall part me from you. I have found you again.

CECILIA. Yes, found what you were not looking for!

FERNANDO. Don't say that!—Oh yes, I was looking for you, you, the one I abandoned, my dear one. Even in the arms of this angel here I found no rest, no joy—everything reminded me of you, of your daughter, my Lucy. Merciful heavens! what joy! Is it true? Is that dear creature my daughter?—I looked for you everywhere. For three years I wandered about. In the place where we used to live I found our house changed, in strange hands, and heard the sad story of the loss of your fortune. It tore my heart to find you gone; I could find no trace of you; sick of life and sick of myself, I donned this uniform and entered foreign service, helped suppress the dying freedom of the noble Corsicans. And now you see me here, after these long and strange aberrations, again on your bosom, my best, my dearest wife!

Enter Lucy.

FERNANDO. Oh my daughter!

LUCY. Dear, good father! If you are my father again.

FERNANDO. Always and forever!

CECILIA. And Stella?

FERNANDO. There's no time to lose. Poor woman! Why, Lucy, why couldn't we recognize each other this morning?—My heart pounded; you know how moved I was when I left you! Why? Why? We could have saved ourselves all this! And Stella! we could have spared her this pain. But we must go. I will tell her that you insist on leaving, that you didn't want to burden her with your *adieux*, that you had to go. And you, Lucy, run over to the posthouse, have them hitch up a carriage for three. The servant can pack my things with yours.—You stay over there, my dear wife. And you, my daughter, when everything's arranged come back here; wait for me in the conservatory; be sure to wait. I'll free myself, say I want to accompany you to the posthouse, see you off and pay the fare.—Poor soul, I'm deceiving you with your own kindness!—We must go!

CECILIA. Go? Please listen to a word of reason!

FERNANDO. Yes, go! Never mind! Yes, my dears, we must go.

Cecilia and Lucy leave.

FERNANDO (*alone*). Go?—Where?—A stab in the breast would open an outlet for all this pain and plunge me into the dull insensibility for which I would now give anything. Are you still here, miserable creature? Remember those happy, happy days when with such self-assurance you prevented a poor devil from casting aside life's burden—how you felt in those happy days—and now! Ah yes, when people are happy—If I had made this discovery an hour sooner, I would have been saved. I would never have seen her again, nor she me. I could have persuaded myself that in these four years she had forgotten me and had overcome her grief. But now? How can I face her? What can I say to her?—Oh, in these moments my guilt, my guilt weighs heavy upon me! Abandoned, both those dear creatures! And I, at the moment I find them again, abandoned by myself! What misery! Oh my heart!

ACT IV

Hermitage in Stella's Garden
Stella alone.

STELLA. You bloom so beautifully, more beautifully than ever, dear, dear place of rest eternal, the rest I hoped for—But you cannot tempt me now—You make me shudder, cool, loose earth, you make me shudder——Oh how often in moments of imagining I have passionately wrapped my head and breast in Death's mantle, stood calmly beside your depths, oh earth, and descending, concealed my aching heart beneath your living cover. There it was to be your task, mold and corruption, to suck dry, like a beloved child, this swelling, overflowing breast and dissolve all my being in a friendly dream—But now!—Heavenly sun, you shine down upon me—it is so bright, so open all around me—what joy it gives me!—He's here again! And in the flash of a moment all creation stands about me full of life—and I too brim with life—from his lips I'll drink new, warmer, more glowing life!—Live where he lives, beside him, with him, in unfailing strength!—Fernando!—He's coming! Listen!—No, not yet!—Let him find me here, beside my grassy altar, beneath my roses! These buds I'll pick for him—here! and here!—Then I'll lead him into this arbor. How good, how good it was that I had it built for two, small as it is.—Here's where my book used to lie, my pen and ink stood there—Away with all that!—If only he'd come!—Deserted so soon? Is he really mine again?—Is he here?

Enter Fernando.

STELLA. Why so late, my love? Where were you? I've been alone a long, long time! (*Anxiously*:) What's the matter?

FERNANDO. Those women put me out of humor!—The mother's a good sort, but she won't stay. She wouldn't tell me why. Let her have her way, Stella.

STELLA. I don't want to keep her against her will. I needed companionship, Fernando, but now—(*throwing her arms about him*:) now, Fernando, I have you!

FERNANDO. Calm yourself!

STELLA. Let me weep! Oh, I wish this day were over! I'm still trembling in every limb! This joy—everything so unexpected and so sudden. You, Fernando! And it's barely happened, barely! This will be the death of me!

FERNANDO (*to himself*). Wretch that I am! Leave her? (*Aloud*:) Let me go, Stella!

STELLA. It's your voice, your loving voice!—Stella! Stella!—You know how I liked to hear you say my name: Stella! No one says it the way you do. The very soul of love in the sound!—How well I remember the day when I first heard you say it, the day when all my happiness began—with you.

FERNANDO. Happiness?

STELLA. I believe you're making a mental count of things. You're counting the dreary hours I brought upon myself because of you. Don't, Fernando, no! Oh, from the moment I first saw you everything completely changed in my soul! Do you remember the afternoon in the garden, at my uncle's? The way you walked over to us? We were sitting under the great chestnut trees behind the garden-house!

FERNANDO (*to himself*). She'll break my heart!—(*Aloud*:) I remember, Stella!

STELLA. The way you came up to us? I don't know whether you noticed that you had captured my attention in the first moment. I at least soon noticed that your eyes were seeking me. Oh, Fernando, and then my uncle brought his music. You took your violin, and while you were playing my eyes could rest on you without embarrassment. I sought out every feature of your face, and then, during a sudden pause, you raised your eyes and looked at me! Your eyes met mine! How I blushed and looked away! You noticed it, Fernando. From then on I could feel you looking at me over the music, often at an inopportune time; for you lost your place, and my uncle couldn't mark time with his foot. Every false stroke of your bow went through me, body and soul. It was the sweetest confusion I ever felt. I couldn't have looked directly at you again for all the gold in Peru. I had to leave to regain my calm—

FERNANDO. True, to the last detail! (*To himself:*) Her memory's only too good!

STELLA. Often I'm astonished at myself: the way I love you, the way I completely forget myself every moment that I'm with you, and yet remember everything as vividly as though it had happened today. How often I've told myself the story, Fernando! The way you sought me out, the way you went roaming through the garden on the arm of my friend, whom you met before me, and she called out: Stella! and you cried: Stella!—I had scarcely heard you speak, but I recognized your voice, and then you both came up to me, and you took my hand! Who was more disconcerted, you or I? One helped the other out—And from that moment—My faithful Sarah prophesied it that very evening—And it's all come true—And what bliss in your arms! If my dear Sarah could see my joy! She was such a good soul, she wept and wept for me when I was so sick, so sick with love. I would have liked to take her with us, when I forsook everything for you.

FERNANDO. Forsook everything!

STELLA. Does that surprise you so? Isn't it true? Forsook everything! You can't take such words from me as a reproach! I've not done enough for you by far.

FERNANDO. What? To leave your uncle, who cherished you like a father and granted your every wish, whose will was your will? Wasn't that a great deal? To give up your fortune, the lands that were all yours, would have been yours, was that nothing? To leave the place where you had lived so long and had been so happy—your childhood companions—

STELLA. And all without you, Fernando? What was it in comparison with your love? Only then, when love dawned in my soul, did I find my footing in the world. It's true, I must confess that in lonely hours I sometimes thought: Why couldn't I enjoy all that with him? Why did we have to flee? Why not keep all I had? Would my uncle have refused you my hand? No! Then why flee?—Oh, I found excuses enough for you! I never lacked for those! And suppose it was just a passing fancy, I told myself—you men have lots of whims—suppose it was just a fancy of his that he wanted to carry off the girl as his secret prize!—Or suppose it was pride and he wanted the girl and nothing else, without anything into the bargain. You can imagine that my own pride made me want to put things in the best light, and so you came off very well.

FERNANDO. This will kill me!

Enter Annie.

ANNIE. Excuse me, m'am! Aren't you coming, captain? Everthing's packed, we're only waiting for you! The young lady was running around and giving orders till our heads were swimming—and now you don't show up.

STELLA. Go and bring them back here, Fernando. Pay their coach fare, but come right back.

ANNIE. Aren't you going along? The young lady ordered a carriage for three, and your servant has loaded your baggage!

STELLA. Fernando, there must be some mistake!

FERNANDO. What does the child know?

ANNIE. What do I know? I'll admit it looks strange that the captain wants to go away with the young lady and leave the baroness behind, seeing she only made your acquaintance at lunch. I suppose that was a tender farewell when you pressed her hand at table.

STELLA (*embarrassed*). Fernando!

FERNANDO. She's only a child.

ANNIE. Don't believe it, m'am! Everything's packed; the captain's going along.

FERNANDO. And where? Where?

STELLA. Leave us, Annie! (*Exit Annie.*) Save me from this horrible embarrassment! I'm not afraid of anything, but that childish talk makes me apprehensive.—You're upset, Fernando!—I'm your Stella!

FERNANDO (*turning and taking her hand*). You are my Stella!

STELLA. You frighten me, Fernando! You have such a wild look.

FERNANDO. Stella, I'm a deceiver and a coward, I can't stand up to you. I can only run away.—I haven't the courage to plunge the dagger into your breast, I try to poison you secretly—murder you! Oh Stella!

STELLA. For God's sake!

FERNANDO (*with rage and trembling*). And not to see her misery, not to hear her despair, I run away!

STELLA. I can't bear it! (*She is about to faint and takes hold of him.*)

FERNANDO. Stella, you whom I hold in my arms! Stella, you who are everything to me! (*Coldly:*) I'm leaving you.

STELLA (*smiling dazedly*). Me?

FERNANDO (*grinding his teeth*). You! I'm leaving with the woman you saw! With the girl!

STELLA. Everything's growing so black!

FERNANDO. And that woman—is my wife!

Stella stares at him; her arms fall.

And the girl is my daughter! Stella! (*Only now does he see that she has fainted.*) Stella! Help! Help! (*He lifts her up onto the bench.*)

Enter Cecilia and Lucy.

FERNANDO. Look, look at this angel! She's gone! Look! Help! (*They try to help her.*)

LUCY. She's recovering.

FERNANDO (*looking at them in silence*). Because of you! Because of you! (*Exit.*)

STELLA. Who? Who? (*Sitting up.*) Where is he? (*She sinks back, looks at those about her.*) Thank you, thank you!— who are you?

CECILIA. Be calm. We are here.

STELLA. You?—You haven't left?—Are you—? God! Who was it that told me?—Who are you?—Are you—? (*Taking Cecilia's hand.*) No, I can't bear it!

CECILIA. My dear love! My angel, I clasp you to my heart!

STELLA. Tell—I must know—tell me—are you—

CECILIA. I am—I am his wife!

STELLA (*springs up, holding her hands over her eyes*). And I? (*She walks up and down in a daze.*)

CECILIA. Come to your room!

STELLA. What are you reminding me of? What is mine? Terrible! Terrible!—Are those my trees that I planted? Tended? Why has everything suddenly become so strange to me?—Cast aside!—Lost! Lost forever! Fernando! Fernando!

CECILIA. Lucy, go and look for your father.

STELLA. No, for God's sake! Stop!—Leave! Don't let him come! Leave—Father!—Husband!

CECILIA. My sweet love!

STELLA. You love me? You press me to your breast?——No, no—let me go!—Cast me aside! (*Embracing her.*) One moment more! It will soon be over! My heart! My heart!

LUCY. You must rest!

STELLA. I can't stand to look at the two of you. I've poisoned both your lives, robbed you of everything—you in misery, and I—what bliss in his arms! (*She casts herself on her knees.*) Can you forgive me?

CECILIA. Don't say that! (*They try to raise her up.*)

STELLA. Let me lie here, and plead and moan to God and to you: Forgiveness! forgiveness!—(*She jumps up.*) Forgiveness? No, give me comfort! comfort! I'm not guilty!—You gave him to me, holy Father in heaven! I held him fast, like the dearest gift from Your hand—Let me be!—My heart's breaking!

CECILIA. Dear, innocent friend!

STELLA (*embracing her*). In your eyes, on your lips I read the message of heaven. Hold me! Carry me! I'm perishing! She forgives me! She feels my misery!

CECILIA. Sister, my sister! Be calm and rest. Just for a moment. Have faith that He who puts these feelings in our hearts, feelings that make us so wretched, can also give us help and comfort.

STELLA. Let me die on your bosom!

CECILIA. Come with me now!

STELLA (*after a pause, drawing away wildly*). Leave me alone, all of you! A whole world of confusion and torment floods my soul, filling it with unutterable pain—It's impossible—impossible! So suddenly! I can't grasp it, I can't bear it! (*She stands there a while looking down, lost in thought, then glances up, sees the other two, shudders and cries out, then flees.*)

CECILIA. Follow her, Lucy! Watch over her! (*Exit Lucy.*) Look down upon Thy children, oh Lord in heaven! Look down upon their misery and their distraction!—Suffering has taught me much. Strengthen me!—If this knot can be loosened—do not cut it apart!

ACT V

Stella's Boudoir. Moonlight

Stella, holding Fernando's portrait and preparing to remove it from the frame

STELLA. Enclose me, fullness of night! hold me! guide my steps! I must, I will leave!—Where can I go, oh where?—Banished from Thy creation! Oh you sacred moon, shall I walk no more where you shine softly down on my tree-tops, where you enclose in fearful, loving shadows the grave of my beloved Minna? Must I leave the spot where all my life's treasures, all my blessed memories are stored?—And you, my burial place, where I have so often tarried in reverence and tears! The place I consecrated for myself, where all the melancholy, all the bliss of my life softly gleams; where I hoped even in death to hover, happily reliving the past with sweet longing—am I also banished from you?—Banishment!—Thank God that your mind is clouded; you can't conceive the thought: banishment! You'd go mad!—So now.—Oh, I'm fainting!—Farewell!—Farewell? To part forever?—The glazed look of death is in that feeling! Part forever! Come, Stella, away from here! (*She seizes the portrait.*) And am I to leave you behind? (*She starts to loosen the nails with a knife.*) Oh, if I could only stop thinking! If I could only part from life in unfeeling sleep or in a transport of tears!——No, live and be miserable: so it is and so it will be! (*She turns the picture toward the moonlight.*) Ah, Fernando, when you came up to me and my heart leapt toward you, did you not sense my confidence in your faithfulness, your kindness? Didn't you feel what a sanctuary had disclosed itself when my heart opened to you?—You didn't shrink back trembling? Didn't faint? Didn't flee? You were capable of despoiling my innocence, my happiness, my life, just for passing pleasure, plucking the flowers and strewing them thoughtlessly beside the way?—What nobility, oh, what nobility!—My youth, my golden days!—You bear deep deceit in your heart!—Your wife!—Your daughter!—And my soul was free, pure as a spring morning!—Everything, everything embodied in one single hope!——Where are you, Stella? (*She gazes at the portrait.*) What greatness! What charm!—That was the look that brought about my downfall!—I hate you! Turn away! go away!—That tender look! so dear!—No! No!—Destroyer!—Me? Me?—You? Me? (*She makes a sudden motion with the knife, toward the portrait, then falls into a chair in a fit of tears.*) Dearest! Dearest!—Oh, I can't help myself!

Enter Servant.

SERVANT. My lady, the horses are at the back gate as you ordered. Your things are packed. Don't forget to take some money!

STELLA. The picture! (*The servant takes the knife, cuts the picture out of the frame and rolls it up.*) Here's money.

SERVANT. But why?

STELLA (*stands silently for a moment, looking around*). Come!

Exeunt.

Living Room
Fernando.

FERNANDO. Get away from me! get away! There it is again, seizing me, driving me to distraction—Everything lies before me so cold, so sickening—as though the world were a void—as though I were to blame for nothing that happens in it——What about them?—Am I not more miserable than you? What claims do you have on me?—So what does all this thinking lead to, eh?—This way, that way! From one end to the other! Everything thoroughly considered and reconsidered! And still the torment grows, more terrible than ever! (*Grasping his forehead.*) A wall here, a wall there! No escape, forward or backward! No hope, no help.—And those two, those three, the best women on the face of the earth? Miserable because of me, miserable without me! Oh, still more miserable with me!—If I could complain, despair, beg forgiveness—if I could spend but one hour in dull hope—lie at their feet drinking in the bliss of misery shared!—Where are they?—Stella, you lie prostrate, you turn your dying gaze toward heaven and moan: "Poor flower that I am, what have I done that You tread me down in Your wrath? What did I do to make You lead this deceiver to me?"——Cecilia! My wife! Oh my wife!—Misery! Deep misery!—What ecstasies unite to make me miserable!—Husband! Father! Lover!—the best and noblest women—yours! Yours?—Can you grasp that, this threefold, unutterable bliss? It alone so moves you, tears you apart! Each one demands the whole of me—And I?—Locked tight, here—deep, fathomless!—She'll be miserable! Stella, you are miserable!—What have I robbed you of? The consciousness of yourself! Your young life!—Stella!—And I'm so cold! (*He picks up one of the pair of pistols lying on the table.*) Yes, just in case! (*He loads the pistol.*)

Enter Cecilia

CECILIA. My friend! How are you? (*She sees the pistols.*) It seems you're going on a journey.

Fernando lays down the pistol.

My friend! You seem more tranquil. May I have a word with you?

FERNANDO. What do you want, Cecilia? What do you want, my wife?

CECILIA. Don't call me that until I've finished. We're all very confused right now, but surely things can be straightened out. I've suffered much, so let's make no rash decisions. Are you listening, Fernando?

FERNANDO. I'm listening!

CECILIA. Take what I say to heart! I'm only a woman, a grief-stricken, sorrowing woman, but there's resolve in my soul. Fernando—I've made up my mind—I'm leaving you!

FERNANDO (*ironically*). Just like that?

CECILIA. Do you think one has to steal away when one leaves what one loves?

FERNANDO. Cecilia!

CECILIA. I reproach you with nothing, and don't imagine that I'm sacrificing so much. Until now, I've grieved over losing you; I made myself miserable thinking about things I couldn't change. I find you again, and your presence inspires me with new life, new strength.

Fernando, I feel that my love for you is not selfish. It's not the passion of a woman who would sacrifice everything to possess the object of her desire. My heart is warm and full for you, Fernando; but it is the feeling of a wife, who, out of love, is capable even of giving up her love.

FERNANDO. Never! Never!

CECILIA. That shocks you?

FERNANDO. You're torturing me!

CECILIA. I want you to be happy! I have my daughter—and in you I have a friend. Let us part without being parted. I'll live away from you, a distant witness of your happiness. You can confide in me, pour your joy and sorrow into my heart. Your letters will be my sole life, and my letters shall seem to you like dear visitors——And thus you'll remain mine, you won't be banished with Stella to some far corner of the earth; we'll love each other, share in each other. Come, Fernando, give me your hand on that!

FERNANDO. This is too cruel for a jest; as a serious proposal, incomprehensible.—Let come what may!—Cold reason won't undo this knot. What you say has a lovely sound, it tastes sweet. If only one did not sense that far more is concealed beneath your words, that you are deluding yourself in trying to still the feelings that are tormenting you with the illusion of comfort. No, Cecilia! My wife, no!—You are mine—I am yours—Why make speeches? Why should I expound my reasons? Reasons are just so many lies. I am yours, or—

CECILIA. Well then!—And Stella?

Fernando shudders and begins to pace wildly back and forth.

Who's deluding himself? Who's deadening his pain with cold, unfeeling, false, temporary comfort? Oh, you men must know yourselves.

FERNANDO. Don't pride yourself on your calm superiority!—Stella! Yes, she is miserable. She'll die of grief if she's apart from you and me. Let her be! Let me be!

CECILIA. Truly, I think solitude would do her heart good, and it would comfort her tender feelings to know that we were united again. Now she's bitterly reproaching herself. She would always think me unhappier than I really would be if I left you; for she judges me by herself. She wouldn't be able to live in peace, wouldn't be able to love, the angel! if she felt that her happiness was stolen from someone else. It's better for her—

FERNANDO. Let her go away! Enter a convent!

CECILIA. But then again I think: why should she be shut away from the world? What sin has she committed that she should have to grieve away the years of her bloom, the years of ripeness and hope, on the verge of despair, separated from the world she loves? And from the man she loves so passionately? And who—am I right, Fernando?—loves her in return?

FERNANDO. What's the point of all this? Are you an evil spirit in the form of my wife? Why are you turning my heart inside out? Why tear to pieces what is already in shreds? Am I not destroyed enough? Leave me! Leave me to my fate!—And God have mercy on you and Lucy! (*He throws himself into an armchair.*)

CECILIA (*goes over to him and takes his hand*). Once upon a time there was a count—

Fernando is about to jump up; she restrains him.

A German count. A sense of religious duty impelled him to leave his wife, his estates, and to set out for the Holy Land.

FERNANDO. Ha!

CECILIA. He was a good man and he loved his wife. He took leave of her, entrusting his possessions to her care, embraced her and departed. He journeyed through many lands, fought, was taken prisoner and sold into slavery. His master's daughter took pity on him, released him from his chains. They fled together. She stood beside him in all the perils of war renewed—her dear warrior! Crowned with victory, he set out for home—to his noble wife!—And the girl who had freed him?—He was a humane soul, believed in humanity: he took her with him. And lo and behold! his good wife, hastening to meet her husband, sees all her loyalty, trust and hopes rewarded, sees him again in her arms. And, round about, his knights, proudly dismounting on their native soil; his servants unloading the prizes of war and spreading them out at her feet. She already sees herself storing them in her cupboards, adorning the castle with them, sharing them with her friends—"My dear, noble wife, you have not yet seen the greatest treasure of all!"—Who is that veiled figure approaching there with her retainers? Gently she dismounts——"Here!" cries the count, taking her by the hand and conducting her to his wife, "Here! behold all this—and her! Receive it from her hands—and from her hands receive me again. It was she who freed me from my chains, she who commanded the winds; she has won the right to me—she has served me, cared for me! I owe her everything—There she is! Reward her!" (*Fernando lies sobbing, his arms outspread on the table.*) With streaming tears the faithful wife threw her arms about the girl's neck and cried: "Take all that I can give you! Take half of him who belongs to you alone—take all of him! Leave all of him to me! Each of us shall have him and neither shall deprive the other—And," she cried, embracing him and falling at his feet, "we are yours!"—They clasped his hands, hugged him—And God in heaven rejoiced in their love and His deputy on earth gave them his blessing. And their happiness and love was encompassed in *one* house, *one* bed, and *one* grave.

FERNANDO. Oh God in heaven, you send us angels in our time of need: give me strength to bear their mighty vision!—My wife! (*He collapses again.*)

CECILIA (*opens the door of the boudoir and calls*). Stella!

STELLA (*throwing her arms about Cecilia's neck*). God! God!

Fernando leaps up and is about to flee.

CECILIA (*detaining him*). Stella, take half of him who belongs to you alone—you saved him—saved him from himself—you have given him back to me again!

FERNANDO. Stella! (*He bows before her.*)

STELLA. I can't comprehend it.

CECILIA. But you feel it.

STELLA (*embracing Fernando*). May I?——

CECILIA. Are you glad I kept you from leaving, you runaway?

STELLA (*embracing her*). You!——

FERNANDO (*embracing both*). Mine! Mine!

STELLA (*clasping his hand, holding him tight*). I am yours!

CECILIA (*clasping his hand, her arm about his neck*). We are yours!

[End of *Stella*, original version.]

For the first Weimar production of *Stella* in 1806 Goethe changed the ending, and in editions after 1816 the play appears under the title of *Stella. A Tragedy*. The new version of the ending begins with Fernando's speech immediately following Cecilia's recounting of the legend of the Count of Gleichen: ". . . *one* house, *one* bed, and *one* grave" (above).

FERNANDO. God in heaven! What a ray of hope!

CECILIA. She is with us! She is ours! (*Going to the door of the boudoir.*) Stella!

FERNANDO. Leave her alone! Leave me alone! (*About to go.*)

CECILIA. Stop! Listen to me!

FERNANDO. We've had enough words. What can be, will be. Let me go! I'm not prepared to face the two of you now. (*Exit.*)

Cecilia, afterwards Lucy, then Stella.

CECILIA. Unfortunate man! Never saying much, never willing to listen to a friendly word of mediation. And she too! I must make this work. (*Calling toward the boudoir:*) Stella! Listen to me!

LUCY. Don't call her. She's resting for a moment, resting after great pain. She's suffering awfully, Mother, and it's her own wish, I fear. I'm afraid she's dying

CECILIA. What are you saying?

LUCY. I fear it wasn't medicine she swallowed.

CECILIA. Don't let my hopes be shattered! God grant that you're mistaken!—How terrible! Terrible!

STELLA (*from the doorway*). Who's calling me? Why are you waking me? What time is it? Why so early?

LUCY. It's not early, it's evening.

STELLA. True, quite true, evening for me.

CECILIA. You shouldn't mislead us this way!

STELLA. Who misled you? You did.

CECILIA. I brought you back. I had such hopes.

STELLA. I have no place to stay.

CECILIA. Oh, I wish I had let you go—let you hurry away, let you travel to the end of the world.

STELLA. I am at the end.

CECILIA (*to Lucy, who has been pacing anxiously back and forth*). What are you waiting for? Hurry! Get help!

STELLA (*detaining Lucy*). No, wait. (*She leans on both of them; they come forward.*) I thought I'd go through life at your side; now lead me to my grave. (*They slowly bring her forward and seat her in an armchair on the right.*)

CECILIA. Hurry, Lucy! Hurry!—Help! Help! (*Exit Lucy.*)

Stella and Cecilia; then Fernando; afterwards Lucy.

STELLA. I *have* been helped.

CECILIA. Oh, I thought it would be so different! I hoped it would be.

STELLA. How good you are, how patient, how full of hope!

CECILIA. What a terrible fate!

STELLA. Fate strikes deep wounds, but often they can be healed. The wounds that the heart inflicts on itself are beyond healing, and so—let me die.

FERNANDO. (*enters*). Was Lucy mistaken, or is this news true? Let it not be true, or I'll curse your noble impulses, Cecilia, and your long-suffering patience.

CECILIA. My heart does not rebuke me. To mean well is better than to succeed. Hurry and bring help, she's still alive, she still belongs to us.

STELLA (*looking up and taking Fernando's hand*). Welcome! Give me your hand, (*to Cecilia:*) and you—give me yours. All for love, that was the motto of my life. All for love, and now, death too. In our happiest moments we were silent and understood each other. (*She tries to unite the hands of the other two.*) Now let me be silent and rest. (*She falls upon her right arm, which is extended across the table.*)

FERNANDO. Yes, we will be silent, Stella, and rest. (*He slowly moves to the table on the left.*)

CECILIA (*agitated and impatient*). Lucy's not coming back, no one comes. Is this house deserted? Is the whole neighborhood a desert? Try to control yourself, Fernando, she's still alive. Hundreds have risen from their deathbed, climbed from the grave. I tell you she's still alive. And even if everyone deserts us, if no doctor comes and there's no medicine to be had, there's still one in heaven who hears us. (*On her knees, near Stella*:) Hear me, oh Lord! Answer my prayer! Preserve her for us, don't let her die!

Fernando has taken a pistol in his left hand and slowly leaves.

(*As before, grasping Stella's left hand*:) Yes she is still alive; her hand, her dear hand is still warm. I won't leave you, I'll hold you with all the power of faith and love. No, it's not a delusion! Fervent prayer is stronger than any earthly help. (*Rising and turning around.*) He has gone, silent and hopeless. Where did he go? Oh, save him from the step his whole stormy life has been leading him to! I must go to him! (*As she is about to leave, she turns to Stella.*) And she—I leave her here helpless. Almighty God! Here I stand, in this most dreadful moment, between two whom I cannot part and cannot unite. (*A shot is heard.*)

CECILIA. Oh God! (*She starts to hurry off in the direction of the sound.*)

STELLA (*struggling to rise*). What was that? Cecilia, you're so far away, come closer, don't leave me. I'm so afraid. Oh, what fears I have! I see blood flowing. Is it my blood? It's not my blood. I'm not wounded, but deathly sick.—It *is* my blood.

LUCY (*enters*). Help, Mother, help! I ran for help, to the doctor, sent out messengers, but oh! I must tell you, quite different help is needed. My father has fallen by his own hand. He's lying there in his blood. (*Cecilia starts to leave; Lucy restrains her.*) Don't go, Mother. Looking won't help, it will only move you to despair.

STELLA (*who has listened attentively in a half-raised position, takes Cecilia's hand*). So this is the way it turns out? (*Rising and leaning on Cecilia and Lucy.*) Come, I feel strong again. Let's go to him. Let me die there.

CECILIA. You're swaying, your knees won't support you. We can't carry you. I have no strength left either.

STELLA (*sinking down beside the armchair*). Then I've reached my goal. You go to him, to the one you belong to. Receive his last sigh, his death rattle. He's your husband. Why do you hesitate? Go, I beg you, I implore you. Your staying here upsets me. (*With feeling, but weakly*:) Remember, he's alone! Go!

Cecilia leaves in agitation.

LUCY. I won't leave you. I'll stay beside you.

STELLA. No, Lucy! If you care for me, hurry, go! go! Let me rest. Love's wings are lamed—they won't bear me to him. You are young and strong. Let duty step in when love falls silent. Go to the one you belong to. He's your father. Do you know what that means? Go! if you love me, if you want to set my mind at rest.

Lucy slowly leaves.

STELLA (*sinking down*). And I die alone.

BROTHER AND SISTER

A One-Act Play

Translated by Frank Ryder

Characters

William, a businessman
Marianne, his sister
Fabrice
Postman

WILLIAM (*at a desk covered with ledgers and papers*). Two more new customers this week! If you keep busy something always comes along, and even if it's not much, it adds up in the end. Besides, play for small stakes and you're always happy, even for small gains; as for the small losses—you can get over them. Now what have we here?

Enter postman.

POSTMAN. A registered letter, declared value twenty ducats, postage due fifty percent extra.

WILLIAM. Fine! Very fine indeed! Charge it to my account.

Exit postman.

WILLIAM (*looking at the letter*). I've been expecting this—and trying all day to convince myself that I wasn't. Now I have just enough to pay back what I owe Fabrice and not take advantage of his kindness any longer. Yesterday he said to me: I'll be calling on you tomorrow. I didn't feel right about that. I knew he wouldn't remind me, and that just makes his presence a double reminder. (*Opening the money pouch and counting.*) In the past, when I was a bit more casual about my business affairs, it was the quiet creditors who were the hardest to face. Anyone who chases after me, and tries to put pressure on me, deserves to be met with arrogance and all that sort of thing. The ones who don't say a word are the ones who touch your heart. They leave it up to you to recognize what's owed them, so their claims have the greatest urgency of all. (*He stacks the money on the table.*) Dear God, how grateful I am to be out of that business and back on a firm footing. (*He picks up a book.*) Your blessing comes to me in these small favors. To me, who squandered your great favors wholesale.—And so—is there any way to express it?—but what you're doing is not for *me*, just as what I'm doing is not for myself. If it weren't for that dear sweet creature, would I be sitting here, checking fractions? Oh, Marianne, if you knew that the one you take for your brother serves you with a different heart, with very different hopes!—maybe!—oh!—it's bitter enough. She loves me—yes, as a brother—no, that's ridiculous, that's lack of faith again, and no good ever came of that.—Marianne, I *will* be happy; and you will be too, Marianne!

Enter Marianne.

MARIANNE. What is it, brother? You called me.

WILLIAM. Not I, Marianne.

MARIANNE. Are you up to some mischief, teasing me out of the kitchen?

WILLIAM. You're hearing things.

MARIANNE. Under other circumstances, maybe. Only I know your voice too well, William!

WILLIAM. Well, what are you doing out there?

MARIANNE. I've been plucking a couple of squabs, that's all. Because I assume Fabrice will be eating with us tonight.

WILLIAM. Maybe.

MARIANNE. They'll be done soon; don't worry, you can let me know later. He'll have to teach me that new song of his, too.

WILLIAM. You like to learn from him, don't you?

MARIANNE. He has a very nice way with a song. And afterwards, when you sit at the table with your head down, I'll take my turn. Because I know it makes you happy if I sing something you like.

WILLIAM. You've noticed that about me?

MARIANNE. Well, who wouldn't notice things about you men? Now if you don't have anything else on your mind I'll be going; I still have a lot to do. Good-bye. Now give me a kiss.

WILLIAM. You can have one for dessert if the roast squab is nicely done.

MARIANNE. It's sinful how rude brothers are. If Fabrice or some other nice fellow had a chance for a kiss they'd jump over the moon, and this gentleman here refuses one I'm trying to give away. Now I'll burn the squabs. (*Exit.*)

WILLIAM. Angel, dear sweet angel! How can I contain myself, how can I keep from throwing my arms around her and telling her everything? Are you looking down upon us, you saintly woman, who put this treasure in my keeping? Yes, they know about us up there, they know all about us! Charlotte, you could not have rewarded my love for you in a more splendid, more sacred way than you did, entrusting your daughter to me on your deathbed. You gave me everything I needed; you brought me back to life. I loved her as your child. And now—my eyes still play tricks on me. I think I'm seeing *you* again. I think fate has given you back to me, rejuvenated, so that I might be with you and live with you, united, as I couldn't—shouldn't—in that first dream of life. Happy, happy! Your blessing, Father in Heaven!

Enter Fabrice.

FABRICE. Good evening.

WILLIAM. My dear Fabrice, I'm very happy; all good things have come my way this evening. Let's not talk about business. Here are your 300 Thalers. Into your pocket they go! You can give me my note back at your convenience. Let's have a good chat!

FABRICE. If you still need them—.

WILLIAM. If I need them again, all right. I'm forever grateful to you, but now take them back. The memory of Charlotte has come to me again this evening, infinitely new and alive.

FABRICE. I'm sure that happens often.

WILLIAM. You should have known her. I tell you, she was one of God's most glorious creatures.

FABRICE. She was a widow when you first became acquainted with her?

WILLIAM. Noble and pure! I was reading one of her letters only yesterday. You'll be the only human being who's ever seen any part of it. (*He goes over to his strongbox.*)

FABRICE (*to himself*). I wish he'd spare me just this once. I've heard the story so often. Usually I'm happy to listen to what he says because it's always straight from the heart. But today I've got quite a different matter on my mind, and I'd particularly like to keep him in good humor.

WILLIAM. It was in the first days of our friendship. "The world seems sweet to me again," she writes, "and I had really cut my ties with it—sweet again because of you. My heart reproaches me, I feel that I may bring misery on us both. Six months ago I was so ready to die—but now I'm not."

FABRICE. A noble spirit!

WILLIAM. This earth did not deserve her, Fabrice. I've told you often how I became a totally different person because of her. I cannot describe my pain when I returned and saw how I had squandered my family fortune. I did not dare to offer her my hand. I could do nothing to make her situation more bearable. For the first time I felt the need to gain a decent livelihood, to pull myself out of the sloth in which I had been living my meager life from one day to the next. I went to work but what good was that? Still I stuck to it and got through one tedious year; at last there came a ray of hope; the little money I started with had grown perceptibly—And then she died—I had to leave. You have no idea what I went through. I couldn't bear the sight of the places where she and I had been together, and I couldn't leave the spot where she was buried. She wrote me just before the end. (*He takes a letter from the strongbox.*)

FABRICE. It's a marvelous letter. You read it to me recently. Listen, William—.

WILLIAM. I know it by heart—and I keep reading it. When I see her writing, the paper her hand rested on, I think once again that she's still present. And she *is* still present! (*A child is heard crying.*) What a shame Marianne can't rest. There she is with our neighbor's child again; she's forever busy tending that boy, day after day, and always disturbs me at just the wrong time. (*At the door:*) Marianne, be quiet with the boy or send him away if he's not behaving. We're trying to talk. (*He stands absorbed in thought.*)

FABRICE. You shouldn't stir up these memories so often.

WILLIAM. It's these lines, these last lines! The departing breath of a dying angel. (*He folds the letter again.*) You're right, it's a sin. How seldom do we deserve to relive the bittersweet moments of our past!

FABRICE. Your fate has always touched my heart. You have told me that she left a daughter—soon to follow her, unfortunately. If only *she* had lived you would at least have had some part of her, some focus for your sorrow and your pain.

WILLIAM (*turning to him, with animation*). Her daughter? She was a dear sweet little thing. She entrusted her to me. Fate has done too much for me! Fabrice, if only I could tell you everything!

FABRICE. Sometime when it's in your heart to do so.

WILLIAM. Why shouldn't I—

Marianne with the little boy.

MARIANNE. He wants to say good night, Brother. You don't have to glare at him that way, or at me either. You always say you'd like to get married and have lots of children. But you can't keep such a tight rein on *them* that they'll cry only at your convenience.

WILLIAM. If they're *my* children . . .

MARIANNE. That might make a difference.

FABRICE. Do you think so, Marianne?

MARIANNE. It would certainly be nice! (*She bends down and kisses the boy.*) I like Chrissie so much; I just wish he were mine! He already knows his letters: I'm teaching him.

WILLIAM. And you think if he were yours he could read already?

MARIANNE. Of course. Because then I wouldn't spend time at anything else all day except dressing and undressing him, teaching him, giving him things to eat, making him beautiful and all that sort of thing.

FABRICE. And your husband?

MARIANNE. He'd be playing right along with us: he'd love him as much as I did. Chrissie has to go home, so he's saying good-bye. (*She takes him to William.*) Here, be nice and give him your hand, a real patty-hand.

FABRICE (*to himself*). She's absolutely charming. I've got to declare my intentions.

MARIANNE (*taking the child to Fabrice*). And this gentleman too.

WILLIAM (*to himself*). She *will* be yours—it's too much, I don't deserve it. (*Aloud:*) Marianne, put the child away; entertain Fabrice 'til supper; I'm going out for a walk, just a block or two; I've been sitting all day. (*Exit Marianne.*) One free breath under the stars, that's all. My heart is so full. I'll be right back! (*Exit.*)

Fabrice alone.

FABRICE. Get it over with, Fabrice. You can carry it around with you as long as you like, it's not going to get any riper. You've made the decision. It's good, it's excellent! You'll keep on helping her brother, and she—she doesn't love me the way I love her. But she can't love with passion and she mustn't. Dear girl! I'm sure she doesn't expect anything but feelings of friendship on my part! We'll get along well together. Marianne! The perfect moment, just what I hoped. I must tell her how I feel—if only her heart doesn't turn against me—her brother's heart I'm confident of.

Enter Marianne.

FABRICE. Did you send the child away?

MARIANNE. I wish I could have kept him here. I just know my brother doesn't like the idea, so I don't insist. Sometimes the little rascal even talks him into letting us sleep together in my bed.

FABRICE. Isn't that a nuisance for you?

MARIANNE. Not at all. He's so wild all day and when I crawl in bed with him he's so good—just a little lamb. A little charmer! And he's as sweet as he can be. Sometimes I just can't get him to go to sleep.

FABRICE (*half to himself*). Sweet, innocent Nature!

MARIANNE. He likes me better than his mother, too.

FABRICE. You *are* a mother to him. (*Marianne is pensive*; *Fabrice looks at her for a time.*) Does the word mother make you sad?

MARIANNE. Not sad—but I was just thinking.

FABRICE. What, my sweet Marianne?

MARIANNE. I was thinking—well, nothing really. I just feel so strange sometimes.

FABRICE. Can it be you've never wished—?

MARIANNE. What kind of questions are you asking?

FABRICE. It's all right for Fabrice to ask, isn't it?

MARIANNE. Wished? Never, Fabrice. And even if such a thought did cross my mind, it was gone again in an instant. To leave my brother would be unbearable—impossible—no matter how attractive the prospect in every other way.

FABRICE. That's very strange. If you lived in the same city together, would that be leaving him?

MARIANNE. Never! Who would manage things for him in the house? Who would take care of him? A maid? Or would he get married? No, that would never do!

FABRICE. Couldn't he move in with you? Couldn't your husband be his friend? Couldn't the three of you have a happy household, a happier household. Wouldn't it be a way of relieving your brother of business worries? What a life that could be!

MARIANNE. You might think so. And when I stop to consider, it's probably true. But then again, on second thought, it doesn't seem right.

FABRICE. I don't understand.

MARIANNE. It's just the way it is. When I wake, I listen to see if my brother is up. If there's nothing stirring, I'm out of bed in a flash and into the kitchen; I start the fire so that the water keeps coming to a boil, over and over, until the maid gets up and takes him his coffee so he has it the minute he opens his eyes.

FABRICE. Little housewife!

MARIANNE. And then I sit down and knit stockings for my brother, and what a business that is, measuring ten times to see if they fit, if they're long enough, if they're right in the calves, if the feet aren't too short; sometimes he loses patience. And what's important to me is not the measuring and fitting. I just want to be around him, doing something, so that he has to look at me occasionally, after he has been writing for a couple of hours, and won't turn into a hypochondriac. Because it makes him feel good to look at me. I can tell by watching his eyes, even though he tries not to let me notice any other way. Sometimes I smile to myself when he acts as if he were solemn or angry. It's a good thing he does, otherwise I'd be fussing over him all day.

FABRICE. He's lucky.

MARIANNE. No, I am. If I didn't have him I wouldn't know what in the world to do. I do all these things for myself, and yet it seems to me that I'm doing it all for him, because even in what I do for myself I'm always thinking of him.

FABRICE. And if you were doing all those things for your husband, how completely happy that would make him. How grateful he'd be and what a family life that would make.

MARIANNE. Sometimes I see it that way in my imagination, too, and I can tell myself long stories, as I sit there and knit or sew, about how it could all work out—and might. But when I get back to reality again, it just won't work.

FABRICE. Why not?

MARIANNE. Where would I find a husband who'd be satisfied if I said, "I promise to love you" and then right away had to add, "But I can't love you more than I do my brother; I have to be able to do everything for him that I did before." Oh, you can see that wouldn't be right!

FABRICE. Later on you'd be doing it partly for your husband; you'd transfer your love to him.

MARIANNE. That's just the trouble. Yes, if love could be paid out or paid in like money, or if it changed masters every three months like a poor maidservant. With a husband it would take time to develop something that's already *here*, something that could never be the same.

FABRICE. A lot of things work out.

MARIANNE. I don't know. When he sits at the table the way he does and leans his head on his hand, looking down and worrying but not saying anything—I can sit for half an hour at a time and watch him. He's not handsome, I sometimes say to myself, and yet it's so good just to look at him. Actually I have the feeling it's partly me he's worrying about; actually his first glance when he looks up tells me so, and that makes a big difference.

FABRICE. All the difference, Marianne. And what if you had a husband who'd worry about you and care for you?

MARIANNE. And that's another thing: you men and your moods. William has his moods, yes, but with him they don't depress me, when from anyone else they'd be intolerable. He has subtle moods but I can sense them sometimes. In his ungracious moments, when he rejects a good, sympathetic, loving expression of feeling, it hurts me—only for a moment actually—and even if I grumble and complain about him it's more because he doesn't recognize my love than because I love him less.

FABRICE. But now what if someone should turn up who'd risk all that and offer you his hand?

MARIANNE. He won't turn up! And then there's the question whether I'd risk it with *him*.

FABRICE. Why not?

MARIANNE. He won't turn up!

FABRICE. Marianne, he has!

MARIANNE. Fabrice!

FABRICE. You see him before you. Shall I make a long speech? Shall I pour out to you all that my heart has so long kept to itself? I love you, you've known that for a long time. I'm offering you my hand; you didn't expect that. Never have I known a girl who had so little idea of the emotions she must arouse in anyone who sees her. Marianne, this is no rash and fiery lover speaking to you. I know you. I have chosen you, my house is ready—will you be mine?—My fortunes in the affairs of the heart have been complicated. I was more than once determined to end my life a bachelor. Now I am yours—do not say no!—You know me; your brother and I are one; you could not imagine a purer union. Open your heart!—A single word, Marianne!

MARIANNE. Dear Fabrice, give me time; I do like you.

FABRICE. Say that you love me! I'll grant your brother his place, I'll be a brother to your brother, we'll join in caring for him. My fortune, added to his, will spare him many an anxious hour. He will take courage, he will—Marianne, I don't want to talk you into something. (*He takes her hand.*)

MARIANNE. Fabrice, it never occurred to me—what an embarrassing position you place me in!

FABRICE. Just a single word! Dare I hope?

MARIANNE. Talk with my brother!

FABRICE (*kneeling*). Angel! Dearest!

MARIANNE (*after a moment's silence*). Good Lord! What have I said?

Fabrice alone.

FABRICE. She's yours!—I really don't need to begrudge the dear child this silly flirtation with her brother. That will gradually shift over to me as we get to know each other better—and he shan't be the loser for it either. It is a wonderful feeling to love someone again, and with luck to be loved in return. It's the kind of thing you never lose the taste for.—We'll be living together; quite apart from that I'd gladly have added long ago to the dear fellow's domestic responsibilities. As brother-in-law it'll be all right. Otherwise he'd become a real hypochondriac, with his everlasting memories and uncertainties, his worries over money, and his secrets. Now everything will be just fine! He'll breathe more freely; the girl will have a husband—which isn't inconsequential—and you'll have a respectable marriage and a wife—which is a lot!

Enter William.

FABRICE. You've finished your walk?

WILLIAM. I've been to the market and up Parsonage Road and back past the Exchange. It's a curious sensation for me to walk through the city at night, when the day's work is done and everyone is either at home, or hurrying home, to rest, and all one sees everywhere is the bustle of tradespeople. I enjoyed watching an old woman in a cheese shop, with her glasses on her nose, weighing out one piece after the other by the light of a little tallow candle, adding or cutting off a slice until the customer had the right weight.

FABRICE. People notice what they're used to noticing. I dare say many walk the streets without looking at old women with glasses, selling cheese.

WILLIAM. You grow to like what you work at, and I've had great respect for tradespeople ever since I found out how hard a Thaler comes when you have to earn it by the penny. (*He stands for a few moments lost in thought.*) I had a very strange feeling as I walked along. So many things came to my mind all at once and all together—and the thing that concerns me in the very depths of my soul—(*He pauses, reflecting.*)

FABRICE (*to himself*). A stupid thing happens to me as soon as he's around. I don't quite dare confess that I love Marianne.—But I have to tell him what happened. (*Aloud:*) William, tell me, you were thinking of moving from here? You don't have much room and it's an expensive place to live. Do you have another place in mind?

WILLIAM (*distracted*). No.

FABRICE. I've been thinking we could make things easier for both of us. I do have my family's house and I use only the upper floor; you could take the lower floor; you aren't likely to marry soon.—You'd have the courtyard and enough office space for your agency; you'd give me a modest sum for rent, and it would be a favor to both of us.

WILLIAM. You're very kind. To tell the truth that's often occurred to me when I came to see you and saw so much unused space, and I have such a worrisome time making do with what I have.—Then again there are other matters.—We'll just have to forget it, it won't work.

FABRICE. Why not?

WILLIAM. What if I do get married?

FABRICE. That could be managed. Single, you'd have plenty of room with your sister; with a wife, you'd be just as well off.

WILLIAM (*smiling*). And my sister?

FABRICE. I'd have room for her in any case. (*William says nothing.*) And even if—. Let's be sensible and talk this over.—I love Marianne. Give me her hand in marriage!

WILLIAM. What?

FABRICE. Why not? Give your consent! Listen to me, brother. I love Marianne! I've thought it over for a long time. She all by herself, you all by yourself—the two of you together could give me all the happiness this world can still hold for me. Give her to me, give her to me!

WILLIAM (*confusedly*). You don't know what you're asking.

FABRICE. Oh, how well I do know! Should I tell you how much is missing in my life and how much I'll have if she becomes my wife and you my brother-in-law?

WILLIAM (*startled; bursting out*). Never! Never!

FABRICE. What's wrong with you? I'm hurt—you seem shocked!—If you are to have a brother-in-law, as you surely will sooner or later, why not me? Someone you know and love! At least I believed—.

WILLIAM. Stop! I can't think.

FABRICE. I have to tell you everything. My fate depends entirely on you. Her heart is well disposed, you must have noticed that. She loves you more than me; I don't mind. She'll come to love her husband more than her brother. I'll take over your prerogatives, you'll take over mine, and we'll all be happy. I've never seen the threads of a plot tied together so beautifully, with such human kindness. (*William is silent.*) And all it takes to settle it—my dear fellow, just give your consent, your word! Tell her that you're pleased, that it makes you happy! I have her word.

WILLIAM. Her word?

FABRICE. Spoken almost in passing, a sort of parting glance, more eloquent than if she had not left me at all. Bashful and loving, willing and trembling; it was so beautiful!

WILLIAM. No! No!

FABRICE. I don't understand you. I don't feel that you have anything against me, and yet you oppose me so. Don't! Don't stand in the way of her happiness—or of mine!—I keep thinking how happy you will be with us! Don't withhold your consent to my hopes, your friendly word! (*William remains silent, in a torment of conflicting thoughts.*) I can't understand you.

WILLIAM. She?—You want her?

FABRICE. What are you saying?

WILLIAM. And she wants you?

FABRICE. She answered as befits a young lady.

WILLIAM. Go! Go away!—Marianne!—I suspected as much! I felt it!

FABRICE. Just tell me—

WILLIAM. Tell indeed!—That was what lay like a thundercloud on my mind this evening. A flash! A clap of thunder!—Take her! The only thing I have, my all! (*Fabrice stares at him, speechless.*) Take her! And to make you realize what you're taking from me—(*Pause. He pulls himself together.*) I told you about Charlotte, the angel who escaped from me, leaving a daughter; her very likeness—and this daughter—I lied to you—she is not dead; this daughter is Marianne!—Marianne is not my sister.

FABRICE. I was not prepared for that.

WILLIAM. I should have been afraid of this, coming from you. Why didn't I follow my heart and shut you out of my house as I did everyone in the first days after my coming here? You alone I admitted into this sanctuary and you have managed to lull me to sleep with kindness, friendship, support, with your seeming coldness to women. Just as I was to all appearances her brother, so I thought your feelings toward her to be truly brotherly. And even when I couldn't suppress an occasional suspicion, I would dismiss it as unworthy. Her sweetness toward you I put to the credit of her angelic heart, which simply saw the whole world with the eyes of love.—And you!—And she!—

FABRICE. I don't want to hear anything more, nor do I have anything more to say. So good-bye! (*Exit.*)

WILLIAM. Go! You carry everything away with you; all my happiness, all my prospects, cut off and broken—the closest and dearest—all at once—the abyss! Fallen, the magic bridge of gold which was to transport me into heavenly delight—Gone!—and because of him, the traitor, who so abused my confidence!—Oh, William! William! Have you been brought to such a pass? Must you be unjust toward this decent fellow? What crime has he committed? Fate, you lie heavy upon me, and you are just in your retribution. Why are you standing there? And you? At this very moment! Forgive me! Haven't I suffered for it? Forgive! It's so long ago! I have suffered endlessly. I seemed to love you both; I believed I loved you; with little attentions and favors I opened up your hearts and made you miserable! Forgive me and leave me—Shall I be so punished? Shall I lose Marianne, the last of my hopes, the essence of my sorrows and cares? It cannot be, it cannot be! (*He stops, silent.*)

Enter Marianne.

MARIANNE (*approaching diffidently*). Brother!

WILLIAM. Ah!

MARIANNE. My dear brother, you must forgive me, I beg you with all my heart. You are angry, I thought you would be. I have done a foolish thing—I feel very strange.

WILLIAM (*pulling himself together*). What have you done, young lady?

MARIANNE. I wish I could tell you. I can't think straight. Fabrice wants me to be his wife, and I—

WILLIAM (*half bitterly*). Go ahead and say it, you're going to consent?

MARIANNE. No, not if my life depended on it! I'll never marry him! I can't marry him!

WILLIAM. How different that sounds!

MARIANNE. Strange! You're not being very gracious, Brother. I feel like going away and staying away for an hour or so, except that I have to get it off my heart right now. Once and for all, I can't marry Fabrice.

WILLIAM (*gets up and takes her by the hand*). What's that, Marianne?

MARIANNE. He was here and he talked so much and told me so many different things that I began to imagine it was possible. He was so insistent; without thinking what I was doing I said he should talk with you.—He took that as a yes, but I felt at that very moment it couldn't be.

WILLIAM. He has spoken to me.

MARIANNE. I beg you with all the strength I can muster, with all the love I have for you, by all the love you feel for me, set things right again, make him understand.

WILLIAM (*to himself*). Almighty God!

MARIANNE. Don't be angry. I don't want him to be angry either. Let's live as we did before—and forever. Because I can only live with you; I want to live with you and you alone. It's something that's always been in my heart and this has brought it to the surface, with terrible force—I love only you!

WILLIAM. Marianne!

MARIANNE. My dearest brother! This past quarter of an hour—I can't tell you what has been running through my heart.—It's how I felt not long ago when there was a fire in a house near the market and at first everything was covered with clouds of smoke, 'til suddenly the fire burst through the roof and the whole house was one mass of flame.—Don't leave me! Don't turn me away, Brother!

WILLIAM. But things can't stay this way forever.

MARIANNE. That's just what worries me so. I'll gladly promise never to marry. I'll always take care of you, always and always. You know, there's an old couple, brother and sister, living across the way; sometimes it's fun to think to myself: what if I'm old and wrinkled like that, if only we're together?

WILLIAM (*holding his hand on his heart, half to himself*). If you can survive this, you'll never again feel cold and anxious.

MARIANNE. It's not the same way with you, I guess. You'll find a wife some time, no doubt, but it would always pain me, even if I tried hard to love her—No one loves you as I do, no one can love you that much. (*William tries to speak.*) You're always so reserved, and it's always on the tip of my tongue to tell you how I feel, and I don't dare. Thank God, now chance has unsealed my lips.

WILLIAM. Say no more, Marianne!

MARIANNE. You mustn't stop me. Let me say everything I have to say. Then I'll go back to the kitchen and sit there at work day after day and just look at you from time to time, as if to say: "You know what I'm thinking!" (*William remains silent, in the fullness of his joy.*) You could have known it long ago, and you have known too, since our mother died and I was always with you, growing up and not a child any more.—You see, what I feel is rather happiness at being with you than gratitude for your more than brotherly care. Gradually you have come to fill my whole heart, my whole mind, so that now it's hard for anything else to find even a tiny bit of space there. I remember well: you sometimes laughed when I read novels; it happened once with Julia Mandeville and I asked whether Henry, or whatever his name was, didn't look like you. You laughed—I didn't like that. The next time I kept still. But I was very serious about it, because in my mind all the characters who were the most lovable, the best, all looked like you. I saw you walking around in the grand gardens and riding horseback, traveling about, and duelling—

She laughs to herself.

WILLIAM. What's the matter?

MARIANNE. I might as well confess to the rest of it: whenever there was a lady who was very pretty and very kind and much loved—and very much in love—that was always me.—Only in the end, when it came to the happy ending, and all their problems were solved, and they got married—I guess I'm really just a simple, good-hearted little chatterbox.

WILLIAM. Go on, go on! (*Averting his face.*) My cup of joy is full and I must drink it to the dregs. God in Heaven, preserve my sanity!

MARIANNE. The hardest of all for me to bear was when two people loved each other and in the end it turns out they're related, or brother and sister—I could have burned Miss Fanny!—I cried and cried! It's such as truly miserable fate!

She turns away, weeping bitterly.

WILLIAM (*his arms suddenly about her*). Marianne! My Marianne!

MARIANNE. William! No! No! I'll never let you go! You are mine!—I'll keep you here! I can't let you go!

Enter Fabrice.

MARIANNE. Ah, Fabrice! You've come at the right time! My heart is free and strong, so I can tell you: I have not given you any promises. Be our friend! I shall never marry you.

FABRICE (*cold and bitter*). I thought as much, William; if you threw your whole weight into the balance I would, of course, be found wanting. I came back to say what has to be said. I give up all my claims; I see that everything is settled; at least I'm glad that I provided the innocent occasion for it.

WILLIAM. At a moment like this don't blaspheme, don't rob yourself of an emotion you'd seek in vain, even if your pilgrimage covered the whole wide world. See this creature before you—she is mine—and she does not know—

FABRICE (*half in mockery*). What doesn't she know?

MARIANNE. What don't I know?

WILLIAM. A lie—now—Fabrice—?

FABRICE (*struck dumb*). She doesn't know?

WILLIAM. That's what I said.

FABRICE. Keep each other, you deserve each other!

MARIANNE. What's that?

WILLIAM (*embracing her*). You are mine, Marianne!

MARIANNE. Good Lord, what is this?—Can I return that kiss?—What kind of kiss was that, Brother?

WILLIAM. Not a restrained and brotherly kiss, in the semblance of coldness; it was the kiss of a lover, eternally and uniquely happy. (*At her feet.*) Marianne, you are not my sister! Charlotte was your mother, not mine.

MARIANNE. You! You!

WILLIAM. Your beloved—and, from this moment on, your husband—if you do not reject him.

MARIANNE. Tell me, how was that possible?—

FABRICE. Enjoy what God himself can only give you once! Accept, Marianne, and ask no questions; you will find time enough to explain things to each other.

MARIANNE (*looking at him*). No, it isn't possible!

WILLIAM. My love! My wife!

MARIANNE (*embracing him*). William, it's not possible!

PROMETHEUS

Dramatic Fragment

Translated by Frank Ryder

Act I

Prometheus. Mercury.

PROMETHEUS. I will not! Tell them that!
And there's an end of it: I won't.
Their will against mine.
One against one—
I'd call it even.
MERCURY. I? Tell that to Zeus, your father?
Tell your mother that?
PROMETHEUS. What do you mean: father, mother?
Do you know where *you* came from?
I did not know that I was standing
Until I saw my feet beneath me;
That I was reaching out
Until I felt these arms extended—
And there they were, watching my steps,
The ones that you call father, mother.
MERCURY. Extending you
The needed help of childhood.
PROMETHEUS. For which they had the obedience of my child-hood—
Shaping the poor young sapling
This way and that way on the winds of their caprice.
MERCURY. Protecting you.
PROMETHEUS. From what? From dangers
They feared themselves.
Did they preserve this heart
From serpents secretly tormenting it?
Steel this breast
To challenge Titans?
What was the forge of my manhood
If not almighty Time,
My lord and yours?
MERCURY. Poor wretch! So much for the gods?
The immortals?
PROMETHEUS. Gods? I am no god—
And I think just as well of myself.
Immortal? Almighty?
What can you do?
Can you compress the breadth
Of heaven and earth into the space

Of my clenched fist?
Can you divide me
From myself?
Can you expand me,
Stretch me out to make a world?

MERCURY. But Fate!

PROMETHEUS. You recognize its power?
So do I—
Now leave me; I'll serve no vassal!

Exit Mercury.

PROMETHEUS (*turns back to his statues, which are scattered throughout the grove*).
Irreplaceable moment!
Dragged by that fool
From your company,
My children!
Whatever stirs within my breast—

He approaches one of the statues, that of a girl.

This breast was meant to swell in answer.
These eyes already speak!
Speak, talk to me, fair lips!
If only I could give to you the gift
Of feeling what you are!

Enter Epimetheus.

EPIMETHEUS. Bitter complaints from Mercury!

PROMETHEUS. If only you'd ignore complainers
He'd have come back uncomplaining.

EPIMETHEUS. Be reasonable, my brother.
What the gods proposed this time was fair.
They'd cede to you Olympus' summit,
There to live and be
Ruler of earth!

PROMETHEUS. To be their steward
And to guard their heaven?
What I propose is better far.
They want to share with me, and I would say
That I have nothing I would share with them.
What I have they cannot rob me of;
What they possess let them protect.
Mine and thine!
And there we part.

EPIMETHEUS. How much is really yours?
PROMETHEUS. Whatever space my energies can fill,
Nothing more nor less!
These stars above, what kind of claim
Have they on me,
That they stare down at me?
EPIMETHEUS. You stand alone,
So stubborn you ignore the joy
There'd be if the gods and you,
Your people, world and heaven all,
Felt themselves whole in spirit, one.
PROMETHEUS. I know, I know!
Please, dear brother, go;
Do what you can but leave me.

Exit Epimetheus.

PROMETHEUS. Here's my world, my all!
Here I know who I am!
Here—all my wishes
Embodied in these figures,
My spirit split a thousand ways
Yet whole in my beloved children.

Enter Minerva.

PROMETHEUS. You dare, my goddess,
Dare to join your father's foe?
MINERVA. I honor my father
And I love you, Prometheus.
PROMETHEUS. And you are to my spirit
As it is to itself.
Has not from the start,
Your word been heaven's light to me?
Always when my soul would speak, as to itself,
Would seem to open up,
Its innate harmonies
Echoing of their own accord—
The words were yours.
So my self was not myself;
A deity was speaking
When I thought I spoke.
And when I thought a god was talking
It was I who spoke.
And thus with you and me,
One in spirit always,

My love for you enternal!
MINERVA. And my presence always with you!
PROMETHEUS. As the sweet glow of dusk
From the departed sun
Rises upward there, softly,
From darkest Caucasus
And bathes my soul with joyous calm—
Vanishing, still ever present—
Just so have my creative powers grown
With every breath I've taken of your heavenly air.
What sort of claim
Do the proud dwellers of Olympus
Think they have
Upon my powers?
They are mine and mine to use.
Not one step farther,
Even for the chief of all the gods!
For them? Do I exist for them?
MINERVA. Those in power think so.
PROMETHEUS. I too can think, my goddess,
And I too have power.—
Still!—Have you not seen me
Often in self-chosen servitude
Bearing the burden they
Made solemn show to place upon my shoulders?
Have I not done my work,
Each daily task, at their behest,
Because I thought
That they could see the past and future too
Within the present,
Thought their command, their guidance
Unselfserving,
Immemorial wisdom?
MINERVA. You served that you might merit freedom.
PROMETHEUS. And not at any price would I
Change places with the bird of thunder,
Clench my master's lightning bolts
Proud in a slave's talons.
What are they?—What am I?
MINERVA. Your hatred is unjust.
Fate's portion for the gods was permanence
And power, wisdom, love.
PROMETHEUS. None of which they hold
In sole possession!

I'll last as long as they.
We're all eternal!
I have no memory of my beginnings;
I have no sense for endings;
Nor do I see the end.
So I'm eternal, since I am!
And as for wisdom—

He shows her about among the statues.

Look at this brow!
Did not my fingers
Make and shape it?
The power of this bosom
Presses back against
The all-assailing dangers that surround it.

He stops at the statue of a woman.

And you, Pandora,
Holy vessel of all gifts
That please
Under the wide sky,
On the endless earth.
Whatever sense of joy revived me,
Whatever solace bathed me
In the cool of shadows,
All happiness of springtime
From the love of the sun,
Whatever tenderness
The sea's soft wave
Pressed to my breast,
And all that I have ever tasted
Of the pure glow of heaven
Of pleasant calm of spirit
All, all that—My Pandora!

MINERVA. Jupiter has promised you
He'd bring them all to life
If you would hear and give assent
To his proposal.

PROMETHEUS. That was the only thing that made me hesitate,
And yet—I was to be the servant, and we
Were all to recognize the Thunderer's overlordship?
No. Let them remain in the bondage
Of their lifelessness;
Still they are free,

And I can sense their freedom!
MINERVA. They *shall* live.
It's up to Fate and not the gods
To give the gift of life, or take it.
Come, I shall lead you to the sources of all life,
Which Jupiter will not close off.
Live they shall, and that through you.
PROMETHEUS. Through you, my goddess,
Live and know their freedom,
Live!—Their joy will be your thanks!

ACT II

On Mt. Olympus
Jupiter. Mercury.

MERCURY. Foul tidings—Father Jupiter—high treason!
Minerva, your own daughter,
Takes up the rebel's cause;
She's led him to the living springs,
Brought his court of clay,
His potter's world
To life around him.
They move like us,
Weaving, exulting, all around him
As we around you.
Zeus, where are your thunderbolts?
JUPITER. They are; they will be!
They *shall* be!
Over all that is,
Beneath the spacious sky,
Upon the endless earth,
My rule prevails.
That tribe of worms augments
The number of my slaves.
If they seek my paternal guidance, good befall them.
Woe betide them if they should resist
My sovereign hand.
MERCURY. All-father and all-merciful,
Forgiver of the crimes of criminals,
All love and praise to you

From all of earth and heaven!
Father, send me that I may proclaim
To those poor mortals born of earth
Your self, your kindness, and your power!
JUPITER. Not yet. In youthful rapture newly born
They think themselves in spirit like the gods.
They will not listen till they need
Your help. So leave them to the life they lead.
MERCURY. No less kind than wise!

Valley at the Foot of Mt. Olympus

PROMETHEUS. Look down, oh Zeus,
Upon my world. It lives,
And I have shaped it in my likeness,
A race to be like me,
To suffer, weep, enjoy, to have its pleasure,
And pay no heed to you—
No more than I do.

The races of men are visible throughout the valley, climbing on trees in search of fruit to pick, bathing in the waters, racing with one another over the meadows; girls are busy picking flowers and weaving wreaths. A man with young freshly cut trees steps up to Prometheus.

MAN. See, here are the trees
As you requested.
PROMETHEUS. How did you get them
Out of the ground?
MAN. I took this sharp stone here
And cut them cleanly at the roots.
PROMETHEUS. Off with the branches first!—
And then drive this one here
Slantwise into the ground
And this one opposite
And tie the tips together!
Then two more here behind
And one more crosswise here on top.
Now the branches from above
Right to the ground,
All tied and woven in,
And sod on every side;
Branches over that,
And more, until no sun,
No rain or wind intrudes.

There, dear son, a refuge and a shelter!
MAN. Thanks, father, thanks a thousand times!
Tell me, may all my brothers live
In my hut?
PROMETHEUS. No!
You built it for yourself, it's yours.
You may share it
With whom you will.
Whoever wants a place to live can build his own.

Exit Prometheus.

Two Men

FIRST. Hands off my goats!
You'll not take one of them.
They're mine, all mine.
SECOND. How so?
FIRST. Last night and all day yesterday
I climbed around here in the mountains,
Worked myself to death
To catch them alive,
Then guarded them all night,
And here with rocks and branches
Penned them up.
SECOND. Well, give me one!
I killed one yesterday myself,
And brought it to the fire to be cooked,
Ate it with my brothers too.
Why do you need more than one today?
We'll hunt again tomorrow.
FIRST. You stay away from my herd!
SECOND. No!

First tries to stop him; Second gives him a push and knocks him down, takes a goat, and is off.

FIRST. Help, help! I'm hurt!
PROMETHEUS (*arrives*). What now?
FIRST. My goats! He's stealing them.
My head is dripping blood.
He battered me
Against this rock.
PROMETHEUS. Just pull the spongy fungus off that tree
And put it on your wound.
FIRST. There—dear father!

The bleeding's stopped already.
PROMETHEUS. Now go and wash your face.
FIRST. What about my goat?
PROMETHEUS. Let the man go!
If his hand is against every man
Then every man's hand will be against him.

Exit First Man.

PROMETHEUS. You've not belied your nature, my children.
You're lazy and industrious,
And gently cruel,
Generously mean,
Like all your brothers in this fate,
Like all the beasts, and like the gods.

Enter Pandora.

PROMETHEUS. My daughter, what's the matter?
Why so upset?
PANDORA. My father!
The things I've seen, my father!
The things I've felt!
PROMETHEUS. Well?
PANDORA. Oh my poor Mira!
PROMETHEUS. What's happened to her?
PANDORA. Feelings I have no name for!
I saw her walking toward the forest glade
Where we so often pick our flower garlands;
I followed her
And when I came down from the hill
I saw her in the valley, sunk down on a grassy spot.
By happy chance Arbar was in the woods.
He took her tightly in his arms
To keep her safe from falling—
And sank, alas, down with her.
Her lovely head fell back;
He kissed her a thousand times,
His lips not leaving hers,
Breathing into her his spirit.
I took alarm, rushed up to them, cried out.
My crying brought her to her senses.
Arbar left her; she sprang up;
And then, with eyes rolled back,
She fell upon my neck.
Her bosom beat

As if to break,
Her cheeks aflame,
Her mouth was parched. She wept a thousand tears.
I felt her knees again grow weak;
I held her, father dear;
All her kisses, all her ardor,
Sent a new and unfamiliar feeling
Coursing through my veins.
Confused, upset,
And weeping, at last I left her,
Left field and forest,
To come to you, my father! Tell me,
What is this thing that so undid her—
And me?

PROMETHEUS. Death!

PANDORA. And what is that?

PROMETHEUS. My daughter,
Many joys have come your way.

PANDORA. A thousandfold—thanks to you.

PROMETHEUS. Pandora, your bosom swelled
To greet the sun in its coming,
The moon in its changes,
And in the kisses of your companions
You knew the purest happiness.

PANDORA. Inexpressible!

PROMETHEUS. In the dance, what force raised your body
Lightly from earth?

PANDORA. Joy!
As every limb, touched by the sound of music,
Moved and stirred and I was swept away on floods of melody.

PROMETHEUS. And all at last dissolves in sleep,
Both joy and pain.
You've felt the burning glow of sun
And parching thirst,
The weariness of knees,
And you have wept to lose your sheep.
And how you moaned and trembled
In the forest when the thorn had pierced your heel—
Until I cured you.

PANDORA. This life's delight takes many forms, my father,
Its sorrow too.

PROMETHEUS. And your heart tells you this as well:
That many other joys are left,
And hurts that you know nothing of.

PANDORA. True! This heart so often longs
To be—oh, nowhere—and yet everywhere.
PROMETHEUS. And still there comes a time when all is fulfilled,
Everything we've longed for, dreamed or hoped
Or feared, my beloved. And that time is death.
PANDORA. Death?
PROMETHEUS. When from the inmost deepest ground
Of being, shaken, you shall feel
All the joy and hurt that ever filled you,
Heart bursting in the storm,
Seeking relief in tears and finding all its flame increased,
When all that's in you echoes, quakes, and trembles,
All your senses fail and leave you,
And you believe that you will faint,
Sink down; when everything about you
Drowns in night, and inwardly, in your own depths of feeling,
You enfold a world:
This is man dying.
PANDORA (*throwing her arms about him*). Oh father, let us die!
PROMETHEUS. Not yet!
PANDORA. And after death?
PROMETHEUS. When all—desire, joy, and suffering—
Dissipates itself in storms of pleasure,
To be in blissful sleep restored,
You'll come to life again, rejuvenated,
To fear once more, once more to hope and yearn.

[At this point Goethe added, in later editions, the Prometheus ode which appears as a separate poem in volume 1, pp. 26–31, of the present collection.]

JERY AND BETTY

An Operetta

Translated by Frank Ryder

Characters

Betty
Her Father
Jery
Thomas

The scene is laid in the mountains of the Swiss canton of Uri.

Mountainous region. In the background a hut by a cliff with a waterfall. To the side a steeply sloping meadow, the end of it hidden by trees. In the foreground at one side a stone table with benches.

BETTY (*carrying two pails of milk slung from a shoulder yoke, comes in off the meadow*).

Little bird, sing brightly!
Blossom, little tree, too!
Hearts are gay and spritely—
Working hard as we do
Day and night.

The linen is sprinkled, the cows are milked, I've had my breakfast, the sun is over the mountain, and Father is still in bed. I must get him up so that I'll have someone to talk to. I don't like having time on my hands. I don't like being alone. (*She takes her distaff and spindle.*) He usually gets up when he hears me. (*Father appears.*)

FATHER. Good morning Betty.

BETTY. Good morning Father.

FATHER. I wouldn't have minded a bit more sleep, but now you wake me up with a cheerful little song, so I can't be angry with you. You are naughty and nice, both at the same time.

BETTY. As usual, Father, right?

FATHER. You should have let me have my rest! After all, you don't know when I went to bed last night.

BETTY. You had good company.

FATHER. And that wasn't nice of you either—to slip into the house so early, as if the beautiful moonlight were making your eyelids heavy. You know poor Jery was here because of you; he sat up with me on the bench till after midnight. I really felt sorry for him.

BETTY. You are always ready to sympathize with him when he hangs around and complains—repeats the same old thing over and over—then says nothing for a quarter of an hour—acts as if he were about to leave—then stays on—and begins all over again from the beginning. I feel quite different. I get bored.

FATHER. But I wish, too, that you would come to some decision.

BETTY. Are you really that eager to get rid of me?

FATHER. No, not that. I'd move in with you; we'd both get along better and be more comfortable.

BETTY. Who knows? A husband isn't always easy to have around.

FATHER. If you're better off, you're better off, that's all. We'd rent out the farm up here and settle down in the valley.

BETTY. But we're used to this! Our house keeps out the wind and the snow and the rain, our meadow gives us what we need. We have plenty to eat and drink all year, and we sell enough so we can afford nice things to wear. We're by ourselves up here and don't have to be civil to anybody if we don't want to. How much better off would you be down in the town, with a bigger house, a nicer panelled parlor, more cattle, and more people around? It only means more to do and more to worry about, and certainly you can't eat any more or drink or sleep any more than you do now. But I *would* like to see you a bit more comfortable.

FATHER. And *I'd* like not having to worry about you any more. I'm getting old after all and I can tell I'm losing my strength. My right arm is getting stiffer and stiffer; I feel the weather more in my shoulder—where the bullet hit the bone. And then, my child, when I finally go, you simply can't carry on alone. You'll have to get married, and you don't know who you'll get for a husband. Now you have a good man offering you his hand. I keep turning that over in my mind; I worry about you, I think about you.

Every morrow,
Some new sorrow
For the children you adore.

BETTY.

Put off sorrow
Till tomorrow
Sorrow's what tomorrow's for.

What did Jery say, by the way?

FATHER. What does it matter? You don't care.

BETTY. I'd like to know if he's said anything new.

FATHER. Nothing new, and he won't have any new business to bring up until you get the old business off his mind!

BETTY. I'm sorry for him; he could be very happy. He's all alone, he has a nice estate from his father, he's young and active; only he wants more, he wants to force someone to become his wife. And it happens to be me! He could have ten girls to pick from in the village. Why does he come up to see us? Why does he want only me?

FATHER. Because he loves you.

BETTY. I don't know what he wants. All he can do is bother me.

FATHER. I wouldn't have any objection to him.

BETTY. I don't either. He's handsome and brave and strong. At the last fair he really threw that stranger who was boasting about his wrestling. I like him very well in most ways. If only men didn't want to get married right away; if only they weren't after you all day long, as soon you're friendly to them.

FATHER. He never came around so much until last month.

BETTY. It won't be long before he's back again, because early this morning I saw him sneaking out to the meadow he owns up in the forest. He never took so much interest in the cattle as he has recently. I wish he'd leave me in peace.—The linen is almost dried out again. How high the sun is! Now what about your breakfast?

FATHER. I'll get it, don't worry. Just take care of lunch in time.

BETTY. That's more my concern than it is yours.

Exit Father.

BETTY. Sure enough! Here he comes. I knew it. Suitors are as punctual as the sun. I'd better start singing something cheerful so he can't launch into his same old tune. (*She finds something to do and begins to sing.*)

The water is flowing,
It never stands still.
The stars in the heavens
Move on as they will.

The clouds are contented
To drift through the sky,
And love is no different—
It soon passes by.

JERY (*who in the meanwhile has come close to her*).

The waters are flowing,
The clouds drift away.
The stars are not like that—
They move, yet they stay.

And that's the way love is,
If lovers are true:
Unchanged in its changes,
The same old or new.

BETTY. What's new, Jery?

JERY. The same old thing, Betty!

BETTY. We have enough old things up here. Bring us something new, why don't you? Where did you come from so early?

JERY. I've been on the upper meadow, to see how many cheeses we have on hand. There's a buyer down by the lake who's looking for some. I think we'll reach an agreement.

BETTY. Then you'll be making a lot of money again.

JERY. More than I need.

BETTY. You can have it as far as I'm concerned.

JERY. Half of it could be yours—or all of it. Think how nice it would be if I'd made a deal and came home and threw the money in your lap.

"Count it over," I'd say, "and put it aside!" Now, when I come home, I have to put my money in the dresser drawer—and for whom I don't know.

BETTY. How long is it till Easter?

JERY. Not long, if you'd give me some hope.

BETTY. Heaven forbid! I was just thinking.

JERY. You'll be the cause of a lot of trouble. Often you've driven me so wild I was ready to marry some other girl just to spite you. And suppose I did and got tired of her right away; suppose I kept realizing: that's not my Betty!—I'd be miserable for the rest of my life.

BETTY. You'll have to marry a beautiful girl who's rich and nice. You never get tired of someone like that.

JERY. I've always wanted you, not someone richer or nicer.

I won't bore you with complaining,
But there's one thing needs explaining:
My whole heart and life have grown
One with you and you alone.

Won't you love me as you used to?
End the misery I'm reduced to?
In my heart you are my own,
I'm forever yours alone.

BETTY. You certainly know some pretty songs, Jery, and you sing them well. You'll teach me half a dozen, won't you! I'm tired of the old ones. Now, good-bye! I still have lots to do this morning. Father's calling. (*Exit.*)

JERY.
Leave me!
Deceive me
Dismiss me!
You'll miss me
In time.
I must go away now—
You're sending me, really—
I just cannot stay now;
I've got to breathe freely.
Deceive me!
Dismiss me!
You'll miss me
In time.

Enter Thomas.

THOMAS. Jery!

JERY. Who's that?

THOMAS. Good morning.

JERY. Who are you?

THOMAS. Don't you recognize me?

JERY. Thomas, is that you?

THOMAS. Have I changed so much?

JERY. You certainly have. You're taller. You look more distinguished.

THOMAS. That comes from leading the life of a soldier. A soldier always looks more distinguished than a farmer. That comes from being treated worse.

JERY. You're on leave?

THOMAS. No. I have my discharge. When my enlistment was over—"Adieu Captain," said I, and went home.

JERY. But what kind of a coat is that? Why are you wearing a hat with braid and carrying a sabre? You still look very military.

THOMAS. In France they call it an *uniforme de goût*, when a person wears something fancy just because he wants to.

JERY. Didn't you like it in the army?

THOMAS. Fine, just fine, but not in the long run. I wouldn't take fifty gold-pieces for my experience as a soldier. You become an entirely different fellow, younger, happier, smarter; you can always get along in any situation, and you know what the world's like.

JERY. How did you happen to come here? Where are you headed?

THOMAS. Things just didn't suit me at home with my mother. So I bought forty head of good Appenzell oxen on credit, all black and brown-black as the night. I'm driving them to Milan. It's a good deal. You earn something and have a good time on the way. I have my fiddle with me—to heal the sick and make the rainy days cheerful. Well, how are things with you, William Tell? You don't look very happy. What's your trouble?

JERY. I wish I could have got away long ago—I wish I could have worked out a deal like yours. I still have money lying around, and I don't like being at home anymore.

THOMAS. Hm! You don't look like a businessman. A businessman has to have a clear pair of eyes in his head. You look sad and listless.

JERY. Oh, Thomas!

THOMAS. Don't sigh, that annoys me.

JERY. I'm in love!

THOMAS. Is that all? I'm always in love, whenever I'm quartered somewhere and the girls aren't too repulsive.

A sweetheart and a glass of wine,
Now who'd be sick in bed?
If you don't drink and you don't kiss,
You're just as good as dead.

JERY. I see you've become like all the others; it's not enough to have fun, right away you have to be crude.

THOMAS. You don't understand, friend! Your condition isn't all that critical. You poor fools—when you feel your first heartthrobs you think that the sun, moon, and stars are about to disappear.

A shepherd once was noted
For time to sleep devoted,
He didn't tend the sheep,
Poor fool, let some girl tease him,
And nothing more could please him—
His heart was drawn out yonder,
To count the stars and wander—
And all he did was weep.
But now that she's consented,
He's got his late-lamented
Thirst, appetite, and sleep.

Tell me, do you want to get married?

JERY. I'm courting the loveliest girl in the world.

THOMAS. When's the wedding?

JERY. We haven't got that far yet.

THOMAS. Why not?

JERY. She won't have me.

THOMAS. That's not very smart of her.

JERY. I'm my own master, I have a nice little estate, a fine house, I'm willing to have her father move in with me, and I'll see that they have a good life.

THOMAS. And she doesn't want you? Does she have someone else in mind?

JERY. She doesn't care for anyone.

THOMAS. No one? She's crazy. She ought to thank God and grab hold with both hands. What kind of stubborn person is she?

JERY. I've been pursuing her for a year now. She lives here with her father. The little farm provides what they need. She's already scared away all the other young fellows. The whole neighborhood is annoyed with her. She gave one of them the brush-off and drove another man's son crazy. Most of them made up their minds in a hurry and took other wives. Only I can't force myself to do that, no matter what pretty girls people say I could have.

THOMAS. You can't keep asking forever. What is a girl like that to do all by herself in the mountains? What if her father dies, what will she do? She'll have to throw herself at the first man who comes along.

JERY. That's right.

THOMAS. You don't understand. You have to talk sense to her—and not too gently at that. Is she at home?

JERY. Yes.

THOMAS. I'll be your go-between! What do I get if I fix you up with her?

JERY. There's nothing you can do.

THOMAS. What do I get?

JERY. Whatever you want.

THOMAS. Ten gold-pieces! I have to ask for something substantial.

JERY. You're welcome to it, from the bottom of my heart.

THOMAS. Now just let me handle it.

JERY. How are you going to go about it?

THOMAS. Cleverly.

JERY. Well?

THOMAS. I'll ask her what she plans to do if a wolf comes along.

JERY. You're making a joke of it.

THOMAS. Or if her father dies.

JERY. Ah!

THOMAS. Or if she gets sick.

JERY. Go on.

THOMAS. And when she gets old.

JERY. Now you're talking.

THOMAS. I'll give her case histories.

JERY. Fine.

THOMAS. I'll tell her that a girl ought to thank God when she finds a fellow who's true to her.

JERY. Excellent.

THOMAS. I'll praise you to the skies. Now run along, run along.

JERY. Life and hope reborn for Jery,
That is what you promise me.
THOMAS. Getting you a girl to marry,
That's no act of charity.

Exit Jery.

THOMAS (*alone.*) Look what can happen to a person in this world. When I went into the cattle business I had no idea that I was going to be a marriage-broker on the side. Let's see what kind of shrew she is and whether she won't listen to reason. The best thing for me to do is to act as if I weren't acquainted with Jery, as if I knew nothing about him—and then I'll make a flank attack on her with my proposition.

Betty comes from the chalet.

THOMAS (*to himself*). Is that her? Why, she's pretty! (*Aloud*:) Good morning, my lovely child.

BETTY. Thank you so much! Would the gentleman care for something?

THOMAS. A glass of milk or wine, Miss, would be most refreshing. I've been driving cattle up the mountain for three hours now, and I haven't found a thing to eat or drink.

BETTY. I'd be glad to oblige, and you can have a piece of bread and cheese as well—with the red wine, a really good Italian red.

THOMAS. *Charmant*! Is this your house?

BETTY. Yes, I live here with my father.

THOMAS. Oh, my! All alone?

BETTY. There *are* two of us. Wait, I'll get you something to drink—or why not come in with me? Why stand outside? You can talk to my father.

THOMAS. Come now, my child, there's no hurry. (*He takes her by the hand, holding her back.*)

BETTY (*breaks away*). What's the meaning of that?

THOMAS. Why not listen to what I have to say? (*He grabs her.*)

BETTY (*as before*). What's the idea? Are we friends already?

THOMAS. Little lady, why the haste?
You're so fair—and shy, too!

BETTY. Most girls lack good sense and taste.
That's no sign that I do.

THOMAS. No, I will not let you free.
Couldn't you be nicer?

BETTY. You're not thirsty—that I see.
On your way!—good-bye, sir!

Exit Betty.

THOMAS (*alone*). That was a poor start! First I should have won her confidence, got settled in, had something to eat and drink, and then started talking. Always in too much of a hurry! How did I know she was going to be so wild? She's as skittish as a squirrel. I'll have to try again. (*Calling toward the chalet:*) There's something else I wanted to say, Miss.

BETTY (*at the window*). Be on your way! There's nothing for you here. (*She slams the window.*)

THOMAS. You rude girl! If that's the way she acts with her suitors, I'm surprised there's even one left. Jery will have a bad time with her. She ought to get a husband who'll yell back at her as loud as she yells at him. Stubborn woman—she thinks she's so safe up here. If anyone decided to treat her badly, she's just have to take it. Someone ought to make her wish she weren't single, and I have half a mind to do it myself. If Jery is watching me, hoping and waiting, he'll certainly make fun of me—even if it isn't all that funny for him. Confound it, she'd better listen to what I have to tell her. At least I'm going to carry out this mission. A retreat would be too much of a disgrace. (*Knocking loudly at the chalet.*) No fooling now, Miss, open up—be so kind as to give me a glass of wine. I'll be glad to pay for it.

Betty (*as before, at the window*). This is no tavern. Get out! We aren't used to this around here. The way you act is the way you get treated. So forget it! (*She slams the window shut.*)

Thomas. Stubborn, silly girl! You think you're so safe up here; I'll show you. Monkey-face! We'll see who'll come to your rescue. Once I've put some sense in her head, she won't be so eager to risk living up there alone. All right then! Since I can't teach her a lesson by word of mouth, I'll give her a practical demonstration. There comes my herd up the mountain. They'll take their midday rest on her pasture. Ha, ha! They'll fix all her meadows for her, they'll trample her land good and proper. (*He calls backstage*:) Hey, there! Hey!

A herd boy appears.

Thomas. It's too hot to drive them any farther up the mountain. Here's a meadow to rest on. Go ahead and drive all the cattle in. Well, why are you standing there, looking surprised? Do what I tell you, understand? This field here. No formalities! And don't let anyone stop you, no matter what happens. Let them graze and rest a while. I know the people here. I'll have a word with them, don't you worry. (*Exit herd boy.*) But what if it gets to the governor? So what, who cares about a little fine? I think the cure should take, and if it doesn't, then we've all had our revenge, Jery and I, and all lovers-and-losers. (*He steps onto a rock close to the water and talks with people offstage.*) Drive the oxen onto the field here. Just pull the fencing down. That's correct, all of it! Boy, in here! All right, have a good time! Chase off the cows over there. Look at them jump when they get driven off their home fields! Take that, you silly girl!

He sits down on a rock, takes out his fiddle, plays and sings.

A quodlibet! Now come along,
Whoever wants to hear:
'Twas Holofernes wrote the song,
It came out just this year.

Father (*hurries out of the chalet*).

What's this? What shameless villainy!
What right have you, you cad?

Thomas. In Poland and in Germany
You'll find it's just as bad.

Betty. You think we're all without defense.
You'll lord it if you can!

THOMAS. A girl with any common sense
Would find herself a man.
FATHER. Just see what gall this fellow's got.
Just wait, you'll get your due!
THOMAS. They say, to split a stubborn knot
Any dull wedge will do.
BETTY. Do I deserve to be abused?
You cad, get out of here.
THOMAS. *Pardon*! You must have me confused
With someone else, my dear. (*Exit.*)
BETTY. This is so shameless!
FATHER. Yet we are blameless!
BETTY. Call all our neighbors
To give us their help! (*Exit Father.*)
My heart is breaking!
Such pain, such aching
Rage—I can't speak
So angry am I—
Yet in anger so weak.

THOMAS (*returning*).

Come now, my beauty,
Just smile on me sweetly,
My herd will take leave.
Of the mountain completely.
BETTY. Back in my presence here?
How do you dare?
THOMAS. Why be so angry, dear,
When you're so fair?
BETTY. Madman!
THOMAS. Sweet angel
From Heaven on high!
BETTY. So choked up with fury,
I almost could die!

He tries to kiss her, she pushes him away and runs indoors. He tries to force open the window; she holds it shut, so he breaks several of the panes and then in a frenzy smashes the rest.

THOMAS (*stepping back cautiously*). Oh, oh! That was too much. Now the game's going to get serious. You could have used better sense on your trial run, my boy. If you're courting for somebody else, you shouldn't shout and raise the roof. The matchmaking I've done in the past has obviously been on my own. In that case there's nothing wrong with dealing frankly—no beating about the bush. What's to be done now? There's going to be trouble. I must arrange an honorable retreat, so that it won't look as if I were afraid. Just be bold—strike up the band—withdraw calmly! (*He walks toward the meadow, playing his fiddle.*)

FATHER. Good heavens! I am furious. What an annoyance! That scoundrel! This is the first time I've felt in my bones that I'm not as strong as I used to be, that my arm is paralyzed, that my feet won't carry me. Just wait, just you wait! Not one of my neighbors will lend a hand; they've all turned against me because of the girl. I call them, I talk, I tell them about it, and no one will take the slightest risk to help me. Yes, it's almost as if they're making fun of me! (*Turning toward the meadow.*) How brash! How insolent! Look at him, walking around, fiddling! Our fence boards torn out! (*Looking toward the house.*) Our windows broken! The only thing he didn't do was plunder the place. Won't any of my neighbors come? I'd never have thought they would take that attitude toward me. But yes, it's true. They're just looking on; there's mockery in their faces. One of them says: your daughter is bold enough, let *her* fight it out with the fellow. Another one says: doesn't she have a man to lead around by the nose, to get his ribs smashed for her? Let her take it—for my son, who left home because of her—that's what the third one says. It's no use. It's terrible, it's disgusting! Oh, if only Jery were around; he's the only one who could save us!

BETTY (*coming out of the chalet; her father goes up to her, she leans on him*). Father! There's no help for us, no protection. Such an insult! I'm completely beside myself. I can't believe my eyes and ears. It's more than my heart can bear.

Enter Jery.

FATHER. Jery, welcome, and bless you!

JERY. What's going on here? Why are you so upset?

FATHER. There's a stranger who's ruining our fields, breaking our window panes, making complete wreckage of everying. Is he crazy? Is he drunk? How do I know, how do I know? No one can stop him, no one. Punish him, drive him away.

JERY. Be calm, my friends, I'll send him flying. I'll see that you have peace. You shall be avenged.

BETTY. Oh, Jery, dear, loyal Jery! How happy I am to see you. Rescue us! You're so brave! There's no one like you!

JERY. Don't stay here. Lock yourselves in the house. Have no fear. Let me take care of this. I'll see that you have your revenge, and I'll drive him away, don't worry.

Exit Father and Betty.

JERY (*alone, picking up a stick*).

I'll instill in
This young villain
Some respect.
To insult her,
Oh how spiteful!
How delightful
To protect! (*He walks toward the meadow.*)
Out now! No quarter!
On to the battle!

As he is about to leave, Thomas walks up to him.

THOMAS. Let's keep this shorter.
I own those cattle.
JERY. Thomas!
THOMAS. Oh, Jery!
Shall I be gone then?
JERY. You were the one then?
Are you insane?
THOMAS. Jery, yes, Jery,
But let me explain!
JERY. Come on, you traitor,
I'm ready to fell you.
THOMAS. I'm still in condition,
That much I can tell you.
JERY. Come on!
THOMAS. I'm coming.
JERY. Off with you, off!
THOMAS. Hear me—be wise!—
One word is enough.
JERY. Ready! I'll batter
Your thick skull in two!
Love, oh my sweet love,
You *will* see me through!

Jery pushes Thomas along in front of him and they exit, fighting. Betty comes anxiously out of the chalet. The two men, still fighting, return to the stage. Each has hold of the other; they are wrestling. Thomas is getting the better of Jery.

BETTY. Jery, Jery,
Listen, listen,
Listen to me, will you?
Help, oh help, oh

Help, my Father!
Please don't let him kill you!

They wrestle and swing each other around; finally Thomas throws Jery to the ground.

THOMAS (*speaking in gasps as he gradually catches his breath*). That takes care of you! You made it hard for me. Doubly hard, because you're a strong fellow and my good friend. Anyway, that takes care of you. You wouldn't listen. In the future, don't be in such a hurry. It's a good lesson for you. Poor Jery! If the fall you took could only cure you of your love! (*To Betty, who meanwhile is busy with Jery—Jery has got up*:) It's because of you he's in trouble, and I'm sorry that I hurt him. Take care of him, bandage him, cure him. He's *met* his match—much luck to him if he *makes* his match in the process. I'm leaving. I can't wait any longer. (*Exit.*)

JERY (*who meanwhile, accompanied by Betty, has come up to the table in the foreground and sat down*). Leave me alone, leave me alone!

BETTY. I—leave you alone? You took my part so loyally!

JERY. I still can't get over it. I fight for you and I lose! Leave me alone, please.

BETTY. No, Jery, you did get revenge for me—even though you were beaten, you won. See, he's driving his cattle away, he's putting an end to his trouble-making.

JERY. And he gets no punishment for it! He walks around acting defiant; he goes away boasting and makes no payment for the damages. I'll die of shame.

BETTY. You're still the strongest man in the whole canton. Even our neighbors recognize how good you are. This was just an accident. You tripped on something. Relax. Don't worry. Look at me! Tell me truthfully, did you hurt yourself?

JERY. I sprained my right hand. It doesn't matter. It'll get better.

BETTY. Let me try to straighten it. Does it hurt? Now, once more. There, that'll fix it. It'll be all right.

JERY. I don't deserve your taking care of me.

BETTY. You went through all of this for my sake. I just don't deserve your taking up my cause so bravely.

JERY. Don't say that.

BETTY. You're so modest. I most certainly don't deserve what you've done. But look, you hand is cut open—and not a word from you.

JERY. Forget it. It isn't important.

BETTY. Take my kerchief, otherwise you'll be covered with blood.

JERY. It'll heal by itself; it'll heal quickly.

BETTY. No, no! I'll fix you a bandage right away. Warm wine is good for healing. Wait, just wait, I'll be right back. (*Exit.*)

JERY (*alone*).

Hope at last, at last is risen.
Heaven opens on my prison.
What a sight!
Through the misty valley's night
Falls the sun's most welcome light.
Let the darkening clouds be parted,
Finish what the dawn has started,
Come, sweet love, and end my plight.

THOMAS (*looking in from the side of the stage*). Listen, Jery!

JERY. Whose voice is that? Have you no shame? Do you dare show up again?

THOMAS. Quiet, quiet! Don't be angry, don't get excited! Listen! I just have one or two things to say to you.

JERY. You'll have a taste of my vengeance, just wait till I've recovered!

THOMAS. Let's not waste our time with empty talk. Listen to me. It's urgent.

JERY. Get out of my sight! You disgust me.

THOMAS. If you lose this opportunity now, it's lost forever. Recognize your good fortune, a piece of good fortune that I gained for you. She's not so snippy as she was. She feels grateful. She realizes what she owes you.

JERY. Are you trying to teach me lessons, you ill-bred fellow, you madman?

THOMAS. You can go ahead and call me names, if you'll only listen to me. All right, I played this crazy trick on her. It was half plan and half accident. Anyway, she finds out that a man with courage is a good source of help. I had to defend myself. It's your own fault that I threw you and hurt you.

JERY. Go on, you won't persuade me.

THOMAS. Look how well everything is going; it's all bound to work out. She's coming around. She respects you—she'll soon love you. Don't delay, don't day-dream, strike while the iron is hot!

JERY. Stop it—and don't bother me anymore.

THOMAS. Anyway, I have to tell you this again. Just be satisfied. You owe it to *me*. All your life you'll have me to thank for your happiness. Could I have carried out your orders any better? What if the ways and means were a bit strange? In the end it did the trick. You have every reason to be happy. Make things right with her. I'll come back, you'll forgive me, and when things are going well with you, you'll even praise me for the idea I had and for the wild things I did.

JERY. I don't know what to think.

THOMAS. Do you believe I wanted to insult her for no reason at all?

JERY. My friend, it was a crazy idea. Let it pass as a soldier's prank.

THOMAS. The main thing is for her to marry you; then it doesn't make any difference how your go-between acted. Here comes her father. Good-bye for now. (*Exit.*)

Enter Father.

FATHER. Jery, what strange turn of events is this? Should I call it bad luck or good luck? Betty is completely changed; she recognizes your love, she honors you, loves you, cries over you. She is more moved than I have ever seen her.

JERY. How could I possibly have expected such a reward?

FATHER. She is bewildered. She stands at the hearth, wrapped in her thoughts, reflecting on the past and how she acted toward you. She realizes how much she owes you. Just don't worry. I bet she'll make up her mind today to do the one thing that will make you and me happy, the one thing both of us wish for.

JERY. Will she be mine?

FATHER. Here she comes. I'll leave so she can be with you. (*Exit.*)

BETTY (*with a basin and some cloth*).

Far too long I've been away now.
Come, let's have no more delay now.
Show me your hand, if you would.

JERY (*as she bandages his hand*).

Lovely spirit, dearest, fairest,
You're so kind that I'm embarrassed.
Ah, the bandage feels so good!

BETTY (*who has finished*).

But your bruises—aren't they aching?

JERY. Cured! With all the care you're taking.
Everywhere your hand has lain
I can feel no further pain.

BETTY. Dear, be honest, not impulsive.
Turn your eyes and look at me.
Don't you find me just repulsive?
Someone whom you loved so keenly
Whom you manfully protected—
By this very one rejected,
Hurt with insult, treated meanly!
If your love for me has faltered,
If your heart's intent has altered,
Let me bear my pain alone.
You shall live in sweet contentment,
While I bear without resentment
All you tell me to atone.

JERY. The waters are flowing,
The clouds drift away.
The stars are not like that
They move, yet they stay.
And that's the way love is,
If lovers are true:
Unchanged in its changes,
The same old or new.

They look at each other. Betty seems upset and undecided.

JERY. Are these signs of some devotion?
Don't let passing inclination
Be prolonged or misconstrued!
Often what seems deep emotion
Is but kindness, inclination,
Tenderness, or gratitude.

BETTY. This is no mistaken notion!
I've had small consideration
For your love and fortitude.
Now I promise true devotion
Trust, oh trust this protestation
Of both love and gratitude.

JERY. Don't worry.
To hurry
's unwise
Your smile is the only
Reward that I prize.

BETTY (*after a pause*).

Can you move your hand around now?
Does it hurt you? Let me see!

JERY (*lifting his right hand*).

No, my hand's completely sound now.

BETTY (*extending her hand*).

Jery, then give it to me!

JERY (*pulling back a bit*).

Doubt or rejoicing,
Which is my story?
Will you stay with me?
Will you be sorry?

BETTY. Trust in me, trust in me.
Yes, I am thine.

From Johann Friedrich Reichardt's composition *Jery und Bäteli* (courtesy of Beinecke Rare Book Library, Yale University).

JERY (*taking her hand*).

I'm yours forever,
And now you'll be mine!

They embrace.

BOTH. Love, oh sweet love,
Joined now by your powers,
Let, oh let our final hours
Be, as were our first, sublime.

Enter Father.

FATHER. Heavens, what *is* this?
Can I believe you?
JERY. Am I to have her?
BETTY. Has he your leave to?
Father?
JERY. Oh, Father!
FATHER. Children—
ALL THREE. Oh, joy!
FATHER. Children, you bring back
My days as a boy.
BETTY AND JERY (*kneeling*).

Give us your blessing!
FATHER. Take all my blessing!
ALL THREE. Blessings and joy.

Enter Thomas.

THOMAS. Dare I intrude here?
Dare I be present?
BETTY. What an impertinence!
JERY. Rude and unpleasant!
FATHER. Heavens, what arrogance!
THOMAS. Give me a word!
I had been drinking, that's
Why it occurred.
Just have your elders
Set my contribution
For fines and the damage.
I'll make restitution.

Aside to Jery:

Twenty will cover
My fee as a lover.

That will be more than
The fine and the costs!

Aloud to Betty:

Marry him!

To her father:

Hear me out!

To Jery:

Speak for me, please!

JERY. Come now, my loved ones,
Forgive him his folly.
This is a day for
All to be jolly!
Come and forgive him!

BETTY AND FATHER (*to Jery*).

I'll do as you say.

To Thomas:

You are forgiven.

ALL FOUR. Oh, wonderful day!

In the distance, the sound of horns. From all sides, all first individually, then together and visible on the rocky slopes:

CHORUS OF REAPERS. Riot! Shouting!
Insurrection!
Uphill, downhill?
Which direction?
Who cares where, though?
Come and help!

JERY, BETTY, FATHER (*in chorus*).

Now see the terrible
End of those horrible
Acts on your part!

THOMAS. Laughable, gullible!
Now that we're finishing
They want to start!

CHORUS (*entering*).

Grim death and murder—
Sounds like from here!

JERY, BETTY, FATHER AND THOMAS.

Love and betrothal.
That's what is here.

CHORUS (*running around*).

Quick, to the rescue!
Where's all the row?

JERY, BETTY, FATHER AND THOMAS.

Quiet, dear neighbors, it's
All over now.

The crowd of people calms down, comes to order, and steps in two groups to either side of the proscenium.

THOMAS (*walks to the middle*).

A quodlibet! Just step this way,
If you would understand:
When wise men all are far away,
The fool is near at hand.
Good friends, I have this word for you—
No more, but it's enough.

Thomas takes a boy by the hand and brings him along to the front of the stage, talking confidentially with him. He sings:

Speak gently when you come to woo,
Don't shout and raise the roof.

(*Thomas continues speaking with the boy, in prose, not verse*: 'Now how did that go? You must know it by heart already.')

BOY. Just speak politely when you woo,
Don't shout and raise the roof.

THOMAS. That's fine, now don't forget,
If you should court,
The moral of this play
Is sweet and short.

THOMAS AND BOY (*duo*).

Speak softly when you come to woo
Don't shout and raise the roof.

Given enough charm and a favorable reception, Thomas and the Boy might venture to address these lines directly to the audience.

CHORUS (*repeats the refrain*).

Meanwhile peace and understanding have been restored in pantomime.

THOMAS.
All now together,
Forgive each other!
I've my reprieve,
And so I shall leave.

ALL.
Peace to the mountains,
Peace to the meadows!
Trees, give them cover,
Cool in your shadows,
So to delight the young
Bride and her lover.
Wedding bells call!
Time will be bringing
Small voices ringing,
Joy to the couple,
Neighbors, and all.
Off we go singing!
Altar bells call!

PROSERPINA

A Monodrama

Translated by Cyrus Hamlin

A barren, rocky region, a cave at the base, on one side a pomegranate tree with fruit.

PROSERPINA. Stop! Stop right now, unfortunate one! In vain
You wander through these barren deserts, back and forth!
Endlessly stretch before you fields of sorrow,
And what you seek forever lies behind you.

Not forwards,
Nor upwards, are your glances meant to turn!
The black cave of Tartarus
Beclouds the lovely regions of the sky,
Where once
To my ancestor's joyful dwelling
With loving eyes I gazed!
Ah! daughter thou of Jupiter,
How deeply you are lost!—

Companions at play!
When all those valleys rich in flowers
Blossomed for us still,
When at the heavenly crystal stream of Alpheus
We splashed and played in glow of evening,
Wove wreaths for one another
And secretly recalled that youth,
To whose head our hearts would consecrate them,
There for us no night could be too deep for discourse,
No time too long,
To tell again our friendly stories.
And the sun
Could not arise more easily from its silvery bed
Than we, when filled with a lust to live,
We bathed our rosy feet in early dew.—

Oh girls! Oh girls!
You who, lonely now,
Distracted, creep along those streams,
Gather up those flowers
Which I, alas, bducted,
Let fall from my lap,
You stand and all look after me, where I disappeared!

They have torn me away,
Those rushing steeds of Orcus;

With iron arms
He held me tight, the unyielding god!
Amor! ah, Amor fled laughing upward to Olympus.—
Do you not, impetuous one, possess
Enough in heaven and earth?
Must you increase the flames of Hell
With your own flames?—

Dragged down
Into these endless depths!
To be queen here!
Queen?
Before whom only shades will bow!

Hopeless is their pain!
Hopeless the fate of the departed,
And I cannot prevent it;
To solemn judgments
Destiny subjected them;
And among them all I err about,
Goddess! Queen!
Myself the slave of destiny!

Ah, this fleeing water
Would I gladly draw for Tantalus,
Satisfy him with lovely fruits!
Poor ancient one!
Punished for provocative desire!—
The wheel of Ixion gladly would I seize,
Put a stop to his pain!
But what can we gods accomplish
For these eternal torments!
Without solace for me and for them,
I dwell among them and behold
The busy work of the poor Danaids!
Empty and ever empty!
How they draw and fill!
Empty and ever empty!
Not *one* drop of water for the mouth,
Not *one* drop of water in their vessels!
Empty and ever empty!
Ah, so too it is with you, my heart!
From what source will you take?—and take it where?

Your peaceful wandering, blessed ones,
May only pass me by;
My way is not with you!
In your weightless dances,
In your deep, dark groves,
In your whispering houses
The living sounds of earth are silent,
Bliss in its fullness
Cannot range from pain to joy.—

Is it on his frowning forehead,
Within his inscrutable gaze?
Can you ever call him husband?
And dare you ever call him else?
Love! Love!
Why did you open his heart
For that one moment?
And why for me,
Since you knew
It would lock itself eternally away again?
Why did he not seize one of my nymphs
And place her next to himself
Upon his lamentable throne?
Why me, the daughter of Ceres?

Oh, Mother! Mother!
How your divinity abandons you
In the loss of your daughter,
Whom you believed to be happy,
Playing, frolicking her youth away!

Ah, certainly you came
And asked about me,
What I needed,
Perhaps a new gown
Or golden shoes?
And you found my maidens
Transfixed at the willows,
Where they had lost me,
No longer found me,
Tearing out locks of their hair,
Lamenting pitifully,
My beloved maidens!—

"Where has she gone? Where?" you called.
"Which way did that villain take?
Shall he, unpunished, desecrate Jupiter's line?
Where does the path lead of his steeds?
Torches here!
Through the night I will pursue him!
No moment will I rest, till I find her,
No path will I avoid,
Neither here nor there."

Your dragons flash their clever eyes at you,
Familiar with all paths, they follow your lead:
In uninhabited wilderness you're driven astray—

Ah, but not to this one place, not here!
Not to the depths of the night,
Untrodden by the immortals,
Where, covered by oppressive terror,
Your daughter wastes away!

Turn upwards,
Upwards along the winged serpentine path,
Upwards to Jupiter's dwelling!
He knows,
He knows alone, the sublime one,
Where your daughter is!—

Father of gods and men!
Do you still repose above on your golden throne,
To which you so often with friendliness
Lifted me up when I was small,
Swinging me in your hands,
Playfully, toward the infinite sky,
So that childishly I trembled lest I float away?
Is it still you, Father?—

Not to your head
In the eternal blue
Of the sky bestreaked by fire,
No, here!—

Lead her here!
So that I may rise up

With her out of this dungeon!
So that Phoebus may bring me
Once again his loving rays,
Luna again may smile
Out of her silver locks!

Oh, you will hear me,
Dear friendly Father,
You once again,
Again, will lift me upwards;
So that, freed from long and heavy suffering,
I may once again enjoy your heaven!

Find comfort, my despairing heart!
Ah! Hope!
Hope pours forth
From stormy night the morning dawn!

This ground
Is no longer rock, no longer moss;
These mountains
No longer full of fear!
Ah, here I find again a flower!
This withered leaf,
It lives still,
Waits still for me,
So that I may enjoy it!

Strange! Strange!
Do I find this fruit here?
Which in the gardens above
Ah! was so dear to me—

She breaks open the pomegranate.

Let me enjoy you,
Friendly fruit!
Let me forget
All my harm!
Again imagine myself
Above, in my youth,
In that dizzying,
Lovely time,
In those fragrant,
Heavenly blossoms,

In those aromas
Of blessed joy,
Which were granted to me
In my delight, my desire!

She eats several seeds.

Soothing! soothing!
Suddenly, what assails me
In the midst of these joys,
In the midst of this manifest bliss
With terrible pains,
With iron hands
Reaching through Hell!—
What crime have I committed,
In my enjoyment?
Ah, why does this first joy
Bring me pain?
What is it? what is it?—
These rocks seem here to beckon more terrifyingly,
To close me in more tightly!
These clouds to oppress me more deeply!
In the distant lap of the abyss
Muted thunder seems to roll, renewed!
And you distant regions of the Parcae
Seem to call out to me:
You are ours!

THE PARCAE (*invisible*). You are ours!
This the decree of your ancestral lord:
Having eaten nothing, you might return;
And the bite of the apple makes you ours!
Queen, we pay homage to you!

PROSERPINA. Did you decree it, father?
Why so? why so?
What did I do, that you banish me?
Why did you not call me
Up to your bright throne!
Why the apple!
Oh, curse the fruit!
Why should fruit be beautiful
If it brings damnation?

PARCAE. Now you are ours!
Why do you mourn?
See, we honor you,
Our Queen!

PROSERPINA. If only Tartarus were not your dwelling,
That I could banish you there!
If only Cocytus were not your eternal bath,
That I might still have
Flames to consign you to!
I, the Queen,
And cannot annihilate you!
In eternal hatred let me be bound to you!—

Draw water, then, you Danaids!
Spin on, you Parcae! and rage, you Furies!
In an equal, eternal, wretched fate.
I rule over you
And for that am yet more wretched than you all.
PARCAE. You are ours!
We bow before you!
Ours! ours!
Exalted Queen!
PROSERPINA. Away! far from me
Keep far your faith and your grandeur!
How I hate you!
And you above all, tenfold I hate you—
Woe is me! I feel already
That hated embrace!
PARCAE. Ours! Our Queen!
PROSERPINA. Why hold out your arms to me?
Reach instead for Avernus!
Conjure forth the pains from Stygian nights!
They will ascend in response to your call,
Not my love.
How I hate you,
My monster, my consort,
Oh, Pluto! Pluto!
Give to me the fate of your damned!
Do not call it love!—
Throw me with these your arms
Into the all destroying pain!
PARCAE. Ours! ours! exalted Queen!

NOTES

Goetz von Berlichingen

First conceived while Goethe was in Strassburg in 1771 in direct response to the autobiography of Gottfried von Berlichingen (1480–1562)—*Lebensbeschreibung des Herrn Götz von Berlichingen*, published in 1731—and under the influence of Herder's program for the renewal of German literature and Shakespeare's historical drama and tragedies (see "Shakespeare: A Tribute," volume 3 of this series, pp. 163 ff.), the initial version of the play was composed in six weeks during the autumn of that year, after Goethe had returned home to Frankfurt. This version, entitled *Geschichte Gottfriedens von Berlichingen mit der eisernen Hand dramatisiert*, was carefully preserved by Goethe in manuscript throughout his lifetime and still survives in the Goethe–Schiller Archives in Weimar. It was published posthumously under Goethe's instructions in the second volume of the *Nachgelassene Werke* in the *Ausgabe letzter Hand* in 1832. The revised version of the drama, undertaken in response to a criticism of the first version from Herder (who complained that Shakespeare had "completely corrupted you"), was published anonymously and without indication of place or date in 1773, privately financed by Goethe and his friend Johann Heinrich Merck. A number of editions followed in quick succession, and the play quickly became famous and ultimately established an entire school of historical dramas using medieval German subjects. Various attempts at stage production occurred, always involving radical cuts and rearrangements of scenes. Goethe himself prepared an abbreviated stage version during 1803/04 in close consultation with Schiller, which received its premiere in Weimar on September 22, 1804, complete with incidental music by Goethe's composer friend Karl Friedrich Zelter. The performance lasted for six hours and was subsequently divided into two parts to be performed on consecutive evenings: Acts I to III on the first night, and Acts III to V on the second, with Act III being performed both times. Subsequently, Goethe introduced further cuts to achieve a manageable version for a single performance, and this was finally published alongside the earliest version of the play in the posthumous works (designated *Bühnenbearbeitung*). The play continues to hold the stage in Germany, at least for intermittent, though always successful performances.

An early translation into English was attempted and published by Sir Walter Scott in 1970, at a time when the Scotsman was a fledgling author and only a beginning student of German. More recently a free adaptation for performance in England was made by John Arden and published under the title *Ironhand* (Methuen Theatre Classics, 1965).

P. 2, Schwarzenberg in Franconia. Almost all the place names and many of the proper names in the play are historically real. Franconia, e.g., was one of the major political divisions of the Holy Roman Empire. Goetz, Sickingen and Selbitz were all "free knights," owing allegiance only to the Emperor. Brother Martin, as the later part of the play reveals, is a veiled allusion to Martin Luther. The peasant uprising appears in its true brutality.

P. 15, Permanent Peace. A Permanent Peace with established courts and procedures was decreed by Emperor Maximilian at the Diet of Worms in 1495, abolishing the custom of unilateral but legally sanctioned "feuds," requiring only cause, challenge, and three days of preparation.

P. 17, To his health. The Abbot makes himself ridiculous by drinking to the health of the Emperor Justinian (died A.D. 565), the codifier of Roman Law, as if he were still alive, and by misconstruing simple Latin (*implicite . . . explicite*).

P. 19, Sachsenhausen. Proverbially boorish town.

P. 20, Post coenam . . . mille meabis. "After eating, stand up, or walk a thousand paces."

P. 28, he was mounted on a white horse. See Shakespeare, *Richard III*, III.iv.

P. 31, Theuerdank. Idealized poem of chivalry, ascribed to Maximilian.

P. 36, Assessor Sapupi. From Goethe's other historical frame of reference, the 18th century. The name is an anagram of Papius, an official of the Imperial Court, discharged for corruption.

P. 41, the Emperor has ordered . . . upon the field. The literal words of the proclamation of the ban, inviting assault with impunity.

P. 82, The world is a prison. See *Hamlet*, II.ii.

EGMONT

In the mid-sixteenth century, the seventeen Provinces of the Netherlands, which were part of the Hapsburg empire, were a center of world trade and brought great wealth in tax monies to Spain. They tenaciously defended their freedom and became open to Protestant teachings. King Philipp II. exacerbated the inquisition and, in 1566, sent to the Netherlands the "Iron Duke" Alba, who, one year later, erected a military dictatorship. Although Egmont, along with William of Orange, opposed iconoclasm, he was executed in 1568. Ultimately, however, the Northern Provinces declared their independence under William of Orange in 1581.

Goethe began work on the drama *Egmont* while he was still living in Frankfurt, soon after the completion of *Goetz*. He based his work primarily on two differing histories: *De bello Belgico* by the Jesuit Famianus Strada (published in Rome in 1632, reissued in Mainz in 1651, the latter serving as Goethe's source); and *Historica belgica* by the Dutchman Emanuel van Meteren (1597 in Antwerp, translated into German in 1627 in Amsterdam, the latter used by Goethe). The play had assumed a definite shape by the time Goethe moved to Weimar in 1775, and he continued to work on it and revise it intermittently during the following years until late 1781. Still incomplete, the manuscript of the drama was taken to Italy by Goethe for a final revision to be published in his collected works, the *Schriften*, for which he had signed a contract with Göschen in Leipzig. *Egmont* was prepared in a final fair copy, which still survives, soon after *Iphigenie auf Tauris* was completed, in the summer of 1787 and sent to Herder in early September. It appeared in vol. V in 1788 and was reviewed in an important essay by Schiller, which resulted in considerable controversy. Initial performances of the play were not successful, and Goethe later suggested to Schiller, after the beginning of their friendship in 1794, that he adapt the play for the stage. Schiller undertook to do this for a visit to Weimar in April 1796 by the famous actor August Wilhelm Iffland. His changes were drastic and not entirely to Goethe's liking, though the version succeeded in the theater. Also well known is the incidental music composed for *Egmont* by Beethoven in 1809/10, the score for which was sent to Goethe by the composer and received polite praise. Goethe also prepared his own stage adaptation after Schiller's death in 1805, but he subsequently restored the original in order to accomodate Beethoven's music.

Clavigo

The drama *Clavigo*, based on the memoirs of the French writer Beaumarchais (specifically the *Fragment of My Voyage to Spain*, published with the fourth volume of the memoirs in February 1774), was composed in one week on a bet (according to Goethe's account in his autobiography), presumably during May of the same year. The play was submitted to the publisher Weygand in Leipzig early in June and appeared later that same month, the first work to include Goethe's name on the title page. *Clavigo* follows very closely the conventions of bourgeois tragedy, introduced to Germany by Lessing (*Miss Sara Sampson*, 1755, and *Emilia Galotti*, 1772) and puzzled readers of *Goetz* and *Werther* by its apparent conventionality. Success in performance was quickly achieved in a number of German theaters during the remainder of the decade, and the play was even performed by the students of the *Karlsschule* in Stuttgart in 1780 with Schiller playing the leading role.

P. 161, Spectator. Addison's and Steele's influential journal of 1711 ff., progenitor of many German "moral weeklies."

P. 164, Buen Retiro. Park in Madrid.

P. 180, santa hermandad. Holy Brotherhood, a fifteenth-century "internal security" agency.

Stella

Little is known about the details of composition for this play, written in Frankfurt during 1775 and circulated in manuscript among Goethe's friends before he moved to Weimar at the end of the year. No literary source is known for what must have been a free invention by Goethe, although some critics have connected the play to the well-known history of the simultaneous erotic attachment half a century earlier of Jonathan Swift to Esther Vanhomrigh and Esther Johnson, whom the satirist referred to with the pseudonyms Vanessa and Stella (Swift's *Journal to Stella* had been published posthumously as early as 1766). The play was sent for publication to a bookdealer in Berlin, August Mylius, by Goethe's friend Merck at the time of the poet's move to Weimar at the end of 1775, and the play appeared in print in January 1776. The play aroused controversy through its ending, where an apparent blessing is given for the *ménage à trois*, and performances were banned. For the premiere performance in Weimar in January 1806 Goethe wrote the alternative, tragic ending, though he included the earlier version a year later in his collected works with Cotta. Only in later editions of his works (1816 on) was the tragic version included. Parodies of both versions were written by the popular playwright August von Kotzebue, the first in 1808 entitled *La Peyrouse*, the second in 1818 entitled *Der Graf von Gleichen. Ein Spiel für lebendige Marionetten.*

P. 204, Rinaldo . . . again. Allusion to one of the heroes of Tasso's *Jerusalem Delivered* (Canto XVI, 18–23), lying in the lap of the enchantress Armida, then watching her put up her hair.

P. 219, there was a count. Cecilia recounts the legend of the Count of Gleichen.

Brother and Sister (Die Geschwister)

According to Goethe's diary, this diminutive play was conceived on the evening of October 26, 1776, as the poet was riding back to Weimar from Jena following a hunt. The text was composed during the two days following and dictated in fair copy on the two days after that, in a manuscript which survives. The work was first published with a few minor changes in volume III of the *Schriften* in 1787. Critics have usually argued for a biographical reading of the play, either referring it to Goethe's developing relationship with Charlotte von Stein or to his close ties with his sister Cornelia.

P. 237, Julia Mandeville. Lady Julia Mandeville, titular heroine of a popular English novel by Francis Brook (German translation 1764).

P. 237, Miss Fanny. Miss Fanny Wilkes, titular heroine of Johann T. Hermes' German novel of 1766, ostensibly based on an English original.

Prometheus (Fragment)

This dramatic fragment in verse was composed during the summer of 1773. Presumably Goethe did not advance the play beyond the two acts which survive. Various sources for Goethe's knowledge of the ancient myth have been proposed, including Aeschylus's *Prometheus Bound*, which Goethe probably did not know in the original at that time, and the article on Prometheus in Benjamin Hederich's *Grünaliches Mythologisches Lexikon* (ed. 1770), along with several eighteenth-century works which mention the myth. Remarkable here is Goethe's experiment in the dramatic use of a free verse form. After moving to Weimar, Goethe gave Frau von Stein the manuscript, from which copies had also been made by the poet Lenz and by Luise von Göchhausen, companion to the Duchess Anna-Amalie. Goethe also composed the famous hymn "Prometheus" out of the material for the drama, presumably at about the same time as its composition. The hymn was subsequently published in 1785 without Goethe's permission by Friedrich Heinrich Jacobi in his famous *On the Teachings of Spinoza*, and Goethe included the poem in his first collection of poems for the *Schriften* in 1789. For decades he had no access to the dramatic fragment, the composition of which he described in Book 15 of his autobiography. Only in 1819 did the copy of the fragment from Lenz's literary remains reach Goethe, and he published it a decade later (1830) in vol. 33 of the *Ausgabe letzter Hand*.

JERY AND BETTY (SINGSPIEL)

The eighteenth-century tradition of German *Singspiel*, to which Goethe made a significant contribution, developed as an amalgam of the Italian *opera buffa*, the French *opéra comique*, and the English *ballad opera*. Musical numbers interspersed with spoken dialogue, all in a fairly light, often satirical manner, prefigure the development of operetta in the nineteenth century, leading in various indirect ways to the American musical comedy of this century. Distinctive masterworks in this tradition, preceding and following the example from Goethe offered here, would be John Gay's *Beggar's Opera* (1728) and Mozart's *Magic Flute* (1791). Goethe's earliest work in this genre was composed while he still lived in Frankfurt (*Erwin und Elmire* and *Claudine von Villa Bella*, both subtitled *Ein Schauspiel mit Gesang*). His most distinctive work as author of *Singspiele*, however, was done in the early years in Weimar for performance by the *Liebhabertheater* of the court: *Lila*, *Die Fischerin*, *Jery und Bätely* and *Scherz*, *List und Rache*. Conceived near the end of 1779, as Goethe was returning from a visit to Switzerland, *Jery and Betty* was written during November and December. Negotiations to secure a proper music for the piece were not fully successful. Philipp Christoph Kayser in Frankfurt was approached first, but he failed to complete a score. Karl Siegmund von Seckendorf was the second choice, who produced the music for the premiere in Weimar the following July. Goethe published a slightly revised text for the work in his *Schriften* (following the fragment of *Faust*!) in 1790, and in the same year Johann Friedrich Reichardt composed a score for the work (a selection from which is reproduced in this volume from the copy contained in the Speck Collection at Yale). This was produced in the Weimar Theater with great success in 1804, soon after the premiere of Schiller's *Wilhelm Tell*. An earlier production in Berlin in 1801 had been achieved by Iffland using Reichardt's music, also with great success. The piece remained in the repertoire in Weimar until 1819.

PROSERPINA (MONODRAMA)

The specialized theatrical genre of monodrama, or melodrama, flourished in the 1770s, following the success of Rousseau's *Pygmalion*. Consisting essentially of a dramatic monologue with musical background music, *Proserpina* appears to have been undertaken in response to a request in 1776 from the composer Christoph Willibald Gluck to Goethe's colleague in Weimar, the author Christoph Martin Wieland, to write a work commemorating the death of his niece, which he might set to music. If this is indeed true, we can only regret that Goethe's text did not secure its musical accompaniment from the great composer. Instead, Goethe inserted the work into his satirical play *Der Triumph der Empfindsamkeit* (1778/9; published in volume IV of the *Schriften*, 1787). The text of *Proserpina* was also published independently in Wieland's journal *Der Teutsche Merkur* in February 1778 as prose, though later it was arranged in the form of free verse. An independent performance was given at the *Liebhaber-theater* in Weimar in 1779 with music by Siegmund von Seckendorf. Goethe's continuing interest in the work is attested by a much later performance in the Weimar Theater in 1815 with new music by a student of Zelter, Karl Eberwein, and an apparently powerful presentation by the actress Amalie Wolf. Goethe praised the event and published an essay on it in the *Morgenblatt* for June 8, 1815. The delicate combination of word, music and theatrical gesture, enhanced by costume and stage design, defined for Goethe in miniature form the highest art of the theater, in the manner which he presumably envisioned much later when composing the *Helena* for *Faust*, *Part Two*.

C. H.

AFTERWORD

Of all the major writers of drama in the Western tradition, Goethe is probably the most widely experimental and generically elusive, the most varied and versatile—perhaps also the most uneven. Unlike his compatriot Lessing he adhered to no well-defined program of exemplary theater. Unlike Shakespeare or Moliere he did not write within a tradition sanctioned by an established national or regional stage. These things scarcely existed in Germany, and their absence was the source of his frequent complaint. Not only the limitations of time and place but also the force of his own creative bent impelled Goethe to experiment and explore. His theater is no monolith, no monument to a unified vision of form and style. It is an ever-changing reflection of life observed, and of the mind that observes it: Protean, all-encompassing, sometimes grand in its sweep of history or symbol, sometimes highly (almost uncomfortably) personal, formally perfect at times and again diffused or fragmentary, ranging in form from musicals and masques to the dramatic pageant of *Faust*, in language from the most "naturalistic" speech to the most elevated and disciplined verse.

The whole corpus, in many cases even the single work, is remarkably like a living organism, growing, changing, constantly subject to revision. In his early years, says one critic, Goethe consciously tried to find a new style for each new subject. No aspect of form or content was immune to change. Relatively few of his plays are the result of a single block of time or a single conception. From the first struggle with the *Faust* to the triumphant end of *Faust II* lies a span of roughly six decades. In this volume we present *Stella* with two radically different endings; some 30 years separate what we might call the tragicomedy from the tragedy. *Egmont* we read in prose; the original verse shows through and can often be scanned. *Goetz* exists in two complete and substantially different versions. We possess four separate versions of his *Iphigenia*. Goethe could work decisively and with astonishing rapidity—*Goetz* in its first version was completed in six weeks, *Clavigo* in eight days—but such energy and productive zeal was as often turned to extensive rethinking and revising as to quick and final execution. The astonishing number of "lesser" works in the Goethean canon is also a witness to his exploration of new and varied paths in the quest for his own substance, his own style. Even relatively slight productions like *Jery and Betty* are an important part of any full picture of the poet; there is a real danger of distortion in a view restricted to the "Olympian" Goethe. The very verse structure of *Jery* is like a proving ground for the virtuoso effects of *Faust*.

Especially in the meager context of contemporary theater, Goethe's wide range of dramatic styles and the "evolutionary" quality of his work might seem to imply a distance from—or a lack of communication with—the stage itself. Not so. Goethe's autobiography bears witness to his youthful fascination with the puppet theater and its traditions. He and his sister "staged" such performances at home. He was an avid theater-goer during his student years at Leipzig. When in 1776 he followed the Duke of Weimar's invitation to be his companion and councilor, he entered a world in which the amateur court theater, sponsored by the Duke's mother, would come to figure as a bright star in a modest firmament. The narrow horizons of the Duchy of Weimar as a political entity scarcely detract from the magnitude of Goethe's achievement. Throughout his later governmental activity, ultimately as minister of everything from mines to museums, he remained the guiding spirit of the Weimar stage: director, producer, actor, dramaturge. It is a double career in the affairs of state and the drama hardly matched since Sophocles, the playwright, politician and general.

For all that, Goethe stands, as a writer of plays, both within and outside the physical limits of the theater. He could and did write with those limits fully in mind: everything from little set-pieces like *Jery and Betty*, one of six such *Singspiele* (operettas) designed primarily to serve the court theater and its aristocratic amateurs, to an experimental "one-acter" like *Brother and Sister*, to the later "classical" drama *Iphigenia*. He also wrote plays that, in anything like their original form, could not be staged. *Goetz* is one. (In many ways it is more like the script for a motion picture!) From the short, in effect fragmentary *Prometheus* or *Proserpina* to the vast pageant of Faust, many of the dramatic works are for reading, not for acting before an audience. If they come to the stage it is apt to be a gesture of retrospective piety and a tour de force. Those who are interested in the historical environment as a partial determinant of such matters will see in this aspect of Goethean drama a reflection of the relatively undeveloped, isolated, and tentative state of the German stage. (One biographer claims that Goethe, who learned greatly from Shakespeare, never saw a Shakespeare play performed.) We are on the whole better advised to see Goethe's drama in the widest possible light: a genre for the representation of the world and the mind, in which persons or aspects of the creative personality appear before *our* mind's eye, to speak or act without narrative intrusions and to tell us, in this self-enclosed but complete microcosm, all we *can* know about life as it is.

As special as the nature of the works is the relationship between

Goethe's life and his dramatic characters, plots, and themes. "All my works are fragments of a great confession," he wrote, and too many of his readers and critics have been seduced into easy equations and trivial or sensational readings. Names and events, attitudes and reactions seem recognizable, the similarities are tantalizing—and were often embarrassing to those of his contemporaries who saw themselves in his mirror. But such connections are veiled, altered, ironic, and ultimately frustrating. Still, in a deeper sense the poet himself *is* always visible, however elusively, behind his characters and plots, quite unlike Shakespeare, who tells us little about himself and infinitely much about the human condition—Shakespeare is the true observer where Goethe is the true revealer. But revealer of what? Not just of his private world. His dramatic art is modeled from life in the personal sense but it far transcends the level of what we think of as "experiences." His drama is in fact a model of the perception of human existence by the experiencing mind: the self, the relationship of self to others, the struggle for freedom and knowledge, the problem of consciousness, the nature of being human. But in most of the works the reference is primarily to the superior individual and to himself as an embodiment of the superior individual, Goethe being no Zola or Dickens.

If the personal equation—the literary work as confession—is ultimately misleading (though attractive) the search for an encompassing framework of theme and meaning is doomed to be at best partial (though doubtless worth the pursuit). Goethe, to be sure, inveighed against such reductive activity. He was annoyed by those who kept asking for the "idea" behind *Faust*: "As if the whole manifold life of Faust could be strung on the meager thread of a single idea!" Whereupon he was agreeable enough to suggest as a guideline "From Heaven through the World to Hell," surely a kind of ironic diversion.

Potentially the most evocative of his own formulations of theme is the famous word of "Shakespeare: A Tribute" (contemporary with some of the early works of the present volume), in which he fixes the essence of the tragic in that mysterious point "where the characteristic quality of our being, our presumed free will, collides with the inevitable course of the whole." (See volume 3 of this series, p. 165.) The remarkable value of this coinage has been almost systematically debased. The easy misunderstanding of "will" and "inevitability" (or necessity), individual "being" and "whole" has led to readings that pit individual will against society, history, class structures, economic trends, collective psychologies, anything that will identify the second term with one or another of the grand determinisms. It has for example led to the almost universal interpretation of the figure of Goetz as a heroic anachronism, in futile conflict with the new (and corrupt) post-feudal national state, as the rebel who succumbs to force majeure and the sweep of history. In part this may be true. But Goetz succumbs also to inner conflicts of loyalty: on the one hand, to the Emperor who is the icon of his free-wheeling independence (because, as Imperial Knight, Goetz owes allegiance only to him) and, on the other, to the essential *spirit* of that very freedom, the liberty to be true to one's individual being, to follow one's will and nature, in effect the first term of the Shakespeare Tribute formulation. It is a conflict that surfaces when the Emperor becomes—or is maneuvered into becoming—the suppressor of Goetz's second freedom, through the ban and the expeditionary force. This, and the breaking of his house arrest, leads to Goetz's recognition of his own responsibility, his own flaws and errors—"I know best what burden lies upon my shoulders"—and to the realization that he is *not* a free agent, either externally or internally. And this recognition is a good deal closer to what Goethe meant by the "inevitable course of the whole."

Thus the literary works of the same period are themselves the best key to this proffered summation. They tell us that the two opposed terms are in fact terms of the individual human being's relationship to reality and to others, of our own perception and self-awareness, of the freedoms and limits of our conduct of life, of the degree to which we see and experience the conditions of our life as, in the words of Benjamin Bennett, "malleable . . . , subject to our arbitrary choice and responsive to our feelings" or as "indissolubly related through the laws of cause and effect"—and thus, for internal and not just external reasons, beyond our control.

The broad evolution of this theme, granted the many relapses into optimism (if, roughly speaking, we take freedom as desirable, necessity or constraint as regrettable), is an increasing diminution of this kind of freedom and a correspondingly tighter set of constraints. Yet Goethe remains virtually unique among the great "tragic" dramatists in rarely abandoning his characters and plots to tragedy in the sense of the Greeks or Shakespeare, that is, to the final unalloyed and cathartic downfall. Through residual hope, or irony, or compensatory image and symbol, the protagonist *seems* at least to live on. This voice is weakest in *Goetz,* stronger in *Egmont*, strongest and summatively so for Faust, who transcends in succession utter spiritual annihilation, a "real" suicide attempt, guilt, and even death itself.

It is the special import of the early and "lesser" works that they show this conflict of self-insight as it evolves from a celebration of the kind of independent will that can indeed shape our destiny, through increasing awareness of the constraints of reality and the obligations of our own nature, finally to a solution or resolution on a different plane. For Goethe the figure of Prometheus was the obvious archetype of the unfettered creating will. Yet it is crucial that we contrast, not equate, Goethe's Prometheus with Aeschylus'. The latter is wholly adamant, foreign to self-pity, confident and defiant. There is in Goethe's figure an undeniable element of the Romantic pose of heaven-storming ambition, combined with the pathos of vulnerability to opposition and defeat, a Prometheanism somewhat more of the word than of the essence, highly self-conscious and even a bit self-pitying, and therefore not Aeschylean.

Beleaguered or frustrated though it may be, a kindred spirit of independence, "humanity," and creativity suffuses *Proserpina*. The defiant goddess becomes the feminine counterpart of Prometheus—and a model for aspiring man: the will to master fate is both divine and necessarily doomed.

Even in the rare cases of "pure" comedy, where the impression is confirmed that things and persons are indeed malleable and where the freedom of will accomplishes its purpose, the recognition remains that in some sense the triumph is an illusion. Goethe could not, in the final analysis, leave *Stella* with both women embracing Fernando: "We are yours!" The later, tragic ending negates such complacency. In *Brother and Sister*, Marianne's final words, "It's not possible," seem at first merely the expression of joy, in the familiar paradox: "so wonderful that it's almost too good to be true." But the linguistic surface is ambiguous, permitting or suggesting a second deep structure: "It *is* too good; it *cannot* be true." This latter reading is in fact an accurate reflection of Goethe's verdict on the triple reconciliation of the earlier *Stella*. It *was* too good to be true.

The vision (whatever its ultimate fate) of freedom, creativity, and expansiveness, the assumed mastery of circumstance and of other people, is at its most intoxicating in the realm where the individual personality intrudes on the world of politics, that is in *Egmont*, but it also animates the world of personal love. Pure, exultant love exists only in a few early poems (of the great ones, "Welcome and Farewell" and "May Song" perhaps) or in a very few of the letters of Werther, though even these are qualified by apprehension and foreboding. What supervenes is the realization of limits, of transitoriness—and of guilt or at least responsibility. Goethe was not above making the biographical equation himself. "Send a copy of *Goetz* to Mlle. . . . She will be to some extent consoled to see that the false lover is poisoned." Hence the sometimes baffling pattern of moth-to-candle, of fatal constriction, that chokes the life of Goetz and the love (and politics!) of Egmont. But the fate of the woman is, in everyday human terms, worse. Often simply a vehicle for the ecstatic freedom of the man, she is equally often abandoned or destroyed. The line leads from Maria in *Goetz* to Marie Beaumarchais, from Stella to Margarete in *Faust*. Few (Clare for one) remain triumphant in the possession or assertion of their love.

Two strategies in the deployment of characters and roles mark most of the dramas, these and the later plays—and the narrative prose as well. They are obliquely related to the conflict of freedom and necessity. The first is evident in the figure of the vacillator, as if the male persona is torn, or condemned to pendulum swings of personality, between two loves, between the two poles of conflicting ideals—or between the vision of freedom and the awareness of necessity. The alternative, also present in the plays, is to be hopelessly immobilized. Hence the figures that vault in an almost manic-depressive fashion from envisioned triumph to defeat or despair or self-destruction: Weislingen, Clavigo, Ferdinand, even Egmont—and of course Werther in the novel and Faust in the great dramas.

The figure of the vacillator is, in its earliest manifestations, jejune enough. Fernando is utterly unable to resist the demands of the moment and perfectly capable of turning his arguments and rationalizations to suit his *vis-à-vis*: his wife at one time, his mistress at the other. He is so totally indecisive as to seem sincere. And this implausible balance is rewarded (in the first version) by the possession of *both* women, which is perhaps appropriate, since he has otherwise demonstrated the capacity to make two women equally miserable. If a literary work is in fact a mirror of the mind of the writer we learn a lot from *Stella* about the youthful Goethe.

Here too Goethe establishes that fateful and pathetic portrait of the good woman found wanting—and aware of her inadequacy: "In the end all I could be for him was a good housewife" (Cecilia in *Stella*). And the role of the restless male, presumably capable of higher things, caged and frustrated: "I've got to get out of here! I was a fool to let myself get caught. . . What couldn't I do? I've got to get out, out into the free world!" (Fernando, as quoted by the Steward). Again it is a sequence which leads par excellence to *Faust*. The great culminating drama is after all contemporaneous, in its genesis, with the early plays of this volume, and the protagonist storms heaven like Prometheus, suffers disillusionment and defeat as do Goetz and Egmont, seduces his simple love as Clavigo does—yet survives all this, plus suicide (Werther's fate) and in a way death itself. Thus the transcendence denied Goetz and only envisioned for Egmont is in Faust achieved. His death, really the gateway to a second immortality after a second life, is the final symbol of the survival of the human drive for greatness, however erring and guilty. It is a necessary, almost a foregone conclusion of a course set in motion by the earliest works. In many ways these first plays (and narratives) cannot be fully understood except as way-stations toward *Faust*—or as way-stations in the evolving creative pattern that leads to *Faust*. And by corollary *Faust* cannot be fully appreciated except in the context of its companions in time and origin, works like those in this volume. (It may also be important to observe here again that the poetic style, the intense virtuosity of form so remarkable in *Faust* is prefigured and "practiced" in works as apparently unassuming as *Prometheus*, *Proserpina*, *Jery and Betty*.)

The other deployment of roles, frequent but not universal in the successive *dramatis personae*, provides, as a foil to the protagonist of divided mind, a less complex, more decisive and practical companion. It is a figure not of higher wisdom or merit but one for whom the conflict of pretended freedom and inalterable design is either non-existent or less compelling. Often the companion sees only the freedom, in a circumscribed vision to be sure. One thinks of Carlos in *Clavigo*, Epimetheus in the *Prometheus* fragment, even (at the humorous level) of Thomas in *Jery and Betty*. Or the "other" may have long since recognized and accepted the forces that limit all such freedom. Of the latter, the most obvious case in point is William of Orange in *Egmont*. Elisabeth in *Goetz* may be another. In these latter two, the companion figure is so persuasive as almost to imply that there *is* another—possibly a better—way of looking at and accomplishing things. As to the former group it seems reasonably clear that, although difficulties attend the hero's course of action, what would happen if his companion prevailed ranges from the disruptive to the disastrous. And always the counter-figure serves largely to illumine the personality in which Goethe was truly interested: the one condemned to awareness of conflict and constraint, the one whose creative freedom in the shaping of life is frustrated in the nexus of inner and outer logic that compels the recognition of our interconnectedness, the individual's non-uniqueness. And once again the line of descent carries through, by way of Pylades (the friend of Orestes in *Iphigenia*) to Wagner in *Faust*.

All the complexity, tension, and conflict of the "personal" level has its correlatives in structure, in thematic development and imagery. The plots of virtually all the plays are marked by a rhythmic alternation between upward surges and abrupt declines, between expansiveness and constriction, between spatial liberation and physical barriers. Distant vistas, whether of the outer world or of the spirit, give way to close horizons; courts and centers of power give away to hearth and home. The opposite pattern of movement is never lacking but it rarely prevails. At its most intense, the force of constriction is manifested in the image or fact of imprisonment. Scarcely a work in this volume is devoid of one or the other, the image or the fact.

In many works the same contrast is evoked by the terms so often used of *Faust I* and *Faust II*: the little world and the greater world. The sphere of everyday relationships, of domesticity and comfortable isolation coexists with the domain of "affairs," of influence and accomplishments. For Egmont it is the world of Clare and that of the court. For Faust it is Margarete's little province and that of the Emperor—or the Cosmos itself. Here again we face the necessary warning: with Goethe, the terms of such oppositions are not to be understood on the surface.

Expansion is not a source of unmitigated pleasure—or not for long. Narrowness is not always stifling. Werther, for example, was profoundly drawn to the little world of Charlotte—for all his fatal attachment to dreams of infinity. Faust, alone in Gretchen's room, cries, "What abundance in this poverty, what blessedness within this prison!" Almost every play in the present volume echoes the theme. Yet, in a further twist, as human limitations and the "inevitable course of the whole" can bring one down harshly and abruptly from the peaks, so too the happiness potentially inhering in the little world can also turn to disillusionment, to entrapment and the prison. And among the outward forms of the latter must be reckoned, despite the charms of domesticity, the institution of marriage.

Only Egmont, really, comes close to living in both worlds. But his greater role as a political leader is dominated—and undermined—by his affability and his trusting nature. And these are attributes more appropriate to the smaller sphere. At the same time there is something undeniably heroic about his little world of love and personal happiness, for Clare surpasses the ordinary in every respect and is in fact more heroic than her lover.

The shadows of constriction and frustration fall nonetheless upon Egmont, and one of Goethe's rare visions of the coincidence of ambition with humane leadership ends in isolation and imprisonment. Egmont's fairest sentiments of liberty are voiced when he is, without knowing it, Alba's prisoner. The whole work can in fact be visualized as a progression of ever narrowing perimeters of place, ending with death in prison, transcended (in terms of the play) by the Victory Symphony. The same is true of Goetz, who moves from heady independence to the self-awareness of limits and obligations, thence to honest surrender in good faith, to betrayal and ambush, to acceptance of house arrest and, after ill-advised and ill-starred escape, to the dungeon and death. The tightening circles in both plays can be drawn like charts, and *Clavigo* is not far removed, as the protagonist is drawn closer and closer to his final entrapment at the bier of his unfortunate Marie.

It would be wrong to end on a note of all-encompassing constriction, and *Egmont* will serve as witness of two countering features almost ubiquitous in Goethe's work as it develops through time. One is the much-discussed and elusive notion of the Daemon.

Among our works, the *locus classicus* is Egmont's famous word about the "chariot of the sun" as an image of destiny:

> As though whipped by invisible spirits, the horses of the sun, Time's horses, run away with the light chariot of our destinies; and we have no choice but to grip the reins with resolute courage and, now to the right, now to the left, avert the wheels from a stone here, a precipice there.

Again the temptation is to read on the surface and say that we are at the mercy of external and alien forces. This may be tolerable as a reading of Hamlet's "There's a divinity that shapes our ends,/Rough-hew them how we will." With Goethe, one is well advised to consider first the meaning from within, just as we must with the dictum about freedom and necessity. Egmont is our witness, for he continues:

> I stand in a high and prominent place and must rise still higher. I have hope, courage, and strength. I have not yet attained the crest of my growth and when I *have* attained the highest point, I shall stand there unwavering, without fear. If I must fall, let a thunderbolt, a gale, even a false step hurl me down into the depths; I shall not be alone there but with thousands of good men.

In other words our fate is in our very personalities, and individuals of the caliber and nature of Goethe's protagonists are compelled by inner necessity to follow the mysterious spirit by which they are inspired—or relentessly driven. It is not a pessimistic or defeatist view, even though it may lead us to our downfall, as Egmont himself realizes. It is rather more a realization that we must carry out our inner destiny: "To thine own self be true," but in a wholly non-moralistic sense, because, if we are "Goethean," we have no choice but to be true to our natures.

Transcending the single personality and therefore perhaps more congenial to the common understanding is a force in its way equally inevitable: the humanizing effect, upon others, of innate purity and integrity of spirit, the contagion of the individual personality in its most "generous" embodiment. This secular miracle becomes, in a sort of compensatory blessing, one of the virtual constants in Goethe's thought. If it is often submerged in the encroaching frailty of the world, that is the measure of Goethe's sad—not tragic—awareness of the common course of human events. The triumph in its most memorable form belongs to Iphigenia, whose truth and radiant influence rescue Orestes from near madness and—once she has determined to risk all by asserting them—subdue the aggressive Pylades, and convert the King from Scythian harshness to (reluctant) tolerance and "humanity." The same force emanates from both Egmont (in his effect on the citizens) and Clare (in her effect on him). It momentarily allows Goetz to trap Weislingen into decency; it radiates from Elisabeth and from Maria. It once emanated from Marie Beaumarchais, but Clavigo's ambitions and follies are too obdurate to be cured. It works, in the figure of Marianne, upon both men in *Brother and Sister*. Prometheus even concedes the benign influence of Minerva. Most often the benefaction is conferred by a woman.

In the ontogeny of Goethe's work the figure of the woman as enlightener and purifier does not develop from the very beginning. In a curious complementarity, it is absent so long as the male is a true vacillator, both irredeemable and successful. The touchstone is Fernando. The relationship of Stella, Cecilia, and Fernando is one of infatuation. The man is, in *Stella* the tragicomedy, rewarded by the possession of both women. He is ennobled by neither. But when the changing geometry of the dramatic work permits it, the good woman can inspire or redeem the errant, beleaguered man. It is a theme which grows from modest beginnings in the works of the present volume, through *Iphigenia*, to its culmination in *Faust*, the last words of which—among the last words of Goethe's creative life—sum it up:

Das Ewig-Weibliche
Zieht uns hinan.
Woman, eternally,
shows us the way.

F.R.

GPSR Authorized Representative: Easy Access System Europe - Mustamäe tee 50, 10621 Tallinn, Estonia, gpsr.requests@easproject.com

www.ingramcontent.com/pod-product-compliance
Lightning Source LLC
LaVergne TN
LVHW102156101026
849957LV00026B/207
9780691292274